Henry Spackman Pancoast

An introduction to American literature

Henry Spackman Pancoast

An introduction to American literature

ISBN/EAN: 9783337202880

Printed in Europe, USA, Canada, Australia, Japan

Cover: Foto ©Andreas Hilbeck / pixelio.de

More available books at **www.hansebooks.com**

AN INTRODUCTION

TO

AMERICAN LITERATURE

BY

HENRY S. PANCOAST

*Author of "An Introduction to English Literature" and
"Representative English Literature"*

NEW YORK

HENRY HOLT AND COMPANY

1898

To my Sisters,

WHO HAVE BEEN IN THIS,

AS IN ALL OTHER THINGS,

MY CONSTANT AND READY HELPERS.

" Democracy is still on trial. It must justify itself or die. Lowell states one of the standards thus : ' Democracy must show its capacity for producing, not a higher average man, but the highest possible types of manhood in all its manifold varieties, or it is a failure.' . . . That this highest type of manhood may be attained in our country, under the existing opportunities of self-development, has been frequently claimed, and if this life be possible, then the expression of it should be also. The highest possible type of literature should succeed the highest possible type of manhood . . . This national literature must be the development, consciously or unconsciously, of all the best literary powers of the best American people. Such a national literature is indispensable to the union of these States—not that union based upon the consent of the governed, and bound by political regulations of their making but the essential union of common sentiments and ideals secured by a common pride in intellectual achievement, and a partnership in patriotism."—*Professor Charles F. Kent's Inaugural Address on Literature and Life.*

PREFACE

THE plan and purpose of this book can be stated in a few words. It is intended as a companion-book to my " Introduction to English Literature," and it has been prepared—so far as the nature of the subject permitted—according to the same general scheme.

The first thing required of a book of this character is that it shall really bring the reader into vital relation with the best works in the literature of which it treats,—that it shall induce him to read or re-read them with both delight and understanding. I have tried to do this by treating our greater authors at comparative length; by making their personality as real and living as I could; by adding some critical discussion of their chief works; and by furnishing study lists containing suggestions for reading and bibliographical references.

Without question our literature does include certain works which we should know not merely because they were written by Americans, but because they are veritably literature. The importance of such romances as *The Scarlet Letter,* such essays as Emerson's *Nature*, such ballads as the best of Longfellow's or Whittier's, is more than national. These works have their place in the mental life of every liberally educated person. It must, however, be admitted that when compared with that of many other nations America's total contribution to the world's literature is both inferior in character and insignificant in amount. If American literature had no claim upon us other than its intrinsic literary value, the proportion of time which it could justly demand from us would be comparatively small. But the study of particular authors and their works is by no means the only reason for a systematic study of our literature. That study has, or should have, an interest for us because of its close and important relation to our national life. Our intellectual growth as evidenced in our literature is a part of our past and the earnest of our future.

Stopford Brooke, in a recent book of his, has said: "True history lies, not in the statement of events of which we cannot be certain how they occurred, but in the statement of how men at any time thought and felt. . . . The history of the race is in the history of what men thought and felt; and it is written, not in annals, not in chronicles, not in State papers, not in the stores of the record offices of nations, but in the literatures of the tribes and peoples of mankind. There is truth worth knowing; all the rest is pleasant enough, but it is only more or less probable in comparison with the certainty we attain when we read a poem or a story of how men thought

and what they felt." * Thus our study means much
more than the study for their purely literary value of
the few masterpieces which are likely to become part
of the common heritage of English-speaking people.
Besides these there are many works which should ·be
studied by every American, if for nothing else, because
of their relation to our national history and ideals.
The *Biglow Papers*, the *Harvard Commemoration
Ode*, Whittier's tribute to Lincoln,—all these, and
others like them, have their place in the education of
American youth. They should be given the fullest
chance to do their work of quickening our national
conscience and lifting us to nobler life. And it is
not books only that help to elevate. The personal
example of such author-patriots as Lowell, Whittier,
and Curtis, of such stainless scholars as Longfellow,
should be a most widespread and potent influence for
good. In a great commercial nation such as ours,
the inspiration from the life and aims of the scholar
and the poet is especially needed to correct the tendency to strive only for the commonplace and the
practical.

Realizing, then, that a large part of the deepest life
of America is recorded in its literature and inseparable
from it, I have accordingly tried to present our
literary history in its true relation to the history of
our people and to make two points especially clear:
first, that our literature is, in its origin, a branch of
that of England, and that its relation to the mother

* "The Old Testament and Modern Life," pp. 195–197.

literature and its gradual divergence from it must be constantly kept in view; second, that our literature, springing up originally in separate English colonies, is in its beginning a literature of sections, and that its history is the history of a gradual approximation towards a national unity of character. The appreciation of this last fact is, in my judgment, an indispensable preliminary to any real grasp of the meaning of our literature's growth.

H. S. P.

GERMANTOWN, Dec. 13, 1897.

CONTENTS

INTRODUCTION

PART I

THE COLONIAL PERIOD. Cir. 1607–cir. 1765

CHAPTER I. THE COLONIES

CHAPTER II. LITERATURE IN THE COLONIES

APPENDIX

TABLES OF LITERARY PERIODS

LIST OF PORTRAITS.

AN INTRODUCTION TO AMERICAN LITERATURE

INTRODUCTION

THE term American Literature, although firmly established by custom, and sufficiently well understood, is, in itself, both inexact and misleading. If we were not acquainted with the meaning which usage has given to the words, we should naturally understand them to include all the literature produced in America, whether before or after its discovery by Europeans. But, rightly or wrongly, the term American literature has received by ordinary use and acceptation a far more restricted meaning. It does not embrace the entire literature of the American continent, as European literature includes that of all Europe; but only that of a definite part of North America—the part now the United States. We dwellers in these United States, holding, as we do, the first place in the Western World, think and speak of ourselves as the Americans, distinguishing Canadians, Brazilians, or Mexicans,—inhabitants as they are of our common continent—by the name of that particular country to which they respectively belong. In the same way, by American literature we mean our literature; just as by the

American literature defined.

American flag we mean our stars and stripes, or by an American citizen, a citizen of the United States. On the other hand, we must remember that American literature does not mean merely the literature of the United States, for it is far older than our national life. It means simply the American branch of English literature set by colonization in fresh earth; it means the continuation of English literature within the limits of what has become the United States, by people English in their speech, English to a considerable extent by inheritance, and English in the original character of their civilization. Of course this literature is now, and has been for more than a century, the product of a politically independent nation, to the making of whose people almost every race and country has now contributed. It is true that our intellectual dependence on England, at first almost unlimited, has gradually lessened, and that for more than a century our Republic has been moving slowly towards self-confidence and independence in literary methods and in thought. Doubtless, as our civilization becomes more compact and mature, as our national ideals grow clearer, our character more firmly set and defined, this divergence between American and English literature will increase, and our coming writers will embody with growing force and distinctness the national life and spirit that will stir around them. But while we may expect to be more and more truly American in the future, we must remember that we were emphatically English in the past; that our literature in its origin was not the voice of a united and independent nation, but the disconnected and stammering utterance of a straggling line of English colonies, fighting for a foothold along the coast of an inhospitable land. For about one half of its entire history,—extending in all over less than three centuries,—what we call American literature was in fact nothing more than one of the colonial literatures of England. Originally the provincial offshoot of the greatest literature of the modern world, American literature has grown up under the shadow of the English, slowly modified by new physical, social, and political conditions. As truly as the American flag represents our political separation from England, so truly does our American literature, in its birth and growth, exhibit our intellectual dependence on the mother-land; a dependence which has been weakened by the development of our national spirit, but which even yet, to a considerable extent, remains.

It is clear that, by reason of its origin, American literature stands in a different position from that occupied by many of the great literatures of the world. The United States is a young nation, but we Americans are not a young people; we are an old people, for our ancestors brought with them a mature civilization when they landed on this new soil to possess and subdue it. One of the most truly national of our poets has spoken of America as that

American and other literatures.

"Strange, new land that yit wast never young."

The literature of Greece reflects the normal progress of a people from the primitive life of a young nation to a state of high civilization and maturity. But unlike Greece, or even England, America has never passed through all these natural stages of a people's growth, and our literature cannot be expected to express them. In certain great departments of literature, in certain materials for the creation of literature, America must of necessity be comparatively or wholly wanting. At no time could we have produced the rude chant, or primitive epic, because when our English forefathers first settled here they had passed far beyond the stage of national development which makes such creations possible. The cultivated Greek was born into a world where beautiful myths and legends were a living part of the very landscape: our writers, living in a land comparatively free from all the hallowed and inspiring associations of the past, can reach the earlier and fresher stages of a race's mental life only by forcing an entrance into an aboriginal world in which we, as a people, have no share. If we would think ourselves back into that dim and legendary land of wonder and beauty which great nations inhabit in their childhood, we must turn, as Longfellow does in *Hiawatha*, to the stories of an alien race, or we must cross the sea and enter the national nursery of the Greek, or Celt, or English. We must therefore think of our literature, not only as a provincial continuation of the English, but as beginning at a comparatively late period in the life of that race of which we are a branch.

But while we may fail to find among the great historic literatures of Europe any one which has come
into existence under conditions exactly similar to our
own, there exists outside of Europe a **True place**
group of rising literatures among which **of American**
ours properly finds a place. The United **literature.**
States is by no means the only country in which
the civilization and literature of England are being
carried forward under new conditions. For centuries, and especially during the last one hundred and
fifty years, the English people have been building
outside of the narrow limits of their island a great
Empire that is now ninety-one times as large as the
mother-land. The English flag waves over tropic
India and among Canadian forests; in Australasia, in
the distant Southern ocean, the English have raised
up a rich, progressive, and powerful state; in half-
mapped Africa is the wonderful spectacle of this
widening English rule. It is not English rule merely,
it is England herself, her Christian civilization, her
institutions, her law, her language, and her literature
that are thus reaching out to the ends of the world.
To-day nearly four hundred millions of people, of
widely different race, language, and inheritance,
acknowledge her supremacy, while to more than one
hundred millions, including the people of the United
States, her language and her literature are native and
inherited possessions. Such facts mark an epoch, not
only in the history of the English people, but in the
history of English literature. This " expansion of
England " means also the expansion of English litera-

ture; it means that the English genius, which has been revealing itself through literature for more than twelve hundred years, has won for its use fresh materials for literary art by coming into contact with new and infinitely varied life. Our true place in literary history is as one of the literatures of this greater England. We have been brought into being by the same great historic movement; we inherit the same civilization, the same traditions, the same classics, the same national traits; we are sprung from the same race, and the speech of Shakespeare—England's poet and ours—is on our lips.

Nevertheless, along with all these points of likeness between our American literature and those of the English colonies, there are certain marked points of difference. Each of the colonial literatures has already a spirit and character of its own, while that of the United States, in addition to all other causes of divergence, has back of it the great fact of our independent national life and ideals.

The world stands but at the beginning of this greater English literature. The creation of it is a world-wide movement, in which we seem destined to bear no insignificant a part. We have a noble inheritance and great competitors; and if, as yet, we have done but little, the long future lies before us. Only the opening chapters in the story of American literature can as yet be told, for we have only begun to build what we hope will be one of the great literatures of the world.

Having gained some idea of the relation which our

literature bears to others in the present and in the
past, let us now try to grasp the general **Periods of**
course of our literary history, and the main **American**
periods into which it naturally divides **literature.**
itself. The literature of a people is but the written
expression of its life. Some men in a nation express
their feelings, ambitions, or ideas chiefly through
their actions; they are statesmen, soldiers, inventors,
merchants: with others, this inner life finds its most
complete expression not in deeds but in written words;
they are poets, novelists, historians, or philosophers.
Both the men of deeds and the men of words have
their part and place, and both classes of men represent
in some degree the hidden central life of the community to which they belong. Since the true life of
a people is revealed to us partly through what it does
and partly by what it writes, its history and its literature are inseparably connected. We can study the
growth of the American people in the fortitude and
courage of its early settlers, in its migration westward
from ocean to ocean, in the deeds of Franklin, Washington, or Lincoln; or we can approach it from
another side, and read its story in the words of the
Puritan preachers, in the oratory of Patrick Henry or
Daniel Webster, and in the books of Emerson, Hawthorne, and Lowell. As the history and the literature
of a nation spring from the same source, the study of
either without the other must be incomplete. In our
study of American literature, therefore, we must first
appreciate its vital connection with the history of the
American people.

American history is the story of the making of a united and independent nation out of a number of scattered and disconnected colonies, and of the building of many foreign elements into the fabric of a great State. It tells us of the planting and growth of these colonies, of their separate life and interests, of their petty jealousy and distrust; it shows us the forces which brought them nearer together and drove them to concerted action; it relates their united resistance to English misrule; their attempt at a confederation of semi-independent States, and the final establishment of a federal government. Through our whole history we can see forces at work which tend to hold back or break up this building of a united people. Thousands of miles of territory have been added to the original thirteen States, many millions of foreigners have brought into our midst a strange medley of races and tongues, one great section of the country has risen in arms against the rest; yet in spite of all dangers our steady and impressive advance towards unity has gone forward, and the substantial integrity, the original character of the nation has been marvellously preserved. Thus one continuous and leading motive of our national history is that progress from diversity towards national unity which finds expression in the country's motto.

The general course of our literary history but follows these broad features in the history of our country at large, so that the main periods of our literary and political history substantially correspond. Thus the literature naturally falls into the following divisions, each of which represents likewise a stage in our historical progress.

I. The Colonial Period, cir. 1607–cir. 1765.

II. The Establishment of Nationality, cir. 1765–cir. 1815.

III. The Literature of the Republic, cir. 1809 to the present day.

I. THE COLONIAL PERIOD—Cir. 1607-cir. 1765

Our literature had its beginning in no one center or community. During the early years of our history the Colonies of the South, of the North, and of the Middle region were separated from each other by the barriers of forest and wilderness, and by their underlying difference in spirit and origin. In each Colonial group, therefore, literature had an independent beginning, and, for a considerable period, a separate development. The crude literary efforts of the several Colonies bear the stamp of their local individuality. Our Colonial literature is consequently a literature of sections, each of which must be studied separately to be rightly understood.

II. THE ESTABLISHMENT OF NATIONALITY—Cir. 1765-cir. 1815

When these isolated Colonies drew together and finally became compacted into a nation, their literature ceased to be wholly a literature of sections, and expressed this new national spirit. The forces which drew the Colonies together politically exerted precisely the same influence on their intellectual and literary life. In the oratory which echoed the common antagonism to England, in the songs and verses of the Revolution, in the effort to manufacture a national literature which followed the establishment of our independence, we see that the spirit of the whole people has become stronger, for the time, than the spirit of any section. In this period, therefore, our literature may be thought of as passing out of the purely local stage, and reaching, at least at times, a national note, under the new fervor of patriotism. This may further be regarded as a transition-time between the old Colonial literature and that comparatively modern and more national literature which begins with the advent of Washington Irving. By 1815, or the conclusion of the War of 1812, the country may be thought of as placed on a firm and permanently independent basis, an era of internal progress and prosperity fairly opening out before it.

III. THE LITERATURE OF THE REPUBLIC
1809 to the present day

Although this period covers less than one third of our entire literary history, nearly all of our most lasting and important contributions to literature have been produced within its comparatively narrow limits. It has been a time of rapid national growth, during which our best energies have been concentrated on the development of our vast material resources, and on the task of building up and governing a great nation. Yet, while the genius of America has thus manifested itself chiefly in active and directly practical pursuits, our progress in literature has been a distinct, if subordinate, work of the epoch. The territory held by the republic has been greatly increased, and our literary life has extended over an ever-widening area. The center of literary production has shifted from place to place along the Eastern Coast. Beginning definitely in the Middle States with the Knickerbocker school, or the writers that surrounded or followed Irving in New York city, the onward movement was taken up about 1830–35 by the great writers of New England, at Cambridge and at Concord. Oliver Wendell Holmes, the last of this group, which includes Emerson, Hawthorne, Longfellow, and Lowell, has but lately left us, and, by his death, definitely ended what has been so far our most memorable literary movement. Before the death of Holmes, however, New England had gradually lost that leadership in literature which she had held during the middle years of our century; new writers have since arisen in the South and in the West, and we may now look forward to a still fuller and wider expression, through literature, of the nation's life.

PART I

THE COLONIAL PERIOD
Cir. 1607–cir. 1765

CHAPTER I

THE COLONIES

OUR American Republic was made by the confederation of English Colonies, joined by the struggle for independence, and welded closer together by the advantages that came to all from union. Our American literature, in its later, or national, stage, was a continuation of the literary beginnings in these several Colonies. However slight the value of this Colonial literature may be, regarded purely from the literary side, when we reflect that these early writers were preparing the way for the greater men who were to come after, we see that their work has an effect and meaning which make it impossible for us to pass it by. We must go back to these Colonies and their literature as we would trace a river to its source: so only can we appreciate the origin of much that we find about us in the United States of to-day.

13

With the single exception of Georgia, the colonization of North America by the English was the work
of the seventeenth century. To know what these

**The
Colonies.**

Colonies were, we must remember what
England herself was during that memorable epoch, for the Colonies were substantially so many offshoots of England set in a new soil.
For Englishmen the seventeenth century was chiefly
a time of civil conflict. Without, Spain had been
humbled; but within, monarchy strove with the rising
spirit of liberty: Cavaliers with Roundheads; the
Church with the Puritan spirit of dissent. The
land was a house divided against itself. Two Englands seem struggling for being within the limits of
one little island, and the whole surface character of
the nation changes as one or the other of the two
contending parties gains control. During the middle
years of the century, or from about 1649 to 1660,
England is a land at least nominally republican in
government, and apparently Puritan in religion.
Its prevailing temper seems sober, austere, perhaps
too often narrow even to fanaticism; it is sombre-
hued, pleasure-fearing, restrained. But after the
restoration of the monarchy in 1660, the prevailing
spirit and character of the people appear to be suddenly transformed. On every side are light-hearted
pleasure-seekers; on every side gayety and color, dis-
soluteness and drunkenness. The nation seems to be
possessed with an incurable levity, and its " merry
monarch " dies with a cynical jest on his lips.

Suppose that representatives of each of these two

Englands, the land of the Puritan and the land of the Cavalier, had been taken out of the con- **Cavalier and Puritan in America.** fusion of conflict, and placed in a new land where each was free to develop untrammelled by the influence of the other. In such a case you would have separate continuations of two distinct and antagonistic Englands. This actually took place in the new land of America.

The first permanent English settlement in this country was made at Jamestown, near Chesapeake Bay, in 1607; the second was at Plymouth, on Massachusetts Bay, in 1620. The first settlement was the beginning of Virginia, the most influential and typical of the Colonies of the South; the second was the beginning of Massachusetts, which came to hold among the New England Colonies of the North a correspondingly influential and typical place. When we examine the objects and composition of these two typical settlements, we find that in a broad, general way they are respectively a continuation of Cavalier and of Puritan England. New England, indeed, is rigidly and exclusively Puritan in its population and spirit, while Virginia and her sister colonies, formed of more mixed elements, are only approximately Cavalier; but, speaking broadly, each group of settlements maintains those rival ideals of social and religious life which during the seventeenth century had fought for supremacy in the mother land.

The chief causes of this diversity of character between two settlements founded almost at the same time are the widely different motives which prompted

their establishment, and the influence of widely
Virginia and the South. different natural surroundings upon the Colonists themselves. In general terms, Virginia was settled for glory or for gold, New England for the sake of religious conviction. It has been said that the one was the "offspring of economical distress, and the other of ecclesiastical tyranny." *

The scheme of colonizing Virginia by the London company had the sanction and support of the royal power. Among the Colonists were adventurers, roving and intrepid soldiers of fortune, gold-hunters, idlers, and "poor gentlemen," made reckless by their necessities. The Virginia enterprise drew such men as a magnet does steel filings, for the New World of the West still shone in the popular imagination as a kind of earthly paradise, where gold could be got without labor. These wild ideas and extravagant expectations were echoed on the London stage, doubtless with a touch of satirical exaggeration, for the theatres were then the "brief chronicles of the time." "I tell thee," says Seagull, in Marston's *Eastward Ho!* (1605), "gold is more plentiful there than copper is with us; and for as much red copper as I can bring I'll have thrice the weight in gold." And he adds to many other attractions of the new land, that "there we shall have no more law than conscience, and not too much of either." † What wonder that

* Doyle's *English Colonies in America :* Virginia, i. 101, etc.
† *Eastward Ho!* Act III. Sc. 3.

the discontented, the bankrupt, and the enterprising looked to such a land as a refuge, a place to repair ruined fortunes, and to risk all on a new chance! What wonder, either, that the statesmen turned to it as a means of relieving the country of some of its superfluous population!

Such, then, were the circumstances which led to the planting of Virginia. But while the first colonists included many from the ranks of the unfortunate, the avaricious, or the criminal, they were later reën-forced by many representatives of the best English stock. After the overthrow of the monarchy in England many of the Cavaliers emigrated thither; there, too, were younger sons of the nobles, and men from the upper and middle classes. From the early days of Virginia we find a touch of the pomp and affluence of an aristocratic society, beside which the pinched and rigid life of New England seems more than ever harsh and meagre. Lord Delaware, one of Virginia's early governors, " came surrounded by the pomp of the Old World, with a train of liveried ser-vants, whose gorgeous dresses must have had a strange effect in the dark Virginia forests." * Moreover, many local conditions helped to develop a society of an aristocratic type. The richness of the soil, and the great importance of the tobacco crop, tended to make the South a region of huge plantations, while the use of slave-labor, which began very early, further increased the wealth and almost despotic power of

* Lodge's *English Colonies in America*, p. 7.

these great landed proprietors. Virginia, during the early half of the eighteenth century, was in many respects a provincial copy of the rural England of that time. The life of the Virginia country gentleman on his broad acres did not greatly differ from that led by the English country squire of the time. The clergy of the Established Church had the low moral tone and lack of spirituality which in the reigns of Anne and the early Georges too often disgraced their English brethren. But life in Virginia was even more lonely and narrowing than in the country districts of contemporary England. There was practically no town life, and the wretched state of the roads was an obstacle to a social intercourse such as was quickening and developing the mental life of Colonial New England. In a community so widely settled, with no great centers of population, the establishment of schools was necessarily difficult. The sons of the wealthy were taught at home, and perhaps completed their education in England, or in the better-equipped Colonies of the North; but among the masses illiteracy was general. We find no trace of that sympathy with popular education which from the first was characteristic of the more northern Colonies, but rather signs of a selfish and aristocratic prejudice against it. In 1671 the royalist governor, Sir William Berkeley, wrote concerning the condition of Virginia: "I thank God there are no free schools, nor printing, and I hope we shall not have these hundred years; for learning has brought disobedience and heresy, and sects into the world, and printing has divulged them, and libels against the best government. God keep us from both." This mediæval policy of keeping the people ignorant in order to repress freedom of thought, and to render the masses subservient to rule, was unfortunately not confined to Berkeley. Throughout the entire Colonial period the South was without any provision for general education.* Even in higher education, reserved of necessity for the sons of the wealthier classes, the South was conspicuously backward.† The printing-press, which stands beside the public school as one of the great agencies of our civilization, was also introduced late, and, even when obtained, was subjected to a supervision stifling to intellectual growth and freedom of thought. There seems to have been no press in Virginia before 1681, more than seventy years after the settlement, and a few years later the governor was instructed by the authorities in England " to allow no person to use a printing-press on any occasion whatsoever." Yet forty years before this the great Puritan John Milton had put forth, in his *Areopagitica*, his daring claim for the freedom of the press, and England had gained that freedom for herself

---

* "There is no indication in the statutes of any desire to provide education, and no system of public schools was even attempted before 1776."—Lodge, *English Colonies in America*, p. 74.

† A college was indeed founded in 1692, at Williamsburg, then the capital of Virginia, called the College of William and Mary; but during its early history it was rather a boys' boarding-school than a college in any proper sense, as nothing was taught beyond the rudiments.

almost at the time she denied it to her Colony. The
entire blame for these unfortunate conditions cannot
fairly be laid to the desire of the English Government
to stifle the free spirit of the people; it is partly
attributable to an aristocratic and autocratic spirit
among the ruling classes in Virginia. Virginia being
in many ways a continuation of monarchical and
Cavalier rather than of republican or Puritan England, there was not that united protest against an
undue authority which would have made its exercise
difficult if not impossible. So that a recent writer
even goes so far as to declare that "thought was not
free in Virginia, religion was not free in Virginia, and
this by the explicit and reiterated choice of the
people of Virginia." *

After reviewing such facts, we must acknowledge
that many conditions of life in the Colonial South
were distinctly unfavorable to any great achievement
in literature. As a rule, great writers have been
dwellers in cities; the best literature is apt to be born
amid the thronging centers of human competition and
activity, where life moves swiftly and with a dramatic
energy and complexity, where thought is called forth
by the incessant pressure of experience, and mind is
quickened by constant contact with mind. Life in
the South was agricultural, isolated; the town, the
focus of mental activity, did not exist. Indeed to this
day it has felt the want of a literary center, comparable to Philadelphia in the early years of this century,

---

* Tyler's *History of American Literature*, vol. i. p. 90.

and to Boston, New York, and Chicago at a later period. The ideal of the upper classes was rather that of the great noble than of the student or man of letters. Besides all this, the deliciously mild and somewhat enervating climate, together with the luxuriant richness of the soil, encouraged a life of indolence. While the intense and wiry New Englander made himself lean over the doctrines of free will and election, or, in the frigid atmosphere of his stoveless meeting-house, listened to long sermons on the future torments of the wicked, the comfortable Virginian laid wagers on cock-fights, or celebrated the victories of the race-track.

Yet, while we are compelled to admit her shortcomings, it is plain that Virginia had many of the elements of a great State. Her faults were mainly those of the dominant class in that early-eighteenth-century England of which she was the colonial representative. On the other hand, life in Virginia was sturdy, healthy, hospitable, and by no means lacking in sterling and manly virtues. The men were brave and chivalric, the women charming and devoted; home-life beautiful, and family affection strong. If the South could not give us many writers of books, it gave us leaders of men, who proved the magnificent qualities of the race in moments of national peril. When the country stood on the brink of the Revolutionary War it was the Virginia Assembly, under Patrick Henry's eloquence, that led the way in which Massachusetts followed; it was Richard Henry Lee, a Virginian, who

The greatness of Virginia.

introduced into Congress the resolution declaring the Colonies independent; above all, it was Virginia who gave us Washington and Marshall. Yet while the South was thus foremost in action, great in the halls of debate, on the battle-field, or in the court of justice, we must look to New England, rather than to Virginia, for the source of our literary and intellectual life. The great Colonies of the South and of the North were to develop on different lines, but it was the ideals of the North that were to have the largest share in the making of the whole nation, and that, at least in a modified form, were destined to prevail.

In studying the character and history of New England we are impressed first of all with the nature of the motive that prompted its settlement, **New England.** for in this motive lies both the cause and the explanation of much that is peculiar in its subsequent life and literature. As a rule, the founding of a colony is the work of a motley crowd of emigrants and adventurers,—an ill-assorted company of men representing almost every shade of social condition, of religion, politics, and moral character. Such, as we have seen, were the elements which the hope of gain first drew to the rich land of Virginia. But the single and unworldly purpose which dictated the making of New England excluded from the Colony all but the few resolute spirits who shared in that purpose, and who were of a temper strong enough to suffer for it. It brought together men of one mind and of one faith, and the State which they created was a wonderfully perfect embodiment of their ideas. "We came hither," wrote one of their clergymen in the early days of the Colony,—"we came hither because we would have our posterity settled under the pure and full dispensation of the Gospel, defended by rulers that should be of ourselves." It was this motive which gave to New England a unity which the other Colonies, with their mixed elements, did not possess. Not only was New England, unlike New York, Pennsylvania, and many of the other Colonies, settled almost entirely by men of purely English stock, but her early settlers were drawn exclusively from those progressive, protesting, and liberty-loving elements in England that in the critical struggle of the seventeenth century saved the nation from tyranny and misrule. It was the Puritan who, almost at the same time, preserved and enlarged the ancient liberties of England and carried liberty over seas to plant it in a new world.

These Puritan builders of New England have left so deep a stamp, not only on that great section that they founded, but on our greatest litera- **The** ture and on the history of our whole **Puritans.** nation, that we must try to do full justice to their character and their ideas. The high average of intelligence and character among the New England colonists is one of the first facts to impress us. A great proportion of them came from Lincolnshire and the neighboring counties, then the great stronghold of Puritanism. They were mostly earnest, thoughtful, God-fearing men, of the middle and yeoman class. The idle, profligate, and disorderly elements which

entered into the making of Virginia had absolutely
no place among them. Some of them belonged to the
ancient landed gentry—men of the class of John
Hampden or Oliver Cromwell, representing the
soundest and finest English stock; * many of these
were graduates of Cambridge, that great university
even then Puritan in its sympathies. Prof. Tyler
says that between 1630 and 1690 there were probably
" as many graduates of Cambridge and Oxford in
New England as could be found in any population of
similar size in the mother-country." † But it is not
merely that they were scholarly men; history shows
them to have been men of endurance and of courage.
Their grand purpose of building in the wilderness a
State which should rest on the foundations of religion
and morality was one likely to attract only the higher
and stancher characters. No wonder that one of
their early preachers declared that " God sifted a
whole nation that he might send choice grain over
into this wilderness."

The character and scholarship of its founders made
New England the most intellectual of all the Colonies;
it left a lasting impress, not on New England only,
but on many a future State in the then unexplored
West, and on the life and thought of the mighty
nation that was to be. It was in New England that
popular education, the only foundation on which a

* " It is no unusual thing for a Massachusetts family to trace
its pedigree to a lord of the manor in the thirteenth or four-
teenth century."—Fiske's *American Political Ideas*, p. 29.

† Tyler's *American Literature*, vol. i. p. 98.

republic such as ours can safely rest, was begun. After the Puritans had provided for the bare necessities of life, after they had built meeting-houses and "settled the civil government," "one of the next things" they "longed for and looked after was to advance learning and perpetuate it to posterity."* As early as 1642 parents were required to furnish their children with at least elementary instruction, and four years later every Colony except Rhode Island had made education compulsory. Certain autocratic spirits in Virginia sought to rest the government on the servile ignorance of the masses; the democratic spirit of New England found in popular enlightenment the true basis of a self-governed State. Even before the establishment of popular schools provision had been made for the higher education. Harvard College was founded in 1636, only sixteen years after the landing of the Mayflower; not, like the college of William and Mary, through the exertions of one man, but by the official action of the authorities. The beginning of this oldest of our colleges, built by the Puritan out of his penury, and set down in the clearing of a wilderness which was not yet wrested from the Indian and the wild beast, is an extraordinary proof of foresight and of loftiness of aim. It showed a trust in the future which time has justified. The college thus founded became a power in the higher life of the little

---

* *New England's First Fruits.* Coll. Mass. Hist. Soc., vol. i., 1st series, 242.

cluster of New England Colonies, and, in later years, in that of the whole nation. It has brought forth great men, and helped to make the little village of Newtown,—rechristened Cambridge in memory of the great university, dear to the Puritan heart,—a center of the greatest literary movement the country has yet seen.*

Apart from this care for education, we find many stray indications of this intellectual quality of the Puritan mind. New England produced the first almanac printed in the Colonies (1639); a humble form of literature, indeed, yet one which in the hands of Benjamin Franklin was to become a characteristic and important medium of popular instruction. New England gave us the first English book printed in North America—the famous *Bay Psalm Book* of Weld and Eliot (1640); she gave us, too, in *The Boston News Letter* (begun 1704), the first, and for fifteen years the only, newspaper printed within the limits of the present United States.

Not only did the Puritans bring with them a decidedly intellectual bent; they found at least some of the conditions of New England life distinctly favorable to mental development. The keen, stimulating atmosphere quickened mind and body with a restless and nervous energy, changing the ruddy,

* " For place they fix their eye upon New-town, which, to tell their Posterity whence they came, is now named Cambridge."— *Wonder-working Providence of Zion's Saviour in New England*, by Capt. Edward Johnson, 1654. (Stedman and Hutchinson's *Library of American Literature*, vol. i. p. 326.)

bulky Englishman into the alert, wiry, quicker-witted
Yankee. There was here no luxurious abundance,
such as that which in the South fostered a life of indolence. An early New England writer says truly
that their company of the elect had not been led into
a land flowing with milk and honey, but into a wilderness, where bare living could only be wrung from
the stony earth by toil. There was nothing to
encourage an almost purely agricultural society, such
as that of Virginia; men must live by their brains,
and so we note the early beginning of manufacturing and other industries at a time when they were
unknown in the fertile Colonies of the South.
Though dwelling in a country of splendid forests, the
Virginian imported his chairs, tables, boxes, even his
wooden bowls, from England; * in the North every
man was a mechanic, and his necessity was the mother
of Yankee ingenuity. There was more social intercourse in New England than in the huge and comparatively isolated plantations of the South. Town
life was pronounced from the first, and half a century after the settlement at Plymouth there were
fifty towns in a population of about eight thousand.
The country was early divided into small districts, or
townships, governed by the town-meeting, at which
every male resident was expected to be present. By
this system of free discussion the men of New England were not only training themselves in democratic
methods of government, but they were developing

* See Beverly on the *Present State of Virginia*, p. 58.

their power to think, and to clothe their thoughts in effective words. Thus climate combined with certain political and social conditions to quicken and develop the New England mind.

But while the tone of New England was conspicuously intellectual, and while conditions favorable to the encouragement of the intellect were by no means lacking, the whole mental life was cramped by an almost complete devotion to questions of theology and points of doctrine. An offence against their accepted religious system was an offence against the State, for the Church and the State were one. The ministers were consequently not mere spiritual guides, but leaders in temporal affairs; no man was permitted to vote unless he were a member of one of the congregations. These founders of a new England had got into a corner of the world, and "with immense toyle and charge made a wilderness habitable," that they might live unmolested in the practice of their faith, and not unnaturally they refused to admit those who differed from them in that faith. They were as intolerant as they were earnest and sincere, for intolerance was the bulwark of their whole system of government. The higher education, designed almost exclusively to prepare young men for the ministry, that "there might be some comfortable supply and succession," was narrowed by a too predominantly theological tone. Hence, as Matthew Arnold has said, "Harvard was calculated in its early days to produce learned theologians rather than men of letters." Thus, with an inspiring if mistaken

thoroughness and vigor, the Puritan undertook to subject life and thought in New England to a minute
supervision and an iron rule; society was under a code
which suppressed extravagance, or what was deemed
affectation, in dress, and which discouraged even
innocent amusements. One Thomas Parker, a minister highly thought of for his learning and goodness,
came down from his study to reprove some of his
relatives who were laughing "very freely" in the
room below. "Consins," he said, "I wonder you can
be so merry, unless you are sure of your salvation." *
The authorities of Plymouth threatened to banish a
young servant-girl as a "common vagabond" because
she had smiled in church. In such a society political
freedom was curiously linked to religious despotism.
Moreover, the conditions of life in the New World
tended to exaggerate certain defects of the Puritan
character. The especial temptation of the Puritan
was to carry his virtues to an excess, and, by the
undue development of his strong and uncompromising
qualities, become self-righteous, fanatical, unchari-
table, and morbid. English Puritans of the highest
type, like John Hampden and the accomplished
Colonel Hutchinson, a lover of music and poetry, preserved a juster balance of nature, and succeeded in
uniting strength, rectitude, and a true religious feeling with a most winning grace and charm. But a
rigorous climate, the hardness, solitude, and perils of
life in the new land, its bitter experiences of hunger,

* Mather's *Magnalia*, vol. i. p. 439.

death, and pestilence, were calculated to intensify
rather than to soften the grimmer and sterner Puritan
traits.   These harsh experiences called out fortitude
and determination, and left but little room for joyousness or ease.   New generations, with no memories
of the charm and beauty of England, grew up to
replace the old; the mother land seemed far off.   The
monotony of life depressed them, and the shadows
deepened.   Held in the iron pressure of such surroundings, the powerful mind of the New Englander,
like that of some mediæval schoolman, became
narrowed by being too inflexibly confined to one set of
ideas, and, intrenched in his own opinions, he drove
from him those whose religious views were different
from his own.   Such conditions were highly unfavorable to the production of a true literature, or indeed
of any form of art.   English Puritanism gave the
world one supremely great poet; but Milton passed
his early years in the evening of a beauty-loving time
—a time of mask and antique pageantry, when the
sounds of feast and jollity yet lingered in the air.
And so Milton added to the inexorable Puritan conscience and an uncompromising seriousness of aim
the artist's love of beauty, color, grace, and joy,—a
love which was partly an inheritance from the
gorgeous Elizabethan age then passing away.   Beauty,
gladness, and the fulness of a comprehensive human
sympathy—without these things art and literature are
starved.   So while in Old England Puritan literature
was cut off by the restoration of Charles II., in
Colonial New England it lived indeed, but lived

pinched and repressed by the lack of the generous and
life-giving conditions without which it is hard for art
to bloom.

Lowell has said that Massachusetts and Virginia
" have been the two great distributing centres of the
English race on this continent." *   Certainly they are the two most conspicuous   The Middle
                                            Colonies.
representatives of two important and contrasted elements which, with others too often unduly
slighted, have gone to make up the nation.   But
these other elements cannot be altogether passed over.
Between the territories of the English Cavalier and
the English Puritan stretched a line of settlements by
no means wholly English, which in character as in
position were midway between these two extremes.
During the early half of the seventeenth century,
while the English were establishing themselves in the
South and North, this rich belt of middle country
was being taken up by other nations.   Holland, true
to the Dutch instinct for commerce, and quick to
perceive the opportunities for trade held out by the
Western world, established trading-posts at the mouth
of the Hudson and further up the river, thus gaining
possession of the finest harbor on the Eastern coast.
A Dutch West India company was established (1621)
and explorations and settlements were made on Delaware Bay and farther inland.   By 1637 the Dutch
had a competitor in the Swedes, who started rival

* *New England Two Centuries Ago.* Prose Works, vol. ii.
p. 14, complete edition.

trading settlements, but gave way to the Dutch about twenty years later (1655).   Finally, when a war broke out in Europe between England and Holland, the whole middle district passed at length into the hands of the English.   Three distinct though kindred races had thus struggled for this middle region, and although it became English at last, foreign elements remained in its population which were not without lasting effects upon its character.   We are better able to understand the character of New York city, and appreciate why it had less literary and intellectual influence in early times than Boston or Philadelphia, if we remember that it was founded as a purely business enterprise by a nation of traders, and that its origin, its wealth and its commercial advantages, have combined to give it an essentially mercantile spirit.

The origin and character of Pennsylvania was widely different.   While there were early Dutch and Swedish settlements within the domain afterwards granted to Penn by Charles II., the real beginning of Pennsylvania was distinctly English.   New York was the child of a Dutch trading company; Pennsylvania the offspring of a desire to institute a better social and religious order, a purpose less selfish and more liberal than that which actuated the Puritans themselves. William Penn, one of the noblest characters in the annals of American colonization, was a man of good birth and education, who had suffered much for his courage and independence in doing what he believed to be right.   The founding of Pennsylvania was in his eyes a " holy experiment."   It was not reared, like the Colonies of New England, on a foundation of narrow exclusiveness; it was to be a refuge for the persecuted and oppressed of every sect. The colony rested not merely on a political but on a religious liberty, and so it welcomed Germans, Scotch, Irish, Welsh, and Huguenots, emigrants of many nations, often attached to strange and curious religious sects. If Massachusetts pointed the way in popular education, Pennsylvania and not New England stands as the pattern of the Republic of the future, that, uniting civil and religious liberty, was to open her arms to mankind. The Puritan built for those of his own faith alone: to him even political rights were determined by religious belief. Penn, with a wonderful humanity and an astonishing faith, founded " a free colony for all mankind."

The people in Pennsylvania were accordingly separated by innumerable differences in race, language, and creed. Some of the sects could boast of learned men, but on the whole this diversity was unfavorable to intellectual progress. There was but little general culture, yet we find Philadelphia making an early provision for education, and prominent from the first in science and scholarship. Like the Puritans, the Quakers had but little sympathy with literature or art from the purely æsthetic side, but they showed a marked fondness for natural science, and intellectual liberty was the very principle of their religion. A school was opened in Philadelphia in 1683, only a year after Penn's landing, and six years later a

Educational and literary conditions in Pennsylvania.

public school was established in which the classics were taught. A printing-press was set up there in 1686, only four years after the founding of the city, and an almanac published by the Philadelphia printer, William Bradford, in the year following. The settlers showed themselves even more prompt than the people of New England in providing for the things of the mind, and we can readily believe that " the early emigrants included in their numbers men of good education and high endowments." In New England, however, education was probably more widely spread over the country districts, while in Pennsylvania it was largely confined to Philadelphia itself.

When we pass in imagination through this line of straggling settlements along the Eastern edge of this **The Colo-** unknown wilderness, we cannot but see **nies in lit-** that, by the very nature of the situation, **erature.** any great and immediate success in literature was for them all but impossible. Not only had they the enormous labor of subduing a continent, of combating Indians, of organizing governments, a work which would absorb the best energies and tax the practical resources of the strongest race, but they had further to overcome obstacles perhaps even more formidable in their lack of educational and literary facilities, in their remoteness from the great centres of culture, and in their very cast of mind. The South was indolent and illiterate, and many among the better classes inclined to despise literature as a profession; New England was intellectual but narrow, and given over too exclusively to matters of theology; New York was mercantile, and its first inhabitants were men of a heavy and phlegmatic race which has made no great contribution to the world's literature; Pennsylvania as a State was behind New England in education, and while Philadelphia was, from the first, a centre of education and culture, its bent seemed rather scientific than purely literary. The Quaker and the Puritan were probably the two most powerful influences back of our educational and intellectual life in the Colonial times, and, while both were excellent, both were distinctly unliterary influences. Emotion and color, the breath of poetry and art, were alike distasteful to the Quaker, while to the New England Puritan, in his " stern precision, even the innocent sport of the fancy seemed a crime." *

* Macaulay's *History of England,* vol. i. chap. ii.

CHAPTER II

LITERATURE IN THE COLONIES

THE beginnings of Colonial literature were what we should expect from such conditions as we have described in the foregoing chapter. In the seventeenth century literature had not yet become a recognized profession in England; what wonder, then, that in the wilds of America men could not give up their lives to letters, but that they wrote only with a directly practical purpose, and as a side interest in busy and stirring lives. The desire of men and of nations to hand down some record of themselves and their doings to those that come after is a deep and general human impulse, and is one of the earliest incentives to literary composition. The early explorers and colonists of America shared in this natural wish to make such a record of what they had seen and done. Consequently many of our earliest books were stories of adventures in the new land, with descriptions of its scenery, and of the strange appearance and customs of its savage people. These books belong to the same class as those which record the voyages of Sir Humphrey Gilbert, Martin Frobisher, Sir Walter Raleigh, and the other great sea-dogs of the Elizabethan time. Then, too, people in England naturally felt the greatest curiosity about the far-off regions in which their kindred had made a home. There was a yet more practical reason for writing books of this kind. The country wanted colonists, and these reports of it were often intended to encourage emigration, put forth very much as we should now issue a prospectus of Alaska or of some sparsely-settled region of the West.

THE LITERATURE OF THE SOUTH

American literature begins in the South, the earliest-settled region of our country, and among its first productions we find books of travel and adventure such as we have just described. It is a book of travel, CAPTAIN JOHN SMITH's *True Relation of such Occurrences and Accidents of Note as Hath Happened in Virginia* (1608), that has gained the reputation of being the first American book. Its claim to this distinction appears to be somewhat doubtful, as Smith returned to England after his exploits in this country and ended his days there. His accounts of American exploration and settlement, therefore, are strictly the books of an Englishman about America, with no more title to be called American literature than Professor Bryce's *American Commonwealth*. But, English or American, we cannot afford to pass over either these books or their author. The famous Captain John Smith was born in a Lincolnshire village in 1580, the very year Sir Francis Drake, the first Englishman to sail round the world, was welcomed home from his famous voyage with great rejoicings. He opened his eyes on a world of gallant exploits and strange adventures in the far corners of the earth. England was ringing with the fame of her great navigators, and Smith, born almost in sight of the sea, tells us that even from his boyhood " his mind was set upon brave adventures." The roving spirit was so strong that when about thirteen he sold his satchel and books, and resolved to run away to sea. His father's death interrupted the execution of this plan; but about two years later he left home for a wandering life full of strange adventures in many lands. As we read of his fighting, his shipwrecks, his romantic rescues by " honorable and virtuous Ladies," he seems to us like some resplendent knight-errant, a hero of mediæval romance, actually alive in that brave sixteenth-century world. On a voyage to Italy he is thrown into the sea by " a rabble of Pilgrims of divers nations," who, " hourly cursing him " for a heretic, swear they will have no good weather so long as he is on board. In a war against the Turks, the ladies longing to see " some courtlike pastime," he successively overcomes three Turkish champions in single combat and cuts off their heads. Unfortunately our chief authority for Smith's life is the narrative of the hero himself, and many believe that his exploits lost nothing in the telling. Probably the childish vanity at times apparent in his writings may be partly due to a dreamy spirit which loved to surround his adventures with that romantic glamour in which his imagination delighted. An old English writer, Thomas

Fuller, tells us that in Smith's old age in London, when beset by poverty, he "efforted [strengthened] his spirits with the remembrance and relation of what he formerly had been and what he had done." * This is as natural as it is pathetic, and helps us to a better understanding of his character and his books. Nevertheless, Smith was no empty boaster, but shrewd and capable, a man for a crisis, and a born leader. The great part he took in American colonization belongs to history; our present interest is in the books in which he jotted down the story of his settlement of Virginia, and his subsequent exploration of New England. Smith was a prolific and, no doubt, a rapid writer; but, like Sir Walter Raleigh, he made authorship merely an incident in a life crowded with dangers and brave deeds. As we might expect, he is not a finished writer; but his books are graphic and entertaining, and full of the vigor and power of the man. If his love of "brave adventure" and the spirit of the artist made him occasionally draw upon his imagination to heighten the interest, at least some of his readers will be secretly thankful for the romance, and pardon the trifling lapses from truth.

The literature of the South during the Colonial era is just what the conditions of life would lead us to expect. There are few books, and fewer authors, and the work produced, while valuable to the historian or interesting to the curious student, shows no exceptional literary

Literature of the South.

---

* Fuller's *Worthies of England,* p. 180 (ed. 1662).

merit or original power.   One of the most vigorous
and graphic bits of prose is an account of the expedition to Virginia of Sir Thomas Eaton, whose ship was
wrecked on one of the Bermudas in 1610.   The story
is told by William Strachy, one of the company, and
the description of the storm is supposed to have
furnished some hints to Shakespeare in the composition of *The Tempest*.   Small as is the amount of
this Southern literature, the portion of it which
can fairly be called American is smaller still.   We
can hardly claim books written during a short stay
in America as a part of our literature, yet if such
books are excluded from these early writings of the
South but little remains.   According to Prof. Tyler,
there were only six authors in Virginia during the
first twenty years of its settlement, " who yet live
and deserve to live."   But of these six we find
that all but one returned to England after a brief
residence.   Nor is this all; this little group of foreign
writers is followed by no strong indigenous growth,
and from 1627 to the close of the century the history
of Southern literature is but little more than a blank.
There are only about eleven writers in the South
before the Revolution, including the six already
referred to, who hold a place, more or less formal, in
literary history, and ten out of the eleven deal with
the history of the country, or relate some personal
adventures, often semi-historical in their character.
Bacon's rebellion in 1675 against the autocratic Governor Berkeley is the occasion of some powerful
verses by an unknown hand, but with this exception

the English poet George Sandys's *Translation of Ovid* (1621–6) is the only notable contribution to literature in the strictest sense. A high authority speaks of this translation as "the first monument of English poetry, of classical scholarship, and of deliberate literary art reared on these shores;"* but when we reflect that it was begun in England and published in London, and that our only claim to it arises from the fact that it was completed during the author's brief stay in Virginia, we can hardly regard it as in any true sense our own.

Looking, then, at this Southern Colonial literature as a whole, we cannot but feel that during this period the affluent and semi-feudal South, with its general illiteracy and its aristocratic denial of freedom of thought, had not begun to create a true and enduring literature.

THE LITERATURE OF NEW ENGLAND

The strongly marked personality of the Puritan is deeply impressed upon the literature of New England, giving it from the first a well-defined and distinctive character. The intense conviction of the reality of the spiritual and the unseen, present as a living force in man's daily life and entering into its smallest and most ordinary details, an inexorable conscience and the rigors of an exacting and often joyless creed, these things create the atmosphere which makes the literature of this great section a thing apart. We are impressed with the large number of books on religious

* Tyler's *American Literature*, vol. i. p. 55.

and theological topics. Besides these larger and more
formal treatises, learned clergymen assail each other
with tracts upon hotly-contested points of doctrine,
and the air is " black with sermons." In such works
we see the provincial branch of that English literature
of theological treatise and pamphlet warfare to which
Milton himself was a contributor. Thus, by putting
three thousand miles of sea between himself and the
fierce disputations that were being waged at home, the
Puritan changed his skies, but not his mind.

Nor is it merely in works of a professedly religious
nature that this especial note of the Puritan is heard:
it recurs at intervals in those diaries and histories
which were written in New England as in the other
Colonies, and repeats itself with still greater distinctness in the stray bits of crude verse that were labo-
riously brought forth amid the chill and hardness of
that sober-minded land.

The first—and as original authorities perhaps the
most important—among the historical writings are
Histories those of WILLIAM BRADFORD (1588–1657),
and jour- the second governor of Plymouth. Brad-
nals. ford was sprung from the yeoman class in
Yorkshire. From his boyhood he had showed a
decidedly religious bent, and, having separated himself from the Church of England, he came to America
on the Mayflower in 1620. He and his fellow-passenger
EDWARD WINSLOW kept a journal which dates from
the day on which they first saw the new land; but
Bradford's more ambitious and important work is his
History of Plymouth, in which he gives a full and

clearly written account of the planting and early history of that colony to 1649.

Side by side with Bradford, the early governor and historian of Plymouth, we may appropriately place JOHN WINTHROP (1588–1649), the governor and historian of the sister colony of Massachusetts Bay. Of good family, a student at Trinity College, Cambridge, the son of a lawyer, and himself bred to that profession, Winthrop is among those choice spirits of scholarly training and sterling manhood who were being lost to England and gained for America by the stringency of Laud and the tyranny and duplicity of Charles the First. His so-called *History of New England* is really an unpretentious journal, a record of every-day happenings, as well as of those momentous events in which he played so great a part. It describes the voyage to America, and gives us, in the form of a simple, personal narrative, much valuable knowledge of the progress of the settlement until 1649. Many a homely incident, as that of the cow that died at Plymouth from eating Indian corn, seems to us but the gossip of a day, yet, like the musty columns of an old newspaper, it helps to bring us closer to the past. In places the style has a genuine freshness and charm. " We had now fair sunshine weather, and so pleasant a sweet air as did much refresh us, and there came a smell off the shore like the smell of a garden." * In such a sentence we

* Winthrop's *History of New England*, vol. i. p. 23 (Savage's ed., 1825).

recognize that captivating turn of phrase which
Stevenson, that great modern master of the prose of
adventure, seems to have learned in part from the
narrative of the old English navigators. Winthrop's
pages furnish many evidences of that belief in the
direct ordering of human affairs by a Higher Power
to which we have already alluded. Two children are
driven into the house by the wind in time to escape
death from a fall of logs, which would have " crushed
them, if the Lord in his special providence had not
delivered them." * Two men, having lost their boat,
are left upon an oyster-bank, and " although they
might have waded out on either side," they are
drowned. " This," Winthrop adds, " was an evident
judgment of God upon them, for they were wicked
persons." † The following account of the extraordinary action of a certain Mr. Glover and its
tragical consequences is not free from an unconscious
humor:

" One Mr. Glover of Dorchester, having laid sixty
pounds of gunpowder in bags to dry in the end of his
chimney, it took fire, and some went up the chimney;
other of it filled the room and passed out at a door
into another room, and blew up a gable end. A maid
which was in the room . . . was scorched, and died
soon after. A little child in the arms of another
was scorched upon the face, but not killed. Two men
were singed, but not much. Divers pieces [firearms]

---

* Winthrop's *History of New England*, vol. i. p. 100.
† *Ibid.*, vol. i. p. 126.

which lay charged in several places took fire and went
off, but did no harm. *Another great providence was,*
that two little children, being at the fire a little
before, they went out to play (though it was a very
cold day) and so were preserved." * Here and there
some chance anecdote or allusion shows us how near
and real religion and conscience were to the people's
life. We are told of a boy of fourteen, who, although
"a dutiful child," becomes "humbled and broken
for his sins," so that he went "mourning and lan-
guishing daily." † A man who is not a church-
member awakes at night with a cry, starts from his
bed, and jumps out of the window into the snow and
runs for miles. The next morning he is traced by
his footprints, and those in search of him see by the
marks in the snow that he has "kneeled down to
prayer in divers places." About seven miles from
home they come upon his dead body.‡ Winthrop
tells the story briefly and without comment, but the
incident has in it a very melancholy and tragic power;
it is full of meaning, and it suggests to our imagination much that is not directly told. The midnight
call to the troubled conscience; the frantic flight
through the winter's night; the strange, silent wit-
nesses to those secret and awful wrestlings in the dark,
—these things force home on us one side of New England life, in all its dark and forbidding reality. It
was the brooding, morbid, but intensely ideal temper

* Winthrop's *History of New England*, vol. i. p. 212.
† *Ibid.*, vol. i. p. 126.   ‡ *Ibid.*, vol. i. p. 214.

of this life that the genius of Nathaniel Hawthorne was to interpret in a generation to come.

We find the same spirit in regard to unseen and spiritual things in the more professedly religious **The Mathers.** books, but of course greatly intensified and less mixed with worldly affairs. A large part of the writing done in New England was the work of the ministers. We have already spoken of their importance in a community which strove to make the law of man coincide with the law of God. As authorized expounders of God's laws they were recognized leaders, and their opinions on political and social as well as on religious matters were regarded with extraordinary deference. As a class, they were incomparably the best trained and most scholarly men in the Colonies, and the incessant writing of sermons helped to give them an alarming facility in composition. Such circumstances combined to make the ministers of New England the nearest approach to a directly literary class.

Perhaps the best illustration of the commanding influence and importance of the ministry in New England is to be found in the famous scholars and **The Mather dynasty.** preachers of the Mather family, who for four successive generations made the pulpit a throne of power. Through RICHARD MATHER (1596–1669), the first in this clerical succession, INCREASE MATHER (1639–1723), his famous son, and COTTON MATHER (1663–1728), his yet more famous grandson, this remarkable family was a growing power in New England life and thought for nearly a hundred years. The Mathers were men of fine presence, of iron constitutions, with tremendous wills, and a capacity for toil that carried them through lives of tireless intellectual labor. Enormous readers and prodigious writers, these three men must have produced in all between five and six hundred works, including tracts, sermons, and pamphlets, besides hundreds of pages of manuscript which remain yet unpublished. The strong family traits are repeated from one generation to another, growing weaker at last in SAMUEL MATHER (1706–1785), the son of Cotton, author and minister like the rest, and the last of the line. Richard Mather, driven by persecution to take refuge in New England in 1635, labored for half a century " as minister of the Church of God." The description given of him suggests dignity and power: " His voice was loud and big; and, uttered with a deliberate vehemency, it procured unto his ministry an awful and very taking majesty." * We are amazed at the tremendous vitality of these men; at their indefatigable energy. Increase Mather lived to the age of eighty-five, and was for more than sixty years " a laborious preacher of Christ." Besides the labors of his ministry, he was for nearly twenty years the acting or actual president of Harvard College, and was during four critical years the representative of Massachusetts to England. With all this he found time to write one hundred and sixty books and tracts, and to read innumerable books—more, probably, than

* Mather's *Magnalia*, vol. i. p. 452.

any American of his day.   Like his father, he seems
to have impressed men with the awe that the New
England minister so often inspired.   We are told that
" he had an awful and reverend manner " in leading
" the public addresses to God," and that his face as
well as his words constrained devotion.*   Cotton
Mather won an even wider distinction than his father
for his miscellaneous learning and literary productive-
ness.   If study could make a great man, it would have
made a genius of Cotton Mather.   He had the largest
private library in the Colonies.   He understood many
languages, and some of his three hundred and eighty-
two published works are written in French, in
Spanish, and in Algonquin.   For over forty years he
occupied the pulpit in the North Church, Boston, at
first as assistant to his father; he was elected Fellow
of the Royal Society—a high honor for a colonist in
those days, and became better known in Europe for
his learning than any American of his time.   Not-
withstanding all these successes, his life, when we
come to know it more clearly, moves us to pity and
regret rather than to admiration, for in spite of sin-
cerely good intentions it exhibited those defects and
mistakes which even in his lifetime New England was
beginning to outgrow.   He was a bright boy, from
whom much had been expected.   Heir to the prestige
and influence of a distinguished family, crammed
with Latin and theology from his precocious youth,

---

* *Annals of the American Pulpit*, vol. i. p. 158.   (Funeral
sermon on Increase Mather.)

surrounded during his early manhood with an atmosphere of deference and adulation, Mather's circumstances naturally tended to make him vain and
overbearing. Besides this, he was a devourer of books
rather than an original thinker or a man of practical
judgment; his retentive memory was stored with a
mass of curious and ill-digested learning, and the
learned allusions with which his works are burdened,
having often but a slight and fanciful connection with
the subject in hand, give his writing an unwieldy and
pedantic tone. There was a consuming earnestness
in this singular character, with the asceticism of some
religious enthusiast of the middle ages. At fourteen
he began the systematic observance of fasts and vigils,
a practice which he continued until late in life. It
was his ambition to resemble a certain rabbi " whose
face was black by reason of his fastings." It was his
habit to make the most ordinary events the occasion
of some spiritual lesson, both for his own benefit and
also for the training of his family. " Two of my
children," he writes, " have been newly scorched
with gunpowder, wherein, though they have received
a merciful deliverance, yet they undergo a smart that
is considerable. I must improve this occasion to in-
culcate lessons of piety upon them, especially with
relation to their danger of everlasting burnings." *
Beginning life full of ambition and zeal, Mather's
later years were embittered by disappointment and
darkened by domestic sorrows. Both tradition and

* Peabody's *Life of Mather*, in Sparks' *American Biography*,
vol. vi. p. 194.

inheritance bound him to a time when the clergy of
New England had wielded a tremendous civil power,
but it was his lot to live when this political power was
fast slipping away. New and more liberal ideas
began to prevail; many were beginning to hold that
the right to vote should be less rigidly restricted to
church-members. So Mather stood committed by all
his life and training to be the champion of a system
of ecclesiastical influence in State affairs, condemned
by the natural laws of growth to pass away. Such a
situation is not without pathos. Under strangely
altered conditions, he fought over again Thomas à
Becket's battle for a lost cause. Lacking, it seems
to us, the help of a lovable and winning personality,
many of Mather's conscientious attempts to assist
others were met with coldness, and, as he complained,
with ingratitude. The man himself, with his pathetic
failures and mistakes, his asceticism, his omnivorous
learning and narrowness of mind, has an interest for
us quite apart from his books, for he is in many ways
the most significant figure in the Colonial history of
his time.

Mather was the last notable representative of a
New England that was breaking up and changing
in accordance with more liberal ideas; in
Mather's work. his writings the traditions and ideals of
that earlier New England survive. In his
most famous book, the *Magnalia Christi Americana,
or The Ecclesiastical History of New England* (1702),
he points the young generation to those traditions
which he thought it wholesome for them to remem-

ber, and those ideals from which he feared they were
inclined to fall away.* He would recall a backsliding
generation by praising the wondrous deeds of their
fathers that begat them, by reminding them that
the hand of God was as truly manifest in the planting of New England as in the departure of Abraham
from Chaldea. "*Tantæ molis erat, pro* CHRISTO
condere gentem,"—this motto, which confronts us
from the title-page of the *Magnalia*, gives us the key
to the spirit in which the history is told. The
Magnalia is a huge, unwieldy work; it passes from
historical narrative to brief biographies of the principal governors and divines of New England, and
includes a review, in eight chapters, of many illustrious
and wonderful providences, both of mercies and judgments. Its pages are as thickly strown with Latin
quotations as a barren New England hillside with
bowlders, and the author's learning is obtruded into
the simplest thought. Even in this intricate and
fantastic style, modelled chiefly after the quaint and

* "Mankind will pardon me . . . if, smitten with a just fear
of incroaching and ill-bodied degeneracies, I shall use my
modest endeavors to prevent the loss of a country so signalized
for the profession of the purest Religion. . . . I shall count my
country lost in the loss of the primitive principles and the
primitive practices upon which it was first established; but
certainly one good way to save that loss would be to do something, that the memory of the great things done for us by our
God may not be lost, and that the story of the circumstances
attending the foundation and formation of this country and of
its preservation hitherto, may be impartially handed unto
posterity."—*Magnalia*, Bk. I., Introd.

somewhat ungainly prose of certain seventeenth-century writers in England, Mather represented a fashion which his contemporaries had already abandoned.

As we see in the *Magnalia* the intense Puritan conviction that God was as truly ordering the destinies of men as in the days when the children of Israel were His chosen people, so in another famous book of Mather's, *The Wonders of the Invisible World* (1692), we find an equally strong apprehension of the personal presence of the powers of evil. This invisible world came very close to him, and he saw in New England the battle-ground for its spiritual hosts. Mather believed that before the Puritans came the land had been the territory of the Devil, where he had " reigned without any control for many ages." The setting up of a kingdom of God within his kingdom had filled him with fury, and he had tried many ways to recover possession. " I believe," Mather wrote, " that never were more satanical devices used for the unsettling of any people under the sun, than what have been here employ'd for the extirpation of the vine which God has here planted." * Foiled in all the more indirect means, the Devil at length came in person with his hosts, and organized a conspiracy for recovering the land. Mather and many others believed that the evil powers had entered into many unhappy creatures, who had been induced to assist him in his plot. The belief in witchcraft was not peculiar to New England, but the brooding and fanatical intensity of the New

---

* *Wonders of the Invisible World*, Sect. I. § II.

England mind gave this dark superstition a peculiar power. We need not tell the story of the witch-trials at Salem—perhaps the most tragic episode in our early history: it is enough to say that Cotton Mather's influence and writings were largely responsible for this horrible delusion. To his excited fancy the devils swarmed in multitudes like the frogs in the plagues of Egypt,* and " Behold! sinners! " he exclaims, " the very devils are walking about our streets with lengthened chains, making a dreadful noise in our ears, and Brimstone, even without a metaphor, is making an hellish and horrid stench in our nostrils." † Painful as are Mather's works on this theme, they yet show us the depth and height of the Puritan nature, at home beyond the borders of the invisible and personifying with the definiteness of Dante's vision the eternal conflict in the souls of men. To the New England Puritan this eternal conflict was the great fact of the world; but he hated iniquity rather than loved mercy, and added to his intense hatred of sin an equally intense satisfaction in the punishment of the sinner. This last trait is strongly shown in that characteristic poem, once widely popular in New England, Michael Wigglesworth's *Day of Doom.*

Before considering this extraordinary work, we must speak briefly of early verse-writing in New England. We should wrong the Puritan if we failed to perceive that, with

Poetry in New England.

---

* Mather's *Wonders of the Invisible World.*
† *Ibid.*

all his outward austerity and reserve, he had yet the
stirrings of a deep poetic feeling latent within him.
Living among the eternal questions of conscience, and
near to the mysteries of the unseen, his life could not
but nourish that spirituality and mysticism which has
continued to characterize the literature of New England. But this pent-up poetry of the New Englander
found no natural and spontaneous outflow in song.
The untaught art by which the people of Scotland
or England shaped and rounded song and ballad into
a thing of beauty and power seemed to have no
place in his composition. The minstrels of early New
England were Puritan divines, who elaborated doggerel epitaphs, and produced the harshest and crudest
versification of the Psalter. This version, commonly
known as the *Bay Psalm Book* (1640), was in general
use for many years among the New England churches.
It is so exceedingly rough and labored that no one
with an ear for poetry can read it without positive
pain, yet it was the work of men who may be fairly
said to represent the best New England scholarship
of their time. Prominent in the undertaking were
Richard Mather, sometime student at Oxford, and
John Eliot, the Apostle of the Indians, who was a
graduate of Cambridge. It seems incredible that
such men should have been incapable of complying
with the ordinary rules of verse-making had they
chosen to do so, and in fact the chief cause of the
roughness of their version was their determination to
sacrifice poetry to the literal accuracy of their translation. They announce in their preface that they

have "attempted conciseness rather than elegance, fidelity rather than poetry"; and the declaration shows the strength and narrowness of the religious feeling in New England, and the comparative indifference to beauty and art. The idea that they were desecrating the Bible they reverenced by converting some of the noblest poetry of the world into childish doggerel had no place in their minds. The verses, accordingly, jostle along like a disorderly mob, instead of marching with the ordered step of an army. When we imagine ourselves within the chill rectangular interior of some Puritan meeting-house, and think of these verses given out line by line, and droned over, without instrumental accompaniment, to some well-worn tune; when we reflect that, sung in this fashion, they were immensely popular throughout New England until shortly before the outbreak of the Revolution,—the æsthetic limitations of Puritanism become more plain.* The memorial verses, usually on

* For general accounts of metrical versions of the Psalter, including the *Bay Psalm Book*, see articles on English Hymnology, The English Psalter, in Julian's *Dictionary of Hymnology*. See also *The Ancient Psalmody and Hymnology of New England*, by Samuel E. Staples; Palfrey's *History of New England*, vol. v., note, pp. 221, 222. The musical deficiencies of early New England congregations should not be overlooked. It is said that "not more than ten different tunes were used in public worship for eighty or ninety years. Few congregations could sing more than five tunes." Coffin's *History of Newbury*, p. 185, quoted by Palfrey, vol. ii.; *History of New England*, vol. ii., note, p. 41. When the music improved, the poetry of the metrical versions improved also.

the death of some minister or governor, are chiefly
remarkable for their frigid quaintness of expression
and their lack of any saving grace of humor.   Thus
the pompous movement of some lines bewailing the
death of Sir William Phips, one of the governors of
Massachusetts Bay, is so suddenly interrupted as to
bring us close to the ridiculous:

> "Our Almanacks foretold a great eclipse:
>   This they foresaw not of our greater Phips."

The following promise is made to the shade of the
departed governor:

> "Now lest ungrateful brands we should incur,
>   Your salary we'll pay in tears, GREAT SIR."*

In some cases we come upon far-fetched compari-
sons, or "conceits," as they were called, such as were
in favor with Donne, Herbert, Crashaw, and other
early seventeenth-century poets in England.   Thus
in some memorial verses we are told that John Cotton
was—

> "A living, breathing *Bible ;* tables where
>   Both *Covenants,* at large, engraven were ;
>   *Gospel* and *Law,* in's heart, had each its column ;
>   His head an index to the sacred volume ;
>   His very name a *title-page ;* and next,
>   His life a *commentary* on the text.
>   O, what a monument of glorious worth,
>   When, in a *new edition,* he comes forth,
>   Without *erratas* may we think he'll be,
>   In *leaves* and *covers* of eternity."†

* Elegy upon the death of Sir William Phips.   Mather's
Magnalia, Bk. II.

† Lines on Cotton, by B. Woodbridge, in Mather's *Magnalia,* Bk. III.

This "mortuary muse," as Lowell calls it, was commonly invoked by those who looked upon the writing of poetry only as an incidental accomplishment, but there is one verse-writer of early New England who produced so large a **Anne Bradstreet.** bulk of verse as to leave us in no doubt of her devotion and constancy to her art. This was ANNE BRADSTREET (1613–1672), commonly known as the "Tenth Muse," from the announcement of her advent in that capacity on the title-page of the London edition of her book of poems. Mrs. Bradstreet herself had no part in the assumption of this lofty title, and it is only right to remember that she constantly expresses the most humble opinion of her work. Mrs. Bradstreet occupied a position of importance in the colony, being the daughter of one governor, Thomas Bradley, and the wife of another. While she was not a poet in any high sense, Mrs. Bradstreet showed such a marked superiority to the verse-makers about her that she justly won a considerable local reputation. Indeed, the great Cotton Mather asserted that her verses would outlast the stateliest marble, and another writer declared that in reading them he was "sunk in a sea of bliss" and "weltering in delight." In these days she has few readers beside the critics, into whose hands she hoped her book would never come. Yet while our earliest woman poet was not a genius, her character and abilities excite both admiration and interest. Before leaving England, at the age of eighteen, she seems to have had the opportunity of gratifying her keen love of reading, and throughout all her life in the loneliness of the crude Western colony, though checked by continual ill-health, and interrupted by the incessant claims of her household duties, the love of learning did not die out within her, but she remained, in the face of every obstacle, a reader, a thinker, and, in her scanty leisure, a writer of prose and verse. To judge her fairly we must realize how distant she was from the great centers of civilization, and remember the many obstacles she had to overcome. Born when Shakespeare's career was just ending and Milton was still in his infancy, the strictness of her religion as well as the remoteness of her situation shut her out from much that was noblest and most inspiring in the literature of that golden time. Besides all this, she was a woman, and, as she writes,

> " Obnoxious to each carping tongue,
> Who says my hand a needle better fits,
> A poet's pen all scorn I should thus wrong,
> For such despite they cast on female wits."

Yet in the teeth of such discouragement Anne Bradstreet wrote the best verses produced in New England in her time. Her works show industry, careful reading, and a religious, thoughtful, and appreciative mind. Her longest, but by no means her best, poem is *The Four Monarchies*, a rhymed history of Assyria, Persia, Greece, and Rome, based on Sir Walter Raleigh's *History of the World*. In her poem on *The Four Elements*, Earth, Air, Fire, and Water dispute together as to which is the most important.* Another poem, the *Four Seasons*, which contains sundry practical and prosaic points about agriculture, seems a dim anticipation of Thomson's *Seasons*. Mrs. Bradstreet was a great admirer of Sylvester's translation of a French poem by Du Bartas called *Divine Weeks and Works*, a long, dull composition much read by the Puritans of that time. She was called by a contemporary "a right Du Bartas's girl," but such a master was not calculated to improve her literary taste. It is in her simple and less bookish verses that she is at her best. Her short poem *Contemplations*, in which really admirable descriptions of nature are mingled with the thoughts that they naturally suggest to her religious and meditative mind, has a genuine poetry in it, absent from her more laborious and less unaffected works. But, on the whole, we should honor and remember Anne Bradstreet, not so much for the intrinsic worth of what she wrote, as for her place in the progress of our history and culture. We must honor her because she was one of the first among us to seriously devote herself to poetry for its own sake, and because her writings and example exerted a salutary and refining influence on others.

In Mrs. Bradstreet's *Contemplations* we have one of the few expressions in poetry of the gentler and sweeter element in New England life, but in MICHAEL WIGGLESWORTH'S *Day of Doom*, hard, dogmatic, and

---

* Curiously enough, this bears a strong similarity to an interlude by John Heywood (1506?-1565), the *Play of the Weather*.

inspired with a fierce religious zeal, the sterner and
Michael more familiar aspect of that life is mani-
Wiggles- fested in all its crude and uncompromising
worth. severity. Wigglesworth's life and character
seem to have little in common with his terrible utterances. Like so many New England writers, he was a
clergyman, and, as far as we can judge, gentle and
kindly. His health was delicate, but, in spite of his
feeble body, he was full of a consuming energy in
good works. Cotton Mather describes him in his old
age as "a little, feeble shadow of a man, beyond
seventy, preaching usually twice or thrice in the week,
visiting and comforting the afflicted, and attending to
the sick, not only in his own town, but also in all
those of the vicinity." Perhaps his love and devotion made him feel all the more strongly the terrors of
that Day of Judgment which his best-known poem
describes. Its rough, doggerel verse is lurid with
graphic and almost exultant descriptions of the eternal
tortures of the wicked, a theme which had attracted
the genius of one of the greatest poets and one of the
greatest artists of the world. We may doubt whether
Dante in his *Inferno* or Michael Angelo in his Last
Judgment had a more intense belief in the awful
reality of the scene they depicted than this obscure
New England Puritan. All was real enough to
Wigglesworth's imagination, but the immeasurable
distance between his halting verses and the works of
the great masters of whom we have spoken tells us
how hard it was for the New England Puritan to
master even the alphabet of the poet's art. Under

the blue Italian skies the very peasant-girls by the impulse of a poetic instinct could utter their loves and longings in song; even in mediæval Scotland the youths and maidens, dancing on the green at twilight, could sing the ballad some poet of the people had made; but in our land it has always been different, and in New England men could preach or act, but they could not sing. So poor Michael Wigglesworth strove to preach what it was in his heart to say, and struggled with his halting, unmanageable verses as best he could. He describes the Day of Judgment coming swiftly on a careless and pleasure-loving world, grown hardened in its sins. He tells of the futile pleas of the heathen, and how they are put to silence; of the infants who, not elected to be saved, are yet assigned "the easiest room in hell." He preaches the everlasting physical torment of the wicked, who, like the condemned in Dante, have no hope of death.

> " For day and night in their despight,
>   Their torment's smoke ascendeth;
> Their pain and grief have no relief,
>   Their anguish never endeth.
>   *   *   *   *   *
> " They live to lie in misery,
>   And bear eternal wo ;
> And live they must while God is just,
>   That He may plague them so." *

It is impossible for us to understand the spirit and motive of such a work unless we are in sympathy with

* *The Day of Doom.* Most of the poem is given in Stedman and Hutchinson's *Library of American Literature*, vol. ii.

those doctrines in which Wigglesworth believed. But
we must remember that such views were preached
Sunday after Sunday from hundreds of pulpits.
Because they were generally accepted, *The Day of
Doom* became, as Lowell declared, the "solace of
every fireside, the flicker of the pine-knots by which
it was conned perhaps adding a livelier relish to its
premonitions of eternal combustion."*

Wigglesworth was about thirty years older than
Cotton Mather, but, like Mather, he saw about him
signs of the breaking up of the more rigid religious
rule of an earlier time, a waning power of the church,
a growing tolerance which to him foreboded disaster
to the Kingdom of Righteousness which the New
England fathers had sacrificed so much to found.
We see how sorely he felt these things in another
poem, *God's Controversy with New England*, which
was published in the same year as his *Day of Doom*.
He treats in this less-known work of " New England
planted, prospered, declining, threatened, punished."
He describes his country, once reclaimed from the
power of Satan, as slipping back into sin, and plagued
and rebuked by God for its offences. If we would be
just to Wigglesworth and others like him, we must
remember that it is much easier for us to condemn his
manner and intolerance than to understand the spirit
of the time in which he lived and the motives which
prompted his work. It seems likely that his conviction of the growing carelessness and wickedness of the
time gave an added zest and fierceness to his picture

* *The Harvard Book*, vol. ii. p. 158.

of the eternal retribution. About him New England seemed, to his eyes, becoming faithless to her high calling, while in Old England the rule of the Puritan had recently been overturned, to give place to the profligate levity of the court of the second Charles. He had the almost fanatical intensity, the rigorous creed of his colony and his time; we can hardly wonder that, gentle and loving as he was, he taxed the slender resources of his uncouth verse with terrible warnings of the wrath that should suddenly overtake the children of disobedience.

We find the same strange contrast between the life and works of JONATHAN EDWARDS (1703–1758), by far the most acute, laborious, and distinguished thinker that Colonial New England produced. Born in East Windsor, Connecticut, where his father was pastor, Edwards gave early **Jonathan Edwards.** promise of extraordinary mental power and of a deep spirituality of nature. The outward course of his life was not materially different from that of many of his brother ministers. Pure, laborious, lofty, and devoted, it was the life of the thinker and the student, full of high aims, if inclined to be morbidly conscientious, over-precise, and austere. Edwards was tall and slender, and, like Wigglesworth, of delicate constitution. His face—if we may judge from his portrait, with its high forehead, mild, meditative eyes, and almost womanly sweetness of expression—is that of the saint and scholar who has lived apart from the vulgar aims and contentions of ordinary men. He was subject to low spirits, but, with a wonderful

capacity for sustained intellectual exertion, he found
the keenest pleasure in working out some intricate
process of reasoning through long hours of solitary
toil.   Many elements of early New England life and
thought meet in him: indeed, it is because he represents so perfectly the different aspects of that life
that he seems full of contradictions which we find it
hard or impossible to reconcile.   He has to an extraordinary degree that high spirituality and beautiful
serenity, that touch of true poetic sentiment, often
buried out of sight or sternly repressed, which were
among the noblest attributes of the Puritan temper.
He has the old Hebraic joy in the presence of God;
and he believes that "a divine, supernatural light is
immediately imparted to the soul by God's Spirit."
Even in his youth, while walking "for contemplation" in a solitary place in his father's pastures, his
soul is filled with high and holy thought.   "And as
I was walking there," he writes, "and looking upon
the sky and the clouds, there came into my mind so
sweet a sense of the glorious majesty and grace of God
as I know not how to express. . . . After this my
sense of divine things gradually increased, and became
more and more lively, and had more and more of that
inward sweetness.   The appearance of everything was
altered; there seemed to be, as it were, a calm, sweet
cast, an appearance of divine glory in almost everything; God's excellency, His wisdom, His purity and
love seemed to appear in everything—in the sun,
moon, and stars; in the clouds and the blue sky; in

the grass, flowers, trees; in the water and all nature
—which used greatly to fix my mind." *

Through the quiet loveliness of this passage we feel
that we are looking into the clear and tranquil depths
of a transparently beautiful nature. The shy spirit
of poetry is shown, too, in his description of Sarah
Pierrepont, whom he afterwards married: " She will
sometimes go about from place to place, singing
sweetly; and seems to be always full of joy and pleasure; and no one knows for what. She loves to be
alone, walking in the fields and groves, and seems
to have some one invisible always conversing with
her." † Yet Edwards's nature was steeped in that
Calvinistic theology in which he had been reared—a
creed which held that the mass of men were irretriev-
ably doomed to everlasting and unspeakable agonies
by what Edwards himself called the " revenging justice of God." His famous sermon, *Sinners in the
Hands of an Angry God*, if possible more terrible and
unsparing than its poetic counterpart, *The Day of
Doom*, filled even a Puritan congregation with awe and
trembling. Edwards loved to dwell on man's inherent vileness and wickedness; he was accustomed to
speak of his fellow-creatures, not as the children of
God, but as loathsome worms and vipers. To the service of Calvinism Edwards brought logical powers of a
high order, and an ideal and philosophic tempera-

* Stedman and Hutchinson's *Library of American Literature*,
vol. ii. p. 374.
† *Ibid.*, p. 382.

ment, so that he seems to us both the sectarian contro-
versialist and the metaphysician.   This is the case in
his most famous work, his essay *On the Freedom of the
Will*, which won for him a high place among the leading minds of the eighteenth century, and exerted a
considerable influence, not only on American, but also
on Scotch and English thought.   To Edwards as a
theologian the absolute freedom of the human will
seemed incompatible with the supreme power or
sovereignty of God as the moral ruler of the world,
and in this essay he has put forth his splendid powers
of argument to disprove the absolute freedom of our
wills.   Everything, he argues, has a cause, and we
choose one thing in preference to another because we
are led to do so by our strongest motive.   The will,
being determined by the strongest motive, is not free.
While Edwards's conclusions are not now generally
accepted, his book holds an honored place in the history of philosophy, and may be regarded as the first
really great and permanent contribution of America
to the thought of the world.

With Jonathan Edwards, the greatest exponent of
its thought and character, we close our survey of the
literature of Colonial New England.   He represents
both its strength and its weakness; its gloomy, inexorable creed, and its zeal for righteousness and
passion for abstract thought.   He is both the spiritual
descendant of Cotton Mather and of Michael Wigglesworth, and the spiritual ancestor of Dr. Channing,
the great leader of New England Unitarianism,
and of Emerson, the thinker of later times.   He

stands the inheritor of the old, which even in his
day was passing, and the forerunner of new developments to come.

THE LITERATURE OF THE MIDDLE COLONIES

In approaching the literature of the Middle Colonies
we feel that we have passed out of the sombre shadows
of Puritanism into a lighter if less stimulating region.
We miss those strong incentives to learning,—the
keen and enthusiastic interest in questions of theology,
and the commanding position given to the ministers;
yet literature, if less earnest, is also less sectarian,
more polished, and more open to the influence of foreign models.   Apart from this, we recognize a general
similarity to a large class of writings already alluded
to in the Colonies of New England and the South.
In this midland belt, as elsewhere, there are books
and pamphlets descriptive of the country, such as
Daniel Denton's *Brief Description of New York*
(1670), and Gabriel Thomas's *Historical and Geographical Account of the Province and County of
Pennsylvania and West New Jersey* (1698); there are
local histories and narratives of adventure, as that
singularly touching and graphic account of his wanderings given by the Quaker Jonathan Dickenson in
his *God's Protective Providence Man's Surest Help
and Defence* (1696).   A careful English student of the
United States has pronounced Pennsylvania " the
most remarkable of all the Colonies after the New
England group "; and so far as the scattered begin-

nings of literature in this central section had any intellectual center, it is to be found in Pennsylvania's
largest and most important city.   Indeed, Philadelphia's progress in education and culture was relatively
more rapid than that of New England, for while New
England was first in these respects in actual time, the
landing of the Pilgrims was about half a century earlier
than that of Penn.   Within a few years after the
foundation of the city, Philadelphia could boast of
scholars and scientists whose high attainments and
broad culture had won them European distinction.
Among them was JAMES LOGAN, who came with Penn
in 1699, a man of generous scholarship and scientific
tastes.   Besides writing a number of Latin essays on
scientific subjects, Logan translated Cato's *Distiches*
(1735), and Cicero's *De Senectute* (1744), the former
probably the first translation of a classic both made
and published in America.   Another man of learning
was GEORGE KEITH, who came to Philadelphia in 1689,
and who was spoken of by a contemporary English
writer as " the most learned man in the Quaker sect,
well-versed in the Oriental tongues and in philosophy
and mathematics." *   A remarkable group of men
bears witness to the city's early preëminence in science.
In JOHN BARTRAM (1699–1777) Pennsylvania produced a scientist that Linnæus, the great Swedish naturalist, pronounced " the greatest natural botanist in
the world."   Bartram made important contributions
to his chosen science, and founded near Philadelphia

* Burnet's *History of My Own Times*, vol. ii. p. 248.

the first botanic garden in this country. DAVID RIT-
TENHOUSE, the astronomer and mathematician, and
THOMAS GODFREY, who invented the quadrant, were
among the other Philadelphians of scientific distinction. Such men, with others of hardly less note,
point to the presence in early Philadelphia of wide
intellectual interests and solid acquirements.

In the field of pure literature the city cannot be
said to have accomplished as much as in science, yet
it produced a number of versifiers who
wrote with smoothness and apparent ease.
Their work is almost entirely an imitation
of the accepted English models, and shows but little
original thought or spontaneous poetic feeling. In
the early years of the eighteenth century Pope had
brought the flowing and monotonous cadence of the
heroic verse to a wonderful excellence. This verse
was immensely popular, to the comparative neglect of
other forms, and it possessed the additional attraction of being easily imitated.* As we glance over the
fugitive verses scattered through the American magazines of the first half of the last century, we come
upon many an obscure reproduction of the trick of
Pope's manner, or, less often, of that of some other
English master. The somewhat frigid but resound-
ing odes of Dryden, Thomson's *Seasons*, Gray's *Elegy*,
or the minor poems of Milton,—such have been the
evident models for some obscure or nameless copyist.

> Poetry in
> Philadel-
> phia.

* See Macaulay's remarks on this point in his *Essay on
Addison*.

Of little or no value as poetry, these verses bear conclusive witness to the origin of much of our early American verse.   Perhaps no English original can be held responsible for the discordant notes of *The Bay Psalm Book* or *The Day of Doom*, but as our verse becomes smoother and more finished it is evidently but a provincial echo, a following of the literary mode of London in a distant part of the English sovereign's domain.   But if such a fact impresses us with our intellectual dependence on England,—and this, we must remember, was only natural under the existing conditions,—it should also lead us to reflect that some Americans, at least, were eagerly familiarizing themselves with the best English classic poets when demands on their time and energies in purely material directions were pressing and incessant.   A good instance of the imitative qualities of this verse, as well as of the real appreciation and reading which it implied, is to be found in the Philadelphia poet THOMAS GODFREY (1736–1763), the son of the inventor of the quadrant, already mentioned. Godfrey seems to have had no direct educational advantages beyond "a common education in his mother tongue."   After leaving school he was apprenticed to a watchmaker, and in 1758 was engaged in the expedition against Fort Du Quesne, but, limited as were his opportunities, his interest and aspiration lay in the direction of painting and poetry.   In 1758 he published a lyric in *The American Magazine*, and rapidly won his way in the public favor.   He died of a fever contracted in the South, at the early age of twenty-seven. If we consider the circumstances under which Godfrey wrote, and remember the general character of our Colonial verse, we cannot but be impressed with the surprisingly high average to which his poetry attains. His poems indeed have but little positive merit, for, like all imitative verse, they do little but remind us of some masterpiece. They are crude in places, and often distinctly juvenile, yet their place in the history of our literature makes them both interesting and important. The youthful efforts of this glazier's son and watchmaker's apprentice show an acquaintance with English poetry greatly in advance of that of the early rhymesters of New England. Here are pastorals after the style of Pope, lyrics which recall Wither and his contemporaries of the early seventeenth century, and an allegoric poem, *The Court of Fancy*, which is patterned on Chaucer's *Parliament of Fowles*. Some of the stanzas in Godfrey's *Court of Love*, while they recall the allegorical descriptions in Sackville, Spenser, or many of the earlier English poets, yet show genuine poetic power. Godfrey's chief claim to be remembered is generally thought to be his blank-verse tragedy of *The Prince of Parthia*, the first drama written in America. This follows the Shakespearean manner as closely as the author's powers will permit—so closely, indeed, that some passages are little more than paraphrases of *Julius Cæsar*, *Hamlet*, and other plays; yet it is not wanting in touches of poetic power.

On the whole, it may be said of this literature of the Middle Colonies, that while it has no such striking and original figures as those of the great Puritan commonwealth, it shows a greater polish, and a wider reading in purely literary directions.   If it has no Cotton Mather or Jonathan Edwards, it has a better balanced and perhaps a wider culture than is to be found in the great Colonies of the North.   Predisposed by religious toleration to a greater liberty of thought than the iron fetters of Puritanism allowed, the ideal State founded by Penn was open in its early years to the influence of the clever but sceptical and unemotional writings which during the later seventeenth and early eighteenth centuries set the standard of English literary taste.   This is the literature on which the provincial taste was largely formed; this is the literature that finds its exponent in Benjamin Franklin.

Culture in the Middle States and New England.

STUDY LIST

THE COLONIAL PERIOD

For general view of the subject see Richardson's *American Literature* and Tyler's *American Literature*.

1. **Captain John Smith**, Life of, by Chas. Dudley Warner (Holt & Co.).   See also Henry Adams' *Historical Essays*.

2. **John Winthrop**, Life of, by Rev. J. H. Twichell, in Makers of America Series.

3. **Cotton Mather**.   A good Life is that by Prof. Barrett Wendell in Makers of America Series.   See also *The Life and Times of Cotton Mather*, by Rev. A. P. Marvin.

4. **Jonathan Edwards**, Life of, by A. V. G. Allen.   See also Holmes's Essay on Edwards in *Pages from an Old*

Volume of Life.   For the philosophy of Edwards, see G.
P. Fisher's *Discussions in History and Theology*.

Selections from the above writers will be found in Stedman and Hutchinson's *Library of American Literature*.

5. History. Palfrey's *History of New England ;* Lodge's
English Colonies in America ; Doyle's *English Colonies in
America ;* Fiske's *Beginnings of New England ;* Cooke's
Virginia, in American Commonwealths Series ; Justin
Winsor's *Narrative and Critical History of America*, vols.
ii.-iv. ; Thwaite's *The Colonies*, in Epochs of American
History Series ; W. M. Sloan's *The French War and the
Revolution*, in the American History Series ; *The Colonial
Era*, by G. P. Fisher, in the same series, contains, in
addition to an admirable historical survey, a useful chap-
ter on the Colonial literature ; Parkman's series on *France
and England in North America* (in 7 parts, published
under separate titles).   Also, the histories of the United
States of Bancroft and Hildreth.

PART II

THE ESTABLISHMENT OF NATIONALITY
Cir. 1765–Cir. 1815

CHAPTER I

THE BEGINNINGS OF NATIONALITY

THE prominent feature of our literature, during the period just sketched, was its lack of unity. The Colonies, distinct in origin and in character, had a spirit of local loyalty and pride, but no feeling of a common nationality. De Kalm, a Swedish naturalist who visited this country as late as 1748, commenting upon this independence of the several colonies, remarks that " each has its proper laws and coin, and may be looked upon in several lights as a State by itself." * Besides all other causes for this isolation of the colonies from each other, was the difficulty of communication in a country so much of which still lay in unbroken forests. Under these conditions, each colony turned to England, rather than to its sister

Colonial diversity.

* Peter De Kalm's *Travels into North America,* vol. i. pp. 262, 263.

settlements, for its material or intellectual supplies. Yet even from an early period conditions were slowly but steadily forcing the English in America to a closer union, and prompting them to a concerted action. Except towards the Atlantic, they found themselves hemmed in on every side by the encroachments of foreign rivals.

Progress towards union.

Florida and the South were in the hands of Spain, while on the far Northwest and West rose the aggressive and ambitious power of France, intent on pushing southward from the Great Lakes along the Mississippi valley. When the menace of France changed to actual conflict, it was but natural that the scattered English should draw closer together and attempt some concerted action against the common danger. Under all the local jealousies and differences between the English colonists was the uniting force of a common interest, the deep instinct of kinship, the bond of the one mother tongue. The great struggle with France for the mastery of the New World, begun in 1689 and continued intermittently for nearly three quarters of a century, thus constantly tended to compact the several Colonies. It was the outbreak of this war with France that brought about the first attempt at a Colonial Congress (1690); it was the renewal of this same war in 1754 which induced Franklin to offer a plan for a permanent Colonial union.

The spirit of nationality fought its way slowly, indeed, against much stubborn and shortsighted local pride. The strength of this local spirit is shown by

the colonies' rejection of Franklin's scheme for union.
Yet the sense of nationality gained ground, if only
under the compulsion of war and necessity.

Hardly was France conquered and the English
supremacy in North America assured before the
colonies were involved in new dangers, which impelled
them yet more powerfully towards union. In the
past, each colony had been more or less closely bound
to England. Virginia, in the early days, had been
far more a part of Old England than of New. But
before the outbreak of the Revolution, Massachusetts,
Pennsylvania, and Virginia—North, Midland, and
South; Puritan, Quaker, and Cavalier—were stirred
to protest by the same indignation against the unjust
exactions of the English Government. When James
Otis, a Boston lawyer, argued in 1761 against writs
of assistance,* and asked boldly "how far the Americans were bound to obey laws they had no share in
making," he spoke not for Massachusetts only, but
for the whole land. When, three years later, he published his pamphlet, *The Rights of the British Colonies
Asserted and Proved*, he wrote for the whole people.
The impassioned eloquence of Patrick Henry expressed the answering sentiment of Virginia. Thus
the South joined hands with the North, while the
North, on its side, did not undervalue this bond of

* Writs of assistance were general search-warrants, in which
the custom-house officer might insert what names he pleased.
For report of Otis's argument, see *John Adams's Works*, edited
by Chas. F. Adams, vol. ii., Appendix A; and *Life of James
Otis*, by Wm. Tudor, Jr., chaps. v. and vi.

a common cause. Bernard, the governor of Massachusetts, declared that Henry's resolutions in the Virginia Assembly against the hated Stamp Act "rang the alarm-bell to the rest of America" (1765). We are told that during the general indignation aroused by this injudicious act, the people, instead of speaking of themselves as colonists, began to call themselves Americans. In the Middle Colonies, the *Farmer's Letters* (1767) of John Dickinson of Philadelphia echoed the patriotic protest of the South and North. So Massachusetts, Virginia, and Pennsylvania stood side by side. Richard Henry Lee, soon to be distinguished as the mover of a declaration of independence, thus summed up the situation: "They wish to make us dependent, but they will make us independent; *these oppressions will lead us to unite, and thus secure our liberty.*"

From about 1765, the year in which an American Congress met in New York to protest against the Stamp Act, the course of our history has been to gradually diminish local jealousies, and to unite separate and discordant elements into a single nation. The slow approaches to this result are matters of familiar history. The heroic struggle of the Revolution; the unsuccessful attempt to carry on the government as a loose confederation of States; the establishment of a truer nationality by the adoption of the Constitution (1787); the patriotic stimulus given by our second war for independence in 1812; the territorial expansion of the new nation; the continued strengthening of the power of the central government,—all these familiar features of our history must be taken into account if we are to appreciate how our national literature was the natural outcome of our national life. Indeed, it may be said that our national life and our national literature were born together, and that the rising Americanism found vent simultaneously in men's deeds and words. From the opening of the Revolution to the close of the War of 1812, when our independence may be considered as having been permanently established, literature had its especial and important share in forwarding the attainment of that national life which the statesman and the soldier were laboring to secure. South and North the idea of country grew in men's minds, bringing with it a new and passionate patriotism. In the agitated controversies and generous ardor of the time, our literature first overstepped the limits of section, and a new era in our literary history began.

Effect of nationality on literature.

There is one man who stands out prominently in this era of consolidation. During the greater part of his life we were still a group of colonies; yet even then he labored to bring about a closer colonial union, and in his later years his work for the united nation was the crowning achievement of his long career. This man, Benjamin Franklin, is so important that we must consider him in a separate section.

BENJAMIN FRANKLIN (1706-1790)

Whether we approach him as philosopher, statesman, scientist, philanthropist, or man of letters, **Franklin's place in our history.** Benjamin Franklin impresses us at last not merely by what he did, but by what he was in himself. We feel his vigor, his originality of mind, his enormous practical ability, his singularly diversified talents, and we are impressed by the man himself as much as by his useful and wonderful career. Numberless pictures have made his shrewd but kindly face familiar to us. Washington wore the powdered wig and queue in vogue among gentlemen at that day, but in the portrait of Franklin the straight, thinnish, gray hair is brushed back from the high forehead and undisguised by wig or powder. We picture Franklin in his later years as a man of somewhat unwieldy carriage, sturdy, inclined to stoutness, and with slightly stooping shoulders, venerable and kind-hearted, but not easy to overreach in a bargain, and full of a humorous appreciation of the weaknesses of others. Even Washington is hardly so real and living to us as is this Philadelphia printer. In his humble origin, in the oft-told story of his rise, through his own push and industry, from the tallow-chandler's boy to the man honored in two continents and successful in a hundred varied enterprises, we are fond of seeing the great example of our national hero, the self-made man. It is said to be the highest merit of a democracy that it offers a free chance to all the men of ability in the community to turn their talents to good use, and Franklin showed us what a man could do for himself in a free country such as ours. "No one," writes a French critic, "began lower than the poor apprentice of Boston; no one raised himself higher, by his own energy, than the inventor of the lightning-rod; no one has rendered more splendid services to his country than the diplomatist who signed the peace of 1783 and secured the independence of the United States." *

Franklin occupies a large place in a momentous period of our national history. His career stretches over nearly the whole of that century in whose great events he bore so large a part. Born a loyal subject of Queen Anne, he died at eighty-four, when the Constitution of the United States had been adopted, and Washington had entered upon his first presidential term. In his early life he spent his energies for the English in the contest with the French; in his later years—the reigning sensation of Paris and the friend of Mirabeau—he labored for America against England as writer and as diplomatist through that "critical period" when our nation was born. Both in our literature and in our history he is thus identified with that period of consolidation at which we have now arrived.

Franklin and the era of consolidation.

Benjamin Franklin, the son of Josiah Franklin, a soap-boiler and tallow-chandler, was born in Boston, Jan. 17, 1706. On his father's side he sprang from

* *Mémoires de Franklin*, écrit par lui-même, traduis de l'Anglais et annotés par Edouard Laboulaye, de l'Institut de France. Paris, 1866.

a humble but sturdy stock, the Franklins having
long had a small holding of land in

Franklin's life. Northamptonshire, England. The eldest
son had followed the trade of a blacksmith
for many generations, and the family had been distinguished by its early Protestantism and determined
independence of thought. On his mother's side
Franklin was descended from Peter Folger, one of the
early New England settlers, whom Mather describes
as "a learned and godly Englishman." Franklin
was the youngest of a large family, and although he
early showed a great capacity for study, his father was
forced to take him from school at the age of ten and
set him to work in the shop, cutting hides, filling
candle-moulds, and running errands. But the boy's
mind was active and inquiring; he disliked the work
and found his resource in books. "From my infancy," he tells us in his *Autobiography*, "I was
passionately fond of reading." Most of the handful
of books owned by his father were works of theological controversy, congenial to the New England mind.
Franklin read the greater part of them, but though
the atmosphere and traditions of Puritan New
England were all about him, the instinct of his mind
and disposition led him to escape into a different air.
Hard-headed and sceptical, Franklin, while born in
that same New England that brought forth the devout
and saintly mystic Jonathan Edwards, early showed
his sympathy with opinions and standards of life
and conduct then common in England, but totally
opposed to the prevailing tone of his surroundings. It

is only by clearly understanding this, that we can
understand the true significance of Franklin's character or of his work as a writer. Thus, although as a
boy he had but very little to spend on books, and
although but few of the contemporary English classics
had then found their way to New England, it was the
study of the leading English writers of the early
eighteenth century, and not of Wigglesworth or
Cotton Mather, that formed his literary style, helped
to direct his thought and taste, and left a lasting impress upon his religious views. The first books he
bought were the works of Bunyan, and in his *Autobiography* he speaks affectionately of Bunyan as
" honest John," and calls him " my old favorite
author." * One of the greatest living prose-writers
of England during Franklin's youth was Joseph
Addison, whose light and graceful style was for years
the model of many English authors. Addison wrote
a number of essays for *The Spectator* (1712–13), a
periodical then very popular in England. A stray
copy of *The Spectator* having fallen in Franklin's
way, he " gave his days and nights to the study
of Addison," and, to improve himself in writing,
endeavored to reproduce the essays in his own words,
correcting his work by a comparison with the original.
But this English influence on Franklin went even
deeper. Puritanism still controlled New England,
but in the mother country its force had long been
spent, and England was passing through a period of

* *Autobiography*, chap. i and chap. ii.

unbelief. The church was worldly and indifferent, the nation lacking in enthusiasm and living faith. It was an age of reason, not of feeling, and many prominent writers were attacking the foundations of belief. The works of two of these sceptical writers, Anthony Collins and Lord Shaftesbury, came in Franklin's way, and helped to unsettle his religious views. He was scarce fifteen when, after doubting on many points, he "began to doubt even of Revelation itself." * Thus both the literary style and the sceptical thought of the England of Queen Anne were a directing and controlling influence on his life and thought.

Meanwhile, Franklin had been apprenticed to his brother James, who was a printer. James published and edited a newspaper, *The New England Courant*, to which Benjamin, then about fifteen, became an anonymous contributor. Having quarrelled with his brother, a man of violent temper, Franklin came to Philadelphia, resolved to push his way unaided. Here he landed, a lad of seventeen, tired, hungry, and friendless, his whole stock of cash "a single dollar, and about a shilling in copper coin." But he had in himself the elements of success—health, youth, industry, business ability, and a shrewd eye to his own interests. The familiar story of his rise need not be retold here; we must note, however, that by a stay of some eighteen months in London, when Franklin was about eighteen, he was brought into

* *Autobiography.*

direct contact with that contemporary English life
and thought which he had already known through the
medium of books. While in London he wrote a
pamphlet hostile to religion, — the publication of
which he afterwards regretted,—and through it met
some of the sceptical writers of the day. Among
others, he was introduced to Bertrand Mandeville, the
author of a cynical book called *The Fable of the Bees*,
at a pale-ale house in Cheapside.

Franklin returned to Philadelphia in 1726, established himself as a printer, and in 1729 became the
proprietor and publisher of a newspaper called *The
Pennsylvania Gazette*. Shortly before this (1728)
he had begun *The Busybody Papers*, a series of
short, moral essays which are evidently the result
of his early study of *The Spectator*. In these papers
he comes before us, after the manner of Addison, as
a censor of morals, and aims to hold up to ridicule
certain follies of the time by exhibiting them in the
person of some imaginary characters. The methods
of Franklin's great model are closely imitated, but the
personages are slightly sketched, conventional, and
lifeless, and we miss the genial warmth and exquisite
grace of the original.

From this time Franklin, by his public spirit,
energy, attention to detail, and wonderful breadth of
interest, became more and more a force in the community. He labored not only for his own generation,
but for posterity. He established a debating club
called the Junto, which developed into the American
Philosophical Society, an organization of more than

national celebrity; he founded the Philadelphia Library, " the mother," as he says, " of all the North American subscription libraries;" he was instrumental in starting the University of Pennsylvania. Equally busy in other directions, he invented the open stove, still called by his name, and in his famous experiment with the kite he " called down the lightning from heaven." Made Postmaster-General in 1753, he greatly improved the postal system, and succeeded in making it not only efficient, but profitable. In 1757 Franklin was again in England, as commissioner from Pennsylvania, and this time remained for five years, meeting Hume and Robertson, the distinguished historians, and many other eminent persons. Franklin returned to England in 1765 as agent for Pennsylvania in matters relating to that province, but the relations between Great Britain and the Colonies were growing difficult and alarming, and his mission grew to one of a wider character.

In 1776, after a short stay in America, Franklin was sent to France as Ambassador of the United States, where he won social as well as political successes which are among the most striking incidents of his wonderful career. In the midst of the airy gallantries of the French court, or all the strange life of old-world Paris, Franklin, with his shaggy cap of marten's fur, his simple dress, his homely wit, moved in his unadorned and solid manhood, the representative, even to many of the Parisians, of a better order of things.

After performing the most signal public services,

Franklin, old, ill, and weary, returned to Philadelphia in 1785. Here he lingered for five years, loved and honored, still active in doing good, so far as his failing strength permitted, until the last. He died at the age of eighty-four, on the 17th of July, 1790.

Franklin was a voluminous and no doubt a rapid writer, as his collected works fill ten large volumes, but the incessant demands upon his time and energy left him little opportunity to devote himself to literature for its own sake. During his long and busy life his pen was seldom idle, but writing with him was usually but the means to an end, a convenient aid to the accomplishment of some definite project. Thus a large proportion of his published work consists of letters, in which, in his clear, business-like, and sensible way, he touches on many subjects,—science, inventions, books, and current politics,—and so unconsciously gives us a glimpse into his alert and eager mind. But work thus written for a specific purpose, while interesting historically, or for the knowledge it gives us of its author, naturally suffers from its temporary character, and can seldom take its place as pure literature.

Franklin as a man of letters.

Franklin's reputation as a writer rests mainly on his *Autobiography*, which has been called "the cornerstone of American Literature," his *Almanac*, and a few of his shorter pieces. *Poor Richard's Almanac* was one of Franklin's great business successes, and is probably the most famous example of the unambitious class of writing to which it belongs. It was begun in 1732, and continued for twenty-five years, soon reaching a circulation, remarkable for those days, of ten thousand copies. In it Franklin speaks through the mouth of an imaginary character, "Poor Richard," or "Mr. Richard Saunders," who is supposed to be the compiler. "Poor Richard" represents himself as always star-gazing, and tells us that he went into the enterprise because his wife Bridget threatened to burn his books and instruments if he did not make some money by his learning. In the pages of his *Almanac* Franklin, under the guise of "Poor Richard," printed year after year those familiar proverbs, sometimes original and sometimes selected, which he apparently regarded as the best practical rules for the conduct of life. Through these homely sayings, so short as to be easily remembered, and so associated with some familiar experience that they reached the dullest intelligence, he preached his cardinal doctrine of industry and frugality as the way to wealth. Such writing may not be literature in the highest sense, but it shows us Franklin; for the rule of life which it advocates was that which the author had long followed, and the way to success which it pointed out was that by which Franklin's own success had been gained. Much as we must admire Franklin's admirable traits, we must admit that in some of the highest qualities he was distinctly wanting. The absence of these higher qualities is apparent in the *Almanac*, as it is in almost all that Franklin wrote. We see that with him success, and the laying up of treasures upon earth, if not precisely the same thing, are at least very close together. He tells us, indeed,

that his object is to make people virtuous, but assures
us at the same time that the road to virtue lies
through the making of money, " it being more difficult
for a man in want to act honestly, than—to use one
of those proverbs—it is ' for an empty sack to stand
upright.' "   He urges us to make money because, if
we are prosperous, people will respect us:

> " Now that I have a sheep and a cow,
> Everybody bids me good-morrow."

He declares that " a ploughman on his legs is higher
than a gentleman on his knees."

Franklin's object was simply to give some practical
help to plain people, and in a limited sense his doctrines and advice are sound.   But from the highest
point of view, it must be admitted that the general
tone of his teaching is mercenary and worldly.   The
exclusive devotion to money-making tends to the
debasement of character; nor is the court which the
vulgar pay to wealth a sufficient reason for concentrat-
ing one's energies on its acquisition.   Moreover, if
Franklin preached wealth as the way to virtue, he was
not insensible to the advantages of virtue as a way to
wealth.   While the highest natures are transported
with a passion for the beauty of holiness, Franklin has
a tradesman's eye for its market value.   " Nothing,"
he writes on the margin of his *Autobiography*, " nothing is so likely to make a man's fortune as virtue."

The *Autobiography* is Franklin's most important
contribution to literature.   It is unfinished, coming
down only to 1757, the year of Franklin's second

visit to England.   Written in the strong, clear,
almost matter-of-fact style which was characteristic of
the man, the book retains an indescribable freshness
and fascination.   Unlike many autobiographies, it
has no posing for effect; it is the direct and simple
record of a remarkable and wonderfully useful life.
But it is even more than this.   Few characters in the
entire range of fiction are more memorable or more
suggestive than that of Benjamin Franklin, and in
the transparent prose of his *Autobiography* Franklin
has half unconsciously given us a character-study
which the greatest novelist or poet would find it hard
to surpass.   Certain faults or mistakes are quietly noted
and regretted, but the pervading tone is one of com-
placent satisfaction, and a willingness is expressed " to
go over the same life from its beginning to the end."

Franklin is often spoken of as a typical American,
the representative of that utilitarian and money-
making spirit supposed to be our leading
national trait.   A Scotch critic calls him

**Franklin's
character.**

" the most practical of philosophers, in
perhaps the most practical of nations "; Jefferson
Davis sees in him the embodiment, not of the nation,
but of New England, and sneers at him as " the
incarnation of the peddling, tuppenny Yankee." *
Both views are not only exaggerated and unjust: they
are based upon a total misunderstanding of Franklin's
real relation to his age.   In his public career Franklin
was a typical American patriot, rightly placed beside

* Quoted by G. W. Curtis in *Harper's Magazine*, July, 1868,
p. 274.

Washington as one of the founders of the Republic; but in his character, his writings, his whole tone of mind and thought, he belonged not to America, but to the England of Shaftesbury, Addison, and Pope. In his scepticism, his cool common-sense, his scientific and intensely practical cast of mind, he is distinctly the child of Old England rather than of New. Franklin's unemotional, unideal temperament had absolutely nothing in common with the sombre fanaticism, the spirituality of the New England which shone through his great contemporary, Jonathan Edwards. Early affected by English books, and a resident for years in the great center of English life and thought, in his literary style as in his opinions he is an Englishman of the age of frigid poetry, shallow irreligion, and the glorification of good sense. In reading Franklin's works confirmations of the correctness of this view continually present themselves. Thus the tone and moral of the *Ephemera*, one of the best of his short pieces, in its allegorical picture of the infinite littleness and insignificance of mankind, are identical with the favorite attitude of Pope and Swift. Franklin, reaching here a higher elevation than he commonly attains, points to the little lives of men with the same contemptuous scorn as that manifest in *Gulliver's Travels* or veiled under the smooth phrases of the *Essay on Man*.

Thus Franklin, to be really understood, must be seen from many sides. Author of one of the first really notable American books, he stands both for our intellectual nearness to England and our political severance from England. We are tempted to admire either too much or too little. If he was one of the least spiritual, he was one of the most incessantly and substantially useful of all great men, and while literature with him was but a side issue, he holds in our literary history a unique and by no means unimportant place.

STUDY LIST

FRANKLIN

1. Franklin's chief claim to literary distinction rests upon his *Autobiography*. The best edition is that edited by John Bigelow. There is a condensed edition in the Riverside Literature Series. Another number of the series contains selections from the writings of Franklin, including *Poor Richard's Almanac*. The *Autobiography* is also included in Cassell's National Library.

2. Biography and Criticism. For a complete list of writings on and about Franklin, see Paul Leicester Ford's *The Franklin Bibliography*. Life of, by James Parton ; by Prof. J. B. McMaster, in American Men of Letters Series ; by J. T. Morse, Jun., in American Statesmen Series. See also Sainte-Beuve's article on Benjamin Franklin in *English Portraits*.

ORATORS OF THE REVOLUTION

As we should expect, the writings of this period of growing nationality are largely of a political and patriotic character. Much intellectual power was put into oratory, a form of literature of peculiar importance in a democracy, and one likely to be developed in the stress of action and controversy. Many of the speeches of these stirring days have been entirely lost

to us, and even the eloquence of such men as James
Otis, Samuel Adams, and Patrick Henry is but little
more than a tradition; yet some passages in the
fragmentary reports of Henry's speeches are perhaps
as familiar to us as any words written or spoken during the whole of this Revolutionary time.   "Our
chains are forged! Their clanking may be heard on
the plains of Boston. The war is inevitable, and let it
come. . . . Is life so dear or peace so sweet as to be
purchased at the cost of chains and slavery? Forbid
it, Almighty God! I know not what course others
may take; but as for me, give me liberty or give me
death."

The speeches of James Otis were likened by his
contemporaries to "a flame of fire," and Richard
Henry Lee was called "the American Cicero." Read
to-day, without the orator's living power of voice and
gesture, these snatches of Revolutionary eloquence
seem stilted and overwrought. But it must be
remembered that while we read them coldly and
critically, when they were uttered a tremendous and
uncertain issue hung over the speaker and his hearers,
and that men's hearts were full of the daring and
defiance of a great resolution.

The political literature of this period was by no
means confined to these gusts of oratory.   The
national crisis produced numbers of politi- Other polit-
cal essays and pamphlets of a more sober   ical litera-
and solid character, which make their   ture.
main appeal to reason and discuss the nature and
principles of government with great ability, clearness,

and a philosophic breadth.   This political writing, beginning during the years immediately preceding the Revolution and including the period of the adoption of the Constitution, shows us a new side of American literary ability.   Hitherto the best intellect of the country, when it turned to writing at all, had largely occupied itself with intricate questions of theology, but, directed in a new course by the necessities of the hour, these political treatises and state papers demonstrated the American strength and capacity in the sphere of government.   As Mr. Charles Dudley Warner says: "It is in the political writings immediately preceding and following the Revolution, such as those of Hamilton, Madison, Jay, Franklin, and Jefferson, that the new birth of a nation of original force and ideas is declared.   It has been said, and I think the statement can be maintained, that for any parallel to those treatises on the nature of government, in respect to originality and vigor, we must go back to classic times."*

One of the most important examples of this order of writing is *The Federalist*, a series of eighty-four essays by Hamilton, Madison, and Jay. The purpose of these essays, written after the close of the Revolution, while the States were loosely held together by Articles of Confederation, is to urge the establishment of a closer union by the adoption of the Constitution.   They came out in a New York newspaper, and were first

The Federalist.

* *Life of Irving*, p. 10.

published in a connected form in 1788, the year before
the Constitution became the fundamental law of the
land. *The Federalist* is written in strong, pure
English, and in the temperance of its tone and its
range of historical illustrations it remains a monument to the learning and breadth of our early statesmen. Its inspiration is the great idea of a strong and
united nation. The following passage may be cited
as a good statement of its leading motive: " Let the
thirteen States, bound together in one strict and indissoluble union, concur in creating one great American
system, superior to the control of all Transatlantic
force or influence, and able to dictate the terms
of connection between the Old World and the
New." *

THOMAS JEFFERSON (1743-1826) of Virginia, the
third President of the United States, and the leader
of the opposite political party to that of
Hamilton, was another notable political   Thomas
writer of the time. Jefferson was a man   Jefferson.
of considerable cultivation, with distinctly scholarly
tastes and high aims. His views on popular liberty
were more radical than those of his great contemporaries, for he had a fuller confidence in the ability
of the people to exercise power with discretion.
Unlike Hamilton and the Federalists, he believed in
greatly restricting the power of the national government and correspondingly encouraging that of the
several States, for he thought that by this means

* *The Federalist.*

greater freedom would be secured to the individual. The century in which Jefferson was born witnessed the outburst of the democratic spirit in the Old as well as in the New World, and Jefferson may properly be classed with certain European thinkers that helped on this movement.

Such writers as Thomas Hobbes (1588–1679) and John Locke (1632–1704) in England, and Jean Jacques Rousseau (1712–1778) in France, had prepared the way for new and sometimes exaggerated views of human liberty and equality. We need not inquire how far Jefferson was influenced by these writers: it is enough to observe that, like them, his tendency was to regard questions of government and human rights from the broadly theoretical or philosophic, as well as from the practical, side. In this he stood apart from the great majority of the American revolutionists, whose resistance to England sprang rather from that instinct of freedom which is inbred in men of English blood than from any definite theories concerning the " rights of man." The New England farmer left his plough to confront the British soldiery at Lexington, but it was reserved for Jefferson, in the opening sentences of the Declaration of Independence, to justify the resistance of the Colonies on the broad foundation of natural and inalienable human rights. In the sonorous introduction to the Declaration, Jefferson puts aside for the time all the particular grievances which were the immediate causes of dispute, and goes back to political principles, which he holds are fundamental and universal. He sets forth the rights of Americans, not under the British Constitution, but by the law of nature; he declares that governments are designed to secure men in these rights, deriving their just powers from the consent of the governed, and "that whenever any form of government becomes destructive of these ends, it is the right of the people to alter or to abolish it." * This belief in the rights of man as man was not a new one with Jefferson when he wrote the Declaration. In some resolutions prepared by him in 1774 he had declared that Parliament had infringed upon both the natural and legal rights of the Americans, and in the same year, in a pamphlet entitled *A Summary View of the Rights of America*, he reiterated this opinion. It was this pamphlet, which took a most advanced ground in regard to the whole question of Colonial rights, that brought Jefferson to the front as one of the leading American political writers. It was widely read, not only in this country but in England, where it was republished in a modified form by the great statesman Edmund Burke. Jefferson's belief in liberty and his confidence in the masses showed themselves in more than one direction. A Virginian and a slaveholder, he was consistent and large-minded enough to champion the cause of the slave, and in an eloquent passage in his *Notes on Virginia*, after recording his protest against slavery, he goes on to prophesy the evil to come. The "liberties" which are the "gift of God" "are not to be violated

* Declaration of Independence.

but with His wrath." "Indeed," he adds,—"I
tremble for my country when I reflect that God is
just: that His justice cannot sleep forever." *   The
same confidence in and respect for man is shown in
Jefferson's efforts in behalf of popular education.   As
in the case of his protest against slavery, this is the
more praiseworthy when we remember the views that
then commonly prevailed on this matter in Virginia
and the South.   No New Englander could write more
earnestly and liberally than did this land-owner of
the "Old Dominion."   "Preach, my dear sir, a
crusade against ignorance; establish and improve the
law for educating the common people.   Let our
countrymen know that the people alone can protect
us against these evils, and that the tax which will be
paid for this purpose is not more than the thousandth
part of what will be paid to kings, priests, and nobles
who will rise up among us if we leave the people in
ignorance." †

As Jefferson was not a speaker, he naturally relied
most on writing as a means of influencing others and
of diffusing his views.   He was a prodigious letter-
writer, some twenty-five thousand of his letters being
still in existence, and these with his public documents
and political tracts compose by far the greater part of
his works.   Besides these he wrote a few short essays
of a more purely literary character, and the *Notes on*

---

* Works, Ford's ed., vol. iii. p. 267.
† Letter to Geo. Wythe, 1786.   Works, Ford's ed., vol. iv.
p. 269.

Virginia, a careful account of the physical features, laws, and general condition of his native State, which contains some passages of considerable literary merit. But, of course, Jefferson, like many of the other founders of the nation, was a statesman first and only secondarily a writer. He wrote his own epitaph; and we may infer from it those achievements of his life upon which he looked back with especial satisfaction at the last. In it he speaks of himself as " Author of the Declaration of American Independence, of the Statute of Virginia for religious freedom, and father of the University of Virginia." Freedom of action, freedom of conscience, and freedom of intellect; the spread of knowledge as the true basis of a State and as the best safeguard for the right exercise of liberty, —these things, in brief, seemed to Jefferson the end towards which the race should move; and it was by his work done in furtherance of these things that he chiefly desired to be remembered.

STUDY LIST

ESTABLISHMENT OF NATIONALITY

1. **Thomas Jefferson.** Works edited by Paul Leicester Ford ; Life, by James Schouler, in Makers of America Series, and by Jno. T. Morse, Jun., in American Statesmen Series.

2. **The Federalist**, edited by Paul Leicester Ford.

3. **History of the Period.** Lives of Hamilton, Jefferson, Madison, Jno. Adams, Samuel Adams, and Patrick Henry, in American Statesmen Series ; John Fiske's *American*

Revolution (2 vols.), and *The Critical Period of American History;* McMaster's *History of the People of the United States,* vols. i.–iii.; A. B. Hart's *Formation of the Union* in Epochs of American History ; and F. A. Walker's *The Making of the Nation* in American History Series.

CHAPTER II

POETRY AND ROMANCE

Our struggle with and triumph over England, followed by the stimulating conviction that we had
actually taken our place among the nations **The young**
of the world, with a long vista of greatness **nation in**
opening before us, put a new and patriotic **literature.**
life into our poetry, as well as into our orations and
political discussions. The period between the establishment of our independence and the close of the
War of 1812 is memorable in European history as
the epoch of the French Revolution and of the rise
and downfall of Napoleon. Generous and impulsive
spirits were aflame with wild notions of social change,
of Liberty, Fraternity, and the " Rights of Man";
and many of these ideas, falling in as they did with
our newly-asserted republicanism, heightened our
patriotic enthusiasm and found an utterance in our
literature. Before the dawn of our Revolution our
attempts at poetry had been few in number and
generally local in their character. The verse of this
new era of our nationality was, at least, abundant in
quantity, ambitious in design, and distended with a
somewhat magnificent sense of the greatness of its
theme. Viewed purely as poetry, the pompous and

101

monotonous epics, or crude, rough-hewn ballads of the time appeal but faintly to readers of to-day, but they claim attention as an important forward step in our national and literary growth. They reflected and furthered the sense that we were one people, born to a great destiny; and never, perhaps, at any period of our history has the pride of national greatness so dictated and dominated American Song. In New England TIMOTHY DWIGHT (1752–1817), JOEL BAR-LOW (1755–1812), and JOHN TRUMBULL (1750–1831), were the principal makers of this patriotic verse. In the Middle States it was represented by PHILIP FRENEAU (1752–1832), HUGH HENRY BRACKENRIDGE (1748–1816), and FRANCIS HOPKINSON (1737–1791), the latter chiefly remembered for his humorous ballad *The Battle of the Kegs*. There, too, JOSEPH HOP-KINSON (1770–1842) wrote his *Hail Columbia*, first sung at the Chestnut Street Theatre, Philadelphia, in 1798. In the South, towards the close of the era, FRANCIS SCOTT KEY (1779–1843) composed our other national song, *The Star-Spangled Banner* (1814). Dwight and Barlow were both chaplains in the army during the Revolution, and were thus brought close to that making of the nation which gives their work its distinctive note. It would be wearisome to do more than allude to the work of this group of Revolutionary writers in the most general terms; but a clear understanding of its general character is neither uninteresting nor unimportant. Three points are worth noting: the length and pre-

Rise of poetry.

tensions of many of their poems; their recurrent note
of patriotism, full of high hopes for the country's
future, and often mingled with the current catch-
words of social reform; and their timid imitation
of the current English poetic forms.   The mere
titles of some of these patriotic poems are sufficient
indications of their theme and spirit.   Timothy
Dwight, a grandson of Jonathan Edwards, and president of Yale College (1795), published a poem entitled *America* in 1772; Freneau and Brackenridge
brought out a poem on *The Rising Glory of America*
in the same year.   Brackenridge's *Bunker's Hill*
appeared in the year our independence was declared,
and Joel Barlow's *Vision of Columbus* in 1785.
Glancing through these poems, we can see how the new
thought of the country's possibilities has wrought on
the imagination of these authors.   In Dwight's *Conquest of Canaän* (1785), a poem of epic proportion,
Joshua is made to preach the " rights of man," * and
foretell the future prosperity of the Republic of the
West.   In that " blissful Eden " men shall

> " Trace juster paths and choose their chiefs divine,
>   On Freedom's base erect the heavenly plan,
>   Teach laws to reign and save the Rights of Man." †

* This favorite phrase occurs in a modified form in Dwight's
Columbia :

> " Thy heroes the rights of mankind shall defend,
>   And triumph pursue them, and glory attend."

Also, more than once in Freneau's *America Independent*
(1778) :

> " If o'er mankind man gives you royal sway,
>   Take not the right of humankind away."

† *Conquest of Canaän.*

Towards the end of John Trumbull's *McFingal*, a satirical poem dealing with the Revolution, and directed particularly against the Tory or English party, the poet declares, in a characteristically American passage, that there is room enough to put Britain into the middle of one of our great lakes, where Lord North standing on the margin would not be able to see land. England's day is declining, America's is to come. The poet sees in the future—

> " Where now the panther guards his den,
>   Her desert forests swarm with men,
>   Her cities, towers, and columns rise,
>   And dazzling temples meet the skies ;
>
>   * * * * * *
>
>   Till to the skirts of Western day,
>   The peopled regions own her sway." *

Barlow's *Columbiad* (1807), an expansion of his already lengthy *Vision of Columbus*, designed to be the national epic, closed with a prayer for that " federation of the world " which Tennyson has pictured as the consummation of human history :

> " Bid the last breath of dire contention cease,
>   And bind all regions in the leagues of peace ;
>   Bid one great empire, with extensive sway,
>   Spread with the Sun, and bound the walls of day ;
>   One centred system, one all-ruling soul,
>   Live through the parts and regulate the whole." †

Unreadable as most of these poems have become, with all their barren flats of mediocrity, they are

---

* *McFingal*, Canto IV.
† Barlow's *Columbiad*.

often, as in the lines just quoted, noble in their ideals.
To readers of that generation they stood for the new-
born America, for the whole land with its boundless
hopes and aspirations, the youthful conqueror of one
of the proudest empires of the earth.

Realizing this, we see also that this new-fledged
and aggressive Americanism did not and could not
create, by a deliberate and conscious
effort, a truly national body of poetry.
True nationality must exist before it can
find a voice in literature, and true nationality is a
thing of slow growth. The colonists were a provincial part of England; they had read English books,
lived on English thought, formed their literary standards on a study of English classics: a declaration of
independence was not an enchanter's wand to change
this at a stroke. Consequently we find the poets of
this period declaiming against Britain, and vaunting
their independence of her, in verses which show by
their careful conformity to English models our complete intellectual subjection to her. During the
period of our Revolution many English versifiers, particularly those of inferior genius and originality, were
still imitating Pope, the ease with which the monotonous rise and fall of Pope's manner could be
reproduced adding, no doubt, to the number of his
followers.* In manner,—that is, in the outward con-
struction of their verses,—Dwight, Barlow, and many
others, are simply Colonial followers of Pope, holding

margin note: National-
ity in lit-
erature.

---

* See what has been said on this point on p. 69, *supra*.

a similar position, except for the nature of their subject, to that occupied by such a versifier as Erasmus
Darwin in England. Barlow, in particular, has caught
Pope's very accent, as in the balanced distribution of
his adjectives, one emphasizing each half of a line.*
In his diction he often reminds us of Pope's contemporary, James Thomson. Trumbull's *McFingal* is
an acknowledged imitation of Butler's *Hudibras*.
Dwight's *Greenfield Hill* (1794), a less ambitious and
more readable poem than his *Canaän*, contains imita-
tions, or direct paraphrases, of Thomson, Goldsmith,
Pope, and probably of Cowper, Dyer, and many other
English poets of the eighteenth century.† The fact
is worthy of notice, that the first considerable efforts
at poetry among us were made at a time when the
English poets naturally selected were not, in most
cases, the best models for a young nation to imitate.
The simple force and pathos of the ballad, the native
music of the song, were almost replaced in the England
of Pope by a style of poetry more artificial, less direct,
full of conventionality, sterile in generous emotions,
the utterance of a sophisticated age, and, as such,

* Cf. the following lines from the *Columbiad*, with some of
the descriptions of nature in Pope's *Windsor Forest*:

> "Beneath *tall* trees, in *livelier* verdure gay,
> Long *level* walks a *humble* garb display;
> The *infant* corn, unconscious of its worth,
> Points the green spire and bends the foliage forth."

† Dwight says in his preface to this poem: "Originally the
writer designed to imitate in the several parts the manner of
as many British poets; but, finding himself too much occupied
to pursue the design, he relinquished it."

unsuited to guide the poetic attempts of a new civilization.

But in the midst of all this imitation, there was the hardly audible tone of a more genuine and distinct poetic voice. Philip Freneau, who turned out much doggerel and indifferent verse for the newspapers, reaches at times, in some lyric like his *Indian Burying Ground*, a level higher than that to which any of his more ambitious brethren attained. His best work is indeed small in quantity, and shines out from a mass of rubbish, but gems like the poem just mentioned, *The Wild Honeysuckle*, and *Eutaw Springs* may be said to hold a permanent place in our literature. Such poems bear the stamp of that originality which is one of the marks of a true poet, and they have an unmistakable grace and delicacy of touch. The English are commonly supposed to be slow to recognize American genius, but Thomas Moore expressed his admiration of Freneau, while Campbell, in *O'Connor's Child*, borrowed one of Freneau's finest lines, and Scott introduced another, but slightly changed, into *Marmion*. Freneau thus received striking proofs of appreciation from three of the greatest English poets of the day. Freneau was probably the earliest of our writers to recognize the Indian as a fit subject for romantic treatment, and in this respect he may be thought of as the forerunner of Cooper, Longfellow, and Simms. In Freneau, then, with all his haste and roughness, we note the slight but positive beginning of a true and higher order of poetry in America.

Hard upon this outburst of patriotic poetry followed the powerful but morbid and fantastic romances of

The begin- ning of romance. CHARLES BROCKDEN BROWN (1771–1810), the first American writer who devoted himself to literature as a profession. Brown may fairly be considered our first romance-writer, although a few stories of very inferior merit had appeared before his work began. He was born in Philadelphia in 1771, and in that city, except for a brief stay in New York, his short life was spent. From his youth his health was delicate, and in a letter written towards the close of his life he declares that he had never known what it was to feel well for more than half an hour at a time. Like many delicate boys, he found his pleasure in poring over books and in the world of the imagination. Much of his time was spent in solitary country rambles. He began to study law, but abandoned a profession whose rigid and practical requirements must have been distasteful to one of his dreamy and romantic disposition. Although sprung from Quaker stock and brought up in the doctrines of that sect, Brown early yielded to the influence of the sceptical philosophy and extravagant social theories that were then dazzling so many ardent spirits. He was greatly attracted by the radical teachings of William Godwin, an English novelist and would-be social reformer, and of Godwin's wife, Mary Wollstonecraft. The strong effect of their influence both on Brown's views and on his literary style is apparent in his writings. The extreme theories advocated by Mrs. Godwin (Mary Wollstonecraft) on the position of women appear to have prompted the composition of Brown's first published work, *Alcuin, a Dialogue on the Rights of Women*. A youthful romance, *Carsol*, in which he depicts a Utopian community, is suggestive of those visions of a new earth in which Godwin and his followers indulged. In his maturer romances Brown's style and principle of composition show so marked a resemblance to the works of the English novelist, that he is often spoken of as "the American disciple of Godwin." *Wieland, or The Transformation*, Brown's first published romance, appeared in 1798. The plot turns on the employment of ventriloquism by the villain of the story, with awful and tragical results. Horrible and improbable as the book is, it contains scenes of unquestionable power. Like much of Brown's work, it has about it a morbid and unwholesome atmosphere, attributable perhaps in part to ill-health, and in part to the fondness for creepy and ghostly subjects, which was a marked trait in the contemporary English school of romance. Brown's other romances, *Ormond, Arthur Merryn, Edgar Huntly, Clara Howard*, and *Jane Talbot*, followed in rapid succession, all except the last appearing within three years after the publication of *Wieland*. On these books, hastily written as they must have been, his reputation chiefly rests.

We have alluded to the influence of Godwin on Brown, but we must remember further that the work of both men was more or less in keeping with the general character of romance-writing then popular. Both wrote before Walter Scott had at least partially

freed the romance from its stilted and unnatural diction, its crude horrors, and gross improbabilities, by
his finer and saner art.   Allowing for some personal
peculiarities, it is to the gruesome and high-flown
school of romance then uppermost—a school of which
Mrs. Radcliffe is perhaps the most familiar exponent
—that Brown belongs.   On the other hand, he aimed
to be American, and to a certain extent he succeeded.
Like Barlow, Dwight, or Freneau, he chose American
subjects.   *Arthur Mervyn* is famous for its graphic
descriptions of the ravages of the yellow-fever in
Philadelphia in 1793; *Edgar Huntly*, the scene of
which is laid in a then thinly-settled part of Pennsylvania, is full of vivid, if somewhat over-colored,
descriptions of the solitudes of mountain and forest.
We are taken, perhaps for the first time in fiction,
into the midst of the perils of our frontier life; we
encounter the panther and the Indian, the latter surrounded with none of Cooper's tinge of romance, but
depicted as the mere wily and bloodthirsty savage.
This choice of a native theme was a deliberate one,
for Brown says in his preface that he is the first to
call forth the reader's sympathy by substituting for
puerile superstitions, Gothic castles, and chimeras,—
the conventional machinery of the English romances,
—" the incidents of Indian hostility and the perils of
the Western wilderness." *   If in this story he distantly suggests Cooper, in his fondness for psychological problems, and in the morbid strain that runs

* Preface to *Edgar Huntly*.

through many of his books, he still more faintly fore-shadows Poe and the yet greater Hawthorne. As has been hinted, the faults of Brown's romances, their unreality, their affected sentiment, their improbability and the like, are often those of the school of writing to which he belonged. Another fault, the confused and inartistic way in which the plots are developed, is probably attributable to the rapidity with which they were composed. In spite of their shortcomings, they have very decided merits. The genuine narrative power in the man triumphs at times over all obstacles, as where Edgar Huntly, who has fallen into a cave while walking in his sleep, is described regaining con-sciousness in darkness and in total ignorance of his surroundings. Brown's romances were among the books that especially directed and fascinated the mind of that greater admirer of Godwin's, the young poet Shelley. When we consider Brown's models, his provincial surroundings, his continuous ill-health, his death at the early age of thirty-nine, and fairly esti-mate what he accomplished under these conditions, we may pronounce him one of our earliest men of genius in the sphere of literature.

Looking back upon the work of such men as Dwight, Freneau, and Brown, it is plain that the conditions which governed the production of poetry and of romance in this time were sub-stantially the same. In both fields we **Poetry and romance.** were struggling to be American, and in both we were still more or less provincial in our subservience to the English mode. Our authors dealt with American subjects, but to learn how to do so they kept their eyes fixed on the example set them by their English brethren. Yet a more original spirit was struggling to emancipate itself, and that spirit was present in the best of these poets, Philip Freneau, and, if to a less extent, in the first of the romancers, Charles Brockden Brown.

STUDY LIST

EARLY POETRY AND ROMANCE

1. Literature. Stedman and Hutchinson's *Library of American Literature;* Moore's *Songs and Ballads of the American Revolution;* Eggleston's *American War Ballads and Lyrics;* Richardson's *American Literature;* Nichol's *American Literature;* Tyler's *American Literature*, his *Literary History of the American Revolution*, and his *Three Men of Letters* (Berkeley, Trumbull, and Barlow).

2. Philip Freneau. *Poems.* "The Wild Honeysuckle," "To a Honey Bee," "The Indian Burying-ground," "To the Memory of the Americans who Fell at Eutaw."

3. Charles Brockden Brown. See article on Brown in *Encyclopedia Britannica*, and Prescott's Essay published in his *Miscellanies;* also Life in Sparks's *American Biography*. For Brown's connection with Shelley and Godwin, see Dowden's *Life of Shelley.*

PART III

THE LITERATURE OF THE REPUBLIC
Cir. 1809–1897

CHAPTER I

LITERATURE IN THE MIDDLE STATES,
1809-1835

MANY of the writers of the period last considered belong to the years of the Revolution, and to that unsettled interval immediately following, before our country was put in a surer and more established condition by the adoption of the Constitution (1787). At such a time, while there was much to arouse patriotism, there was much to awaken anxiety, and the poet had to look to the promise of the future from the midst of many difficulties and dangers that threatened the very life of the young State. But after the Constitution had placed the nation on a firmer basis by strengthening the hands of the central government, many of these dreams of the poet seemed in a fair way to be fulfilled. The need of a truer nationality had compacted the loosely confederated Colonies into a firm and indissoluble union. Three new States, Vermont,

The growth of the republic.

113

Kentucky, and Tennessee, had been added to the original thirteen between the adoption of the Constitution and the close of the century. In 1801 Louisiana was purchased, and the United States asserted her power and dignity in a war with the Barbary pirates in defence of her growing commerce. In 1802 Ohio was admitted as a State. The rising republic again asserted herself in that contest with England, which has been called the Second War for Independence. This war greatly strengthened our national confidence and self-respect: it proved that the American Union was not an experiment, but an accomplished fact; and it was followed by a growth of patriotic pride and a deepening realization of the meaning of our national existence. At the close of the war the people were jubilant, and the country blazed with bonfires. In the first flush of patriotic enthusiasm our national song, *The Star-Spangled Banner*, was composed. While we were thus vindicating our national position abroad, the nation was still further extending its borders. Louisiana became a State in 1812, and in the years succeeding the second war with England the sturdy young republic was thrusting out her arms and gathering vast stretches of territory to herself. Between 1816 and 1821, Indiana, Mississippi, Illinois, Alabama, Maine, and Missouri were added to the Union,—six States within six years. The country's strength and greatness gained on the imagination, while the petty rivalries and jealousies, which were a remnant of the old Colonial exclusiveness, grew weaker, and the idea

WASHINGTON IRVING

of State sovereignty began to fade before the larger
conception of a great Republic, whose dominion
should stretch from sea to sea. This advance of the
country in territory and importance was accompanied
by a marked improvement in our literature, and that
national spirit which had quickened our oratory and
poetry to new life continued to exert an increasing
influence. Indeed, it is not until this time that
American literature can be fairly said to have taken
a place among the literatures of the world. It is true
that before this a few writers, such as Jonathan
Edwards, Franklin, Freneau, and Brown, had produced notable works, which had made some impression
on foreign readers; but on the whole it must be
admitted that up to this time we had made but a
slender addition to the great body of literature, and
that at the opening of this century American books
and their authors were commonly unknown or despised
beyond the provincial limits of our own land. This
was changed by the group of writers whose work we
are now to consider: Washington Irving (1783–1859),
James Fenimore Cooper (1789–1851), William Cullen
Bryant (1794–1878), and their associates.

WASHINGTON IRVING (1783–1859).

Washington Irving is the first in point of time of
our greater men of letters. We read his books to-day,
not because they help us to understand a past stage in
our mental life and growth; not merely because they
were a force in broadening the thoughts and enlarg-

ing the sympathies of a past generation; but because
they have the enduring interest that belongs to true
literature, and so delight and amuse us as they did the
readers of an earlier time. Irving is almost the first
American writer of whom this can be truly said. We
approach the works of nearly all the others that have
been mentioned, as a task; we may find in them much
that is curious, profitable, or entertaining; but on the
whole we read them with a certain effort and lay them
down with a sense of a duty done. But Irving is still
so fresh, so living, so companionable, that in turning
over the pages of his sketches or his histories, after
toiling through the dusty volumes of his predecessors,
we feel that we are at length among the first of the
moderns, and that we have gained a more familiar
ground. Chaucer is often spoken of as the " father
of English poetry,'' although there were many English
poets before him; and in some such way Irving,
while he had many predecessors, may be thought of
as the father of our American prose.

The man who thus stands at the threshold of the
greater period of our literature was lovable and
Irving's   kindly, and his life was as beautiful and
life.   as wholesome as his books. His father,
William Irving, a Scotch sailor from the Orkney
Islands, had married an English girl and settled in
New York city. He entered into business there some
years before the outbreak of the Revolution, and
there Washington Irving, the youngest of eleven
children, was born in 1783, the very year of the birth
of our Republic. " Washington's work is ended,''

Irving's mother is reported to have said, "and the child shall be named after him." One anecdote of Irving's childhood impresses itself on our imagination. When he was barely out of petticoats, a Scotch servant of the family took him into a shop which Washington had just entered. "Please your honor," she said, pointing to her little charge, "here's a bairn was named after you." The President put his hand on the head of his little namesake and gave him his blessing. "The touch," says Mr. Charles Dudley Warner, "could not have been more efficacious, though it might have lingered longer, if he had known that he was propitiating his future biographer."* Irving's early surroundings seem far from favorable to the development of genius. New York was then a provincial town, inferior to either Philadelphia or Boston in size, importance, and culture. It had suffered severely from the British occupation during the Revolution, when nearly half the town had been burned. Dutch was still spoken, although the use of English was becoming more and more established; and the old Dutch life, which was to furnish Irving with material for some of his best work, still lingered in the town, and held its place yet more firmly in the scattered dwellings of the neighborhood. The commercial spirit ruled, education was backward, and there was but little literary or intellectual life. Irving's early opportunities for education appear to have been limited. He left school before he was sixteen. In

* Warner's *Life of Irving*, p. 23.

addition to the ordinary English branches he had learned some Latin,—his nearest approach to a classical education. But, like Mountjoy in one of his sketches, he was a reader and a dreamer. At ten he was stirred by a romantic Italian poem, read in translation; at eleven his boy's imagination was sent voyaging over seas by the adventures and travels of Robinson Crusoe and Sinbad the Sailor. He would linger about the pier heads and watch the " parting ships " with " longing eyes." His father had the strictness so common to the Scotch, and Irving would steal out secretly for a forbidden taste of the theatre, returning home at nine for family prayers. At sixteen he began to study law, but his health was delicate, and after he had taken several trips in this country in hopes of improving it, his family decided to send him to Europe, that he might have the benefit of the sea voyage. Europe has become so much nearer and more familiar to Americans in these days of rapid ocean-travel that we are likely to undervalue the influence on Irving's career of what was for those times an unusual experience.*

Before Irving, hardly one of our native-born writers had any knowledge of the older civilizations, except that which reached him through the imperfect medium of books or correspondence. Franklin and Jefferson are conspicuous exceptions; but for the most

* " So late as 1795, a gentleman who had been abroad was pointed out, even in the streets of the large cities, with the remark, ' There goes a man who has been to Europe.' "—McMaster's *History of the People of the United States*, vol. i. p. 51.

part our men of letters had never been beyond the
limits of the comparatively crude surroundings and
limited life of a new community. Irving had the
natural susceptibility of the artist to beauty and
romance; he was young, and his restricted life and
quiet surroundings must have made the change to the
wonders of France and Italy, the throngs of London
and the delights of Paris, all the more impressive.
He was abroad for two years—learning French,
haunting picture-galleries, listening to music, meeting
celebrities. He saw the great actors John Kemble
and Mrs. Siddons; he saw the fleet of Nelson sweep
by in search of the French, and a year later he saw
the body of the dead admiral lying in state at Green-
wich. Shortly after his return home in 1806, Irving
made his first considerable attempts at writing.
Together with his brother William and J. K. Paulding, who became a writer of some distinction, he con-
ducted a fortnightly periodical called *Salmagundi*.*
The paper, like Franklin's *Busybody*, was an open
imitation of Addison's *Spectator*, long the accepted
model for periodical writers; it has also points of
resemblance to Goldsmith's *Citizen of the World*.
Like the *Spectator*, the little paper aimed to ridicule
the follies and reflect the passing life and fashions of
the town; it was light, good-natured, and popular,
and a creditable production for that time. Many of
the sketches which Irving contributed to it were really

---

* Salmagundi is a dish composed of a variety of ingredients;
hence a miscellany or collection of pieces of various kinds.

'prentice studies in subjects which he afterwards elaborated in his masterpieces, and this fact gives them
more than a temporary interest. In the mean time
Irving had completed his legal studies. He was good-
looking, good-humored, and popular, and he entered
into the social pleasures of Philadelphia, Baltimore,
Washington, and Albany, as well as of his native
city, with a youthful zest. He had thus a wider
experience of American life than a writer would have
been likely to gain under the more isolated conditions
of the Colonial times. In the midst of this gay life
a sorrow came to Irving, which he carried with him
until his death. This was the death of Matilda
Hoffman, whom he had loved with a beautiful and,
The "His- as he showed through his long life, with
tory of New an unchanging affection. When the blow
York." fell, Irving was engaged upon a humorous *History of New York*. After he had recovered
from the first shock of grief, he completed his work
in hopes of finding some distraction from his trouble.
The appearance of this book in 1809 is a landmark
in our literature. It is more than the first masterpiece of American humor: it marks the appearance
of our first great man of letters. Behind it stretch
the long years of Colonial dulness; after it the
path leads almost without a break to the writers
of to-day. The *History of New York* is a serio-
comic history of that city during the government
of the Dutch. Like some of the greatest English
satires, it is a burlesque on the heroic manner of the
classic epics; but besides this, it is a parody on the

pedantry and long-windedness of a certain local historian. Scott declared that he had never found anything so closely resembling the manner of Dean Swift, the greatest and most merciless of English satirists. The comparison was a natural one, and intended to be a compliment; but we are nearer the truth if we admit that Irving had produced an essentially original book, good enough to stand alone, without hanging on to the skirt of any English classic. Certain passages, where the satire becomes more direct and pointed, as in the sarcastic justification of our treatment of the Indians, may remind us of the great English master; but the resemblance is slight and accidental. A large part of Irving's humor is a simple overflowing of fun; his great sense of the oddities and absurdities of his fellow creatures seems only to warm his heart to them the more. Where Swift is venomous, Irving is kindly; where Swift is profound, Irving skims lightly over the surface; his laughter is without malice, and his jests leave no wound. But the originality of the *History of New York* lies not only in the peculiar flavor of its humor. Perhaps the most wonderful thing about the book is the way in which the little Dutch settlement is made alive and real to our imagination. Irving lived in a land where the past seemed as plain and as ordinary as daylight; yet he had somehow contrived to invest the apparently commonplace annals of his native town with all the fascinations of an age of fable, and with the romantic coloring of a legendary time. Out of fragmentary and unpromising materials he had created, in a crude,

new country, a new world of the imagination. He
may almost be said to have manufactured antiquity
and forcibly attached it to New York. The *History*
is the first book in which Irving takes us to this
delightful region. We are in a world of ponderous
Dutch burghers, fat and phlegmatic, slow-witted and
oracular, where the most redoubtable achievements,
in the golden age of Governor Wouter Van Twiller,
were eating, sleeping, smoking, drinking, and saying
nothing, and where the burgomasters were chosen by
weight. The placid town of Manhattan rises before
us, its wooden houses with their gable ends of yellow
and black Dutch brick; its patriarchal burghers dozing
in the sunshine or by the fireside over their eternal
pipes; its bovine inhabitants unvexed by learning, or
by those inequalities in intellect which are the occasion
of emulation and strife. "There are two opposite
ways," says Irving, "by which some men make a
figure in the world: one by talking faster than they
can think; and the other, by holding their tongues
and not thinking at all." The last, we may infer,
was the method of the governor and not a few of his
subjects, in those days of tranquillity. To call such
a world into being, endow it with a charm of its own,
and relate its history with an unfailing and kindly
humor, was to show one's self a literary artist. The
History of New York was received with enthusiasm;
but Irving did not immediately follow up his success.
His family were in easy circumstances, so he was able
to continue a pleasant social life so congenial to his
kindly but observing temperament. He had an

interest in his brother's business, and in 1815 he left
for England to look after the affairs of the firm. The
enterprise was not prospering, and Irving devoted
himself to its management with a faithfulness greatly
to his credit.

In 1816 the firm failed, and Irving turned to
literature for support. The first result of this
definite choice of his career was *The*
Sketch-Book, which appeared almost simul- The "Sketch-Book."
taneously in America and England. Ten
years had passed since the publication of the *History*
of New York, and we miss in *The Sketch-Book* the
unrestrained and almost boisterous fun of its pre-
decessor. On the other hand, its tone is gentler,
more thoughtful, more refined, and suffused with
that indescribable repose and charm so characteristic
of its author's maturer work. It consists of sketches
of various aspects of English and American life,
sometimes in the form of a personal reminiscence,
sometimes of a short story. The book belongs to
that eighteenth-century school of essay-writing of
which Addison is the great example; but, like the
essays of Goldsmith or Lamb, Irving's sketches have
a flavor of their own. His *Westminster Abbey* equals,
if it does not surpass, Addison's famous essay on the
same subject; and such sketches as the series on
Christmas at Bracebridge Hall, or *The Country*
Church, remind us of the days of Sir Roger de
Coverley. Two of the best pieces in the book deal
with American themes: *Rip Van Winkle* and *The*
Legend of Sleepy Hollow. In them Irving returned

to that delineation of the Dutch life of New York
which he had so happily begun, and actually gave to
the banks of the Hudson that added charm of myth
and legend almost unknown in our land. *The Sketch-
Book* was a triumph, not only for Irving, but for
American letters, and from this time Irving's place
and career were substantially assured.

Irving now entered upon a long life of literary
production, which we cannot here trace in detail.
Contact with Spanish life, while attached
to the American Legation at Madrid, **Histories.**
turned his interest into a new channel, and resulted
in his *Life of Columbus* (1828), a more solid and
ambitious work than he had yet attempted, and in
his *Companions of Columbus* and his *Conquest of
Granada.*   Another book inspired by this stay in
Spain was the *Tales of the Alhambra* (1829), written
after a residence in that old palace of the Moors.
None of these Spanish studies is superior to the
Conquest of Granada in an Old-world and romantic
charm.   Irving was not a deep thinker, nor, in a
strict sense, a great scholar.   He did not attempt to
write history as a philosopher or as a scientific student
of political or social conditions: he wrote it with the
living delight of an artist, conscientious as to the
accuracy of his facts, but moved by the dramatic and
human interest of incident and character, and by the
romantic fascination of his theme.   Those who consider the dryness of a history a good test of its value,
naturally look askance at Irving's richly-colored pictures of chivalric days; but his magical touch has

helped to recreate for us a chapter in the splendid
past of Spain, and thousands have felt through him
the gallantry and pathos of the last stand of the
Moors, who, but for him, would have passed it by
unheeding.

After spending a few years in England, during
which he was given the honorary degree of D.C.L.
by Oxford University, Irving returned to America in
1832. During the seventeen years of his absence the
country had gone forward with astonishing rapidity.
Thousands had poured westward from the Atlantic
States, pushing the frontier of settlement farther and
farther back into the wilderness. Wealth was increasing, and the introduction of the steamboat had given
unsuspected facilities for transportation and intercourse. Irving explored the wonders of this new
territory in a journey through the South and West,
the results of which he later embodied in his *Tour of
the Prairies* (1835).

Irving's disposition was affectionate and domestic.
He had seen and learned much in his wanderings: he
now longed to rest in a home of his own. He accordingly bought a small place on the banks of the
Hudson near Tarrytown, close to the spot which
his *Legend of Sleepy Hollow* had made famous.
Here he established himself in a quaint Dutch cot-
tage, built about a hundred years before by one of the
Van Tassels. It was a "little, old-fashioned stone
mansion, all made up of gable-ends." Among its
attractions was a queer old weathercock which had
been brought from Holland, and in time the walls

were covered with ivy grown from a slip that had
come from Melrose Abbey. Irving called the place
"Sunnyside," a name pleasantly in keeping with his
sunshiny and almost boyish spirits. He reluctantly
left his retreat in 1842 to go to Madrid as ambassador;
but except for this period of enforced absence it
is with "Sunnyside" that the remainder of his life is
associated.

Although Irving was fifty when he retreated to his
"roost," or rest, at "Sunnyside," he continued to
write industriously and with but little intermission
for the quarter of a century of life that yet remained
to him. Among the most noteworthy of these later
Lives of works are his *Life of Goldsmith*, and
Goldsmith his final task, the *Life of Washington*.
and Wash- The first of these is one of the most per-
ington. fect and enjoyable literary biographies in
our language. It is based on a larger English work,
and it does not profess to give us new information.
Its charm lies rather in the kindly warmth of appreciation that pervades it, in its latent humor, and in
the easy flow and beauty of its style. The shiftless
but lovable Goldsmith has strong points of resemblance to Irving's greatest contribution to the characters of fiction—that most graceless, amiable, and
lovable of vagabonds, Rip van Winkle. Such a subject was one to arouse Irving's sympathies and to call
out his best powers.

To write a successful life of Washington demanded
abilities of a widely different kind. The career of a
great soldier, statesman, and patriot must be closely

related to large national issues; such a biography
is part of a nation's history, and it demands the
historian's largeness of view. Such a subject was
less directly within the scope of Irving's peculiar
genius. The book was in five large volumes, and
appeared between 1855 and 1859. It was written
towards the close of Irving's life, when he had less
vigor than formerly to complete so large an undertaking, and he himself complained that the work dragged
sadly towards the last. The book, if not the most
characteristic of Irving's writings, is nevertheless well
done. It is the result of careful research; it is simple
and direct in style, quiet and well-balanced in tone,
and it brings Washington before us with undeniable
fairness and power. With the *Life of Washington*,
Irving's work ended; he died at " Sunnyside " within
a year after the final volume had been given to the
public.

Irving's literary career covers an eventful half-
century in our literary history. When he began to
write, the literature of the imagination
could hardly be said to exist among us, **Irving's Work.**
and the puritanic gloom which darkened
so many of our productions was unrelieved by any
kindly light of humor. In England, American
books were almost universally despised or ignored.
Before Irving laid down his pen, a second and
yet abler group of writers had succeeded that to
which he himself belonged; and our literature had at
length won for itself a hearing and a respectable foot-
ing beyond the seas. Irving had no inconsiderable

part in bringing about this great change. He is commonly said to be the first writer to make our literature respected abroad. Thackeray called him " the first ambassador whom the New World of Letters sent to the Old," and added that he taught millions of his countrymen to love England. It was thus no small part of his work that he helped the two greatest English-speaking nations of the earth to understand and appreciate each other. As a writer, his literary sense was finer and more delicate, his art altogether on a higher plane than that of any American who preceded him. Irving's temperament was quickly responsive to his surroundings. He had a healthy enjoyment in the beauty of the world and the society of his fellow-creatures; he had a shrewd perception of that which lent itself to literary treatment; being touched alike by the odd or ludicrous, and by the quaint, romantic, and picturesque. Hence his writings are obviously inspired from without rather than from within, and his descriptions of Dutch, English, Spanish, and wild Western life are the reflections of his successive experiences. A great part of the fascination of Irving's writings is due to the fact that they are the expression of a singularly pure and lovely nature. The love he inspired in both England and America was due not merely to his writings, but to himself. Like Rip van Winkle, he was by nature something of a loiterer; he became a worker later from a manly sense of duty. But from both his character and works a certain masculine harshness and power, characteristic of sterner and stronger souls, are

notably absent. He draws us to him by a humor that
is free from bitterness, by his unfeigned goodness,
and by his love and sympathy for all mankind. He
wrote modestly of his aims: "If I can now and then
penetrate the gathering film of misanthropy, prompt
a benevolent view of human nature, and make my
reader more in good humor with his fellow-beings
and with himself, surely—surely I shall not then
have written entirely in vain."

STUDY LIST

IRVING

1. Essays. "The Country Church," "Westminster
Abbey," "Stratford-on-Avon," and the Christmas Series,
in *The Sketch Book;* and the "Interior of the Alhambra"
and "The Alhambra by Moonlight" in *The Alhambra.*

2. Stories. "Rip Van Winkle," "The Legend of Sleepy
Hollow," and "The Spectre Bridegroom," in *The Sketch
Book;* "Dolph Heyliger" and "The Stout Gentleman" in
Bracebridge Hall; "Wolfert Webber" in *Tales of a Traveller.* The stories in *The Alhambra* will be found delight-
fully suggestive of the *Arabian Nights.* Selections from
the *Sketch Book* are published in the Riverside Literature
Series (Houghton, Mifflin & Co.). G. P. Putnam's Sons
publish a specially annotated "student's edition" of *Tales
of a Traveller*, *The Alhambra*, and *The Sketch Book.*
Another edition of the *Tales of a Traveller*, annotated by
Prof. Matthews and Prof. Carpenter, is published in Longmans' English Classics.

3. Life of Oliver Goldsmith; Conquest of Granada.

4. Biography and Criticism. Life, by his nephew,
Pierre M. Irving; by David J. Hill, in American Authors
Series; by Chas. Dudley Warner, in American Men of

Letters Series. For criticisms, see Whipple's *American Literature;* Curtis's *Literary and Social Essays;* Howells's *My Literary Passions;* Lowell's *Fable for Critics;* Thackeray's "Nil Nisi Bonum," in the *Roundabout Papers;* and *Studies of Irving,* containing essays and addresses by C. D. Warner, Bryant, and George P. Putnam.

JAMES FENIMORE COOPER (1789-1851)

The quality of Irving's genius is another proof that American literature is, as a whole, but the continuation of English literature under new conditions. He works in an atmosphere of Old-world culture, and shows no trace of that largeness of design and crudeness of execution, of that unregulated power, which belong to the vigorous but undisciplined period of youth. His style, formed on the best English models, has that high finish and careful restraint characteristic of an ancient civilization. The subdued tone of much of his work may be compared to that of a mild and tranquil afternoon in autumn, when everything is suggestive of quiet, contemplation, fulfilment, and repose. His inspiration is from the past rather than from the future. Even in the midst of the eager rush of young America his first instinct is to turn to the life and legends of a time that has gone by.

With Cooper, on the other hand, Irving's fellow-worker in the building of a national literature, the case was almost precisely the reverse. While not free from foreign influences, Cooper is far more independent of them, and in his sympathy with a primitive life, his crudity of style, his lavish vigor, he

JAMES FENIMORE COOPER

represents, as Irving could not do, the stirring spirit of
a young people. Cooper himself had the masculine,
fighting temperament of the man of action. He lived
a more stirring out-of-doors life than that which usually falls to the lot of men of letters, so that both by
nature and experience he was fitted to be the novelist
of incident and adventure.

James Fenimore Cooper was born in Burlington,
New Jersey, a sleepy old town on the Delaware, in
1789. He was destined, however, to spend
his early years in far different surround- **Cooper's life.**
ings, for when he was only about a year
old his father, who owned a large tract of land in a
then unsettled region of New York near Otsego
Lake, turned his back on civilization and settled
there with his family. In his novel *The Pioneers*
Cooper has given us a faithful picture of this region
as he knew it in his childhood. It lay on the outer
edge of settlement, and the axe had made but few
clearings in the dense woods that shut in the lake.
Westward stretched the solemn and almost unbroken
wilderness. So remote was it, that a panic was at one
time created in the little settlement by rumors of an
Indian outbreak. Cooper was thus made familiar
from childhood with the surroundings and incidents
of border life, and his after-work bears witness to
the depth and accuracy of these first impressions.
And to a woodsman's knowledge of the woods he
added a seaman's knowledge of the sea. Dismissed
from Yale College for some boyish outbreak, it was
decided that he should enter the navy. He accord-

ingly spent about a year on a merchant vessel as a
common sailor, this being then the customary training for a naval career. After about three years in the
navy he married, and, yielding to his wife's wishes,
resigned his commission and returned to country life.
His active disposition found an interest in farming.
For ten years after his retirement from the navy he
showed no inclination towards a literary career, and
up to the age of thirty he had published nothing.
Even then his sudden plunge into authorship was due
to accident rather than to any literary or bookish
tastes. Impressed with the shortcomings of a story
of English life he had been reading, he said impulsively that he believed he could write a better story
himself. His wife challenged him to prove it, and
with little or no thought of publication he began a
novel to justify his claim. He was encouraged to
complete the venture, which appeared under the title
Precaution in 1820. The scene was laid in England,
probably because the original intention was to outdo
an English novelist on his own ground. The book
was published anonymously, and was popularly believed to be the work of an Englishman. It met with
some favor, but chance had led Cooper into the draw-
ing-room conversations of polite society, a region
particularly unsuited to his powers, and he had no
real knowledge of the upper-class English life which
he attempted to describe. It is probable that Cooper
would not have repeated his experiment had not some
of his friends accused him of lack of patriotism in
thus abandoning his own country for a foreign theme.

To vindicate himself from this charge Cooper wrote a
second novel, *The Spy*, a story of our Revolution, which
was published in 1821–22. In its way the publication
of *The Spy* is almost as memorable an event in our
literary history as the publication of Irving's *History
of New York*. Cooper had found a subject congenial
to his powers, and had begun to do for the American
novel a work comparable to that of Irving in his
especial sphere. The importance of the book was
almost instantly recognized. A writer in the *North
American Review* for 1822 declared that Cooper had
" laid the foundations of American romance," and
that he was the first who " deserved the appellation
of a distinguished American novel-writer." He had
proved, the same critic continued, that the novelist
might find in American life a suitable and practically
new field for his art. But the success of *The Spy*
went far beyond the verdict of the critics, for Cooper
at his best got directly at the large body of readers.
In spite of our provincial deference to English opinion,
America delighted in it without waiting for foreign
sanction, and it was read with eager pleasure in England and France. The success of *The Spy* was not
altogether due to the novelty of its subject. With
many of Cooper's characteristic faults, it has also his
characteristic merits. It is full of scenes that show
the vigor and dash of his narrative power; and its central character, the humble pedler Harvey Birch, cool,
brave, incorruptible, quick in resource in times of
peril, is a noble example of that homely heroism in
the portrayal of which Cooper excelled. Cooper's

originality in choice of subjects was even more strongly shown by his next stories, *The Pioneers* and *The Pilot*, both of which appeared in 1823. The former is a story of the woods, the latter of the sea. Thus almost simultaneously Cooper showed himself master in two new spheres of fiction: in one of them he stands almost without a rival; while in the other, although he has had many followers, he has seldom, if ever, been excelled.

Cooper left home in 1826 for an extended stay in Europe. Several books were the direct outcome of his travels, but none of them rank with his best work, as, unlike Irving, all his truest inspiration came not from the Old World, but from the New. After his return to the United States in 1833 he engaged in a number of bitter and unfortunate controversies, which made him extremely unpopular for many years. An intense patriot, he found many things on his return to his own country which he thought should be amended. With the highest intentions, he was combative, devoid of tact, and both acutely sensitive to criticism himself and outspoken in his criticism of others. But unwise as he may have been in entering into these disputes, our strongest feeling is one of admiration for the unfaltering manliness, ability, and courage with which he contended almost single-handed against his detractors. During these years he wrote rapidly and incessantly, producing some of his best and some of his poorest books. In addition to many novels he published a careful and excellent *History of the United States Navy* (1839). He died at Cooperstown in 1851, in the midst of those scenes of his boyhood which he had made famous.

The real greatness of Cooper as a romance-writer has been much obscured by his obvious faults and by the changes in literary taste.   His style is full of defects, for he wrote rapidly, **Cooper's work.** often carelessly, and he lacked literary training.   He was successful only within certain limits, and frequently failed because he did not recognize his limitations, and, unlike his own *Pathfinder*, sought to go beyond his gifts.   The lack of judgment, which often led him to attempt what he was unfitted to perform, has made his books of most unequal value, and the mixture of so much that is inferior tends to blind us to his genuine excellence.

While it would be absurd to ignore Cooper's faults, readers of to-day seem to be much more in danger of forgetting his merits.   His familiar title " the American Scott " is apt to make us undervalue his original power.   His method indeed is naturally similar to that of the great master of modern romance, but it must not be forgotten that Cooper distinctly widened the sphere of romantic fiction by carrying it into new fields.   Scott found his inspiration in feudalism; Cooper in the untamed freedom of the wilderness and the sea.   Scott had predecessors in his delight in the Middle Ages, but Cooper wrote practically as a pioneer, and added a new domain to literature.   Through him the hardy and adventurous life of our western frontier first took its place in fiction; he it was who made the crafts and cruelties of Indian warfare, the obscure heroism of the backwoodsman, the interminable solitudes of the American forest, a reality in the imagination of Europe. Cooper's best and most comprehensive picture of border-life is of course to be found in his famous " Leatherstocking Tales," so called from one of the many names given to the hero. These books, *The Deerslayer* (1841), *The Last of the Mohicans* (1826), *The Pathfinder* (1840), *The Pioneers* (1823), and *The Prairie* (1827), to name them in the order in which they should be read, are, taken together, Cooper's greatest contribution to literature. Cooper styled them "a drama in five acts:" it would probably be more accurate to call them a rough prose epic of the deeds of a New-World hero, nobler intrinsically than Achilles or Æneas. The stories show us this simple-hearted hunter and scout, Natty Bumppo or Leatherstocking, at five successive stages of his long and hazardous life. We see him on his first war-path, humble as one who has not been proved; we see him in the fulness of his marvellous skill and sagacity; and we see him finally when age has come upon him, his friends dead, his very dog feeble and toothless, his famous rifle, Killdeer, out-of-date, and ready, like its owner, to be laid aside. To thus show the life and development of a single character in five successive novels is a memorable achievement, and the success with which this has been accomplished is one of Cooper's highest claims to distinction. Pure-minded, simple-hearted, ignorant of books, but skilled in every sign of the forest; with a deep sense of religion, half primeval, half Christian,

with an aboriginal nearness to nature and an inveter-
ate hatred of towns,—Leatherstocking has rightfully
taken his place among the noblest and most original
of the great characters of fiction. And Leatherstocking is more than interesting to us as an individual; like most of the great characters which the
human imagination has created, he interests us partly
for himself and partly because of what he represents.
He is as distinctly a typical product of our border life
as Rob Roy is of the forays of the Scottish Highlands
or Achilles of the heroic age of Greece. He is a
national hero: young as we are, he is ours. Living
beyond the fringe of civilization and moving in front
of the wave of settlement, his life is indirectly associated with that subduing of the West which is perhaps the most wonderful and heroic achievement of
the American people. The greatness of this national
movement, while it enters into the Leatherstocking
stories only as a kind of secondary motive, yet gives
to the whole a certain dimly recognized breadth and
epic largeness of tone. In 1740–45, when in the
Deerslayer its hero begins his career, Otsego Lake is
yet unmapped by the king's surveyors; in the
Pioneers, some sixty years later, the country about it
has been taken up by the settlers, and the old hunter,
compelled to retreat before them, grumbles that he
loses himself in the clearings; finally, in *The Prairie*,
which carries us to a period just after the Louisiana
purchase of 1803, we are shown the emigrant train of
the indefatigable settler pushing into the treeless
plains of the far West. Leatherstocking's part in this

advance is not that of the settler but the pioneer; he even grumbles to find the settler following at his heels; yet, like Daniel Boone, he is a heroic figure in one of the heroic episodes of our history.

And as Cooper, in these and other stories, is the novelist of the American forest, so, in such a novel as *The Pilot*, he is as truly the novelist of the sea. Here, too, he is distinctly original in his choice of subject. The life of the sailor had indeed been incidentally introduced into English stories before his time: it entered into *Robinson Crusoe*, into the *Humphrey Clinker* of Tobias Smollett, and shortly before Cooper wrote *The Pilot* Scott had touched on it in *The Pirate*, although with a landsman's ignorance of nautical affairs; but Cooper is admittedly the first writer of genuine sea-stories, and in this the creator of what was virtually a new order of fiction. In both of these great regions of his art, the woods and the sea, Cooper is remarkable for the truth and vividness of his descriptions of nature in her unconfined and uncontaminated beauty and power. He had lived with nature from a child, and if his descriptions of her lack literary finish, this is more than made up by that intense feeling of reality which his life-long understanding of her enabled him to convey. He is so true in this that he makes us live in the scenes he describes, for the smell of the woods is in them and the salty breath of the sea. Nor is Cooper to be despised as a painter of character. Of course his heroines are commonly but lay-figures for the development of his plots; of course he was incapable of presenting human

nature, and especially civilized human nature, in all
its delicate shades of difference; but in one region he
was supreme. It was his to show us the plain, unlet-
tered man, with something of the primitive hero under
his humble dress; and Harvey Birch, Pathfinder, or
Long Tom Coffin, stands worthily beside those great
kindred creations Adam Bede and Jeanie Deans.

The action of his stories often lags; as a rule, his
plots are crudely constructed and improbable; but he
rises to a crisis, and his dash and vigor in single scenes
cannot well be surpassed. We find it hard to parallel
the dramatic force and manly power of such descriptions as that of the wreck of the Ariel in *The Pilot*,
the defence of the cave in *The Last of the Mohicans*,
or the discovery of the body of Asa in *The Prairie*.

High-minded, robust, manly, such qualities fitted
Cooper, full of faults and prejudices as he was, to be
a truly national writer. He represented us in a way
that even Irving could not, for through him the
readers of Paris or London forgot for a time the spirit
of the Old World to identify themselves with the
spirit of the New.

STUDY LIST

COOPER

1. **Works**. Cooper's "Leatherstocking Tales" are house-
hold works, and need no recommendation. In addition,
The Spy and one or two of the "Sea Tales," such as *The
Pilot* and *The Red Rover*, should be read. *The Last of the
Mohicans*, edited, with Introduction and Notes, by Professor
Richardson, is published in Longmans' English Classics.

2. Biography and Criticism. The only biography of
Cooper is Professor Lounsbury's *Life*, in the American
Men of Letters Series. See also the introductions to the
"Leatherstocking Tales" and the "Sea Tales," in the
edition of Cooper's novels edited by his daughter, Susan
Fenimore Cooper (Houghton, Mifflin & Co.). Considerable
information is to be found in T. S. Livermore's *History of
Cooperstown.* For criticism, see Bryant's Discourse on
Cooper; Lowell's *Fable for Critics;* and an interesting
allusion in Thackeray's "On a Peal of Bells," in the
Roundabout Papers. For an extreme criticism of Cooper,
see "Fenimore Cooper's Literary Offences," in *How to Tell
a Story; and other Essays*, by Mark Twain.

WILLIAM CULLEN BRYANT (1794-1878)

Although a few creditable lyrics had been produced
before his time, Bryant is the earliest of our greater
poets, and fairly deserves his title "the Father of
American Song." He stands with Irving and Cooper
at the beginning of the modern period of our literature, holding somewhat the same relation to its poetry
that Irving does to its prose. Bryant is associated
with the group of writers commonly known as the
"Knickerbocker School," which during the first
quarter of the century made New York the literary
center of the country. But while his career identifies
him with New York, he belongs to New England by
birth, inheritance, and early surroundings. He came
of sound Puritan stock, his ancestors on both his
father's and his mother's side having come over in
the Mayflower. He was born at Cummington, a

WILLIAM CULLEN BRYANT

quiet town in western Massachusetts, in 1794, and
grew up in the simple, hard-working,
wholesome atmosphere characteristic of **Bryant's life.**
New England a century ago.   In his description of the neighborhood of Bryant's early home
George William Curtis writes that " the very spirit
of primitive New England brooded over the thinly-
peopled hills and in the little villages and farms." *
Drawn to nature by an instinctive sympathy and surrounded by her influence, the boy came to know her
as a naturalist and to love her as a poet.   He tells us
that from his " earliest years " he was a " delighted
observer of external nature."   Two other influences,
both of them characteristic of early New England,
were about him from his youth—religion and books.
He was brought up in the solemn if severe faith of
his Puritan ancestors, and he was a reader, especially
a reader of poetry, from his childhood.   After a year
at Williams College he studied law, but only to
abandon it for literature, as Brockden Brown, Irving,
and so many others had done before him.   His literary tastes declared themselves very early.   Shortly
after he left college, when not yet eighteen, he wrote
Thanatopsis, the noblest verse produced in America
up to that time.   When a law-student he was rebuked
by his preceptor for reading Wordsworth's *Lyrical
Ballads* instead of Blackstone's *Commentaries on the
Laws of England*.   He worked manfully at his profession, for it was not in him to shirk an obligation,

* Commemoration address on Bryant in 1878.

but his verses suggest to us the effort it cost him.
Shortly after his admission to the bar in 1815 he
wrote sadly that the bright vision which had once
come to him in the silence of nature had faded in the
atmosphere of the world.   In 1817 *Thanatopsis* appeared in the *North American Review*, followed by
another masterpiece, *To a Water-fowl*, in the year
following.   These contributions brought him at once
into notice, and he was asked to write the annual poem
for the *Phi Beta Kappa* Society at Harvard.   This
poem, *The Ages*, was published with several others in
1821, the year of the appearance of Irving's *Sketch-
book* and Cooper's *Spy*.

After an honest effort to get on in his profession,
Bryant came to New York and accepted the post of
joint editor of the *New York Review and Athenæum
Magazine* (1823).   This periodical, a new venture,
proved to be short-lived, and in 1826 Bryant became
associate editor of *The Evening Post*.   From this
time journalism absorbed a large part of his time and
energies.   His connection with *The Evening Post*
stretched over more than half a century, and through
that long and critical period he did his work con-
scientiously and well.   Living in the tumult of a
great city, the sanctifying presence of nature was with
him to the end.   Through all the exacting duties of
journalism he found rest and pleasure in turning from
the discussions of the hour, or the heat of political
controversy, to those influences of the woods and fields
and open sky which had been his earliest inspiration.
These seasons of escape and refreshment found from

time to time an expression in his verse and determined
its prevailing tone.   In *A Winter Piece* he alludes to
that instinct which seems from the first to have sent
him to the woods to be healed :

> " When the ills of life
> Had chafed my spirit, when the unsteady pulse
> Beat with strange flutterings, I would wander forth
> And seek the woods. . . .
>   While I stood
> In Nature's loneliness, I was with one
> With whom I early grew familiar,—one
> Who never had a frown for me, whose voice
> Never rebuked me for the hour I stole
> From cares I loved not, but of which the world
> Deems highest, to converse with her."

As nearly all of Bryant's inspiration comes from the
same source, his poetry is for the most part the utterance of a single mood.   He did not develop or improve
as a poet; from the first he is master of his especial
style, and the spirit of his earliest verse is the spirit
of his last.

Bryant became a prominent and dignified figure in
the social and intellectual life of his adopted city.
Various collections of his poems had appeared from
time to time, and in 1870–71 he published a blank-
verse translation of the Iliad and Odyssey, which has
that nobility and dignity peculiar to his poetic
manner.   His long life extends over nearly the entire
history of our strictly national literature.   When he
was born Franklin had only been dead four years,
and Brockden Brown had not published his earliest
romance; when he died in 1878, the work of Emerson,

Longfellow, and their great contemporaries was nearly ended, and a yet later generation, the writers of our own day, were pushing to the front. Before Bryant had finished his work, Irving and Cooper, the other members of that early triumvirate, had passed away. Bryant alone remained, honored by his successors as the patriarch of our national literature. Bryant is not only the earliest of our greater poets: he stands alone in our literature by the individual tone and quality of his work, having absolutely no predecessors in America, and founding no school. *Thanatopsis* was not merely the greatest poem written in America up to the time of its appearance: it was totally distinct in manner and spirit from anything which we had heretofore produced. The poem has that classic severity, dignity, and noble seriousness for which so much of Bryant's best work is remarkable. Its theme is at once simple and comprehensive; the solemn fact of death, divested of those painful associations which make us tremble, stands out against the illimitable background of nature, as a part of the universal plan. There is no direct promise of immortality, but we are elevated and sustained by the contemplation of the unfailing natural processes of birth and decay. At the close the injunction to live worthily rings in our ears like a trumpet-call. There is nothing distinctly Christian in the poem, but in its high seriousness and in its uncompromising call to duty it is in keeping with the essential inner spirit of the English people from the

Bryant's work.

days of the Anglo-Saxon gleemen to those of Milton
and of Browning. The verse has a majestic movement
adapted to its solemn theme:

> "The hills
> Rock-ribbed and ancient as the sun ; the vales
> Stretching in pensive quietness between ;
> The venerable woods ; rivers that move
> In majesty, and the complaining brooks
> That make the meadows green ; and, poured round all,
> Old ocean's gray and melancholy waste,—
> Are but the solemn decorations all
> Of the great tomb of man."

Quite apart from its meaning, the sound of this
verse, with its suggestions of Milton, of Shakespeare,
or of Wordsworth, tells us that American poetry has
reached a new stage in its development. The influence of Pope had ceased to be supreme in England
some time before Bryant wrote *Thanatopsis*. During
the latter half of the eighteenth century a new school
of poets had asserted themselves, who discarded Pope's
favorite metre, and wrote with a fresh inspiration of
nature and of man. This movement against Pope
and all that he represented culminated in the poetry
of Wordsworth and Coleridge during the end of the
last and the early part of the present century. But
while the English poets were rebelling against Pope
the American verse-writers continued to imitate him,
and Bryant is the first among us to show decidedly by
his spirit and metre that he had cast him off. In a
juvenile poem Bryant himself was one of Pope's many
imitators, but he came under the spell of Words-

worth, and in *Thanatopsis* we see that the new spirit already dominant in England has at last reached us here. Thus Bryant's real predecessors are not American, but English. He is the spiritual descendant not of Dwight or Barlow, but of Milton, Cowper, and Wordsworth. But although from this aspect Bryant represents the English influence on our literature, he is both truly American and individual. A true poet can be affected by foreign influences without becoming a servile copyist. There is no reason to suppose that Bryant's delight in nature was less inborn than that of Wordsworth himself; nor can we doubt that while both Bryant and Cowper take sanctuary in nature from the turmoils of the streets, the impulse to do so was as genuine in the one case as in the other. This genuineness of Bryant's is shown in the truth of his natural descriptions. Nothing is borrowed from books or introduced for mere effect; he brings before us our country as he had known and loved it from a boy. He celebrates the yellow violet and the goldenrod, flowers that had never bloomed in English song. While Cooper was making our American landscape familiar through fiction, Bryant was giving it, for the first time, a place in poetry. Through his verse we enter the dimly lighted woods, with their familiar lessons of renewal and decay; we see the unsullied winter landscape of New England, the myriads of ice-crystals glittering in the sunlight; or we are carried in the wake of that great Western emigration to where the slopes of the prairies stretch in soft undulations under the drifting shadows of the clouds. Bryant does more than describe such scenes: he is fond of drawing from them some solemn if familiar lesson; he clothes them with his own meditative and often sombre spirit. In this characteristic seriousness he is not only close to the English race-temperament: he is American in so far as he expresses, although without theological bias, that section of English Puritanism which made its stronghold in New England.

As a poet Bryant possesses great excellence within a strictly limited range. He is even more exclusively the poet of nature than Wordsworth; throughout his poetry warmth, human interest, and human passion are almost absent. He wrote but little verse, and never really surpassed his two early efforts, *Thanatopsis* and the *Ode to a Water-fowl;* yet though he did not advance, he maintained an exceedingly high standard until the last. Within his own narrow limits, as a meditative poet, as a descriptive poet of nature, and as a master of blank verse, remarkable for its loftiness, nobility, and repose, he occupies an exceptionally high position among the poets of America; and even outside of our national limits, in that almost world-wide English literature of which ours is but a part, he has won a place which, if minor, is both honorable and secure.

STUDY LIST

BRYANT

1. Poems. "Thanatopsis," "The Ages," "To a Water-fowl," "Green River," "A Winter Piece," "The Death of the Flowers," "The Yellow Violet," "The Prairies," "Song of Marion's Men," "A Forest Hymn."

2. **Biography and Criticism.**   Life, by Parke Godwin ;
by D. J. Hill, in the American Authors Series ; by John
Bigelow, in the American Men of Letters Series.   Curtis's
Literary and Social Essays ; Stedman's *Poets of America ;*
Whipple's *Literature and Life,* and *Essays and Reviews,*
vol. i. ; Lowell's *Fable for Critics.*   J. Alden's *Studies in
Bryant,* in the Literature Primers Series, is a useful little
book for an analytical study of Bryant's poetry.

MINOR WRITERS OF THE MIDDLE STATES

While Irving, Cooper, and Bryant were the leaders
in the making of our national literature, we must
remember that the full strength and importance of a
literary period such as that to which they belonged
cannot be measured by the work of its greatest writers
alone.   The natural desire of a young nation to create
and possess a literature which should truly represent it
was a strong incentive to a considerable number of
native writers who strove to describe the American
landscape or depict the novel conditions of American
life.   The three great leaders whose work we have
just studied were consequently only the strongest and
completest representatives of a literary activity in
which many minor authors shared, and the men by
whom they were surrounded worked under the same
conditions, and helped forward, each after his own
fashion, the same general result.   Having studied the
period during which our national literature took shape
in the work of its greatest writers, we must now
endeavor to look at it from a more general and comprehensive point of view.

Let us look at our literary history as a whole, from the time of the Revolution to about the middle of the present century, and ask ourselves how this important epoch is related to that long Colonial era of preparation which preceded it.

We have already seen how the force which raised up and strengthened our oratory, our poetry, and our prose during this first stage of our national history, was the ever-increasing sense of the dignity and meaning of our national life. But this spirit of patriotism could not eradicate those deep-seated differences between section and section, which had been present from the first. While sharing in the wider national life, each section of the country retained its own peculiar character and aims. Local loyalty and local jealousy remained. We had a political center in our national capitol; but no city could hold a similar relation to our intellectual and literary life. In France and England the condition has been widely different. For the past five or six hundred years London has been so distinctly the focus-point of English thought that her literary history is almost identical with the national life itself. In the brief life of our literature, on the contrary, the intellectual center has continually shifted from one section of the country to another. When we regard the rise of our national literature from this aspect, we are chiefly impressed by the small part played in it by New England, the most scholarly and intellectual of all the original Colonial groups. The period under review is clearly remarkable for the temporary transference of literary leadership from New England to

the South, and from the South to the Middle States.
When the Revolution and the critical years that succeeded it brought forth our great orators and political
writers, although New England and the Middle States
were neither silent nor uninfluential, the real superiority lay with the South. From the South came two
of the greatest political productions of that epoch—
The Declaration of Independence, and the *Constitution of the United States.** New England gave us
James Otis, Samuel Adams, and Fisher Ames; together
with the Middle States she gave us Franklin; but the
South gave Patrick Henry, Thomas Jefferson, Madison, Lee, and Monroe. John Marshall, the Chief
Justice of the United States during a most critical
period of its history, a man of far-reaching influence
and some literary gifts, was, like many of the Southern leaders, a son of Virginia.

Aside from oratory and politics, in spite of the
early literary superiority of the Puritan, the foundations of our really national literature were laid in the
Middle States. Poetry really found its voice, not in
the pretentious efforts of the New Englanders, Barlow,
Trumbull, or Dwight, but in the verse of the Philadelphian William Clifton, or yet more indubitably in
a few lyrics of the New Jersey poet Philip Freneau.
In romance, through the stories of Charles Brockden
Brown, the Middle States were not only in advance
of the rest of the country, but were practically without a rival. In the first quarter of the present cen-

---

* *The Federalist*, which may be ranked as the third, belongs
in part to the Middle and in part to the Southern States.

tury the leadership of the middle region of the country became even more marked, and in that great section New York succeeded Philadelphia as a literary center. The view of the Southern poet Edgar Allan Poe on this matter must be received with caution, as he was disposed to undervalue the literary group in New England, still it is worth noting that he wrote as late as 1846: "New York literature may be taken as a fair representation of the country at large. The city itself is the focus of American letters. Its authors include perhaps one fourth of all in America and the influence they exert on their brethren, if seemingly silent, is not the less extensive and decisive." * If we apply these remarks to an earlier period than that of which Poe wrote, they can hardly be thought exaggerated. From the literary advent of Irving in 1807 to the decisive entrance of Longfellow and Emerson about 1836, the work of our greatest men of letters was centered in New York. Two of our then most famous authors, Irving and Cooper, were sons of the Middle States; the third, Bryant, chose New York city as the sphere of his literary career. Besides the greater lights, there were many others of lesser magnitude. To New York belong the two poets FITZ-GREENE HALLECK (1790–1867) and JOSEPH RODMAN DRAKE (1795–1820), united in their friendship and their work.

Halleck, like Bryant, was of New England birth and descent, but a New Yorker by adoption. Drake

* *The Literature of New York.* Poe's Works, Stoddard's edition, p. 435.

belonged to the great metropolis by birth as well as by residence. These two writers began their work in 1819, the year of the publication of Cooper's *Precaution*, with the *Croaker Poems*, a witty and satirical chronicle of New York life which may be compared to Irving and Paulding's *Salmagundi*. The best verses of Halleck, although somewhat rhetorical and declamatory, have an undoubted spirit and vigor. They stand in somewhat the same relation to poetry of a less noisy and more subtle order that a good brass band bears to a symphony orchestra. He once said to Drake, "It would be heaven to lounge upon the rainbow and read Tom Campbell," and his verses suggest the martial music of Campbell's battle-lyrics, or the telling but showy rhetoric of Byron. His *Marco Bozzaris* has been declaimed by innumerable schoolboys. Halleck visited Europe in 1822, and some of his best poems are due to his foreign impressions. Among them are his tribute to *Burns* and his *Alnwick Castle*, the home of the great family of Northumberland. In the latter there is that intrusion of a satirical humor into the very fortress of romance, that sudden half-cynical drop from poetry to prose, which is not only characteristic of Halleck but of the American spirit, a spirit destined to reappear later and in a more aggressive form in the writings of Mark Twain.

One poem of Halleck's stands quite apart from those we have mentioned: his tribute to the memory of his friend Drake, which has a simplicity and a directness which speak of genuine sorrow. The young

(margin note: Fitz-Greene Halleck.)

poet whose loss is here commemorated died of consumption at twenty-five, cut off in the opening of a career which was full of promise.   He is chiefly remembered as Halleck's friend and co-worker, and as the author of a spirited

Joseph Rodman Drake

lyric, *The American Flag*, and a longer poem, *The Culprit Fay*.   The first of these holds a high—perhaps the highest—place among our national songs. The verse has a stirring and martial music, and when we get beyond the somewhat strained and over-elaborate figure in the opening stanza, the poem gains in power as it becomes more simple and direct.

> "Flag of the brave! thy folds shall fly,
> The sign of hope and triumph high,
> When speaks the signal-trumpet tone,
> And the long line comes gleaming on.
> Ere yet the life-blood, warm and wet,
> Has dimmed the glistening bayonet,
> Each soldier eye shall brightly turn
> To where thy sky-born glories burn ;
> And, as his springing steps advance,
> Catch war and vengeance from the glance."

The Culprit Fay is the story of a fairy condemned to do penance for loving a mortal.   It is slight, pretty, and fanciful, perhaps over-ingenuous.   It follows the traditions of fairy poetry and suggests the famous description of Queen Mab in Shakespeare's *Romeo and Juliet*, or the quaint fancies of Drayton's *Nymphidia*.   Here and there are delicate and beautiful bits of natural description and an occasional strain that, as Professor Beers has observed, recalls the melody of Coleridge's *Christabel*.

Another prominent member of this New York or " Knickerbocker " group was NATHANIEL PARKER WILLIS (1806–1867), a light but pleasing writer once

N. P. Willis.   widely popular.   Like Bryant, Willis early won distinction by his verse; like Bryant, he left his native New England and became an editor in New York.   Here, however, the resemblance ends, for Willis, " all *natty* and jaunty and gay," as Lowell described him, was essentially a writer for the day and not for posterity.   His thin, fluent verse has no trace of Bryant's somber dignity and concentrated power, but some of his shorter poems are still worthy of a place in our anthologies.   His service to our prose was a more important one.   By his stories, sketches, and reminiscences of travel, written in an easy, sprightly way, but in the careful spirit of the artist and with a genuine feeling for style, he helped to raise the standard of workmanship and refine the public taste.   Many other New York writers of the time must be passed over, or given but the merest mention here.   Among these were SAMUEL WOOD-WORTH, a magazine editor, remembered for his single poem *The Old Oaken Bucket;* GEORGE P. MORRIS, a New York journalist born in Philadelphia, the author of several homely, simple lyrics, as *Woodman, Spare that Tree;* and JULIAN C. VERPLANCK, a lecturer and critic.

Although our literature thus had, for the time, its center in New York, it must not be inferred that the other parts of the country were entirely unproductive. While New England could boast of no writers com-

parable to the greatest of those in the Middle States,
we note the signs of the great literary awakening of
New England which was near at hand. The *North
American Review*, destined to be for years the mouth-
piece of the best thought and scholarship of the
country, was founded in Boston by an ambitious
group of young men in 1815. A new spirit, the realization of the beautiful, was softening the crude but
intense and vigorous intellect of the Puritan. WASH-
INGTON ALLSTON, the painter, returned from Europe,
filled with the charm of the Old World, to lecture on
art. RICHARD HENRY DANA (1787–1879) in his
ambitious and once well-known poem *The Buccaneer*,
and in some unpretentious verses, *The Beach Bird*,
showed a true poetic instinct. Such poets, with JAMES
G. PERCIVAL and CHARLES SPRAGUE, were promises of
a time when the New England genius should really
free itself in song.

Nor was the South wholly silent in this awakening.
EDWARD C. PINKNEY (*Rodolph and other Poems*,
1825) trilled his airy love-lyrics like a descendant of
some seventeenth-century cavalier, or commemorated
Indian maidens among the trees; while WILLIAM
GILMORE SIMMS tried his 'prentice hand at poetry,
fortunately to abandon it later and become one of the
most popular of early Southern story-writers.

We naturally ask ourselves why it was that New
England, originally superior to the sister Colonies in
education, intellectual force, and literary production,
should have failed to keep the lead during those
years when, with the quickening of the nation's

life, a higher and more truly national literature was
taking form.   Clearly it was not because
of any weakening of the Puritan mind, for
a few years later, in the days of Emerson,
Hawthorne, and Longfellow, New England
not only re-established her superiority, but
exhibited a new literary power differing from and
surpassing anything she had shown herself capable of
hitherto.

Causes of the loss of New England leadership.

The causes of literary movements often lie too deep
to be fully understood, but the most obvious causes of
this shifting of the literary center may be briefly suggested.   It is not hard to see why the South should
have come to the front in an era of oratory and political discussion, for the conditions under which a
Southern gentleman lived fitted him to excel as a
political leader and a man of affairs.   The warmer and
more unrestrained Southern temperament found a
natural expression in the fervor of oratory, and the
Southern proprietors ruling over their broad acres, or
taking a large share in the conduct of the State, were
trained to command.   The same conditions which
made Virginia the mother of statesmen made her the
leader in a time when the best productions of our
literature were political in tone.   It is equally clear
why the superiority of the South, so marked in this
especial sphere, should not have extended beyond it,
for in the general diffusion of education the South
was still backward.   In purely literary cultivation the
supremacy lay neither with the South nor with New
England, but first with Philadelphia and afterwards

with New York, the two greatest cities of the Middle
States. The more closely we look into it, the more
we become persuaded of the high cultivation of Philadelphia during the later Colonial times and the early
period of the Republic, as compared with the other
parts of the country. This cultivation was, and still
is, so reserved and unobtrusive that it has been often
undervalued and overlooked. For more than a century, while it remained the capital of Pennsylvania,
Philadelphia was the first town in the Colonies in
commercial, political, social, and literary importance.
Until 1830 it was the first city in population. From
1790 to 1800 it was the seat of the national government, and at the close of that period it had " gathered
a more agreeable society, fashionable, literary, and
political, than could be found anywhere except in a few
capital cities of Europe." * The Irish poet Tom
Moore, who visited Philadelphia in 1804, was taken
into the little band of literary men grouped about
Joseph Dennie, who edited a magazine called *The
Portfolio*. Moore was so much impressed with Dennie
and his friends, the " sacred few," as he calls them,
that he pronounced Philadelphia the only place in
America " that could boast of a literary society." This
view is no doubt hasty and extravagant, but it has in
it an element of truth. Dennie and his co-workers,
while not great men, were the most active and promising group of writers then in the country. Far more
convincing than this foreign judgment is the record
of the city's actual achievement. Philadelphia had

* Adams's *History of the United States*, vol. i. p. 119.

the most famous men of science, the best libraries, the first and best subscription library in the country. In more directions than can here be mentioned the city was the pioneer. Our earliest drama was written in the "Quaker City." The first monthly magazine (1741) and the first daily newspaper were started there. *The Portfolio* (1801–1827) before mentioned, and afterwards *Graham's Magazine* (1841–1857), were in their day among our leading periodicals.* More than any other of our great cities, Philadelphia was the publishing center of the country, and gave Americans the earliest and best reprints of the English and Latin classics. Even from a very early period of its history there are indications that in Philadelphia, if scholarship was less profound, there was a wider acquaintance with the lighter forms of literature.† Yet although the city could boast of some creditable writers, it showed on the whole a cultivated appreciation of the works of others rather than a marked creative or original power. It ceased to be the national capital, and its literary supremacy gradually passed to New York, which, as the century advanced, surpassed it in wealth, population, and commercial importance.‡

* On this subject see *The Philadelphia Magazines and their Contributors, 1741–1850*, by Albert H. Smyth.

† See what has been said on this subject on pages 67–72 *supra*. The Philadelphian William Clifton (1772–1799) is a good example of the early aspirations towards poetry and culture.

‡ From the time of the opening of the Erie Canal in 1825, which connected New York with Lake Erie by way of the Hudson River, the growth of the city was very rapid.

While these two great cities of the Middle region
thus successively led the way, the New England
genius was still retarded by the narrowness and lack
of general cultivation which resulted from the strictness of its religion. Professor McMaster tells us that
in 1784 the Puritanical taste of the readers of Boston
was still strong, and that their principles forbade
them to read many of the greatest English writers.
We shall see in the next chapter the effect of the
emancipation of the New England mind from these
narrow ideas in the rise of the greatest group of
writers the country has yet produced.

CHAPTER II

LITERATURE IN NEW ENGLAND, 1835-1894

From about 1830–40 New England entered upon a long period of literary supremacy. The intellectual awakening which preceded and accompanied this literary period began in Boston and its vicinity, and Boston rapidly distanced New York as a literary center, as New York had distanced Philadelphia. Between 1826 and 1840 nearly all of the great New England writers of this period had definitely begun their work. Longfellow published his first collection of poems in 1826. Holmes began his work in 1827, and Hawthorne in 1828. Emerson, Prescott, Lowell, Whittier, and Motley all followed between 1830 and 1840. The expression of the New England mind in the works of this group of writers constitutes, as a whole, our most memorable contribution to literature; it is one of the greatest and most lasting achievements of our American civilization.

The intellectual leadership thus gained by New England was not in one but in many directions; it did not consist merely in the productions of a group of men of genius, but it had back of it the impetus of a widespread popular movement. Theology had been from the first the dominant force in New England,

160

and this literary epoch was closely related to a sweep-
ing reaction, which began in the early years of the
century, against the old theology.   This reaction was
the rise of Unitarianism.   We need not speak here of
the purely religious or doctrinal side of this movement.   Quite apart from this, it had a most important
influence on literature.   In the early days of New
England men were compelled or expected to think and
believe on all points as the ministers bade them.   The
Unitarian movement brought with it the assertion of
individual opinions, and promoted the greatest freedom of thought.

To measure the force and significance of this movement we must recall the iron dogmatism, the severity,
and the narrowness from which it was a reaction.
The men of early New England may fairly be called
fanatical, narrow-minded, and superstitious; but at
their worst they were a strong race, limited and confined by restrictions of their own making.   They had
great powers, undeveloped or unused, a deep reserve
of poetry, and a capacity for independent thought.
The Puritan, as one of the greatest of the New England poets described him, was a man who fought
with a prayer on his lips: a man of dry, "unwilling
humor,"

> "With a soul full of poetry, though it has qualms
> In finding a happiness out of the Psalms";*

a soul tender beneath an outside roughness,

> "That sees visions, knows wrestlings of God with the will,
> And has its own Sinais and thunderings still."*

* Lowell's *Fable for Critics*.

These men had put the largest part of their intellectual force into damnatory sermons or theological arguments; they had been cramped and unequally developed by the lack of a truly liberal culture, their gentler and æsthetic side had been repressed and starved. Yet the effort of the Puritan to rear a group of States in a new world, where men's thoughts and acts should be made to square with a set standard, resulted, as might have been expected, in "an intellectual Declaration of Independence." Restiveness under discipline and restraint grew even in the days of Wigglesworth and Cotton Mather. In the Unitarian movement, which took an organized form about 1815, the New England mind, long checked, was in open revolt, until, in the teaching of Emerson, we find the opinion of each individual held up as superior to all external authority or guidance. As Unitarianism directly tended to promote intellectual freedom, its relation to literature was naturally both direct and important. Associated at first with Harvard College, Unitarianism had a distinctly literary side, and the duty of a wider culture was almost one of the articles of its creed. According to a competent authority, its "most remarkable quality" was "its high social and intellectual character." * The earliest of its leading preachers, J. S. Buckminster, in an address before the Phi Beta Kappa Society in 1809, lamented the decline of scholarship, urged the importance of a deeper and more exact knowledge, and declared that

---

* Adams's *History of the United States*, vol. ix. p. 183.

New England was on the threshold of a new intellectual era.* William Ellery Channing (1780–1842), the greatest organizer of the movement, advocated the study of foreign literatures, and dwelt upon the need of a more generous culture. "Self-culture," he said, "is religious. . . . The connection between moral and intellectual culture is often overlooked." †

Nor was it merely that Unitarianism was the means of helping many in New England to gain that richer and fuller cultivation, the lack of which had retarded its free and harmonious development. It must be further noted that the doors were thus opened to foreign literature and thought at a time when English literature was on fire with new life and inspiration, when the Old World was in the ferment of fresh enthusiasms, new philosophies, and strange social ideas. The *idealistic* or *transcendental* philosophy had recently arisen in Germany, and had been brought from thence into England by Coleridge. The general tendency of these transcendental thinkers, or *transcendentalists* as they were called, was to regard thought, or spirit, and not matter, as true reality. One of them spoke of all this universe about us, which seems so solid and substantial, as but the thought of God made apparent. They laid great stress on man's intuitions, and on the presence of God's spirit in man and in nature. These lofty and spiritual conceptions were readily absorbed into New England thought, for they harmonized with the mystical and somewhat

---

* Buckminster's Works.   † Address on Self-culture.

visionary strain in the Puritan character. Edward Everett, the orator, returned from Germany in 1820, and lectured on this German thought, and it also found its way into New England thought through the works of Coleridge and afterwards of Thomas Carlyle. In more purely literary directions the foreign influences of the time were no less stimulating. Since the time of Pope the whole spirit of English literature had been sweetened and renewed by a spirit of tenderness and charity. Such great poets as Burns, Wordsworth, and Coleridge had shown a new power to feel, a new sense of the sacredness and beauty of nature, and of the worth and dignity of man. Finally, the love of humanity, and the growth of a democratic feeling, were prompting aspirations and attempts to introduce better social systems, and in these hopes some of the advanced thinkers in New England afterwards came to share. Thus, released from the weight of formalism and asceticism, and at the same time quickened and uplifted by influences of a most congenial and stimulating character, the New England mind ceased to expend itself wholly on theology, and asserted through a group of great writers those literary powers which had been so long suppressed.

RALPH WALDO EMERSON (1803-1882)

In its great literary epoch, the reserve power, the stored-up energy and repressed sympathies of New England, first found an adequate outlet in literature. We can detect the throb of the strenuous New England

RALPH WALDO EMERSON

nature in its early history and under the stiffness and
pedantry of its early writings, yet we feel that the
Colonial Puritan has in him much that he never really
puts into written words. The barriers to progress and
to expression once swept away, the inherent force in
this great section of our country enabled it in a few
years to distance its competitors in the Southern and
Middle States. It was not perhaps so much that the
Middle States went backward in literary production,
although this was to a certain extent the case, as that
New England, her restrictions once removed, shot
suddenly ahead.

Geographically, this literary manifestation of New
England centers at Cambridge, in that group of
scholars to which Longfellow and Holmes belong, and
at the quiet old neighboring town of Concord, which
is associated with Emerson and Thoreau. The greatest
individual force in the movement, so far as the influence of any one man is concerned, is to be found in
the life, character, and work of Emerson. By this we
do not mean that Emerson was a greater writer than
any of the men who surrounded him; his relative
merits as a writer are a matter for individual opinion:
we mean that he was the most representative of the
whole movement, and that he was the most influential
in shaping its form and character. To say best what
men all around one are laboring more or less ineffect-
ually to define and put into words, is to become a
prophet in one's own country. Emerson did this, and
perhaps this personal power to stimulate and inspire,
and to make the vague more tangible and effective,

was the greatest element in his work.   The testimony of his famous contemporaries, his wide and enduring influence as a lecturer, the immense veneration which he awakened in New England, all bear witness to the power that went out from him as a man as well as a writer.   Hawthorne said that "his mind acted upon other minds of a certain constitution with a wonderful magnetism, and drew many men upon long pilgrimages to speak to him face to face."*   Lowell, who belonged to a somewhat later generation, recalls the effect that Emerson's thrilling voice had on him in his young manhood.   He "brought us life," Lowell declares; he was to generous youth "the sound of the trumpet that the young soul longs for."†   One cause of this power lay in the fact that Emerson found the right word for ideas and enthusiasms which the men about him were laboring to put in tangible form.   He stood and spoke for the peculiar temperament and for the intellectual traditions of New England as modified and enlarged by the new spirit of his age.   Like the best spirits of his time and locality, he is widely receptive of foreign influences.   He draws inspiration from the poetic thought of Plato, from the German idealists, from the mystical seer Swedenborg, from the Eastern religions, from Coleridge and the nature-poetry of Wordsworth; yet with it all he retains every native peculiarity, and his words have the unmistakable local flavor of New England.   He is not a typical

---

* "The Old Manse" in *Mosses from an Old Manse*
† Essay on *Emerson the Lecturer*.

American, as Lincoln was, nor even as Lowell was.
Spare, angular, hard-featured, with lean jaws and
thin, firm lips, he is distinctly the product of New
England. By inheritance and disposition he represents it in its spirituality, its purity, its nervous
energy, its intellectual chill and vigor,—in its limitations and its strength.

Ralph Waldo Emerson was born in Boston in 1803.
By actual inheritance the most distinctive
intellectual life of New England for gen- **Emerson's life.**
erations back was summed up in him. He
was sprung from one of those families of ministers and
scholars which Holmes has called the "academic"
families of New England. He could count a minister
among his ancestors on both his father's and his
mother's side, for eight generations. His father, the
pastor of the First Church of Boston, was a Unitarian
and a friend of Channing. For the first thirty years
of his life Emerson seemed as though he were destined
to continue this ministerial succession with but little
deviation from the family pattern. He went to the
Boston Latin School and to Harvard, where he graduated in 1824. He taught school, studied divinity,
became a minister, and in 1826 was called to the
Second Unitarian Church of Boston as associate
pastor. In its outward features this is the biography
of hundreds of "academic" New Englanders. But
the young Emerson had grown up in a ferment of
strange doctrines. His philosophy was carrying him
beyond the limits of the teachings of Channing and
his associates, and even in the Unitarian pulpit he felt

himself constrained. He differed with his congregation upon an important point of doctrine, and in 1832, after a frank avowal of his views, he felt it right to resign his charge. It was a courageous and manly course, for it involved the sacrifice of a promising career for what Emerson believed to be the truth.

In 1833 Emerson went abroad for about a year, meeting Carlyle, among many other famous men, and laying the foundations of what proved a long and memorable friendship. After his return to this country he settled in 1834 at Concord, Massachusetts, in the old-fashioned house that Hawthorne has celebrated under the name of the " Old Manse." Emerson was then about thirty; nearly half a century of life was yet before him,—the quiet, uneventful life of a thinker, scholar, and teacher,—and during all this long period Concord remained his home. Few spots in all our country are more hallowed or inspiring than the little town that thus became the center of Emerson's influence. There on the banks of the Musketaquid, a tranquil stream that glides with almost imperceptible flow through the green meadows, the first patriot blood was shed in our war for independence. There, in the same room in which Emerson wrote his *Nature*, Hawthorne wrote his *Mosses from an Old Manse*. There, too, on a high ridge in the great cemetery, Hawthorne is buried, while Emerson lies near him, a mighty block of New England granite for his headstone, the pines of New England casting their brown needles over his grave. Near by is Walden Pond, on whose wooded shores Henry Thoreau, Emerson's

eccentric disciple, built his hut in search of simplicity
and solitude.

In the winter after his settlement at Concord Emerson began his career as a lecturer, delivering courses
in Boston and in many towns throughout New England, and gradually coming to find in the lecture plat-
form a pulpit from which he could speak his thought
free from all external control. The year 1836 is
notable in his history and in that of our literature.
It was in this year that Emerson composed his *Concord
Hymn*, one of the best and most popular of his
shorter poems, in honor of the farmers " embattled "
in the cause of liberty; in this year, too, he published
his first book, *Nature*, which contains much of the
essence of his teaching. There is probably very little
strictly original thought in this famous book; its
originality lies rather in the freshness and vigor of the
form in which old ideas were embodied. There is
this indescribably quickening quality in most of Emerson's work, so that an old thought seems vitalized by
his touch, and acts on us as a spiritual tonic. The
book deals, in a rapt and poetic fashion, with the relations of nature, or the so-called physical universe, to
the life of man. From the consideration of Nature as
the minister to man's temporal and bodily needs we
rise to a view of Nature as the teacher and inspirer of
his spirit. The book is permeated with the ideal
philosophy of the Germans, with the nature-poetry of
Wordsworth and the nature-teachings of Carlyle.
Emerson, too, like his great German and English
predecessors, sees in this varied spectacle of Nature

but a manifestation of God to the soul. "The world is a remoter and inferior incarnation of God, a projection of God into the unconscious. . . . The foundations of man are not in matter, but in spirit." But along with the re-announcement of such ideas we find that resonant note of self-reliance and hopeful courage eminently characteristic of Emerson himself. Why, he complains, should we look backward? "The sun shines to-day also. There is more wool and flax in the fields. There are new lands, new men, new thoughts." "Build, therefore," he concludes, "your own world." Such words are instinct with the stirring spirit of a young land; they make us feel how habitually Emerson turned his face towards the rising sun.

This same spirit of resolute self-reliance, pointing us to to-day as a new day, is shown in Emerson's next important work, *The American Scholar*, an oration delivered before the Phi Beta Kappa Society in 1837. In it we are taught that the true scholar, while he uses all the learning of the past, must yet, before all, see and think for himself. Our day of apprenticeship to the learning of other lands is gone by. "We will walk on our own feet; we will work with our own hands; we will speak our own minds." With Emerson no authority is sacred but the guidance of one's own spirit. "Every mind," he writes, "has a new compass, a new North, a new direction of its own"; and in such utterances we can measure the extent of the rebound from that iron dogmatism of his Puritan forefathers which sought to conform every thought and impulse to its will.

As Emerson's stimulating powers became more generally recognized, he gradually became the center of a group of thinkers known as the "transcendentalists." The so-called "transcendental movement" which those followers of the new light inaugurated may be regarded as an outgrowth and extension of New England Unitarianism. It was largely indebted to the ideal philosophy of the recent German thinkers, and on its humanitarian side it adopted and endeavored to put into practice certain wild notions of social reform. Severely practical as it may seem, the high-strung New England nature has a strong tinge of the visionary, and the transcendentalists included some long-haired prophets who confused and mystified themselves and their hearers with high-sounding and "Orphic utterances." In spite of frequent assertions to the contrary, Emerson himself does not always escape the prevailing tendency to disguise a comparatively familiar thought in mystical and oracular phrases. Charles Dickens declared that he was given to understand when in Boston "that whatever was unintelligible would certainly be transcendental." * Lowell has pricked some of the inflated extravagances of the time with the keen point of his humor. "Not a few impecunious zealots abjured the use of money (unless earned by other people), professing to live on the internal revenues of the spirit. Communities were established everywhere, where everything was to be common but common sense." †

* *American Notes.*   † Essay on Thoreau.

Two direct results of this "transcendental move-ment" were the establishment of *The Dial* (1840), a

"The Dial." magazine for the promulgation of the new doctrines, and the founding of Brook Farm, an agricultural and industrial community intended to exemplify the ideal state of society. Immense hopes and unselfish efforts were centered in *The Dial.* Emerson was a frequent contributor, and for a time its editor, some of his best-known prose and verse appearing first in its pages. It gathered the leading transcendentalists about it: George Ripley, a scholarly Unitarian minister, afterwards the head of Brook Farm; Margaret Fuller, its first editor, and a woman of wide acquirements, who was called the "priestess of transcendentalism"; A. Bronson Alcott, mystic and vegetarian, who chopped wood and contributed "Orphic sayings," which were at least sufficiently unintelligible for the most transcendental taste. With these were many more equally distinguished, so that *The Dial* shows us this remarkable movement in all its fervor. Carlyle thought that the writers for *The Dial* seemed in danger of "dividing themselves from the *fact* of this present universe." Vulgar fact, however, overtook them, and after about four years money difficulties brought the enterprise to an end.

Transcendentalism had a humanitarian as well as a philosophic and religious side, and it was this

Brook Farm. humanitarian zeal to better the world that took shape in Brook Farm. We need not consider here whether this desire to re-organize society sprang up spontaneously in New England, or whether, like the transcendental philosophy, it was partly the result of foreign influences. In either case, it was in accord with certain aspirations and theories of the time. Nearly half a century earlier Coleridge and Southey had planned to found an ideal community on the banks of the Susquehanna, and since that time thinkers both in England and in France had preached this doctrine of social reconstruction, or, as in some cases, striven to put it into practice. Consciously or unconsciously, Brook Farm embodied the essence of these foreign ideas. The Association secured about two hundred acres of land at West Roxbury, some nine miles from Boston, and started there a community which should combine the teaching and study of literature and science with agriculture and other industries. The enterprise was carried on in the face of increasing practical difficulties for about five years. Emerson was not a member of the community, although interested in its progress.

This much has been said about New England transcendentalism and some of its manifestations, because Emerson is its best exponent and its chief representative. We must, however, leave these more general subjects and return to Emerson himself. The remainder of his tranquil life, greatly influential as it was, requires but little comment. From time to time he added to his published works a volume of essays or a book of poems. He made a second trip to Europe in 1847, and summed up his impressions of England in his *English Traits*. He continued to write and to lecture occasionally until towards the close of his life. He died April 27, 1882.

We have spoken of Emerson's subtle and wide-spread influence, and have referred it partly to the

Emerson's work.
fact that he fitly represented the New England mind during a certain important phase of its thought, and partly to the magnetic attraction of his pure and exalted character, the " intellectual gleam diffused about his presence like the garment of a shining one." *

But the great writer or thinker works not merely for his own generation but for succeeding generations. He represents not merely a set of men, or a single community, but something common to man. To reach a really just estimate of Emerson as a writer, it would be necessary to put aside, for the time, this personal, and therefore comparatively temporary, aspect of his work, and judge of his writings as a thing apart and distinct. We are forced to determine how far he succeeded in communicating to his written works that quickening power which he himself exerted; how far his poetry and his prose are likely to survive that wave of transcendental enthusiasm which produced them. This separation of the permanent influence of Emerson's writings from the personal influence of Emerson himself time only can really accomplish; but in the meantime we must be on our guard against accepting without reserve the eulogies of his imme-

---

* Hawthorne, *Mosses from an Old Manse:* " The Old Manse."

disse followers, who wrote under the spell of his living voice and presence.

Without entering upon Emerson's probable place among English writers, we can here only speak briefly of the general character of his work. He speaks to us as poet and as essayist; but in either case his work has much the same essential qualities. In both poetry and prose he is emphatically the philosophic and religious teacher, the lover of nature; but dwelling in clear, bracing, rarefied atmosphere, remote from human passion and human sorrow. In both his prose and poetry, too, we find that lack of a rounded and even excellence, that absence of the power to construct a work which should be great not in detached passages, but as a whole, which is admittedly one of his most serious defects. Emerson's verse has undoubtedly an individuality and distinction rarely found in our poets. It has admirable qualities, but radical shortcomings, which show, it is to be feared, the inborn limitations of Emerson himself. It is the creation of the brain rather than the utterance of the heart; it fails in a warm, living, generous humanity; above all, the lines in not flow and sing themselves, as those of a true poet do, but the muses seems half-frozen in the instrument. When Emerson was a boy at singing-school a single exhibition of his vocal powers induced the teacher to tell him that he need not return. He lacked the musical faculty, and we can hardly read one of his longer poems to the end without being irritated by some harsh or limping line.

Emerson, in his prose, if an inconsequent, is an

immensely stimulating writer. His mind seems to have the edge and glitter of highly-tempered steel. His short, terse, epigrammatic sentences pierce us like so many separate sword-thrusts. The intense, nervous vitality of the New Englander snaps and sparkles in his abrupt and oracular utterance. Brilliant, with a tiring, unrelieved brilliancy, his light, like that of the electric spark, may prick but cannot warm. He writes with a conscientious minuteness of homely things, " the meal in the firkin; the milk in the pan";* nevertheless, his sympathy with the every-day problems and experiences of men and women is theoretical rather than real and spontaneous. In reality he has that abstraction and equable serenity possible for those who survey life from the mountain-peaks of philosophy. He has an invincible hopefulness; but we miss in him that bond of tenderness, that sense of comradeship that we have with the great souls who have bled and stumbled on the common highway. He remains coldly intellectual; absolutely unimpassioned, as though man were but a superior thinking-machine, the tension of his thought renders his work singularly lacking in the quality of repose. These and other limitations are evident in his prose; and while his work abounds in wise maxims, and in memorable and noble passages, we may agree with Matthew Arnold in refusing to place him with the greatest masters of style.

Yet Emerson stands squarely among the great men of our century. His voice reaches us from the

---

* *The American Scholar.*   Compare the whole passage.

heights, unworldly, clear, and pure. It is a great
thing that our rich and commercial America, in the
abundance of its material successes, should have
brought forth a teacher of such unsullied life and lofty
purposes, who bore unswerving witness to the worth
of the things which are not seen. This was his work
and mission, a great and beautiful one, to quicken our
spirit, to increase our hold on the spiritual and
eternal. We may well be proud when we read what
a French writer has written of him: "In this North
America, which is pictured to us as so materialistic, I
find the most ideal writer of our times."

STUDY LIST

EMERSON

1. Essays. "Nature" and "The American Scholar," in
Nature; Addresses and Lectures; "Uses of Great Men,"
and "Shakspeare; or, The Poet," in *Representative Men;*
"Self-reliance," "Friendship," "History," in *Essays*, 1st
series; "Character," in *Essays*, 2d series. *English Traits*
may also be read, both for the fairness of its criticism and
the glimpse it gives us of Emerson's personality.

2. Poems. "Concord Hymn," "Walden," "Threnody,"
"The Snow-storm," "The Rhodora," The Humble Bee,"
"Boston Hymn," "Voluntaries," "The Past," "Wood-
notes," "Forbearance."

3. Biography and Criticism. Life by James Elliot
Cabot; by Dr. Holmes, in American Men of Letters Series;
by Dr. Richard Garnett, in Great Writers Series; by Prof.
Herman Grimm, in Makers of America Series. Whipple's
Recollections of Eminent Men; Curtis's *Literary and Social
Essays.* For criticism, see Lowell's essay, "Emerson, the

Lecturer," in *My Study Windows;* Stedman's *Poets of America;* Henry James's *Partial Portraits;* Augustine Birrell's *Obiter Dicta,* 2d series ; Morley's *Critical Miscellanies,* vol. i.; Whipple's *American Literature.*

4. For an account of "Brook Farm" see Frothingham's Life of *George Ripley,* in American Men of Letters Series ; also, Higginson's Life of *Margaret Fuller Ossoli,* in the same series.

HENRY W. LONGFELLOW (1807-1882)

We have said that Emerson widened the narrow boundaries of New England thought, enlarging the channels for the freer flow of European ideas, but the Puritan nature required something in addition to this emancipation of the intellect for its full development. It needed beauty, sentiment, warmth, and the grace of romantic associations. The general tone of life throughout the New England States had been upright and hard-working, but severely practical, colorless, and plain. There was little within the blank walls of the whitewashed meeting-house to touch the sense of beauty,—little within the scope even of the more cultivated on which the imagination could live. The English Puritan had desecrated cathedrals, he had let in the white daylight through windows which had once been radiant with the pictured stories of saints and martyrs; the American Puritan had alienated himself from the grace, joyousness, and inspiration of much of the world's best poetry, living his meager existence, indifferent or antagonistic to a world of beauty and power to him almost unknown. These

HENRY WADSWORTH LONGFELLOW

1

sterling, hard-featured men needed to grow in this
power to feel; they needed to have this daily life—
too often crude, petty, and rigid—expanded and
softened by that nameless charm of poetry, legend,
and art which with the consecration of a long past
and a thousand beautiful associations make up the
magic of the Old World. This need of the refining
and cultivating grace of Europe was not indeed
peculiar to New England; to a greater or less extent
it was a need of the country at large. It is true that
in prose Irving had communicated to his countrymen
some of this fascinating flavor of the older civilizations, but in poetry it first began to diffuse itself
through the verse of Longfellow, steeped in the fra-
grance of a romantic past. Longfellow was, indeed,
the poet of many national themes—of Indian life and
legend, of the early Puritan settler, of the parted
Acadian lovers; nevertheless, his absorption of European influences, and his power to infuse this foreign
leaven into our American life, remains his especial
work and mission. Few lives are more stainless,
untroubled, and complete than that of this sweet-
natured and placid master of tranquil song. It moves
with an even flow, like the poet's own singing, clear,
melodious, and pure; the life of a quiet, gentle
scholar, of high aims steadfastly pursued and worthily
accomplished; deepened and disciplined by the inevitable sorrows, but without fret, or hindrance, or
stain. There have been many greater poets than
Longfellow, but few who followed so faithfully Milton's precept that the poet's life should first be a true

poem; few whose lives were a more perfect preparation for the full use of their best gifts. This beautiful adjustment between Longfellow's life and work is,
perhaps, the thought that impresses us most deeply in
studying the story of the man himself.

Henry Wadsworth Longfellow was born in 1807, in
Portland, Maine; a beautiful town with elm-shadowed
streets and a wide outlook over the sea.
Like Emerson and Bryant he sprang from **Longfellow's life.**
the old New England stock. William
Longfellow, the founder of the family in New England, settled in America in 1676. On his mother's
side the poet could boast an even longer descent from
that John Alden and Priscilla whose story is told in
The Courtship of Miles Standish. Longfellow's
father was a lawyer of cultivation and high standing;
he was a friend and former classmate of Channing's,
and in sympathy with his religious views; his mother
was a lover of poetry with a sensitive and imaginative
nature. With such parents, and with exceptionally
beautiful surroundings, all the conditions of Longfellow's boyhood were favorable to a full and natural
development. He had ready access to books, and
turned to them with eagerness, but at other times he
loved to look across the gleaming bay to the islands
that were the Hesperides of his " boyish dreams," or
to wander in the woods, thinking those " long, long
thoughts " of youth that tell of the stirring of the
soul. Even as a boy the unknown beyond the water
had charms for him; and he warmed at the

> "Spanish sailors with bearded lips,
> And the beauty and mystery of the ships,
> And the magic of the sea."*

Longfellow came of an active and soldierly race, but all his tastes and aspirations were bookish, and from the first he was a typical man of letters. As a trembling and expectant boy of thirteen he had found his way to the poet's corner of the *Portland Gazette*. In 1822 he went to Bowdoin College, entering the same class with Hawthorne. Here he studied hard and continued to write verses, while his ambitions gradually fixed themselves definitely on a literary career. "The fact is," he writes to his father in 1824, " I most eagerly aspire after future eminence in literature; my whole soul burns most ardently for it, and my earthly thought centers in it." † In those days it was even more hazardous than at present to trust to literature for support, and Longfellow's father was naturally impressed with the practical obstacles to his son's choice. A fortunate circumstance, however, unexpectedly opened the way. It had been decided to establish a professorship of modern languages at Bowdoin College, and Longfellow, who had impressed the trustees by his high character and ability, was offered the position with the understanding that he should first study in Europe to prepare himself for his duties. In that day the world for an American youth was commonly narrowed down to his own immediate

---

* See his poem *My Lost Youth*.

† *Life of Longfellow*, edited by Samuel Longfellow, vol. i. p. 53.

surroundings; it was an unusual as well as fortunate chance which thus enabled the young poet of nineteen, impressionable, eager, and receptive, to come so early under the spell of the Old World which was to color so much of his future thought and work. We can conjecture the vividness of these foreign impressions from *Outre-Mer*, the book in which he recorded his wanderings; we can learn from it, too, the ardent spirit in which he approached the Old World. He tells us that it was to his imagination " A kind of holy land, lying afar off beyond the blue horizon of the ocean; and when its shores first rose upon my sight, my heart swelled with the deep emotions of the pilgrim when he sees afar the spire of his devotion." *

Longfellow left home in 1826, and remained abroad about three years. By the end of that time he had made himself proficient in French, Spanish, Italian, and German; he had widened his horizon by foreign scenes and experiences, and gained the means of access to the great literatures of the modern world. In 1829 Longfellow settled down to his duties at Bowdoin College, working with his accustomed steadiness, and winning popularity as a teacher by the peculiar charm and gentleness of his disposition. In 1831 he married Miss Mary Storer Potter, whose death in 1835 was his first great sorrow. We come near to this great grief through some lines in Longfellow's poem *The Footsteps of Angels*, in which he speaks of his wife as

---

* *Outre-Mer.*   The Pilgrim of Outre-Mer.

" the being beauteous
Who unto my youth was given,
More than all things else to love me,
And is now a saint in heaven."

Shortly before this, in 1834, Longfellow had been appointed Professor of Modern Languages at Harvard. To further prepare himself for his new duties, he again visited Europe, spending some time in the north, and studying Swedish and other northern languages. In 1836 he established himself at Cambridge, and entered upon his new duties in the year following. This old town, during those years the center of much of our best culture, was hereafter to be his home.

The years that followed Longfellow's return from his first European tour had been also years of literary activity, but it was almost wholly in the direction of prose. His work during this **Literary work.** period is obviously an outcome of his studies and his foreign experience. Thus we have *Outre-Mer* (1835) with its reminiscences of France, Spain, and Italy, and the prose romance of *Hyperion* (1839), the story of the Continental wanderings of a very youthful sentimentalist, Paul Flemming. The book last named, the scene of which is laid chiefly in Germany, is filled with the spirit of mediæval romance, moonlight, castles, and impassioned moods and a generally fervid and ecstatic one which comes near, at least, to sentimentality. This is the atmosphere we encounter in certain romantic German writers, and the book suggests to us how largely Longfellow was affected, not only here but elsewhere, by the

German spirit. During these years of prose writing Longfellow contributed scholarly papers and a few short poems to the magazines, but his only considerable work in poetry was a translation from the Spanish of Coplas de Manrique.

Up to 1839 Longfellow's reputation as an original poet had rested chiefly on verses scattered through the newspapers and magazines, but that year, which had been marked by the appearance of *Hyperion*, is also notable for the publication of his volume of collected poems *The Voices of the Night*. The book is a memorable one in the history of our literature. It had a wide and immediate popularity; some of the poems, like *The Psalm of Life* and *Excelsior*, sinking deep into the people's life. From this time it is to poetry that Longfellow's efforts are almost exclusively directed, and by volume after volume he steadily won for himself a more and more assured place. In 1843 he married Miss Frances Appleton, and until her tragic death in 1861 his life was full of high serenity and great achievement. After this second sorrow he still continued his scholar's life of study and literary labor, but with an increasing sense of loneliness he came to patiently look forward to the end. This peaceful and expectant spirit shines out in his last volumes, *Ultima Thule* (1880) and *In the Harbor* (1882); it is the note of a beautiful old age. Long ago had he looked " o'er sunlit seas " toward the shining Hesperides, his " land of dreams '; now in sight of the tempestuous islands of the North, he sings:

" Ultima Thule ! utmost isle ;
    Here in thy harbors for awhile
    We lower our sails ; awhile we rest
    From the unending, endless quest."

He died tranquilly at Cambridge, on the 15th of March, 1882.

We have said that as Emerson uttered foreign thought with the unmistakable twang of Yankee speech, adding to it a certain accent and independence of his own, so Longfellow was before all else the medium through **Long-fellow's work.** which we received the grace and beauty which had grown up so slowly in an older world. It requires no extended study to show us the truth of this in Longfellow's case. As a translator he domesticates chosen poems and fragments from many literatures among us. He brings us, in his faithful and musical renderings, which in themselves are distinct contributions to literature, treasures from the poets of Germany, France, Sweden, Spain, Italy, and ancient Rome. In magnitude his translation of the *Divine Comedy* of Dante is of course his most important work as a translator, but we are further impressed by the breadth of his range and sympathies. But he not only brought Europe to us as a translator, we must note further the large proportion of his original poems which deal with, or are suggested by, foreign themes. The *Tales of a Wayside Inn* is a collection of stories supposed to be told by a group of friends about the hearthstone of the old Red Horse Inn at Sudbury, Mass. Out of the twenty-one stories that compose the poem, only four

deal directly with American themes. The rest relate
to many lands, and often take us back to a distant
past. Among the shorter poems *The Belfry of
Bruges* and *Nuremburg* are good examples of this
foreign flavor. Nor is this all. Even in the poems
which treat of national subjects we can often detect
the power of these foreign influences on the poet himself. A passage in a French poet suggests the refrain
in *The Old Clock on the Stairs*, while that in *My Lost
Youth* is the haunting "echo of a Lapland song."
The metre of *Hiawatha*, perhaps his most distinctly
American poem, is borrowed from the Kalevala, a
national epic of Finland. It is also to be observed
that this cosmopolitan flavor in Longfellow is more
than a mere fondness for other lands or other literatures; it is in accordance with his deliberate conviction
in regard to the true scope of a national American
literature. In *Kavanagh* he ridicules and refutes the
theory, so rife in the days of Barlow and Dwight,
that in order to be national our literature must be
a local production, shut in to American themes.
Originality is not to be gained by remaining ignorant
of the best that has been thought and done in the
world. On the contrary he says, "Let us throw all
the windows open; let us admit light and air on all
sides." * And in the *Tales of a Wayside Inn* he
recurs to the same prevalent notion of nationality in
literature to combat it again.

---

* *Kavanagh*, chap. xx, p. 115. See the allusion to Hamlin
Garland's presentation of an opposite view on p. 325.

"Poets—the best of them—are birds
Of passage ; where their instinct leads
They range abroad for thoughts and words,
And from all climes bring home the seeds
That germinate in flowers or weeds." *

But while Longfellow was himself a "bird of passage," laden with precious seeds from many climes, he is, though not our most distinctively American, from one aspect our most representative poet. Other American poets are more vigorous, more passionate, more patriotic than Longfellow, but none has appealed so widely to the great mass of our people, or won so universal a welcome in England. It is not a light thing to write songs that go straight to the heart of millions, and yet never stoop to win favor by a single suggestion of anything that is vulgar, or trivial, or base. Scholar as he was, Longfellow was before all the people's poet. He is the laureate of the simpler emotions, the wholesome domestic affections: pure, melodious, absolutely easy of comprehension, his comparatively restricted range of thought and mood keep him in accord with the sympathies of a large number of readers. With none of the Puritan vigor, he has the strong Puritan conscience, and he is essentially the preacher of homely morals, a counsellor and helper such as the people love. Thus, in actual fact, Longfellow, in the years of his greatest influence, was more truly the poet of our democracy than an eccentric

* *Tales of a Wayside Inn.* Part III. Interlude after "The Musician's Tale." Read the whole passage.

genius like Walt Whitman, whose chants are seldom heard beyond the most exclusive literary circles.

Having spoken of Longfellow's life, and the widespread and beautiful influence of his verse, it only remains for us to speak briefly of his poetry itself. Clearly his place is not among the great poets of our language. We can feel the same natural limitations in his character and in his work. He gave us all there was in him to give, but, while he was gentle, scholarly, and lovable, there is an intensity, originality, and power which it was not given him to possess. It is no disparagement to Longfellow to say that his poetry lacks those profounder and intenser notes, or that it has but little basis of deep or original thought. But if Longfellow is not among the greater poets, among the humbler singers who are the comforters and inspirers of multitudes his place is high, and, we may hope, secure. Poetry which, like Longfellow's, is unaffected, wholesome, and near to the popular sentiment, has a good chance of outlasting verse of a far more complex and ambitious character. The lovely idyll of *Evangeline*, for instance, is but a simple story, simply told. But its theme is one of lasting power over men's hearts: the strength of woman's devotion, the might of a love which "hopes and endures and is patient." In the beautiful background of nature through which the story moves, in the gentle and serene beauty which floods all the poem, we recognize the fine artistic instinct which gives permanence to a work. But excellent as are many of Longfellow's longer poems,

perhaps he is at his best in his ballads and songs. By
its picturesqueness, lyrical movement, and concentrated power, the *Skeleton in Armor* rightfully takes
a high place among the finest ballads in the language.
By this, and such other ballads as the *Wreck of the
Hesperus*, Longfellow stands, in at least one depart-
ment of poetry, among the best masters. Nor should
we be unmindful of the more delicate and softer charm
of many of his lyrics, *The Bridge, Rain in Summer,
My Lost Youth*, and many more, or the high excellence of such sonnets as *Nature* or *Dante*. In the
change of fashion in poetry, it is doubtful whether the
excellence of these things is now fairly estimated by
the critical reader. However this may be, there can
be no question about the great place which Longfellow
holds in the progress not merely of our literature but
of our people. His life and work together stand in
our thought as a true poem, and we honor him as one
who, while he may not have been a " puissant singer,"
yet left the world " the sweeter for his song."

STUDY LIST

LONGFELLOW

1. **Poems.** "Evangeline," "The Courtship of Miles
Standish," "Paul Revere's Ride," "The Skeleton in
Armor," "The Wreck of the Hesperus," "A Psalm of Life,"
"The Light of Stars," "The Village Blacksmith," "Rain
in Summer, ' "The Bridge," "The Day is Done," "The
Arrow and the Song," "My Lost Youth," "The Children's
Hour," "Morituri Salutamus," "Nature," "My Books."

2. **Biography and Criticism.** Life by Rev. Samuel

Longfellow (3 vols.); Life by E. S. Robertson, in Great Writers Series. R. H. Stoddard's *Homes and Haunts of our Elder Poets;* H. E. Scudder's *Men and Letters;* Stedman's *Poets of America;* Curtis's *Literary and Social Essays;* W. E. Henley's *Views and Reviews;* Whipple's *Essays and Reviews,* I. ; Whittier's *Literary Recreations.*

NATHANIEL HAWTHORNE (1804-1864)

From Emerson, the thinker, and Longfellow, the poet, we pass to Hawthorne, the master of romance. Emerson gave expression to the ideal and visionary side of the New England intellect; Longfellow ministered to a latent sense of beauty; but Hawthorne is probably the completest and most discerning interpreter of the inmost spirit of New England Puritanism. Others may have given us more graphic and realistic pictures of the outward appearance and conditions of early New England life, but none has penetrated so deeply beneath the surface or so marvellously laid bare the workings of its soul. Hawthorne stands in a double relation to this Puritan spirit. Sprung from a Puritan ancestry, from one aspect he inherits and shares himself in certain Puritan traits: yet, like the New England of his time, he has outgrown its bygone intolerance and severity, and from another aspect he expresses the revulsion against them in all its reactionary force. In this way he is consequently as representative, though not as personally influential, as Emerson himself.

When we regard Hawthorne from the first of these two aspects, or as an inheritor of the past, we see how

NATHANIEL HAWTHORNE

deeply his life and character are rooted in his native
soil.   The Hawthornes were among the first settlers;
William Hawthorne, the founder of the American
branch of the family, having come to this country
with John Winthrop in 1630.   For generations they
had lived in Salem, a spot which seems the very heart
of New England Puritanism, the most tragically
puritanical of the New England towns.   There the
"dark and haughty Endicott," the destroyer of the
Maypole at Morton's Mount, ruled in the early days
of the Colony; there Quakers were persecuted; there
Roger Williams preached, and from there that great
"apostle of toleration" was intolerantly driven out.
More than all, Salem was a center of that dark chapter
in the history of Puritanism, the witchcraft delusion,
and there the unhappy victims of that tragic frenzy
were tried, tormented, and put to death.   An ancestor
of Hawthorne's was judge in one of these witch-trials,
and tradition said that he had brought a curse upon
himself and his descendants because he would show
no pity.   Hawthorne himself refers to the persecuting
spirit displayed by his ancestors, and adds: "I, the
present writer, hereby take shame upon myself for
their sakes." *   Such was the somber background of
Hawthorne's genius.   Born in Salem, July 4, 1804,
nearly all his boyhood and a part of his later years
were spent in that old home of his ancestors, and his
brooding and keenly sensitive nature was thus forced
into contact with the melancholy memories of its past.

* Introduction to *The Scarlet Letter.*

The shadows of that past lie across his work. According to his own declaration, which, however, we must not take too literally, he had "all the Puritanic traits, both good and evil." The truth appears to be that while he belonged to a new era which had outgrown the intolerance and harshness of the earlier times, he yet shared in much of its deepest spiritual life. Hence those obscure problems of existence, the mystery of sin, the influence of the spiritual and the unseen, which fascinated many an early New England thinker, often became in Hawthorne's stories the actual basis of the work. He writes in the spirit of the artist, he does not force his moral on us in set terms; but if we penetrate to the center of his creations of wonder and beauty we find that in the heart of the romance is hidden a sermon. Such traits surround his works with a peculiar atmosphere, the spiritual atmosphere of the finest spirits of New England.

But while Hawthorne thus recreated the vanished past of New England and at the same time expressed in his own nature those essential elements in its spirit which had come down to his own times, he also shared in that liberality and tolerance which distinguished the leaders of his own generation. He realized all the shortcomings of Colonial Puritanism, and portrayed its " grim rigidity " with an unsparing severity. He has no part in the Puritanic formalities and restraints, but is keenly responsive to Nature and beauty; thus his description of " the Sylvan Dance " in *The Marble Faun* is a veritable prose idyll of a Golden Age. For a moment the conventional constraints of an artificial life are flung aside; Donatello, the Faun of the woods, has made Miriam a child of nature like himself, and they dance in the checkered sunshine with the simple, overflowing joyousness of children. In such scenes, rare as they are amidst the shadows that darken so much of Hawthorne's work, we see his deep if wistful sympathy with health and youth and all the gladness and the freedom of the world of nature. In the early part of *The Scarlet Letter* we are told of a wild-rose bush which had sprung up just outside the iron-spiked door of a Puritan prison, and the soft pure color of those delicate pink blossoms seems doubly beautiful to us against that dark, inexorable background. This picture with its suggestive contrast may be remembered as a symbol of the peculiar genius of Hawthorne himself.

Only the general outline of Hawthorne's life can be given here. As a boy he seems to have been a great reader, but high-spirited, and inclined to neglect the routine of his appointed studies. Long-fellow's boyhood has been spoken of as that of the born man of letters. Hawthorne's **Hawthorne's life.** was rather that of the man of genius. By a brief residence in Maine he early developed a taste for solitude, easily understood in one of his shy and reticent nature. After graduating from Bowdoin College in 1825, he spent twelve years in Salem, reading, writing stories, many of which he burned and some of which he published, and becoming, in his own familiar phrase, " the obscurest man of letters in America." * Like

* Preface to the *Twice-Told Tales.*

many other great masters of prose, he appears to have won that delicate finish and refined beauty which distinguished his style by laborious and incessant effort. *Fanshawe*, his early romance which he afterwards suppressed, shows but little trace of his peculiar power.

The real beginning of Hawthorne's work, so far as any true recognition of it is concerned, dates from the publication of the first series of his *Twice-Told Tales* in 1837. In 1841 he became a member of the Brook Farm community,* but found farm-labor and romance-writing hard to reconcile. Recording this experience in his journal, he writes: "After a hard day's work . . . my soul absolutely refuses to be poured out on paper"; and adds that in his opinion a man's higher nature "may be buried and perish in a furrow of the field just as well as under a pile of money."† Nevertheless the Brook Farm episode proved a not unfruitful one in the end, for his experience there furnished materials which Hawthorne used later in *The Blithedale Romance* (1852). In 1841 he married, and settled at Concord in the "Old Manse."‡ Thus happy in his marriage and surrounded by conditions favorable to his genius, he speaks of himself as "translated to another state of being." Under these kindly influences he composed some of the best of his short stories, which appeared with others previously published in his *Mosses from an Old Manse* (1846). In

Brook Farm.

---

* See pp. 172–173, *supra.*
† *American Note-Book* (June 1, 1841).
‡ See p. 168, *supra.*

the same year he was forced to leave his paradise, as he playfully called it, by an appointment to a post in the custom-house at Salem. Brought thus sharply into daily contact with that practical and business side of life from which he was by nature so much apart, Hawthorne, as he tells us, set himself to gather what profit was to be had from it.* He was in no mood for writing during the three years he held this place, but it was during this time that his great romance *The Scarlet Letter* took shape in his mind. It was not until he was removed from office by one of those changes which are a blot on our politics that he was able to carry out the idea over which he had been brooding. The publication of *The Scarlet Letter* in 1850 showed that Hawthorne had reached a new stage in his career. The first of his longer romances, it proved his ability to take a theme similar to those in many of his short studies, and successfully handle it on a larger scale. *The Scarlet Letter* was followed by *The House of the Seven Gables* (1851) and the *Blithedale Romance* (1852). These, with *The Marble Faun* (1860), are his four great romances.

In 1853 Hawthorne was appointed Consul at Liverpool by President Pierce, formerly his classmate at college. During the four years he held this position he published nothing. Released from his consular duties, he spent three years travelling in France, Italy, and part of England. Some of the results of these seven years of European experience are embodied in Haw-

---

* "The Custom-house," Introduction to *The Scarlet Letter*.

thorne's later works, the English, French, and Italian
Note-Books, and *The Marble Faun*, a story the majestic background of which is Rome, with its weight of
memories, its ruins, its art, and its past.

Hawthorne returned home in 1860. For a time he
worked vigorously, but before long it became evident
that his strength was failing. It is pathetic to remember that the theme of his last romance, which he did
not live to finish, was the elixir of life, the magic
draught by which man's days on earth might be per-
petually prolonged. He died May 19, 1864.

One of the first facts to impress us in a general
survey of Hawthorne's work is its unmistakable originality. Among American writers there are a few who
resemble him, but none who really contest
his supremacy in that shadowy region he
has made so peculiarly his own. In all
English literature we can hardly recall a single prose-
writer, with the possible exception of Thomas De
Quincey, whose work shows any similarity of tone.
Probably Hawthorne has most in common with certain romance-writers of Germany, but in the literature of the English language he stands practically
alone. The peculiar quality which thus sets Hawthorne's work apart must be felt, for no analysis can
adequately explain that positive but undefinable impression which his romances produce. It may be
said in general, however, that it is due partly to
the originality of his aim, and partly to the refined
beauty and subtle suggestiveness of his style. Unlike
most writers of fiction, Hawthorne's chief object is

Hawthorne's
work.

not to depict a certain phase of life in its external
aspect, or even to present to us certain characters: it
is rather to study the working of certain spiritual elements or forces in human life by showing us their
operations in a given case. His interest centers in
some moral problem or some spiritual truth, and he
tells his story or creates his characters so as to study
the problem or illustrate the truth. Sin, for example,
is a constant element back of human life and action,
and two of his greatest romances are minute and contrasted studies of the nature and workings of this
terrible force. In the first of them, *The Scarlet
Letter*, he traces the effects of sin on a group of characters—the effect on one soul of a sin discovered and
punished, the effect on another of a sin concealed.
He shows its noxious effect, not only on the original
transgressors, but on the souls of others. On the one
hand it awakens an unholy passion for revenge, and
transforms a man into a fiend; on the other, as an inheritance by that law which visits the sins of the
fathers upon the children, it is mysteriously mingled
with the nature of a child.

The second of these books, *The Marble Faun*,
raises the old question of the reason for sin's very
existence. Roger Chillingworth in *The Scarlet Letter*
was utterly corrupted by sin, but Donatello in *The
Marble Faun*, sinning not deliberately but impulsively,
attained through remorse and repentance a deeper
and fuller life so,—as in Eden,—sin destroys the
primitive innocence but brings knowledge. Is sin,
then, permitted as a means of growth? The question

is asked but not answered. Now these two books are admirable examples of Hawthorne's aim and method. In each the result is not a sermon, but a work of art, for the moral problem is not crudely stated, but diffused throughout the whole substance of the work; yet so completely does this spiritual element pervade Hawthorne's work that we feel ourselves transported in his romances to a world which is somehow unfamiliar. It is like a familiar landscape metamorphosed at the touch of moonlight, filled with unaccustomed lights and shadows, and vague with things but dimly seen. While, as in *The Scarlet Letter*, the forms of the grim-visaged Puritans move before us with their "steeple-crowned hats and sad-colored garments," they seem but as phantoms to us beside our haunting sense that the true reality is the spiritual and the unseen. Men and women, their joys and sorrows, are thus comparatively unreal to us in Hawthorne, because he so constantly regards the visible and external as a symbol or a manifestation of the obscure world of thought and spirit. Hawthorne may consequently be regarded as the master of a kind of romantic allegory. Spenser in his *Faërie Queene* made his knights and ladies represent or personify the various virtues and vices, but Hawthorne works more subtly than this. He does not embody any sin or any temptation in a human shape, but reveals it as a purely spiritual energy acting through and in the lives and souls of men. Thus the ideal temper which distinguished Emerson distinguished Hawthorne also; but in the one it was expressed through philosophy, in the other it put on the glorified garment of art. "The idealist," wrote Emerson, "speaking of events, sees them as spirits." Such an idealist was Hawthorne, the voice of the deepened life of New England, and perhaps the greatest writer that we have yet given to the literature of the world.

STUDY LIST
HAWTHORNE

1. Sketches. "The Old Manse," "Birds and Bird-Voices," in *Mosses from an Old Manse;* "Sunday at Home," "A Rill from the Town Pump," "Sights from a Steeple," in *Twice-told Tales.*

2. Short Stories. "Legends of the Province House," "The Gray Champion," "The May-pole of Merry Mount," "Endicott and the Red Cross," "The Minister's Black Veil," "The Gentle Boy," "Wakefield," "The Great Carbuncle," "David Swan," "The Ambitious Guest," in *Twice-told Tales;* "The Birthmark," "Rappaccini's Daughter," in *Mosses from an Old Manse;* "The Snow Image" and "The Great Stone Face," in *The Snow Image and other Twice-told Tales.*

3. A Wonder Book ; Tanglewood Tales.

4. The Scarlet Letter ; The Marble Faun.

5. Biography and Criticism. *Nathaniel Hawthorne and his Wife,* by Julian Hawthorne (2 vols.) ; *A Study of Hawthorne,* by G. P. Lathrop. Life, by Henry James, in English Men of Letters Series ; Life, by Moncure D. Conway, in Great Writers Series ; "Hawthorne," in J. T. Fields' *Yesterdays with Authors; Recollections of Hawthorne,* by Horatio Bridges. See also Curtis's *Literary and Social Esays;* Leslie Stephen's *Hours in a Library,* 1st. series ; R. H. Hutton's *Essays in Literary Criticism;* Whipple's *Character and Characteristic Men;* G. Barnett Smith's *Poets and Novelists.*

OTHER WRITERS OF THE NEW ENGLAND GROUP

So far we have confined our attention to three of the representative writers of the New England group. But if we would appreciate the magnitude and importance of this great period of New England literature, we must look at it also as a whole; we must try to gain some conception of the large number of distinguished writers connected with it, and of the extent and variety of their work. It is remarkable to consider how little America had done in certain branches of literature when this period opened, and how much it had accomplished through the labors of these writers before it closed.

Besides the three writers already studied, the period gave us three who are justly grouped with them: James Russell Lowell, Oliver Wendell Holmes, and John Greenleaf Whittier. Before it, while we had produced respectable chroniclers or writers of biographies, we had done almost nothing in the higher branches of historical writing. The period gave us four of our most eminent historians: Prescott, Motley, Bancroft, and Parkman. Among many other scholars and literary critics we may mention Ticknor, the historian of Spanish literature; the essayists E. P. Whipple and Henry Tuckerman; the Greek scholar Felton; the profound student of English, Francis J. Child, editor of the Scotch and English Ballads; and Charles Eliot Norton, the Dante scholar and the critic of Art. Prominent among the older men of this group is that strange, shy haunter of the woods, Henry D.

Thoreau; ill at ease in the midst of conventionalities and at home in the wilderness, the preacher of a simpler and more unfettered life. There, too, were men of a yet broader and nobler type: George Ripley, the devoted laborer at Brook Farm; and George William Curtis, the patriot, orator, and man of letters. Indeed we must not think of this movement as purely literary; its foundations were laid in character, and it was strong on its moral and political sides. Mrs. Stowe's terrible picture of slavery in *Uncle Tom's Cabin*, and the eloquence of the abolitionist orators, Wendell Phillips and William Lloyd Garrison, did a great work in helping to arouse the nation's conscience. These are but some of the great names which might be mentioned; one writer crowded after another, and the period still lingers with us to-day in Thomas Wentworth Higginson and Edward Everett Hale.

If we are inclined to wonder at the power thus suddenly put forth, we must remember that besides the especial causes already alluded to there lay back of the whole movement the shrewd sense, the spiritual vision, the sound manhood, and the moral impetus of a great race. So it is that this time of awakening life comes to the bleak region of New England like the coming of spring. Warm airs heavy with the odors of some Southern land blow softly over her rocky fields, and the grass is starred with flowers; warm suns thaw the ice of her frozen streams, and the waters are poured out in a flood.

The time is too full of activity, the literature too abundant, for us to be able here to do more than select a few of the eminent writers worthy of study, and speak of them only with comparative briefness.

JAMES RUSSELL LOWELL (1819–1891) holds among the rest a position which is both lofty and distinctive.

James Russell Lowell. Like so many of his great contemporaries, he came of a family which had been associated with the higher side of New England life since the early days of the Colony. Among his ancestors were clergymen, judges, and men eminent for their practical ability and public spirit. His father, a minister of a church in Boston, was a man of sterling worth and energy, and Lowell, like Longfellow, grew up in the midst of cultured surroundings, enlarged by a free access to the best books. Nor were books the only influence about him; the present as well as the past was alive with inspiration, for New England was pressing forward under the spur of new ideas. Lowell graduated from Harvard in 1838. Five years before this William Lloyd Garrison had definitely begun the agitation for the immediate freeing of the slave by the establishment of his abolitionist paper, the *Liberator*. Two years before Lowell's graduation, Emerson had become the center of the transcendentalists by the publication of *Nature*. Thus when the future poet of the *Biglow Papers* came to manhood the Northern conscience was aroused and the Northern intellect quickened to an intenser life by its enthusiasm for the thought of new teachers. By nature Lowell was dreamy and poetic, and an ardent lover of beauty, but he had in him a vast reserve of strength. He had the keen humor, the shrewd obser-

JAMES RUSSELL LOWELL

vation and practical sense, the capacity for righteous
indignation and patriotic devotion, which fitted him
to be the champion of a great cause. In the first flush
of his generous and high-souled youth, when a strong
nation was rousing herself to face a coming crisis,
Lowell's nature gained a manly force and earnestness
in this uplifting and invigorating air. The growth of
his character under these influences is reflected in his
earlier poems. Studies of different types of women,
comparable to certain early efforts of Tennyson, give
place to poems of a stronger and sterner strain. We
have indeed the excellent but somewhat imitative
treatment of Old World themes, the poems on classical
subjects such as *Rhœcus*, or *The Shepherd of King
Admetus;* the mediæval *Legend of Brittany*, the softened beauty of which recalls the languorous atmosphere of Keats; but we have also the expression of a
deep conviction that the poet of our new land must
be the poet of freedom and human brotherhood, that
he must put aside the properties of " silken bards,"
and speak his new message in the power of his manhood.

> "Our country hath a gospel of her own
>   To preach and practice before all the world—
>   The freedom and divinity of man."

Few Americans have felt so deeply as Lowell the
true ideal of our democracy. He not only loved our
country for what it was; he saw its faults, and yet rose
to the high conception of what it might be in the history of mankind. It is the strength of his moral fiber
and the noble ardor of his patriotism that gives his

verse its resonant and distinctive character. So in the
midst of his classicism and mediævalism his *Stanzas on
Freedom*, the first of his antislavery poems, ring out
like the call of a trumpet.

> " They are slaves who fear to speak
> For the fallen and the weak ;
>
> *   *   *   *   *
>
> They are slaves who dare not be
> In the right with two or three."

At a time when to be an Abolitionist was to invite
ridicule and unpopularity, Lowell was one of those
who dared to be in the right with a few. *The Present
Crisis*, inspired by the question as to the introduction
of slavery into Texas, then recently annexed to the
United States, contains lines that sent a thrill through
the manhood of the North. The young poet had
come, like Childe Roland in Browning's poem, to the
door of our Dark Tower of shame, and dauntlessly he
set the " slug-horn to his lips " and blew his note of
challenge. If the past is with the poets of the Old
World, the future belongs peculiarly to the poets of
the New, and *The Present Crisis* is aflame with the
feeling that, as Emerson had declared, " to-day is a
new day."

> " New occasions teach new duties, Time makes ancient good
>   uncouth ;
>   They must upward still and onward who would keep abreast
>   of Truth."

In such a strain there sounds the magnificent confidence, the indomitable resolution, of a young land; it
is the true voice of our America.

In 1846 the poems which made up the first series of Lowell's great satiric masterpiece, *The Biglow Papers*, began to appear in the *Boston Courier*. Up to this time Lowell had been the poet of love, beauty, and patriotism; his work had been full of a high seriousness; but in the *Biglow Papers* elements of his genius which had yet found no expression in his verse became suddenly apparent. The poems were inspired by our war with Mexico, which was believed to have been undertaken in order to gain new territory for the extension of slavery. They are written in the Yankee dialect, and are supposed to be the work of Hosea Biglow, "an up-country man, capable of district-school English," but in the habit of relapsing into his homely native speech when strongly moved. A pedantic Mr. Wilbur, the pastor of the First Church at Jaalam, is introduced under the guise of editor. Probably no one was more surprised than Lowell himself at the success of this novel experiment; he was surprised at the power of the weapon he had made, and when the slavery question reached its climax in civil war, a second series of Biglow Papers was added to the first.

Taken as a whole, the *Biglow Papers* form one of our most noteworthy contributions to literature. It is often said, and quite truly, that no other country but New England could have produced them. Hawthorne embodies the Puritan spirit; Lowell here brings us face to face with the every-day Yankee, in undeniable flesh and blood. Lowell loved the flavor of the common speech, and by a single effort he has lifted the twang, the drawl, the quaint phrases of the down-east countryman, into literature. From this aspect the *Biglow Papers* are local; but they are much more—they are among our few distinctly national poems, more fully and truly American than *Hiawatha* or *The Courtship of Miles Standish*. While they represent New England, they also represent much that is best in the American people—the clear-sightedness, the shrewd humor, the essential right-ness on great moral issues, which are deep-seated in our democracy. Lowell might have expressed the views advanced in the *Biglow Papers* in that scholarly phrase or that elevated verse which would have been his own natural medium, but he believed that the moral sense of the plain average American man was sound and true; and so, instead of speaking for himself individually, in his own way, he instinctively chose to speak as a plain man of the people, in homely, pithy phrase. Hence we have in the *Biglow Papers* not the scholar writing from his library, but the voice of the nation. As a work of art the poem holds a high and distinctly unique place among the satires of the language, differing widely in form and spirit from the satiric masterpieces of Dryden, Pope, Butler, or Byron. The mixture of humor and deadly earnest is a national trait, and the *Biglow Papers* differ from many English satires in mingling wit and absurdity with a genuine poetic beauty and a spirit of the in-tensest patriotism. There is a wide range from such incisive verses as *The Pious Editor's Creed* and *What Mr. Robinson Thinks* to that idyll of the farm-house kitchen, *The Courtin'*, or the truth and beauty with which the New England landscape is made real to us in *Sunthin' in the Pastoral Line*, or *Hosea Biglow to the Editor of the Atlantic*. In all we recognize an element unfortunately rare in the pure and melodious strains of our American verse, the note of a masculine strength. When we add to the poems of patriotism already mentioned such masterpieces as *The Washers of the Shroud*, and the noble but more unequal *Commemoration Ode*, written at the close of the Civil War, we realize that Lowell is virtually the laureate of our Republic, the poetic voice of our national life and ideals.

We have so far spoken of Lowell as the poet of patriotism, but to pass over his poetry of a wholly different kind would be to give an entirely wrong conception of his work. He could be nobly strenuous or inimitably humorous; but he had also an intimate knowledge and deep love of nature, a tenderness and a delight in beauty, and this gentle and more dreamy side of his sensitive nature also uttered itself in his verse. So, with a rare delicacy of perception, Lowell could turn aside from the great present questions and, like his "musing organist," could "build a bridge from Dreamland for his lay." The poet of the *Biglow Papers* is thus the poet of *The Vision of Sir Launfal*, with the passionate nature poetry of its prelude; of the love-sonnets; of *The Dandelion ;* of *In the Twilight*, perhaps the most subtle and beautiful of all the shorter poems. Reading such poems, we know that Lowell was able not only to "blow through bronze," but also to "breathe through silver"; yet, filled as they are with the poetic spirit, we feel at times that the poet has not fully mastered the secret of his art.   His life was crowded with many interests; he did not consecrate himself to poetry with the exclusive devotion of Tennyson; and his work has an inequality absent from the art of that great master.   We are often disturbed by a false or jarring note, and miss at times the magical phrase.   Yet Lowell was a genuine poet, and we see this in the advance he makes in the sweetness and perfection of his work.   To the end we see him gaining greater finish and delicacy, and some of his most perfect if not his strongest poems are among his last.

Lowell began his work as a poet, but from the first he had been a wide reader, absorbing books with the scholar's enthusiasm and the poet's sympathy and in-sight.   As he approached middle age this scholarly side of his mind began to find more direct expression. In 1854 he delivered a course of lectures on the British Poets at the Lowell Institute, and in the year following was appointed to succeed Longfellow in the chair of Modern Languages and Literature at Har-vard.   After preparing himself, as Longfellow had done, by a foreign trip, he entered on the duties of his professorship in 1857.   The twenty years of college work which followed were years of intense and loving toil.   George William Curtis tells us that in these years Lowell sometimes studied fourteen hours in the day, so " relentless" was his devotion to study.   This period of scholarship is notable for Lowell's work as

prose-writer and literary critic, and the best results of
his studies and his university work were condensed
into essays which are the finest addition America has
yet made to the literature of criticism. Like his
verse, Lowell's prose is alive with a characteristic
audacity and variety; there is no even and colorless
excellence. The essays are filled with an intense individuality. All is poured out in profusion—the irre-
pressible daring humor, the wealth of learning, the
quaint memorable phrase, the homely telling allusion;
and in all there is vigor, freshness, and unconven-
tionality. He has explored the whole range of English
literature, and brought many of its greatest masters
nearer to our sympathy and understanding. He
delights to give us, as in the monumental essay on
Dante, the fruit of years of loving toil. In Lowell's
prose there is a delightful sense of ease and power;
lacking a classic finish, it has a warm humanity, and
it often reaches a grace and felicity of manner that is
the delight of lovers of style. Lowell's literary criticism is the more remarkable because America has been
and is singularly deficient in this branch of literature.
England has had dozens of capable critics during the
last half-century, while among us Lowell stands almost
alone,—"the only critic of high rank," as one writer
asserts, "that our literature owns." During the
twenty years of his professorship at Harvard, Lowell
was one of the founders and, for the first five years,
editor of the *Atlantic Monthly*, and later one of the
joint editors of the *North American Review*. These

two periodicals have had a most important part in our literary development.

Lowell was not only poet, scholar, and critic, but back of all his varied interests he was the patriot, the wise, large-hearted citizen; and in this more than anything else we find the basis of his life and work.   In the fullness of his splendid powers he was called upon to represent his country.   He was first Minister to Spain and then to England, being sent to Madrid in 1877 and transferred to London in 1880.   His residence in England was far more than a great social triumph.   His charm, wit, tact, and learning made him everywhere liked and honored.   He came, as he said, as a distant cousin, but went back as a brother. He was in demand as the chosen orator on great public occasions; he made the aptest of after-dinner speeches. But through all this, pleasant as it was in itself, he accomplished a great purpose never lost sight of: he changed and raised the English idea of America, and brought the two greatest English-speaking countries nearer together.   In these later years of his life he was conspicuously the public servant; many of his speeches are more or less occupied with political themes, and many of his matured opinions are summed up in his address on *Democracy* in 1884.

Lowell was our strongest if not our best poet, our greatest critic, and one of our greatest scholars. Through his many-sidedness he is our most representative man of letters, the true dean of the faculty. We admire him for all these things, but we admire him even more for that greatness of character which was

OLIVER WENDELL HOLMES

the basis of them all. "We value character," says Lowell himself, "more than any amount of talent." *
So while it is much that Lowell should so fitly represent American letters, it is yet more that in himself he should represent and stand for American manhood; a shining example for us who come after, a demonstration that our democracy with all its shortcomings has yet the force to be the maker of men.

Another notable member of this Cambridge group, the last to leave us of all the greater New England writers, was OLIVER WENDELL HOLMES (1809–1894). Versatile as he was, physician, poet, lecturer, novelist, and "autocrat" of that immortal "breakfast-table," the distinctive share which Holmes took in his epoch is unmistakable almost from the first. Passing to Holmes from Emerson, Hawthorne, or Lowell, we are aware that he is of a slighter intellectual build; that his especial faculty is not so much depth or power, as an inimitable lightness, deftness, and grace. In a word, while he is many other things, he is pre-eminently the humorist, the kindly, keen-witted, fun-loving spirit, whose audacious flashes of merriment startled the solemn gloom that had so long hung heavily over New England. We have grown to look upon humor as one of our most distinguishing national traits, and as fellow-countrymen of Josh Billings and Mark Twain we regard it as a dominant element in our literature. But up to the advent of Holmes our higher literature

Oliver Wendell Holmes.

* Essay on Rousseau.

had, with the exception of Irving, been uniformly serious. It would, of course, be little short of impious to look for levity in the New England of Michael Wigglesworth and Jonathan Edwards, but even outside of Puritanic limits our authors who wrote best seldom smiled. As Mr. George William Curtis expresses it, " the rollicking laughter of Knickerbocker was a solitary sound in the American air until the blithe carol of Holmes returned a kindred spell."* Yet the spell that Holmes' keen wit exercises over us, while perhaps akin to that which charms us in the rich humor of Irving, is far from being absolutely the same. The pages of Irving are luminous with a softer, warmer glow, while those of the New Englander, while not untouched by pathos, sparkle with a sharper and colder light. In this, as in all things, Holmes was the true child of the great section which produced him, and, like so many of his contemporaries, he shows at almost every point the force and persistence of those traits which went to the making of New England. He exemplifies in himself the truth of his own doctrine of the strength of inherited influences. The blood of some of the best and oldest families of New England, the Wendells, the Olivers, the Quincys, ran in his veins. Among his ancestors was that fluent poetess Mistress Anne Bradstreet, "The Tenth Muse."

Thus Holmes was indeed the son of New England, but in a yet stricter and more especial sense he was the child of that exclusive culture focussed in and

* *Literary and Social Essays*, p. 218.

about Boston. Born almost under the shadow of Harvard, in the days when Cambridge was a quiet country village, he received his collegiate and his early medical training at that great university. Early associations and friendships had a lasting power over him; his attachments were broad and deep-rooted. After spending some years abroad in order to continue his medical studies at Paris and Edinburgh, he returned to Boston, becoming henceforth, except for a few brief intervals, a fixed and notable part of the city's social and intellectual life. As a college boy he had been the class poet; as a man he was peculiarly the "laureate of Harvard" and of Boston. Year after year he celebrated the reunions of his class in his witty, unfailing verse, and one of his latest poems was occasioned by the introduction of the trolley-cars into his beloved town. With that town everything combined to inseparably associate him; he was a part of its life by his affectionate hold on its past, by those gifts of wit, kindliness, and personal charm which made him so long its pride and ornament. And as Walter Scott loved Edinburgh, as Dr. Johnson or Charles Lamb or Dickens loved London, so Dr. Holmes loved Boston, and that placid suburb where his life began. Few authors have put more of their personality into their writings. Whether he wrote prose or verse, medical lectures, or "medicated novels," the result in any case was but an overflow of the man himself. For a generation he was one of Boston's cherished talkers, and in his works he simply indefinitely enlarges his audience and talks in print. His best and most characteristic work in prose, *The Autocrat of the Breakfast-Table*, and its successors, consist of snatches of fragmentary conversations and reflections, in which the chief talker is readily identified with the author himself.

Holmes first won fame as a poet. As a very young man he wrote his spirited verses *Old Ironsides*, a ringing protest against the proposed breaking up of the veteran war-frigate the Constitution, a ship which had borne an honorable part in the War of 1812. The appeal went straight to the people's heart; it was taken up throughout the country, and laid the foundation of the poet's reputation. In 1836, the year of the appearance of Emerson's *Nature*, Holmes read a longer and more ambitious composition, *Poetry, a Metrical Essay*, before the Phi Beta Kappa Society. In this same year he published his first volume of poems, which included *The Last Leaf, The Treadmill Song*, and other familiar pieces. Holmes' muse, if not often very lofty, was always surprisingly prompt and available. A fluent versifier, with an easy, agreeable flow of meter, with wit, good-fellowship, and enough real feeling to serve as a corrective, he became incomparably the best and the most popular of our writers of poems for especial occasions. It is said that forty-seven per cent of his poems were thus written, as it were, to order, in honor of the most various celebrations. The dedication of a cemetery, or a State dinner; the meeting of a medical association, or the anniversary of an agricultural society; centennial and semi-centennial celebrations, and a long succession of

class-reunions,—on all such occasions Holmes showed
his happy gift of putting into verse the fitting words.
A greater poet might perhaps have done it less easily,
but for the occasion Holmes did it inimitably well.

If, however, we look at Holmes' total poetic work,
we shall probably conclude that his final place among
our poets is likely to rest upon a very few poems.
Light, graceful, humorous, or absurd, he is distinctly
a minor poet, accepting his limitations, and apparently
claiming for himself no higher title. Once, in *The
Chambered Nautilus*, he rises into the larger, nobler
air; it is doubtful whether he has elsewhere reached
an equal height. But it is not given to all poets to
be in the "grand manner," and the especial place and
value of the less lofty singers should not be slighted
or overlooked. The masters of the slighter forms of
society verse,—of the lyric of wit, fun, or fancy,—
have their assured place, even if it be on the outskirts
of the poetic realm. We cannot be always at the
highest tension, and, as Holmes himself says,

> " A page of Hood may do a fellow good
> After a scolding from Carlyle or Ruskin."

By certain poems—not many, indeed, but memorable—Holmes holds an assured place among verse-
writers of this lighter kind. *Dorothy Q.*, which has a
fineness and pathos not incomparable to that of Austin
Dobson; *The One-Hoss Shay*, *La Grisette*, *The Last
Leaf*,—such verse rightly entitles Holmes to be ranked
in that charming company to which Prior, Hood,
Praed, and Thackeray belong.

Holmes was nearly fifty before he made any important contribution to prose. When the *Atlantic Monthly* was started, in 1857, Lowell assumed its editorship with the understanding that a set of articles should be contributed by Holmes. Lowell's foresight was amply justified. The arrangement gave us *The Autocrat of the Breakfast-Table*, a book which placed Holmes among our most brilliant and charming writers of prose. By a guiding instinct, or a happy accident, Boston's famous talker had here hit upon—or perhaps we may rather say created—a literary form which showed his mastery in his own domain. The book purports to be the record of the table-talk of a Boston boarding-house. It is indeed less a conversation than a monologue in a dramatic setting; variety, humor, and human interest being furnished by the casual introduction of the various boarders, whose remarks or questions serve to bring out the Autocrat's best wit and wisdom. Such a plan allows the author the widest liberty; we have at once a greater ease and discursiveness than in the more formal essay, and at the same time an underlying connection not found in the scattered thoughts or meditations of certain great classic writers. *The Autocrat of the Breakfast-Table* was followed from time to time by other works of the same general character: *The Professor at the Breakfast-Table* (1859), *The Poet at the Breakfast-Table* (1873), and *Over the Tea-Cups* (1890). The series is full of Dr. Holmes; it reveals his alert, restless intellect, darting from grave to gay,

Holmes' prose.

touching and adorning all with liveliness and sympathy.

The same rambling and conversational quality which in the Breakfast-Table Series is so great a merit, detracts from the entire success of Dr. Holmes' novels, as it tends to interrupt the story and unduly obtrudes the personality and opinions of the author. His three novels, *Elsie Venner* (1860), *The Guardian Angel* (1868), and *A Mortal Antipathy* (1885), contain interesting presentations of character, striking situations, and an abundance of shrewd reflection, but they are rather the curious studies of the physician and thinker than masterpieces of story-telling. Each of them is a minute inquiry into the effect of some innate or hereditary influence on human character and action. It is suggested in *Elsie Venner* that in some cases a purely physical condition for which the individual cannot be held morally responsible may be the cause of a moral defect, and the two remaining stories turn also on this problem of moral accountability. It is dangerous, if fascinating, ground; it takes us into that debatable region where body and spirit touch and interact, and where we are led to ask how far the thing which we are and do is determined by the forces without or the personal power within. The fact that this subtle question should have attracted Holmes so strongly, is another illustration of his intensely New England cast of mind. His ancestors had approached the problem of evil tendencies or human accountability as theologians, and discovered predestination and original sin. The same deep problems fascinated Holmes, but he approached them as a physician and a scientist, in the reactionary and modern spirit of his time.

Although we cannot dwell here on the work of Dr. Holmes in medicine, it must be remembered that he gave to this his chosen profession a great part of his energy. He made numerous and important contributions to medical literature; he was Professor of Physiology and Anatomy at Dartmouth College for two years, and held the same chair at Harvard for thirty-five years (1847–1882). It is enough to say here that even into his medical lectures he carried the genial, winning grace of that personality which, underlying all his varied activities and successes, gives its distinctive flavor to his work.

Emerson, Longfellow, Lowell, and Holmes were inheritors of generations of scholarship. Europe was **J. G. Whittier.** open and familiar to them, and their wide culture gave them the key to the treasures of her literature and her past. In certain ways JOHN GREENLEAF WHITTIER (1807–1892) is closely associated with this group of poet-scholars, but, on the whole, he stands apart from it by his origin, his education, and the prevailing character of his work. As has been pointed out, Emerson, and the great writers who surrounded him were, for the most part, the outcome of Puritanism as then transformed and liberalized by the power of new ideas; Whittier, on the contrary, was a Quaker and sprung from Quaker stock. To the close of his life the " Quaker poet " held fast to the tranquil faith in which he had been reared, and the religious spirit of many of his poems is neither that of

JOHN GREENLEAF WHITTIER

Emerson nor of those Calvinistic teachers whose iron creed Emerson had cast off. By religion, by inheritance, and in some respects by temperament, Whittier is thus outside of Puritanism, that most dominant influence in the life and literature of New England.

A further point of separation is to be found in the character of Whittier's early life and surroundings. The lives of his great New England contemporaries in poetry were mainly identified with cities. They knew and loved nature, indeed, yet they habitually viewed life from the midst of the charmed circles of culture in Boston, Cambridge, or Concord. Whittier was country-born and country-bred. He grew up a simple New England farmer's boy, taking his share in the beautiful, homely labors of the barn-yard and the field. Emerson and his circle were college-bred; they belonged by birth to the "academic aristocracy" of New England. The meagerness of Whittier's early training at the country-school near by was supplemented by a year of hardly-earned instruction at a neighboring academy. His ancestors were a simple, upright, hard-working people, his boyish surroundings devoid of luxury or of any especial incentives to culture. Whittier is thus, in a peculiar sense, the poet of the people and of nature. He comes to us out of the very heart of rural New England. To the farmer, nature is not merely an occasional source of pleasure; he lives in daily dependence upon her, brought by his calling into direct and wholesome dealings with her processes of growth. Born to farm labors, the knowledge of nature was Whittier's birthright, and not even

Lowell with all his subtler sympathies can bring us so close to the New England landscape, or make the life of the New England farmer so idyllic and so real.

The Whittier homestead, pictured for us by the poet in *Snow-Bound*, stood in the valley of the Merrimack River, in the northern part of Essex County, Massachusetts. In this plain New England farmhouse the family had dwelt for generations. The situation is remote and solitary; the hills shut it in, their wooded slopes "ridging" the west. Here Whittier was born, December 17, 1807. The poet in him woke early, and as a boy he found help and inspiration in the songs of that greater genius of the farm, Robert Burns. The Scotch ploughman spoke to the heart of the New England farmer's boy, and, as Whittier declared, he saw the world with new eyes:

> "New light on home-seen Nature beamed,
>   New glory over Woman;
> And daily life and duty seemed
>   No longer poor and common.*

When he was about twenty, through the influence and encouragement of William Lloyd Garrison, then at the beginning of his career, Whittier left the farm to make journalism his profession. For the next twelve years (1828–1840) his duties called him to various places: for a time he was in Boston, then in Haverhill, then in Hartford, and later in Philadelphia. His early association with Garrison, his love of freedom, and his deep hatred of cruelty and oppres-

* Whittier's Poems: "Burns."

sion, all combined to make him the indomitable opponent of slavery, and he stands side by side with Lowell as the poet champion of the cause of the Abolitionists. With his gentle, loving, and sensitive nature, Whittier, like Lowell, had that power of just wrath possible to men of a pure and lofty type. Mingled with that peculiar twilight serenity so characteristic of those of the Quaker sect, there was a stern zeal for righteousness like that in the great Hebrew prophets, a martial dash and vigor that passes into the swinging beat of many of his best ballads, and sets our blood astir. Thoroughly in earnest, Whittier gave not only his songs but himself to the antislavery cause. He was one of the secretaries of the antislavery convention; he edited *The Pennsylvania Freeman*, faced hostile audiences, confronted riotous and abusive mobs, in the strength of his conviction and his cause.

Leaving Philadelphia in 1840, Whittier sold the homestead on the Merrimack, and settled at Amesbury, a small town in its vicinity. Here and in his beautiful country-place near Danvers, not far from Boston, he spent the long remainder of his life. Thus, except for the brief interval of his journalistic work, made stirring and eventful towards its close by his gallant battle for the slave, Whittier's life was passed in those country surroundings which give to his verse so much of its freshness and charm.

The course of Whittier's life is accurately reflected in his poetry. Burns had led him to see a hitherto unsuspected beauty in familiar surroundings. He sought as a youth to convert the Indian into a hero of romance, and to claim for poetry the scenes and legends of New England. At first the result was but very partially successful, and he himself declared in after years that Mogg Megone, the hero of one of these early efforts, suggested " the idea of a big Indian in his war-paint strutting about in Sir Walter Scott's plaid."* Another Indian poem, *The Bridal of Pennacook*, is less of a failure, but hardly a success. If Whittier cannot compete with Longfellow in his treatment of Indian legend, he has found in the records of the early settlers of New England materials for ballads which at least compare favorably with Longfellow's best work on similar themes. Among such poems are the splendid ballad *Cassandra Southwick*, and the story of the days of witchcraft, *Mabel Martin*. Spirited and admirable as are these studies of the past, Whittier is above all the painter and revealer of his own time. He stands out pre-eminently as the poet of the antislavery contest, the poet of rural New England, and the poet of a tranquil and comprehensive religious faith. We will speak briefly of these three elements in his work.

Regarded strictly as poetry, many of Whittier's antislavery lyrics fall below the level of his best verse. They show earnestness, sincerity, and vigor; but Whittier was slow in mastering the technical requirements of his art, and these poems, often written for an occasion and in the heat of the conflict, were in-

* Collected Works, ed. 1888, vol. ii. p. 325.

tended to serve a practical and immediate purpose. Fame could wait; his cause could not, and it was more than fame. So Whittier simply used verse as another weapon in the fight he was waging; in his antislavery verses, widely read through the newspapers, he spoke directly to the hearts of the people, and he did his work. Nevertheless the effectiveness of these poems in a great national crisis is one thing, and their permanent value in poetry another; and from the latter aspect we often find in them a genuine but too declamatory passion, rather than an enduring poetic form. They have, moreover, that diffuseness which is admittedly one of Whittier's most serious artistic shortcomings. Yet once, at least, in these poems Whittier reached a height to which the best of our poets seldom attain. Among the mass of prose and poetry produced by our Civil War, the *Laus Deo*, a song of praise and triumph for the abolition of slavery, must rank with the few really great and lasting contributions to literature. Through all its exultant lyrical movement we feel the throb of the great bells; it is alike a song of victory and of thanksgiving, and like that ancient chant of Miriam, it is a perfect union of those two great emotions, patriotism and praise.

> " It is done !
> Clang of bell, and war of gun,
> Send the tidings up and down.
> How the belfries rock and reel !
> How the great guns, peal on peal !
> Fling the joy from town to town."

The antislavery poems were an episode, if a dramatic and important one, in Whittier's career; his poems which record the New England farm-life came out of a lifetime of association and an intimate understanding and sympathy. Whittier's intense feeling for New England may be compared to that filial devotion to country which permeates the work of Scott or Burns. Other countries may be fair, but the poet with this deep feeling for the land of his birth knows that one only can satisfy his needs. We know that Whittier spoke in all sincerity when he wrote of his bleak New England:

> "Home of my heart! to me more fair
> Than gay Versailles or Windsor's halls,
> The painted, shingly town-house where
> The freeman's vote for Freedom falls." *

It is this intimate knowledge and lifelong love of New England that has made Whittier in an especial sense her poet. He sets us down in the midst of her, and we see, as for the first time, that life of the New Englander glorified and yet startlingly real. Thus in the *Barefoot Boy* he shows us the careless ranger of the fields, with his sunburned face and torn hat-brim; there is the country schoolhouse, the sumach and blackberry vines about it, and within the warped floor and battered seats. Then in *Telling the Bees*, one of the most perfect and suggestive of the shorter poems, there is the quaint local custom, touched by a

* *The Last Walk in Autumn,* xxi.

universal pathos against the homely but beautiful
background of the farm-house.

> "This is the house, with the gate red-barred
>   And the poplars tall ;
>   And the barn's brown length, and the cattle-yard,
>   And the white horns tossing above the wall."

To describe such scenes both truthfully and poetically requires power of no mean order, and to this
power Whittier added sympathy with the lives of
those who toil. In the series entitled *The Songs of
Labor* we are made to feel the dignity and nobility
of man's toil, when "the working hand makes strong
the working brain." The lives of the fishermen of
the stormy northern coasts, of the lumbermen in the
wintry solitude of a Maine forest, are entered into
with a democratic spirit meant to show "the unsung
beauty" underlying "common things." The most
perfect expression of all this side of Whittier's genius
is probably to be found in *Snow-Bound*. The poem
comes to us with the directness of a personal experience; it is an actual part of life, and thus built on
solid and enduring foundations. Only one household
is brought before us, but we feel that in portraying
this, one side of our American life has been given a
lasting interpretation in literature. The genius of
Whittier has lifted the New England farmhouse in
winter into the great world of poetry, as the genius
of Burns did the humble, godly home of the Scotch
cotter, or that of Cowper the domestic comforts of an
English fireside. We share in the "nightly chores,"

the morning task of cutting a path through the snow-drift; we see the "prisoned brutes" in the barn; at night we pass indoors and join the little group about the blazing fireplace. All is real and true; every detail is brought before us with a loving sureness of touch which reminds us of the painstaking minuteness of some old Dutch painter. Without stretches the New England landscape, bleak, snow-covered, solitary; the wind sweeps over it and we hear the sleet with its "ghostly finger-tips" tap the pane. It is a veritable idyll; and it is as distinctly ours as an idyll of Theocritus is Greek, or as Tennyson's idyllic poems of English country life are English. It is at once true in every familiar incident and particular, and yet filled with that grace and meaning which the true poet teaches us to discern in familiar things.

Finally, we find in Whittier a deep and tranquil religious feeling, finding definite expression in one important group of poems, but passing beyond this, and pervading more or less fully the whole body of his work. This religious spirit is at the farthest remove from the gloom and severity of the Calvinistic creeds; it is a spirit of peace, light, love, and childlike trust. Not unmindful of the questionings of his age, this confidence suffices the poet until the end.

> " I have no answer for myself or thee,
>   Save that I learned beside my mother's knee;
>   ' All is of God that is and is to be;
>   And God is good.' " *

* Whittier's Poems. " Trust."

It is this spirit of trust that illuminates with a serene radiance that most finished and beautiful poem, *The Eternal Goodness*. On the purely artistic side Whittier had many technical shortcomings. His instinct for form was not always fine enough to balance the deficiencies of his early training, and the preacher and reformer in him sometimes injured the poet. On the other hand, he gained as he grew older a greater mastery of his art, and he has reached at times an extraordinary height of poetic excellence. In all cases we feel his sterling manhood, his singleness of purpose; and we should realize that after all deductions he has a genuineness, an elevation, and an original force which win for him a high place among our poets.

So far we have dwelt almost exclusively on the work produced by the great writers of New England, within the limits of poetry, romance, and literary criticism. But even a brief survey of the Golden Age of our literature would **The Historians.** be incomplete without some mention of what has been accomplished in the fields of learning and scholarly research. In reality this work is of an exceedingly high order. In poetry and even in fiction, branches of literature which demand the highest creative or imaginative power, the work of the American writers, creditable as it is, is as a whole distinctly inferior to that of their English contemporaries. It is childish to allow our judgment in this matter to be warped by any fancied loyalty to country, for the truest patriotism lies in seeing clearly our national shortcomings and striving to amend them, not in blindly insisting that they do not exist. In the field of historical writing, however, no such admission is required, for the works of our best American historians are fairly entitled to be ranked with those of the greatest English historians of the time. The American mind is quick and versatile, but it has shown a truly surprising willingness to labor slowly and diligently in original investigation.*

In addition to thorough knowledge and accuracy, the great New England historians have not been wanting in a fine feeling for style and in a true literary instinct. One of these, GEORGE BANCROFT (1800–1891), had, indeed, the faculty of the historical investigator in larger measure than the faculty of the literary artist; yet his *History of the United States*, a monument of careful industry, remains, with all deductions, an invaluable and scholarly work. This history, in twelve volumes, the first of which appeared in 1834, covers the Colonial and Revolutionary periods, treating them with such fullness and exactness that it has taken its place as a standard authority.

George Bancroft.

WILLIAM HICKLING PRESCOTT (1796–1859), whose earliest work, a *History of the Reign of Ferdinand and Isabella*, was published three years after the first volume of Bancroft's history, possessed in a wonderful degree not only the

W. H. Prescott.

---

*This has been so marked of late years as to attract the notice of one of the most acute of our English critics. Bryce's *American Commonwealth*, vol. ii. p. 631.

patient spirit necessary for careful and painstaking research, but also the imaginative power to present the dry facts thus discovered in a picturesque and delightful narrative. This was the more remarkable when we consider under what disadvantages he labored. When quite a young man an accident made him almost blind. After travelling abroad for two years, vainly seeking relief, he returned to America, and with the help of a secretary bravely began the work upon which he had set his heart. For the next twelve years he was occupied in writing the *History of the Reign of Ferdinand and Isabella*. This was followed (1843) by a *History of the Conquest of Mexico*, and four years later by the *Conquest of Peru*. After this he wrote three volumes of his *History of the Reign of Philip II.*, but he did not live to complete it.

Prescott, like Irving, had come under the fascination of Spain in the days of her greatest power, when she was laying the foundations of her empire beyond the seas. His selection of the Spanish conquest in South America as a subject was a particularly happy one; for, in addition to the fact that this great era of discovery possesses an especial interest for Americans, it was a theme which afforded a fine opportunity for graphic description. Few novels move us more deeply than Prescott's vivid story of the perilous escapes, the trials, the hardships, and the daring of this band of romantic adventurers, discovering and conquering a new world, gorgeous with the rich and brilliant coloring of tropical life, and filled with a fabulous wealth and treasure long dreamed of by Old-World explorers. Prescott's work as a whole maintains a high order of excellence, but in this fascinating book the nature of his subject has enabled him to give us a peculiarly poetic and rounded production. The daring exploits of Cortes and his little band; the extraordinary richness of the kingdom they subdued, and the tragic fate of its unhappy ruler,—all these combine to give the story the unity and poetic quality of a great epic. Although, in the light of recent knowledge, critics have questioned some of Prescott's statements, his histories are, in nearly all essential points, to be relied upon as correct, and we may still take pleasure in the thought that, in the wonderful pictures he has given us, truth has not been sacrificed to effect.

Another great historian of this New England group, JOHN LOTHROP MOTLEY (1814–1877), after graduating at Harvard studied for several years

J. L. Motley.

at the German universities. He then returned to Boston and chose law as his profession. Law was soon abandoned for literature, and in 1839 he published an unsuccessful novel, *Morton's Hope*. In his next venture he made use of some of the historical materials he had begun to collect; but this second novel, *Merry Mount*, while not devoid of merit, was like the first a literary failure, and Motley came to the conclusion that his vocation was that of the historian. Having made this decision, he did not hesitate in the selection of his subject. His view of history was essentially that of one who believed in free institutions and in popular rights. In looking back over the past his sympathy and interest went out to the great mass of people rather than to the little group of kings and nobles. For one of his temperament and convictions, the disregard of human rights, the cruelty and oppression of a tyrannical ruler, or a popular uprising in the cause of freedom possessed a peculiar attraction and an underlying significance. The struggle of the race towards liberty impressed him as a leading element in modern history, and he aspired to become, in part, its historian. As such he may be regarded as an exponent, from the historian's point of view, of those principles which are the foundation of our Republic.

The stubborn and successful struggle of the Dutch against the bigotry and tyranny of Philip II. was interesting in Motley's eyes, not merely because of its heroic or dramatic incident, nor wholly because it was a fight for liberty, but because, as he saw it, it was a step towards the wider establishment of human rights; an episode in the drama of progress, the full meaning of which had not been fully perceived. As he writes in his Preface: "To all who speak the English language the history of the great agony through which the Republic of Holland was ushered into life must have a peculiar interest, for it is a portion of the records of the Anglo-Saxon race—essentially the same, whether in Friesland, England, or Massachusetts." And again: "'To maintain,' not to overthrow, was the device of the Washington of the sixteenth century, as it was the aim of our own hero and his great contemporaries." *

Motley planned a series of histories which, under the general title of *The Eighty Years' War for Liberty*, was to include *The Rise of the Dutch Republic*, *The United Netherlands*, and *The Thirty Years' War*. He did not live, however, to fully carry out his design. He soon realized that it was impossible to carry out his tremendous undertaking in this country, and in 1851 he went abroad with his family in order to investigate original manuscripts, and to visit the chief places connected with his work. The untiring labor which he expended for many years in the most minute and painstaking researches shows the earnest devotion of a great scholar. He not only read in different languages the greater part of the authorities which the best libraries had collected on his subject, but obtained permission from various governments to look into their private archives and state papers. He spent months over illegible, unpublished correspondences, and at one time he employed one secretary in London and kept two more busy at the Hague, while he himself was at work in Brussels. Many would have been appalled at the overwhelming mass of material thus brought to light, but Motley showed his judgment and critical faculty in the wise selection of what he most needed. Throughout all his work we find a broad grasp of the most important features of the subject, and the relation between the social and political conditions of a nation and its life at a given period is clearly brought out.

* Preface to *The Rise of the Dutch Republic*.

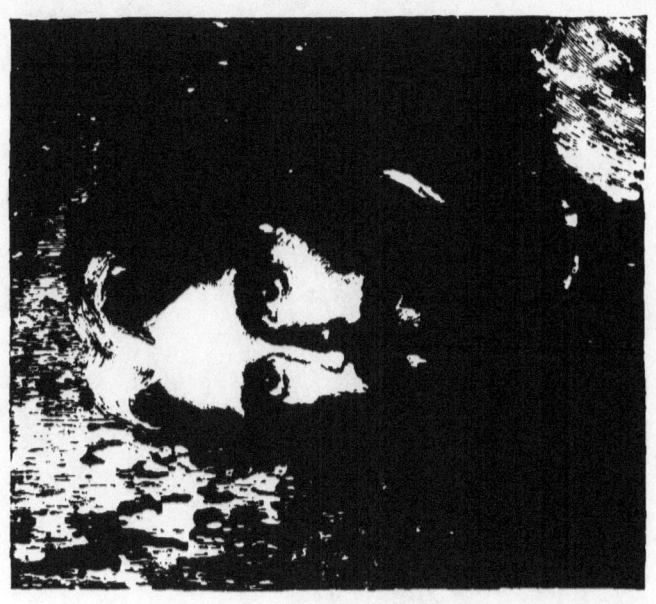

JOHN LOTHROP MOTLEY

FRANCIS PARKMAN

Motley's style, which suggests that of Carlyle, is notably vigorous and brilliant, and certain passages are filled with sarcastic humor. Prescott excelled in the orderly movement of his narrative, but Motley possessed a dramatic instinct which enabled him to seize upon some revealing situation and bring it vividly before us. This same dramatic power shows itself also in his delineation of character; certain figures stand out with life-like distinctness, and we can almost imagine ourselves alongside of those men and women of the past in whose company, Motley himself wrote, he was spending all his days.* When *The Rise of the Dutch Republic* was published in 1856, it was enthusiastically received, not only in his own country, but in England and on the Continent, where it was translated into three languages. *The United Netherlands* still further increased the reputation which Motley had gained by his first history, and it is indeed to be regretted that he should not have lived to complete the last of the great series he had planned.

If we have found that for various reasons the works of these three great historians are of especial interest to Americans, the subject chosen by FRANCIS PARKMAN (1823–1893), the last historian of this group, is no less deserving of their earnest attention; and the successful manner in which he has treated it has placed him in the front rank of our prose writers. Parkman seems to have definitely decided upon his life-work while still a student, for he determined then to devote himself

Francis Parkman.

* Holmes's *Memoir of Motley*, p. 69.

to the writing of history. Like Motley, he planned a
great series which was to be united by one central
idea. In Parkman's case this theme was the conflict
between England and France for the possession of the
New World. He realized how much depended upon
the result of this momentous struggle; that the whole
character of America's civilization was at stake at this
critical period of her career. Filled with the enthusiasm of a great purpose, Parkman determined not
only to make himself familiar with state papers and
published authorities, but to live for a time among
the Indians and make a study from life of their character and savage customs. In 1846 he went out west
to the Black Hills of Dakota, and, joining a tribe of
Sioux, suffered the hardships and privations of a wild
life, for which he was physically unfitted.* He
returned with invaluable material and a personal
knowledge of the Indian which was of immense service
to him in his work; but his health had become seriously impaired, and besides this drawback he had, like
Prescott, to contend with partial blindness. When
the difficulties under which these two men labored are
taken into account we cannot but be impressed with
their wonderful courage and perseverance, and look
with increased admiration on their masterly productions. Parkman was a conscientious workman, and
his style, while perhaps a trifle highly colored and
ornate, is picturesque and full of descriptive power.
The following titles of his principal works in their

* In *The Oregon Trail* (1847) we find thrilling accounts of
these Western adventures.

historical sequence will indicate more definitely the scope of his undertaking: *Pioneers of France in the New World; The Jesuits in North America; La Salle, or the Discovery of the Great West; The Old Régime in Canada; Count Frontenac, or New France under Louis XIV.; A Half-Century of Conflict; Montcalm and Wolfe; The Conspiracy of Pontiac and the Indian War after the Conquest of Canada.*

The later history of our country seems often lacking in romance; but the period of which Parkman treats is touched with the glamour of chivalry, which stands out in sharp contrast against the broad background of the wilderness and the wild passions of aboriginal life.

The kindred arts of oratory and literature stand in a somewhat peculiar relation. The power of the orator and the power of the writer are similar but distinct. The great speaker, **The Orators.** holding his hearers, perhaps, by some quality of voice or some indefinable compulsion of manner, may say nothing which will stand the test of being read as literature; the great writer, on the other hand, able to stir the hearts of thousands by his printed words, if brought face to face with an audience may be incapable of holding the attention of a single hearer. But while the arts of oratory and of literary composition are thus distinct, many great orations outlast the occasion which produced them, and, even though no longer enhanced by the personal spell of the speaker, possess, independently of it, a durable quality which places them among the masterpieces of literature.

During her years of intellectual leadership New England led the country in oratory also, and the work of her succession of great orators belongs, at least in part, to literature. We have said that in the Revolutionary period and during the early days of the Republic the supremacy in oratory lay with the South. But as the present century advanced and the country passed into the shadow of those anxious years when slavery threatened the very existence of the Union, it was New England that gave America, in DANIEL WEBSTER (1782–1852), her greatest orator. It was New England also that gave us Edward Everett (1794–1865), the master of a finished and scholarly eloquence; Wendell Phillips (1811–1884), and Charles Sumner (1811–1874), the orators of the Abolitionists. It only increases our admiration for the part that New England oratory played at this critical stage of our national history, to remember that Webster had formidable antagonists in John C. Calhoun and other orators of the South. Through Webster, New England forced home to the conscience of the nation the conviction that at all sacrifices the Union must be preserved. This conviction was the central note of Webster's career. He did not exaggerate when he said in the most celebrated of his political speeches, the *Reply to Hayne:* "I profess, sir, in my career hitherto, to have kept steadily in view the prosperity of the whole country and the preservation of our Federal Union. It is to that Union we owe our safety at home and our consideration and dignity

Daniel Webster.

abroad. It is to that Union that we are chiefly indebted for whatever makes us most proud of our country.'' The effect of such words went far beyond the walls of the Senate; they even went beyond the generation to which Webster belonged. Such famous passages, included in countless schoolbooks, read and declaimed throughout the country by thousands of schoolboys, had an inestimable influence in moulding the opinions and determining the future actions of those that came after,—those whose part it was to maintain the Union when imperilled by the Civil War. Beginning life as a farmer's boy in New Hampshire, Webster's tremendous personal and intellectual force, joined to his phenomenal abilities as an orator, pushed him rapidly to the front. For thirty years he '' stood at the head of the bar and of the Senate, the first lawyer and the first statesman of the United States.'' *
He has been dead for nearly half a century, yet the personal power that was a part of the man has not ceased to impress us. Even Carlyle, the devout admirer of sheer strength in a man, felt this nameless force in Webster, and, in spite of a predisposition against anything American, has left his tribute to him on record. '' As a logic fencer, advocate, or parliamentary Hercules,'' he writes, '' one would incline to back him at first sight against all the extant world.'' And after describing the '' amorphous crag-like face,'' and the '' black eyes under those precipices of eyebrows,'' he concludes: '' I have not traced as much of

* Lodge's *Life of Webster.* American Statesmen Series, p. 347.

silent Berserker-rage, that I remember of, in any other man." *   Webster's speeches are more than triumphs of oratory.   For us of a later generation the eloquence of his great southern contemporary Henry Clay (1777–1852), like that of Patrick Henry, is little more than a tradition; but the masterpieces of Webster, with their strength of thought, their marvellous keenness and clearness of argument, their command of language, and their strains of a sonorous and splendid rhetoric, have passed into our literature.   Everett had the grace of a more perfect culture, Phillips and George William Curtis were noble and ardent speakers, but we can still feel the half-latent and almost incomparable personal force that lay behind Webster's words; the strength of an intellectual giant, so abundant that it seems never fully put forth.   One other

Webster and Lincoln. and yet greater man, Abraham Lincoln, impresses us with this overwhelming sense of restrained power.   We feel it back of his compact and strongly-built sentences, which, free from all affectations of rhetoric, and unimpeded by a superfluous word, go straight to the mark, and find their place in the heart and conscience of the nation.

As we look back upon the work of these great orators of New England as a whole, from Webster to Sumner and Phillips, as we recall its sterling quality and its incalculable effects upon our national history, we see that it was by no means the least important

* *Carlyle-and-Emerson Correspondence.*   Edited by C. E. Norton, vol. i. p. 247.   Carlyle also refers to Webster in the same volume, p. 19.

part of New England's service to the country at large.
To all that the Puritan gave us we add this also. We
appreciate that in those years of her full strength
New England not only wrote our greatest poetry, our
best histories, and our keenest political satire; that
she not only charmed us with her humor, and led the
way in scholarship, but that, beside all this, she gave
us men who, in a time of national uncertainty and
peril, could lead opinions and control events by their
genius for speech.

GENERAL SURVEY OF THE LITERATURE OF THE NEW ENGLAND GROUP

Before finally taking leave of these New England
writers, and passing to their contemporaries in the
Southern and Middle States, it seems desirable to
emphasize some of the thoughts suggested by their
work as a whole.

The supremacy of New England as a literary center
extended approximately from 1836 to 1870 or 1880.
It is true that some of the greatest writers of the
group entered the field before 1836, and that a number died between 1882 and 1892; it is true, further-
more, that Holmes, the last summoned, lingered until
so late as 1895; nevertheless the dates above given
fairly indicate the period when New England was the
center of our best literary activity.

In the second place we observe that this supremacy
of New England is more strictly the supremacy of
Massachusetts. It is Massachusetts which produced
almost all the eminent writers of the period, and in

Massachusetts, the great strongholds of the literature, Boston, Cambridge, and Concord, lie but a few miles apart. Longfellow, the son of Maine, is indeed a conspicuous exception; but even Longfellow is identified with Cambridge rather than with his native place. In reflecting upon this striking fact we cannot fail to be impressed with the important influence that the concentration of learning and culture at certain points exercises upon literary production. The success of the writer is largely dependent upon favorable conditions; ordinarily he needs the stimulus that comes from association with men of kindred tastes and ability; he is helped by a nearness to the great publishing-houses and magazines, and by the whole stir and movement of the intellectual and social life around him.

Boston afforded such conditions; Cambridge, emphatically a university town, brought together a chosen company of scholars; while Concord, not too distant from this center to make intercourse difficult, gave to the more shy and solitary spirits the charms of natural beauty and historic association.

In the third place we notice that this New England literature is not only produced almost entirely within the limits of a small district of the oldest of the New England Colonies, but that it is largely the work of those who represent by descent and inheritance the early Puritan settlers. The leaders in letters, Emerson, Longfellow, Hawthorne, Holmes, Lowell, and many more, are men who traced their descent to the early days of the Colony; men sprung from the old

Puritan stock, with the blood of generations of scholars in their veins. Whether we like it or not, the fact remains that in New England the oldest and so-called "best" families, the families of pure English stock, have given us our greatest men of letters.

And we may mark in the fourth place the lofty and stainless lives of these poets and scholars of New England. There was a time in the history of English literature when the great majority of writers lived in alternate poverty and excess; there was a time when the gift of poetic genius was associated with a career of reckless dissipation and a miserable death; but in their purity, self-culture, and nobility these American men of letters set an example to the world. They have been excelled in the greatness of their genius, but no group of writers in the whole history of literature has surpassed them in the greatness and beauty of their lives. We Americans may think with just pride of Emerson's lofty serenity of spirit, of Lowell's well-balanced nature and sterling manhood, and of Longfellow, the gentle, loving scholar, wearing through all the allotted term of years "the white flower of a blameless life." As we regard the great writers of New England on this personal side, we see that the incorruptible Puritan stock from which they came was calculated to produce not merely men of powerful intellect, but men of marked uprightness and nobility of character.

Nor can we fail to notice that in these New England writers the angularity and roughness of the Puritan character have been smoothed and softened by the grace and loveliness of foreign civilizations. The New Englanders of the earlier time were provincials, fenced off not only by their creed but by their condition from any direct knowledge of the world beyond the seas. But in the generation to which Emerson belonged we find a sudden change, the effects of which are immediate and far-reaching. With hardly a single exception, the great New Englanders of Emerson's time visited Europe, and the subtle influence of Europe is visibly at work in them, moulding their character, and coloring their thought, their writings, and their lives. Something has been said as to the effect of this direct contact with Europe on the writers of the Middle States. What has been said of the deep impress left on Irving by foreign travel applies with equal or perhaps even greater force to the men of New England. The old days of Colonial isolation were over; throughout all this period the increase in wealth and leisure, the growing delight in foreign scenes, and the astonishing improvements in the facilities for ocean travel were steadily bringing the New World into closer and more familiar relations with the Old. In itself this was enough to make a new era in our literature. No wonder that, in conjunction with many other causes, it made an era in the literature of New England. Think for a moment of some of its direct results. To cite only a few examples, it gave us Longfellow's *Outre-Mer* and *Hyperion*, as well as a large number of his poems; Lowell's *Cathedral*, Emerson's *English Traits*, Hawthorne's *Our Old Home*, and Holmes's *Our Hundred Days in Europe*.

In fiction it furnished inspiration and background for *The Marble Faun*, and in history it unlocked to Motley the stores of fresh material, and made the scenes of his narratives real and familiar to his mind.

But even beyond this direct effect of European travel upon our literature there lies its pervading and even more important influence on the lives and thoughts of the writers themselves. It goes deeper than that direct effect apparent in any particular works. Longfellow, Lowell, and Hawthorne were different men because they knew Europe. Its life had entered into theirs; they had grown by it, and it naturally became a part of the influence which they exerted on our cruder social and intellectual life.

Finally, we must remember that this literature of New England is, above all, the characteristic expression of that particular locality which produced it. It is neither national nor foreign in its essential spirit; it is New England. Much of it is as essentially distinct from the literature of the other sections of our country as the literature of Scotland is from that of England; and whatever it may have received from Europe, it remains Puritan at heart. To understand it, we must strive to enter into the spirit and traditions of New England, realizing at the same time that all the writings produced within this great section form but a chapter in the many-sided development of American literature as a whole.

ADDITIONAL STUDY LISTS AND REFERENCES FOR NEW ENGLAND WRITERS.

Lowell. 1. *Poems.* "The Vision of Sir Launfal" (compare Tennyson's treatment of the same subject in the "Holy Grail "), "Commemoration Ode," "An Incident in a Railroad Car," "Stanzas on Freedom," "The Present Crisis," "To the Dandelion," "In the Twilight," "The First Snowfall," "The Rose: A Ballad," "The Washers of the Shroud," "The Optimist," "On the Capture of Fugitive Slaves near Washington," "At the Commencement Dinner," "A Fable for Critics"; and the following from the *Biglow Papers:* "What Mr. Robinson Thinks," "The Pious Editor's Creed," "The Courtin'," "Sunthin in the Pastoral Line."

2. *Essays.* "On a Certain Condescension in Foreigners," "Shakespeare Once More."

These essays are suggested simply as being suitable for the purpose. Where all are so excellent, selection is extremely difficult.

3. *Biography and Criticism. Recollections and Appreciations of,* by Francis H. Underwood; *Letters,* edited by Charles Eliot Norton (2 vols.); Stedman's *Poets of America;* Haweis's *American Humorists;* Curtis's *Literary and Social Essays;* Henry James's *Essays in London;* "James Russell Lowell;" Whipple's *Outlooks on Society, Literature, and Politics;* "Lowell as a Prose Writer;" William Watson's *Excursion sin Criticism;* "Lowell as a Critic;" Barrett Wendell's *Stelligeri, and other Essays Concerning America;* "Mr. Lowell as a Teacher."

Holmes. 1. *Poems.* "Old Ironsides," "One-Hoss Shay," "The Chambered Nautilus," "Dorothy Q.," "Musa," "Treadmill Song," "The Last Leaf," "The Music Grinder," "La Grisette," "The Oysterman." (Compare Thackeray's ballad-form.)

(Much of Dr. Holmes's poetry is of the nature of *Vers de Société*, which has been well defined as "the expression of common sentiment and common feeling in graceful but familiar rhyme." Prior and other eighteenth-century poets were particularly successful in this kind of writing ; but its popularity has not been confined to any particular age. Among the modern writers, Mr. Frederick Locker-Lampson (died 1895) and Mr. Austin Dobson have probably been the most successful producers of this kind of verse. An interesting article on this subject is "English Fugitive Poets," by G. Barnett Smith, in *Poets and Novelists* (Appleton, 1876). See also *Lyra Elegantiarum*, edited by Mr. F. Locker-Lampson (1867).)

2. *The Breakfast Table Series.* Of these the *Autocrat* is the best. As the book is of a fragmentary character, a fair idea of it may be gotten from representative passages.

3. *Novels.* If any of the novels are read, *Elsie Venner* will probably best repay perusal.

4. *Biography and Criticism. Life*, by W. S. Kennedy, and by E. E. Brown ; *Life and Letters*, by John T. Morse, Jr. (2 vols.). Stedman's *Poets of America ;* Curtis's *Literary and Social Essays ;* Haweis's *American Humorists ;* Whipple's *Essays and Reviews*, vol. i.

Whittier. 1. *Narrative and Legendary Poems.* "Cassandra Southwick," "Barclay of Ury," "Skipper Ireson's Ride," "Telling the Bees," "Maud Muller."

2. *Poems Subjective and Reminiscent.* "The Barefoot Boy," "Snow-Bound" (compare this poem with Burns's "The Cotter's Saturday Night"), "In School Days."

3. *Religious Poems.* "The Eternal Goodness," "In Quest," "Trust."

4. *War-time Poems.* "Barbara Frietchie," "Laus Deo," "Massachusetts to Virginia."

5. *Personal Poems.* "Ichabod," "Burns."

6. *Biography and Criticism. Life and Letters*, by

Samuel T. Pickard (2 vols.); Stoddard's *Haunts and Homes of Our Elder Poets;* Stedman's *Poets of America;* Whipple's *Essays and Reviews*, vol. i.; Barrett Wendell's *Stelligeri*.

The Historians. (It is impossible to enjoy or appreciate our great historians merely by reading selections from their works. As soon as possible the student should make himself acquainted with each of these writers by a careful reading of at least one of his works. The following suggestions are made for his future guidance, but the list might profitably be increased:)

1. BANCROFT. (*a*) *History of the United States.*

(*b*) *Biography and Criticism. Century Magazine*, vol. ii. p. 473, article by Wm. M. Sloane; Griswold's *Prose Writers of American Literature.*

2. PRESCOTT. (*a*) *Conquest of Mexico ; Ferdinand and Isabella.*

(*b*) *Biography and Criticism.* Life of, by G. Ticknor ; Edward Everett's Oration on, in Everett's *Orations;* Essay on, in *Essays and Reviews*, vol. ii., by Whipple.

3. MOTLEY. (*a*) *Rise of the Dutch Republic.*

In addition to the works of Motley mentioned in the text, his unfinished *Life of John of Barneveld* is worthy of notice, both on account of Barneveld's connection with the period which Motley treats, and for the masterly way in which the character is presented.

(*b*) *Biography and Criticism.* Memoir of, by O. W. Holmes ; *The Correspondence of*, edited by George W. Curtis ; Article on, in *Recollections of Eminent Men*, by E. P. Whipple.

4. PARKMAN. (*a*) *Conspiracy of Pontiac.*

(*b*) *Biography and Criticism.* Griswold's *Prose Writers of America*, p. 679 ; *Authors at Home;* Personal and Biographical Sketches of American Writers, edited by J. S. and J. B. Gilder (1888).

5. **Webster.** (*a*) *Webster's Great Speeches and Orations,*

published by Little, Brown, & Co., Boston (1879); Works
of, in 6 vols., with biographical sketch by Edward Everett;
" Reply to Hayne," in *Orations and Arguments by English
and American Statesmen*, edited by Cornelius B. Bradley.

(b) *Biography and Criticism.* Life of, by George T.
Curtis; Life of, by Henry Cabot Lodge, in *American
Statesmen Series.* For his style, see Whipple's *American
Literature*, and Whipple's *Essays and Reviews*, vol. i.

Whittier's poem "Ichabod" is of interest, as it represents
the unfavorable view taken by the abolitionists of Webster's
later political course.

CHAPTER III

LITERATURE IN THE SOUTH

On the whole the literature of England is that of a Northern people. The early Continental surroundings of the English people in a bleak, rain-drenched, storm-swept region were conducive to earnestness and melancholy rather than to that simple joy of life natural to those who dwell under a fairer and more southern sky. In spite of many modifying foreign influences, the early race-traits of the English have maintained their place with a dogged persistency, and we still find that a subdued or sombre coloring, a deep seriousness, a masculine vigor, rather than a lightness and grace, continue to characterize much of their best work. But when the English settled Virginia, when they established themselves in the Carolinas and in Georgia, this ancient Northern race found itself transported into the midst of Southern conditions. In place of the duller skies of England, clouded with a soft haze or obscured by a curtain of fog, they were set down in an atmosphere of transparent brilliancy, in a land where the mighty woods were bright with gaily-plumaged birds, where the heavens spread above them a luminous dome of blue in which at night the

248

stars glittered with wonderful radiance. In New
England this same Anglo-Saxon race fought storm,
privation, and peril after the manner of their fathers;
they were still a people of the North. But another
branch of this English stock came under a softer
and less bracing atmosphere: they came into a mild
and luxuriant region, a land of rich fields of rice and
cotton, reaching down to semi-tropical Florida, with
its winding bayous, its glowing wealth of flowers, and
the Northern English literature came under the
gentler influences of the warm and passionate South.

It is only within a very recent period, in such story-
writers as Geo. W. Cable, Lafcadio Hearn, and Thos.
Nelson Page, that the effect of these new conditions
on literature has really become apparent, for until
after the close of the Civil War the independent
literary development of the Southern States was retarded by causes which have already been partially
explained. The provision for general education in
the South long continued painfully inadequate.
Among the upper classes, the languorous climate, the
possession of great estates crowded with slaves whose
constant attendance relieved their masters from the
necessity of making personal exertion—all these things,
working in an aristocratic and conservative society,
tended to foster among the more educated a life of
splendid ease. Slave-labor, the richness of the soil,
and the structure of Southern society, all tended to
make the South largely dependent on agriculture; so
while outside its limits new industries were springing
up, the South, holding tenaciously to old ways, fell

farther and farther behind the other sections of the country in the rapid march of national prosperity. As manufacturing and commerce shot ahead in the Northern and Middle States, as the young West flung all its magnificent and impetuous energy into the utilization of its superb resources, the South, entrenched in its traditions and its chivalry, self-centered in its semi-feudal and Old-World picturesqueness, was left an anomaly in the midst of the eager life of an enterprising, money-making republic.

Such conditions told heavily in many ways against literary production. From the first, literature had suffered from the lack of town life. "Jamestown had perished, Williamsburg never grew, Richmond did not attain much size until long after Northern cities had become centers of books and intelligence." * During the present century, while Charleston, Richmond, and New Orleans were locally important and influential, the agricultural South had no such centers of literary activity as Philadelphia, Boston, and New York, successively the strongholds of literature and culture. Moreover, in a society where there was no adequate system of popular education, and where class feeling was strong, one who belonged to the masses had little chance to excel in literature, while one who belonged to the classes was unlikely seriously to devote himself to it, or, even should he do so, was unlikely to succeed.

There was indeed no lack of intellectual ability

* *Pioneers of Southern Literature* : " A Glance at the Field," by S. A. Link, p. 11.

inherent in the South, as her early records in law, statesmanship, and oratory abundantly prove; but the best powers of her leading minds were not put forth in a literary direction. A gentleman of the landed or aristocratic classes was apt to regard literature as a graceful accomplishment rather than as a serious and exacting profession. Thus one writer tells us that in Charleston literature was often thought of "as the choice recreation of gentlemen, as something fair and good, to be courted in a dainty, amateur fashion, and illustrated by *apropos* quotations from Lucretius, Virgil, or Horace."* Another Southern writer declares in a similar strain that "literature stood no chance because the ambition of young men of the South was universally turned in the direction of political distinction, and because the monopoly of advancement held by the profession of the law was too well established and too clearly recognized to admit of its claim being contested."†

Another potent cause was doubtless the dearth of influential publishing-houses. Poe, the greatest genius the South has given to literature, was driven to depend largely upon Northern publishers and Northern magazines for his support, and even the Southern writers who have risen into prominence during very recent years have almost invariably done so through the medium of the great publishing-houses and magazines of the North. The primary

* Paul Hamilton Hayne, quoted in W. P. Trent's *Life of Simms.*

† *The Old South,* by Thomas Nelson Page, p. 67.

causes of this unfortunate condition were probably the lack of general culture and literary appreciation in the South. Publishers, magazines, and authors are alike dependent for their support upon the readers and buyers of books, and when culture is the monopoly of the few, the conditions are all unfavorable to literary production.

If this absence of the diffusion of education lay at the root of the trouble, another radical drawback seems to have been the conservative spirit and behind-the-age tastes among the cultivated few. Many a Southern library contained but little later than the English classics of the earlier eighteenth century, and Pope in poetry and Addison in prose were accepted as the standards of correctness and elegance. We cannot but contrast this with the New England of Channing and Emerson, agitated by the latest wave of German thought, and quickly responsive to the fervor of Coleridge or Carlyle. So, comparatively cut off from the fresh current of ideas abroad, isolated by its peculiar social system and ideals from the rest of the country, yet prone to disregard or discourage an independent literary expression, the South, before the war, was heavily handicapped.

It is but just to the South to understand clearly the disadvantages under which it labored, for when the facts are understood, instead of asking why its contribution to literature was not more important, we are surprised at the amount it accomplished. Our tendency is to slight the work of this great section, and give to that of the Northern writers a somewhat undue prominence. A more impartial survey shows us that the warm, imaginative Southern nature, sympathetic, beauty-loving, romantic, has made notable additions to our literature in the past, and that it is likely to prove a yet more important element in our national literature in the future.

Two characteristics of the Southern literature of this century are precisely what the social conditions just described would lead us to expect. In the first place, a large proportion of the **The Writers.** best writing, especially during the earlier part of the period, is produced by men who are not professional men of letters, but whose chief energies are spent in other fields. Thus JOHN MARSHALL, whose *Life of Washington* (1804–1807) has been called " the first great contribution to American historical literature," * was one of our greatest jurists and the Chief Justice of the United States. WILLIAM WIRT, favorably known by his *Life of Patrick Henry* and *Letters of a British Spy*, was long a lawyer in active practice, and Attorney-General under Monroe and Adams. EDWARD COATE PINKNEY (1802–1828), some of whose slight and sentimental songs echo the lyrics of the English cavalier poets of the seventeenth century, was also a lawyer, and this list of those whose powers were thus diverted from literature might be greatly enlarged.

In the second place we are impressed with the fact that there are no groups or schools of writers such as

---

* Cooke's *History of Virginia*, American Commonwealths Series, p. 490.

we find gathered about a common center in Boston or New York. Men of talent and of literary tastes and ambition appear in South Carolina, Virginia, Georgia, and Louisiana, too often to fight almost single-handed the unequal battle against poverty, indifference, or neglect. It is consequently difficult to gain any comprehensive idea of Southern literature, as its history is so largely a record of comparatively isolated careers.

Prominent among the early Southern writers of the century is JOHN PENDLETON KENNEDY (1795–1870), a native of Baltimore. His three novels, *Swallow Barn, a Story of Rural Life in Virginia* (1832); *Horse Shoe Robinson, a Tale of the Tory Ascendency* (1835); and *Rob of the Bowl* (1838), present to us a vivid and pleasing picture of some characteristic aspects of Southern life. Kennedy is another example of the prevailing tendency to subordinate literature to other interests, for, like so many of his literary contemporaries, he led the active life of a lawyer and statesman

J. P. Kennedy.

Another novelist, WILLIAM GILMORE SIMMS (1806–1870), stands apart from the men to whom the writing of books was but a side issue, as the first Southern writer of distinction to follow literature as a profession. This circumstance, involving as it did a long and gallant struggle with adverse conditions, gives him an important place, aside from the intrinsic value of his writings, as the pioneer among the Southern men of letters. Simms was a man of fine physique and vigorous personality, his character was noble and impetu-

William Gilmore Simms.

ous; he had an instinctive delight in the active and
adventurous side of life, and described it in many a
stirring romance with a true sympathetic power. He
was born in Charleston, and became in after years an
important influence in its intellectual and literary life.
Simms's life began in struggle and uncertainty, for
his father had become financially involved, and moved
from place to place in the effort to repair his broken
fortunes. The boy's early opportunities for education
were scanty. He never went to college, but from the
first he was an ardent reader. At eight years of age
his lifelong passion for writing had already declared
itself. As a youth, he was a druggist's apprentice;
then he studied law, and was admitted to the bar in
1827. But before this he had published two volumes
of youthful verse, and an irresistible inclination urged
him towards literature. After several other ventures
in verse Simms published *Martin Faber*, 1833, the first
of that long succession of romances of adventure on
which his chief claim to be remembered rests. The
best of these stories deal with the Colonial life of the
South, or with that life during the succeeding period
of the Revolution. While far from being a finished
writer, Simms had great qualifications for such a
task, an enthusiastic love for his State and a close
acquaintance with its scenery, a pride in the history
of his section, and an intimate knowledge of its past.
Behind all this lay the genuine narrative power and
vigorous spirit of the man.

Simms is distinctly inferior to Cooper, with whom
he inevitably suggests comparison; yet his best stories

form a kind of companion study to Cooper's work, depicting as they do the same period of our national growth under Southern instead of under Northern or Western conditions. In his portrayal of the Indian character Simms is probably more truthful than Cooper, whose Indian heroes, if more romantic, are, it is to be feared, more ideal. Among Simms's many books, *The Yemassee* (1835), which deals with an Indian outbreak in Colonial South Carolina, and *The Partisan* (1835), a story of the Revolution and the exploits of Marion and his band, may be mentioned as good examples of his powers. Charleston may be thought of as the nearest approach the South had to a literary center in Simms's time, yet Charleston was slow to recognize him, and he was often forced to look to the North for help and encouragement. Many of his works were published in New York, and once on returning from a trip to that city he declared bitterly that he was surprised to find the North so warm and the South so cold. But Simms was a man of generous, helpful temper, and, although nearly ruined by the Civil War, he did all in his power for the younger literary men who were trying to force their way to the front.

Among them were the poets PAUL HAMILTON HAYNE (1830–1886) and HENRY TIMROD (1829–1867), both of whom were natives of Charleston and members of this Charleston group. Unlike Simms, Hayne was a college graduate, the heir to a moderate fortune, and the inheritor of an ancient name. He became a contributor to several

Hayne and Timrod.

Southern magazines, but like so many of his contemporaries, he entrusted his first volume to a Northern publishing-house (Poems: Ticknor & Fields; Boston, 1855). He had studied law in his youth, but he gave a lifetime of single-minded effort to his art. His poetry is melodious, graceful, and carefully wrought, but while not precisely imitative, it is often close in form and manner to certain English models. Like Keats and William Morris, he is touched by the beauty of the classic and romantic ideals, and his narrative poems have an undeniable smoothness and charm. He also excelled as a sonneteer.

The memory of his lifelong friend Henry Timrod is closely associated with Hayne. The two poets were schoolfellows in Charleston, and in their early youth they frequently attended the literary reunions at the hospitable home of Simms. Timrod died at thirty-eight, and left but a slender volume of verse behind him. Hayne far surpassed him in range as well as in the amount of his poetic production. Nevertheless there is in Timrod a more distinctly Southern atmosphere and a stronger note of personality. We are inclined to associate Hayne with that amiable English poet Leigh Hunt; but Timrod has an originality which makes him the precursor of the Southern genius, Sidney Lanier. Thus *The Cotton Boll*, with its vista of the wide expanse of snowy cotton-fields bathed in the dazzling sunlight, and its defiant note of challenge to the North, is both suggestive of Lanier and distinctly the product of the South. In many of Timrod's poems we are delighted with descriptions of nature that betray a close observation and genuine sympathy; indeed all of Timrod's work has this genuine quality. There is nothing bookish or second-hand about it; it speaks rather of a fresh and independent grasp of life.

In reviewing the work of this little group of Charleston writers we must remember that, in common with other Southern writers, their prospects were blighted and their free development checked by the desperate struggle of the Civil War. At the outbreak of this desolating contest Charleston was just beginning to be, in a lesser degree, the Boston of the South. The number of ambitious periodicals started within its borders between 1828 (*The Southern Review*) and 1842 (*Southern Quarterly*) bears witness to the literary aspirations of at least some of its leaders, even if the short life of most of these enterprises points with equal certainty to the lack of a reading public. But when Simms had led the way and by his gallant fight made literature more possible as a profession for those who came after, the very life of the South was absorbed in the four tragic years of war. While the war furnished a theme to many a Southern poet; while Hayne, Timrod, and many others sang their songs of battle with an intense conviction of the righteousness of their cause, rivalling that of Whittier or Lowell in the North,—the Civil War was, on the whole, a heavy blow to the rising Southern literature. In the midst of that life-and-death struggle, with the Northern arms on their soil, men had neither time nor money for the patronage of literature, nor the desire to turn aside from the one issue which claimed them. And to many a promising Southern writer the war brought little short of financial ruin. It reduced Simms, who was living in affluence, to the bitter necessity of toiling at hack-work for a bare living; it swept away Hayne's fortune and forced him to depend upon his own exertions; it brought Timrod to the verge of actual starvation, involving him in difficulties from which he was released only by death. When we think of the odds against which these Southern writers contended, and then recall all those favoring circumstances in which the genius of Longfellow and many another member of the New England group was enabled to reach its full development, we cannot but wonder what the South might have accomplished for our literature under equally advantageous conditions.

Apart from this little coterie of Charleston writers were the Virginia novelists JOHN ESTEN COOKE (1830–1886) and MARY VIRGINIA TERHUNE (1837–), better known under her pseudonym of Marion Harland. Cooke portrayed the stately and aristocratic life in old Virginia, essaying to do for his native State what Simms had accomplished for South Carolina, Hawthorne for Colonial New England, or Irving for Knickerbocker New York. Some of his later romances, such as *The Wearing of the Gray*, deal with the Civil War, in which Cooke himself took part. He also wrote some biographies and an excellent history of Virginia. *The Virginia Comedians* (1854), which has been pronounced "the best novel produced in the South before the war," * gives

Virginia.

* This is the verdict of both Prof. Richardson and Prof.

an interesting picture of the courtly society at Williamsburg, the old capital, under the ancient régime. The book, however, belongs to an era in novel-writing that has passed away, and to the modern taste the style is high-flown and extravagant, while the humor often seems to come dangerously near to the absurd. Marion Harland, who, though born in Virginia, has spent a great part of her life in the North, has also depicted Southern life. Her books, which are quieter and more finished in tone than those of Cooke, gained a well-deserved popularity.

Besides the writers which Virginia has given to literature, she has the distinction of having produced and sustained the *Southern Literary Messenger* (Richmond, 1835–1864), the best-known literary magazine of the South. Compared with our leading periodicals of to-day it impresses us as amateurish and provincial, yet it was of inestimable advantage to many a rising Southern writer, and an important factor in literary development. As Thomas Nelson Page, one of the best of the recent writers of Virginia, remarks, "It had much to do with sustaining the unstable Poe, and with developing nearly all those writers of the South whose names have survived." *

Georgia, although deficient in large towns, and without a literary center, has made most important additions to the literature of the South. It has

Beers. Thomas Nelson Page, on the other hand, expre ses a preference for the later novels.

* "Authorship in the South Before the War," in *The Old South.*

enriched our literature of humor with the graphic *Georgia Scenes* of A. B. LONGSTREET, and, in our day, with the restful fun and shrewd wisdom of JOEL CHANDLER HARRIS.   To Georgia we owe another recent writer, RICHARD MALCOLM JOHNSTON, whose short stories are widely and favorably known.   In poetry it has given us Dr. FRANK O. TICKNOR (1822–1874) and SIDNEY LANIER (1842–1881), the latter, in the opinion of many, the greatest literary genius the South has yet produced.   Dr. Ticknor lived the self-sacrificing life of a kindly, hard-worked physician, but in the scant leisure which the duties of his profession allowed him he wrote some poems—less known than they should be—which deserve to live. One of these, *Little Giffen*, which commemorates one of the otherwise unknown heroes of the war, has a concentrated force and directness which make it not unworthy of comparison with some of Browning's shorter narrative poems.   Lanier's work is of so great importance as to demand a separate mention.

In Louisiana, literature has been notably influenced by the large French element in the population, and so pronounced is this influence that some of its most important contributions to literature have been written in French.   But in more recent years, Louisiana, with Indiana and Kentucky, has helped onward the rising literature of the far South.

From this general survey of the place of the Southern States in the making of our national literature we must pass to a fuller consideration of two leading writers, Edgar Allan Poe and Sidney Lanier.

STUDY LIST
SOUTHERN LITERATURE

1. Songs of the South, edited by J. T. Clarke, with an introduction by Joel Chandler Harris (Lippincott, 1895), contains a selection from Southern poets from Colonial times to the present day. *War Poetry of the South*, edited by Wm. Gilmore Simms (New York, 1867).

2. Southern Literature, by Louise Manly (Richmond, 1895), contains a pretty full collection of Southern writers, with brief biographies, and short extracts from their works ; but it gives little or no idea of the historical development of Southern literature, or of the conditions under which it has been produced. *The Old South*, by Thomas Nelson Page, contains an article on Authorship in the South before the war, and is valuable in general for a study of Southern conditions from a Southern point of view.

Dr. Frank O. Ticknor, Henry Timrod, and Paul Hamilton Hayne, by Samuel A. Link, in the little series of studies entitled *Pioneers of Southern Literature*.

There is also another series by Wm. Malone Baskervill, entitled *Southern Writers*.

For reference to Virginia in particular, consult Cooke's *Virginia* in the American Commonwealths Series. See also "English Culture in Virginia," by W. P. Trent (Johns Hopkins University Studies, vol. vii. p. 198).

EDGAR ALLAN POE (1809-1849)

Probably no writer in the history of our literature has been the subject of such active controversy as Edgar Allan Poe. As a man he has had bitter assailants and indignant defenders; he has alternately been loaded by his defamers with unmeasured abuse, and presented to us by his generous advocates as one driven to his ruin by "unmerciful disaster"; an

EDGAR ALLAN POE

unhappy genius, worthy of our pity and our tears. As
a poet his place has been almost equally a matter of
dispute. Some critics of eminence have placed him
in the first rank among the poets of America, while
others, impressed by the narrowness of his range and
his lack of a broad basis of thought and emotion, have
considered him as a clever craftsman, chiefly remarkable for his skill in the employment of certain metrical
and melodic effects. Other writers, again, contend
that the true view is to be found in some middle
region between these extremes. In all this confusion one thing at least is certain—Poe is one of the
few American writers who somehow have succeeded
in arresting and holding the attention of the world of
letters. At least one of his productions, *The Raven*,
is among the most widely known short poems in the
language; his short stories have been enthusiastically
received, especially in France; and whatever we may
think of his character, his aims, or his work, Poe is
one of the men about whom the student of literature
is bound to have an opinion.

Only the main facts in the story of Poe's unregulated and unhappy life need be given here. We have
said that the poets of the New England group were
remarkable for the nobility and purity of their lives.
From first to last they impress us with a steadfast-
ness and strength of purpose which springs from a
solid basis of manhood; when sorrow overtakes them
they meet it with fortitude, and they are secure in
the power of self-control. From whatever cause,
Poe's life and character, when placed beside that of

Longfellow or of Lowell, stand out in sharp and tragic contrast. Among our American men of letters Poe is peculiarly representative of that unfortunate class of men of genius which in England includes Marlowe, Burns, and Byron; men whose just balance was destroyed, and whose lives were wrecked at last by the association, with their great gifts, of ungoverned emotions, weakness of will, and a morbid outlook on the world. We need not take it upon ourselves either to blame or to excuse; we are simply called upon to realize the facts of Poe's life so far as they help us to appreciate the tone and spirit of his work.

Poe's place in our literature is one of peculiar isolation. Of Northern birth but of Southern ancestry, he belongs by common consent among the writers of the South; yet his writings, unlike those of Simms, Timrod, and their associates, have no distinctively Southern background. He is not bound to any one section, but wanders in his unsettled and struggling career from city to city, trying his fortune with equal ill success in Boston, Richmond, Baltimore, Philadelphia, and New York. Unlike Irving, Emerson, or Longfellow, he belongs to no literary movement or coterie: distantly resembling Hawthorne in his prose tales, his deepest ties are with trans-Atlantic writers; in his own country he stands essentially alone.

Poe's life.
Poe came of an old and honorable Maryland family. His father, David Poe, married an actress, and himself went on the stage. Their profession took them to Boston, and there Edgar Allan Poe, the second of

three children, was born on the 19th of January, 1809. Two years later the death of both parents within a year left the children, the eldest only five years old, wholly unprovided for. Poe's mother had died in Richmond, and the child was charitably received into the family of his godfather, Mr. John Allan, a wealthy merchant of that city, who treated him with kindness, and, as he grew up, made liberal provision for his education.

The Allans spent some time in England, placing Poe in a school near London, and on their return to Richmond he entered the University of Virginia (1826). So far, it must be admitted, Poe's opportunities had been far greater than his early misfortunes would have led us to expect; but at college, while he distinguished himself as a scholar, he developed an unfortunate propensity for gambling, involving himself in debts which Mr. Allan finally refused to pay. His benefactor accordingly took him from college and put him into business in Richmond. But the drudgery of the counting-house was repugnant to Poe's tastes; he was doubtless impatient of control, and he forfeited his opportunity a second time by running away to Boston and enlisting in the regular army, where he served with some credit for two years.

Soon after his arrival in Boston he had taken the first step in his literary career by the publication of a small book of verse, *Tamerlaine and Other Poems* (1827). This was followed two years later by a second venture, *Al Araaf Tamerlaine, and Minor Poems* (1829). At this time English poetry had just

passed through a fervid period of romance and sentiment, and these early poems of Poe's show that he
was affected by the prevailing spell of Byron and
Moore. As Mr. Stedman says: "Poe, growing up
under the full romantic stress at the end of the
Georgian period, . . . inevitably copied the manner
and structure of poems he must have known by
heart."* Moreover, one of Poe's morbid temperament, with an unwholesome fondness for melancholy,
must have found something peculiarly attractive in
Byron's congenial gloom.

In 1829 Poe effected a partial reconciliation with
Mr. Allan, who again gave his aid by securing his
admission to West Point. This third opportunity
was also wilfully thrown away. Poe neglected, and
finally utterly disregarded, his military duties, and as
a result was court-martialled and dismissed in 1831.
Thus again thrown on his own resources, for he could
expect no further aid from Mr. Allan, Poe settled in
Baltimore, and, after one or two years of struggle,
entered upon the hard task of supporting himself by
his pen. His first literary success was his story of
the *MS. found in a Bottle*, which won him a prize of
one hundred dollars (1833). In the year following
Mr. Allan died, without making provision for his
former ward, so that Poe was left, as he said, "penni-
less, without a profession, and with very few friends."
Nevertheless in 1835 he married his cousin, Virginia
Clemm, a girl of thirteen. It is but just to say that

* Stedman and Woodberry's ed. of Poe, vol. x.; Introd.,
p. xx.

Poe was devotedly attached to his wife from first to last, and that she and her mother faithfully shared his poverty and disappointments, and were patient with his faults. Even at this time he yielded habitually to that passion for drink which was at last his ruin. He was in great destitution when through the influence of J. P. Kennedy he obtained employment on the *Southern Literary Messenger*, which had just been started. From this time he led an unsettled, hand-to-mouth existence. He was connected from time to time with various magazines, and he became widely known as poet, story-writer, critic, and editor. The illness of his wife, who died in 1847, drove Poe, if we accept his own account, to greater excesses. At all events his habits grew worse, and in addition to excessive drinking he became addicted to the use of opium. From these causes, and probably because his peculiarities of temperament made him difficult to get along with, Poe's engagements with the various magazines and periodicals with which he was successively connected were usually of short duration. With numerous opportunities, with friends disposed to advance his interests, with undoubted ability, and with great readiness as a writer, his poverty somehow kept pace with his growing reputation. Almost to the last he cherished great plans; if he worked irregularly, he yet worked hard and rapidly, and he has left his impress upon our poetry and our prose; yet his life, extenuate it as we may, is a melancholy record of weakness and error, from the dissipations of his college days to its awful close. In

1849, having become engaged to be married to a Mrs. Shelton, he came to Baltimore to bring Mrs. Clemm to the wedding. While there he was found overcome by drink or opium, and dangerously ill. He was taken to a hospital, and there a few days later he died.

Poe claims our attention as a critic, a poet, and a story-writer. His critical work, while sometimes acute and discriminating, especially when he deals with the technicalities of composition, is, on the whole, of passing rather than of lasting importance, and adds but little to his permanent reputation. He had not, as Lowell had, the breadth of view and the solid basis of scholarship which are such important elements in any enduring work of criticism. Lacking these great essentials, Poe was not free from a taint of petty jealousy, and at times he suffered his personal likes or dislikes to influence his critical judgments. A conspicuous example of this is found in his series of papers on *The Literati of New York*. On the other hand, he did good service, as in his recognition of the genius of Hawthorne, and if his work in this direction is not of the highest quality, he must be recognized as among the influential critics of his time.

Poe as a writer.

Poe's critical writings have already fallen into a comparatively subordinate place, and it is on his work as poet and romance-writer that our estimate of his genius must really rest. Judged by this, the best that he has given us, we cannot but acknowledge his very positive limitations. He is neither profound nor

As poet and romance-writer.

varied; he is powerless to uplift, to inspire, or to console. His fame rests, not on his ability to do many things, but on his power to do a few things almost incomparably well. The reasons for his success within certain positive limits are singularly definite and comprehensible, and we can enumerate the magic gifts which the fairy godmother of genius bestowed on him in his cradle.

He was endowed with that power of close analysis, of logical and consecutive thought, which we associate with a mathematical and keenly intellectual mind. While this is by no means his greatest gift, it shows itself unmistakably in one side of his life and work. It is seen in his power of deciphering cryptograms, and in the cleverness with which, as in *The Gold Bug*, he involves his readers in a tangle in order to delight them with his skill in unravelling it. The clearness of his reasoning powers is shown in his detective story, *The Mystery of Marie Roget*. He was able to foretell correctly the plot of Dickens's *Barnaby Rudge* after reading the first few chapters, and nearly half a century ago he could predict the present era of tall buildings in New York city. The same hard intellectual temper is shown in his interest in science, of which he made use in fiction somewhat as Jules Verne did in later years.

Poe was further endowed with great narrative power of a certain kind. He could tell a story rapidly and vividly, filling it with a marvellous reality and thrilling interest. One of the best examples of this side of Poe's genius is the minute and horrible story of adventure, *The Narrative of Arthur Gordon Pym.* In such stories Poe is the follower of that great master of realistic story-telling, Daniel Defoe.* But while possessing this kind of narrative power in a high degree, Poe used it sparingly, for in many of his best stories his primary object is not the unfolding of a plot, but the revelation of a mood or the production of a single effect. This ability to combine the incidents and accessories of a story so that they all work together to deepen a single impression upon the reader's mind and imagination was one of the greatest with which Poe was endowed. From this aspect the nature of his art may well be styled "pictorial," for in many of his best studies, both in poetry and in prose, he resembles a painter who subordinates everything to the production of one harmonious color tone.

With Poe, this tone or total effect is gradually produced by the introduction of a number of minute and highly suggestive descriptive details, each touch, directed to the same end, intensifying the effect of what has gone before, until the whole work is filled with the spirit or atmosphere which takes hold of us with an extraordinary and ever-increasing power. *The Fall of the House of Usher* is a good instance of Poe's success in this particular method of composition. The mood of passive grief which the story embodies is associated with and interpreted by melancholy images of neglect, decay, and death. Our appreciation of the mental condition of the unhappy master of the House is intensified by the sombre and mournful

* See Stoddard's ed. of Poe's Works ; Introd., vol. i. p. 11.

background to the story, ineffaceably imprinted on our imagination,—a doomed house, crumbling into ruin, with its vacant, staring windows; the whole structure an image of desolation set in the midst of a deserted and indescribably dreary landscape. The spectral trees about it, with their stark, white branches, the gray sedge, the black tarn,—all these insensibly combine to create that unity of effect which makes a landscape of Poe's as individual, after its own fashion, as a picture of Corot's. And as the command of neutral tints is shown in the subdued tone of this picture, so the command of color-effects is conspicuous in *The Masque of the Red Death*. There, each room in the prince's suite is ablaze with a color of its own: blue or purple, green or orange, white or blood-red, the light streams through the stained glass of the Gothic windows. This same pictorial quality reappears in certain of Poe's poems. We recognize it in *Ulalume*, with its autumnal fall of decay and death, " with its dank tarn of Auber," its mists, and its withered leaves; we recognize it in *The City in the Sea*, that disordered vision of a citadel of Death, whose " Babylon-like walls " are lit by no rays from heaven, but by a strange light from the "lurid sea."

Fine as such conceptions are, they are remotely suggestive of a theatrical striving after scenic effects; they seem to rise from an unwholesome imagination. Shadowy, fantastic, distorted, they make us feel that (to borrow Poe's own phrase) in the spell he casts over us there is—

> " Much of madness and more of sin,
>   And horror the soul of the plot." *

Yet, within the confines of the grotesque and terrible, Poe has few superiors. He rules over this sombre, miasmic, melancholy region, full of waste places, of ruins, and of stagnant waters, haunted by broken hopes and " leaden-eyed despairs."

In addition to Poe's pictorial power and closely associated with it is his mastery of one especial mood —the mood of a passionate and hopeless grief. Much of his best prose and poetry consists of studied and highly artistic variations on a single theme—sorrow for the death of a young and beautiful woman. *The Raven, Annabel Lee, Ulalume,* and *For Annie* are familiar examples of this in his poetry; *Ligeia, Berenice,* and *The Fall of the House of Usher* in his prose. The underlying theme is variously treated: it may take form as a simple lyrical expression of grief, as in *Annabel Lee,* or all the wonderful resources of Poe's pictorial art may be employed to enhance it, as in *The Fall of the House of Usher;* but in either case we can detect the fundamental similarity.

Finally, Poe was endowed with still another gift, —a gift of musical utterance, which gives to his verse a charm and melody of its own. Shallow in its thought, narrow in its range, almost devoid of true human sympathy, Poe's poetry has made a secure place for itself largely by an undefinable fascination that he somehow found in the lingering beauty of his

* Verses in *Legeia.*

musical utterance. Critics have pointed out that this especial haunting quality of Poe's verse is mainly due to his use of what are technically known as the refrain and the repetend, the first a familiar poetic device, the second not wholly unknown before Poe's time. The refrain is the recurrence at stated intervals of a particular word or phrase; the repetend, as employed by Poe, is the immediate repetition of a line in a slightly modified form. Stedman, who has given much attention to the subject, thinks that Poe was aided in his characteristic employment of these two metrical effects by certain passages in Mrs. Browning and in Coleridge. At all events there is an originality as well as beauty in Poe's use of these effects, and we feel that by his use of what had been done before he virtually created a new thing. Whatever the source of his music, Poe's verse has that unmistakable note of personality which is one of the marks of a true poet. It is no small matter to have added anything to the technique of English verse, and when we reflect upon the wild power of Poe's imagination, upon his lyrical and descriptive gifts and marked individuality of tone, we must assign him, in spite of all that we miss in him, a place among our poets which is both distinctive and secure.

Our final estimate of Poe's work as a whole will depend upon our view of the true function of the artist. He believed that the artist's highest work and mission was to give pleasure; he defined poetry as " the rhythmical creation of beauty," and declared that " unless incidentally " it had " no concern what-over with duty or with truth." He put forth all the resources of his genius: his intellectual subtility, his feeling for the weird, the sublime, and the grotesque, his sense of color, his sense of sound,—he manipulated all these as a skillful craftsman for the building of works of wonder and beauty. He probably did all that it was in him to do. If we are satisfied that he was right in his aims and in his theory of art, we can ask nothing more. But if we believe that the spiritual and moral are vital elements in the greatest art, if we think that conscience and truth and duty have their place in its temple, we are forced to conclude that the limitations of Poe's own nature, the painful inadequacy of the man himself, have left ineffaceable marks upon the quality and character of his work, and prevented it from reaching an excellence to which it might otherwise have attained.

STUDY LIST

POE

1. Poems. "The Raven," "The Bells," "The City in the Sea," "Ulalume," "Annabel Lee," "The Haunted Palace," "Eulalie."

2. Tales. "The Black Cat," "The Fall of the House of Usher," "The Gold Bug," "William Wilson," "Ligeia," "The Masque of the Red Death."

3. Biography and Criticism. The best life of Poe is the one by George E. Woodberry in the American Men of Letters Series. The edition of Poe's works edited by R. H. Stoddard contains a very good memoir by the editor. An edition, which will probably become the standard, has re-

cently been published under the editorship of G. E. Wood-
berry and E. C. Stedman.   It contains a Life of Poe and a
critical estimate of his work.   See also Stedman's *Poets of
America;* Andrew Lang's *Letters to Dead Authors;* and
Edmund Gosse's *Questions at Issue*—the article " Has
America produced a Poet ? "

SIDNEY LANIER

Without question, Poe's greatest successor in poetry
among the writers of the South is Sidney Lanier.   In
surveying the scattered and difficult beginnings of
Southern literature before the war, Poe's melancholy
figure stands as on a solitary eminence; in any general view of that literature during the years of civil
contest and the period immediately succeeding, Lanier
holds, at least in poetry, a correspondingly important
place.

In passing from the earlier to the later writer we
cannot but be impressed by the sharp contrast between
them in character, in life, in work, and in ideals of
art.   It is true that Lanier's life, like Poe's, was one
of struggle and hardship; but the obstacles which
confronted Lanier were not of his own making, and
his whole career is a manly warfare with adverse conditions, fought out with unfaltering will and unswerving purpose, until the very end.   Beset by difficulties,
he makes us feel that for a man of his strong and
courageous spirit the weakness of failure is impossible.

Sidney Lanier was born at Macon in 1842, in that
middle region of Georgia which has already given so

much to literature.   His father, Robert S. Lanier,
was a lawyer; his mother's ancestors were
Lanier's life.   honorably associated with the history of
Virginia, and by her thrift the family
lived plainly but comfortably.   The boy's two ruling
passions, music and literature, showed themselves in
his earliest years; he found his way to books with the
instinct of the born reader, but, as he himself tells us,
even before he could write legibly he could "play
passably well on several instruments."   At fourteen
he entered Oglethorpe College, a neighboring institu-
tion, then of no great importance.   A few weeks after
his graduation, after he had passed four years in what
he calls "the uncongenial atmosphere of a farcical
college," the country was on the edge of the Civil
War.   Already the "two figures of music and of
poetry" had taken their place in his heart, but in
1861, then a boy of nineteen, he enlisted as private
in the Macon Volunteers.   Throughout the entire
struggle he served bravely and faithfully; he bore
his part in the battles of Seven Pines, Drewry's Bluffs
in the seven days' conflict about Richmond, and in the
bloody battle of Malvern Hill; he was also on the
signal service, and detailed for duty as a mounted
scout.   Captured and imprisoned for five months, he
found himself at the close of the war without a profession, almost without money, and with his health
seriously impaired.   Yet through all and under all he
had kept unchanged his boyish devotion to the two
arts .of poetry and music.   Years of struggle lay
before him.   At one time he tried to support himself

by teaching; at another he was clerk in a hotel; for a
time, at his father's wish, he studied law.   In 1867
he published his first book, *Tiger Lilies*, in which he
records many of his experiences in the war and many
of his youthful hopes and aspirations.   In the same
year he married Miss Mary Day, entering upon a life
of happiness and sympathy the high influence of
which is hinted at in some of his most beautiful poems.
But, content at home, at the very outset of his literary
career he had to begin that long and depressing
struggle with disease which ended only with his death.
In 1868 he had a hemorrhage from the lungs, and his
work henceforth was done, with many intervals of
critical illness, with the fatal shadow hanging over
him.   Putting aside his father's offer to join him in
practicing law at Macon, he determined to devote
whatever time and health were left him to carrying
out the great purpose of his life.   Accordingly, in
1873, he settled in Baltimore, having obtained the
position of first flute in the Peabody Symphony
Orchestra.   From this time he remained "engaged
always in a threefold struggle—for health, for bread,
and for a literary career."   The odds against him
were heavy; he was comparatively unknown, but,
faithful to his ideals, he persisted in writing poetry as
he thought it should be, without regard to what the
public might like or demand.   After some disappointments, *Corn*, his first important poem, found a place
in *Lippincott's Magazine*, through the discrimination
of Mr. John Foster Kirk, at that time its editor.
The connection proved a fortunate one.   *The Sym-*

phony, *The Psalm of the West*, and other poems appeared in the same magazine, and in 1877 a collection of his verse was published by the Lippincotts.

Lanier had a deep conviction of the worth and high seriousness of the poet's art. He asserted that Poe " did not know enough," and felt that the fullest and most perfect art must rest on a solid basis of thought and knowledge. From the time of his settlement in Baltimore he had therefore set himself to a careful and extensive study of English literature, and the outcome of this study was first a number of lecture courses on literature at private schools and elsewhere, and finally an appointment as lecturer at Johns Hopkins University. Two books, *The Science of English Verse*, an exposition of his theory of the principles of versification, and *The English Novel*, are made up of lectures originally given in the course of his duties at the University. Besides his teaching and his music he had to rely upon a considerable amount of miscellaneous literary work in the hard " struggle for bread." He wrote a descriptive handbook of Florida in the interests of a railroad company, and towards the close of his life edited, for young readers, *Froissart* and several other noble old classics. Always his high ideals were before him, but, as he says in one of his earlier letters, his head and his heart were often full of poems which the " dreadful struggle for bread" would not give him time to put on paper. In 1881, when the hard task of getting a living was growing easier, and when he could at length count on some long-looked-for leisure, to give his genius yet

fuller utterance, the disease with which he had contended so long finally struck him down. Brave to the
last, he wrote *Sunrise*, one of the most beautiful of
his poems, when consumed with fever and under the
immediate expectation of the end. He died a few
months later, September 7, 1881, and, in his wife's
words, "that unfaltering will rendered its supreme
submission" to the Will of the Highest.

Before attempting to judge of Lanier's work as a
poet, it is well to remember the disadvantages under
which he labored and the difficulty of the
task he set himself. We must think of
him passing from a small country college
to the battle-field; of his long fight with sickness and
poverty; of his burden of uncongenial work, his
struggle for recognition, his intense longing in the
midst of restricted surroundings for a fuller life in the
quickening atmosphere of art and culture. We must
remember how he wrote to Bayard Taylor in 1875
that his life had been "a mere drought and famine"
for the want of such an atmosphere. We must
remember, further, how beyond all the hindrances
from without lay the inner difficulty of perfecting
new theories of the poetic form, and of expressing
those noble ideals of art which he strove to realize.

The higher the view a poet takes of his vocation,
the greater the demand upon his powers; the loftier
the purpose, the greater the strength required for its
accomplishment. To Lanier, with his single-minded
consecration of his efforts to a great ideal, Browning's
words are strikingly applicable:

" That low man seeks a little thing to do,
    Sees it, and does it;
This high man, with a great thing to pursue,
    Dies e'er he knows it."

So far as his poetic form is concerned, Lanier came as an innovator, and was brought face to face with those difficulties which confront all who seek to discover and apply new principles of composition. He believed that there was an underlying analogy between the musical and the poetic form, the full possibilities of which poets had as yet failed to appreciate, and he sought to carry more fully into poetry certain princi_ples of musical composition. He had not time to fully work out his ideas; much of his work was doubtless experimental; and it is probably for this reason that we find in it an eccentricity of expression apparently due to his imperfect mastery of his methods. In itself it was no light task to perfect a new method of poetic expression; but Lanier's was not the nature to rest content with the mastery of any novelty of form. To him the poet was one of the world's spiritual helpers and guides, and art the revelation through a beautiful body of a beautiful soul in the work. In this, as in all other respects, Poe and Lanier are fundamentally opposed. To the one, as has been said, truth and goodness were incidental and unimportant elements in art; to the other they were the very breath of its life. True art, in Lanier's eyes, is " inexorably moral." " Unless you are suffused with truth, wisdom, goodness, and love," he writes, " abandon the hope that the ages will accept you as an artist." The ideal of Milton or of Browning is not more noble than Lanier's; their aims are no higher, their solemn consecration of themselves to serve in art's high temple is not more complete.

When we thus take into account his limitations and the largeness of his aims, it does not surprise us that Lanier's poetry impresses us as frequently involved and incomplete. It lacks simplicity; there is often a sense of strain and effort, a painful absence of that ease which comes with the highest powers. Yet with all difficulties of utterance there is in it an inspiring loftiness of thought, a deep sympathy with the life of nature, and at times a wonderful lyrical and poetic beauty. It has, moreover, that accent of originality which among our American poets is rare indeed. In his close fellowship with nature, as in the *Hymns of the Marshes*, he seems to merge himself in the great sum of her life. He has given us the glow and quiet of the Southern landscape, as in the *Tampa Robins*, or *A Florida Sunday*. A true patriotic feeling for the greatness of our country, a sense of the meaning of its past and of the possibilities of its future, is shown in his *Psalm of the West*. He can speak out strongly and boldly too, as in *The Symphony*, against that taint of business dishonesty and those too-material aims which are corrupting the life of our Republic. Few poets have dealt with this side of our modern life at once so truthfully and so poetically; few have shown a deeper sympathy with the cramped lives of the poor, shut in too often from those

> "Outside leagues of liberty,
> Where Art, sweet lark, translates the sky
> Into a heavenly melody."

The true poet of the South, he is the poet of a chivalrous reverence for women; the poet of all high emotions. He it was who sang

> "When life's all love, 'tis life : aught else,
> 'tis naught."

He is a foe to the hard intellect unsanctified by love and tenderness; a foe to the mercenary and the base. Under the open sky, by the corn-field, or in the clover of the Pennsylvania meadows, he protests against the hardness, the sharpness, the mercantile spirit, that debases our American life. To love of nature, love of country, and love of man Lanier adds a power of poetic expression which at times is both fine and true. As has been said, he did not reach the limit of his powers or the full mastery of his art, yet he has shown us in his *Revenge of Hamish* that he could rival the best of our poets in the ballad-form; and in such lyrics as the songs in *The Jacquerie, My Springs*, and in *The Song of the Chattahoochee* he has given us single poems worthy to endure. With all its shortcomings, Lanier's work is a noble and beautiful addition to American poetry, the full worth of which is not yet generally recognized, and there is none among all our poets whose life is more stainless, more lofty, and more inspiring. He unites the Southern warmth to the Northern intellect, and if the coming writers of the great region to which he belongs bring

to their work an equal self-consecration to high ideals;
if they strive, as he did, to strengthen the full
Southern nature with the rigid discipline of thought
and knowledge,—we may have a work accomplished
which this poet of the new South left but begun; we
shall have a literature more glowing, more passionate,
and perhaps even more enduring than that of the New
England school.

STUDY LIST

LANIER

1. Poems. "The Song of the Chattahoochee," "Tampa
Robins," "Revenge of Hamish," "My Springs," "The
Ship of Earth," "The Psalm of the West," "Song for 'The
Jacquerie':" "*The hound was cuffed, the hound was
kicked*"; "Corn."

2. Biography and Criticism. *Lanier*, by Wm. Malone
Baskervill (in the series entitled "Southern Writers,"
published by Barbee & Smith, Nashville); Memorial, by
Wm. Hayes Ward, prefixed to edition of Lanier's *Poems*,
edited by his wife; Article by Merrill E. Gates, in the
Presbyterian Review, vol. viii. p. 669.

CHAPTER IV

THE LATER WRITERS OF THE MIDDLE STATES

WE must now return to that middle region of our country in which, as we have seen, the higher and more enduring literature of the Republic had its beginning. It will be remembered that the

Contemporaneous rise of literature in the different sections. leading writers of this section, Irving, Cooper, Bryant, and their associates, who were the true founders of our national literature, did not end their work until about the middle of the century. Cooper, who died in 1851, was the first of this great triumvirate to depart. Bryant, who lived on, the patriarch of American letters, until 1878, was the last. These Middle States pioneers thus lived to see the sudden appearance of the yet greater school of writers in New England, and the fight against adverse conditions made by the rising literature of the South.

It helps us to take a broad view of the literary history of our nation as a whole when we reflect that Cooper wrote for nearly a quarter of a century after the appearance of Longfellow's first published book of poems (1826), and that Bryant lived fourteen years

284

after the death of Hawthorne, and no less than twenty-nine years after that of Poe. A careful study of chronology will make it plain that, although they belonged to an earlier generation than that of Emerson or of Poe, these pioneer writers of the Middle States and the literary leaders of New England and the South yet worked for a considerable period side by side. It is all the more necessary for us to remind ourselves of this, because the method of study which we have followed tends to create a different impression in our minds.

In order to show the independent life and growth of literature during the present century in these different sections of our country we have been obliged to consider successively the literature of the Middle States, New England, and the South. But literature did not perish in New York and Pennsylvania when it triumphantly asserted itself in New England, and its advance in New England was largely contemporaneous with its contest against many difficulties in Virginia and the South. In time yet another literature was added to that of the three older sections—the literature of the growing West; and all these have developed separately, yet connected by those underlying bonds which render them in many ways so truly one. So we have at least four sections, each having its distinct literature and its distinct intellectual life, and each having its share in the wider and more varied movement of American literature as a whole. As we thus survey the whole field of our literary activity, during a period of some twenty or thirty years after the middle of the century, we see New England first at the height of its power, then gradually losing to some extent its leading place; we see New York distanced, yet continuing to produce work of a high order; we see the South, and finally the West, pressing forward and widening the area of our literary production.

In the middle section the early leaders were not without successors. With the possible exception of Walt Whitman, some of these later men were equal to any one of the three great writers who preceded them, yet they continued, in their own way, the work of those whose labors were nearly done. Pennsylvania gave four poets, born in "four successive years"— T. BUCHANAN READ (1822–1872), GEORGE HENRY BOKER (1823–1890), CHARLES GODFREY LELAND (1824–), and BAYARD TAYLOR (1825–1878).

Read, a landscape-painter, who passed much of his life abroad, composed, besides many larger works, some really notable short poems.

T. Buchanan Read.

His *Sheridan's Ride* is among the most popular of our war-poems, but two lyrics, *Drifting* and *The Closing Scene*, have a far higher poetic beauty. The last-named poem, with its subdued autumnal tone, has a grace and finish which remind us of the refined and delicate verse of Collins or of Gray.

Boker was a Philadelphian, long prominently identified with its literary life. He wrote creditable sonnets and some good lyrics; a number of his poems were inspired by the Civil War. He is also favorably known by his plays.

George Henry Boker.

His work as dramatist places him with the very few recent English poets who have succeeded in producing dramas which while not deficient in poetic excellence yet meet the actual requirements of stage representation.

Leland, also a Philadelphian, owes his popularity chiefly to the *Hans Breitman Ballads*, a collection of amusing verses of rather transient interest, in the dialect of the Pennsylvania Dutch.

C. G. Leland.

Bayard Taylor, the youngest of this group, is in many ways the most notable. He was born in 1825, in Chester County, a region in the neighborhood of Philadelphia, of thriving farms with comfortable farm-houses solidly built of gray stone, and of capacious barns. The district had been early settled by the English Quakers, and its people, with the thrift, simplicity, and inflexible uprightness of the Quaker, were not free from the rigidity and the narrowness in matters of art which characterize the members of that sect. "They hung no pictures on their blank walls, nor listened to the touches of sweet harmony. No line of beauty ever disturbed the peace and the decorum of their sober meeting-houses." * Taylor came of a long line of Quaker ancestry, but he was also partly German by descent. He himself thought that it was this foreign element in his inheritance, this "strain of distant and dead generations," that asserted itself in him, filling

Bayard Taylor.

* Smyth's *Life of Bayard Taylor*, p. 7. American Men of Letters Series.

him with warmer life and strange longings, and making him impatient even from his boyhood of the narrow horizon and bare lives of those about him. From whatever cause, in the midst of the ordered quiet and monotonous toil of a provincial community, this Quaker farmer's boy was eager to know and to see; impatient to grasp all that life had to give. When he was but ten years old the longing to visit foreign lands had already taken possession of him; by the time he was nineteen this longing had become a definite purpose. Through some newspaper verses he got a foothold in literary circles, and he became further known by the publication in 1844 of *Ximena*, a small book of poems. Determined to see Europe, he succeeded, probably more by his energy than because of these literary ventures, in inducing several newspaper editors to engage him to write them letters from abroad. Some of them paid him in advance, and with only about one hundred and forty dollars he started on his tour. It was a daring venture; it meant privation and self-denial, but in Taylor's case it meant also sudden success and fame. He was abroad two years, travelling on foot and paying his way by his letters to the *New York Tribune* and other papers, —a crude, courageous, eager-hearted country-boy, thrown on his own resources, and educating himself by all that he felt and saw and all that he overcame. The literary outcome of this astonishing trip was his *Views Afoot, or Europe seen with Knapsack and Staff* (1846), the first of his many books of travel, and the beginning also of his literary success. The book tells the story of Taylor's adventurous wanderings with simplicity and directness. It shows the quick power of the reporter to observe, and of the poet to appreciate; but, more than all, it is an object-lesson in what can be accomplished by sheer pluck and strength of will. The public were quick to see its merits, and six editions were sold in the first year.

In 1847 Taylor settled in New York, joining that circle of literati in which Bryant, Willis, and Halleck were the ruling spirits, and thus taking his place in the literary succession. Cooper still lived in his home near Otsego Lake, and Irving at Sunnyside was not far from the metropolis. Taylor's life during the years that followed was one of restless and varied activity, full of tireless labor and keen enjoyments. He toiled at journalism; he became widely and favorably known as a popular lecturer; he wrote books of travel, novels, and poems. "His intellect," says Professor Smyth, "was of that activity that it gave him trouble not to work." * But from time to time he would vanish from out the circle of these familiar interests, and disappear into the strange life of other lands. In 1851 he made a memorable journey to the East, pushing his way far up the Nile into regions then but little known, journeying, a bronzed and bearded traveller, through Syria, Palestine, and Asia Minor. "I have a Southern soul, it seems," he wrote in his Diary, "for I feel strongest and happiest where the sun can blaze upon me." † He was an ideal traveller,

* Smyth's *Life of Bayard Taylor*, p. 184.
† Quoted in Smyth's *Life of Taylor*, p. 90.

and in the course of his roving life he visited India, China, Japan, and Arabia, and made his way through Norway and Lapland into the regions of the far North. His energies were dissipated on many ambitions. As he grew older, he aspired, as Walter Scott had done, to found a great home for his family. He built a large house at "Cedar croft," in his native Chester County, only, like Scott, to burden himself with debt.

Under all his varied interests, his deepest wish was to prove himself a great poet; but although he published many poems, to the public he was pre-eminently the explorer, lecturer, and writer of travels. Some of his most ambitious poetry was produced during his later years. His translation of Goethe's *Faust* (1870–1871) has become a classic, and the notes and comments are a monument to his minute and scholarly study of the great German poet. This work alone would entitle Taylor to be long remembered. Two poems of this period, *The Prophet* (1874) and *Prince Deukalion* (1878), though among the longest and most ambitious of Taylor's poetical compositions, have added little to his reputation. The last great project of his life was to write a life of Goethe, a task for which he was singularly fitted, and his appointment in 1877 as minister to Berlin seemed to open the way for the carrying out of this undertaking. But when leisure and opportunity seemed thus at last at his command, his splendid health, which had carried him buoyantly through a lifetime of toils and hardships, at length deserted him, and he died at Berlin, December 15, 1878, leaving his work undone.

Taylor impresses us as a man who would probably have reached a yet higher level in literature if he had possessed a greater singleness of aim. His temperament was inquiring, free, and ardent; from the narrowness of provincial **Taylor's work.** life he came early into contact with half the civilizations of the world. Most of his life was given to an endeavor to enlarge his range of experience, and to the receiving of those new impressions which crowded in on him from every side. Successful in many fields, overburdened by the pressure of work, and distracted by the variety of his objects, we need not wonder that he did not reach in poetry that full measure of success for which he longed. "His life," says Mr. Stedman, "was consecrated to poetry, yet not devoted to it"; * but the highest rewards of the poet may not be thus lightly won. Taylor himself seems to have realized that he had allowed himself to be turned aside too often from his highest calling, for he writes regretfully,

"And still some cheaper service claims
  The will that leaps to loftier call ;
Some cloud is cast on splendid aims,
  On power achieved some common thrall." †

Whatever Taylor might have done in poetry under other conditions, or if his life had been prolonged, he has undoubtedly done enough to win for himself a highly creditable standing among our poets of the second rank. As a rule, his verse, while easy and melodious, lacks concentration and individuality. We meet nothing that jars upon our ear or offends our taste, but we find little that arrests our attention

---

* *Poets of America*, p. 409.   † Poems : *Implora Pace*.

or that remains with us long after the book is closed. Yet certain poems of Taylor's have in full measure that indefinable poetic quality which we often miss. The fruits of his later wanderings, the *Poems of the Orient*, are full of beauty. The famous *Bedouin Song* in this series ranks with the best of our lyrics, and *Nubia* is among the masterpieces of sonnet literature. The *Song of the Camp* and other shorter poems show that Taylor at his best was a true poet; indeed it is probable that the mass of his inferior work has done much to obscure his real merit and to prevent his receiving his due. Among the longer works, *Lars, a Pastoral of Norway*, may be mentioned as a most charming idyllic poem, worthy to be placed beside *Evangeline*. In spite of the immense popularity that Taylor's travels enjoyed in their day, in spite of the fact that his best novel, *The Story of Kennet*, deals truthfully with a phase of Pennsylvania life which has had but little recognition from the story-writer, it is by his best work in poetry that Taylor is likely to be longest remembered.

Besides the group of poets just spoken of, the Middle States produced during this period some distinguished scholars and prose-writers. Among the earliest of these was HENRY REED (1808–1854), who was lost in the wreck of the ocean steamer Arctic, and who held a professorship at the University of Pennsylvania from 1835 until his untimely death. Professor Reed was a sympathetic and enthusiastic student of English literature; his sense of what was

Prose-writing and scholarship.

Henry Reed.

excellent in poetry was quick and delicate, and he did much to enlarge and refine our literary appreciation. He was among the first, if not actually the first, of American critics to appreciate the charm of Wordsworth's poetry, and his friendship with both Wordsworth and Coleridge made him peculiarly fitted to interpret the work of these poets and their theory of composition. His edition of Wordsworth, which first appeared in 1837, did much to make the poet better known to American readers. He also edited the poems of Gray, and several other standard English works. After Reed's death several of his courses of lectures on literary subjects were published under the supervision of his brother.

Our present plan of study excludes the criticism of living writers, but two scholars of this middle region, although still in the fullness of their powers, cannot be passed over altogether without mention. HENRY C. LEA (b. 1825), a Philadelphian, is the author of *A History of the Inquisition during the Middle Ages* (1888), and of other mediæval studies. HORACE HOWARD FURNESS (b. 1833), also a Philadelphian, holds a prominent place among Shakespearean students. His Variorum Edition of Shakespeare's plays, which has been in course of publication since 1870, is a splendid monument to American scholarship, and is generally accepted on both sides of the Atlantic as the best planned and most complete edition of England's greatest poet. Side by side with the work of Dr. Furness we may place that of THOMAS R. LOUNSBURY (b. New York, 1838), whose scholarly study of Chaucer is a noteworthy addition to the literature which has gathered around Shakespeare's great predecessors in English poetry.

Among these Middle States writers is one who claims exemption from all ordinary standards, a man whom it is equally impossible to classify or **Walt Whitman.** to put aside—WALT WHITMAN, the most unique and puzzling figure in American letters. Somehow there suddenly appeared out of the business activity and dead-level prosperity of this equable middle region a man who is believed by his admirers to be the greatest poet, the most genuine voice, of our democracy. He had, as Bayard Taylor thought, "a colossal egotism." He aspired to "define America, her athletic democracy" to foreign lands, to teach her what she veritably is and what she may become. He declared that these new States needed a new poetry, untainted by the feudalism and the worn-out beliefs inseparable from the literatures of Europe; he abandoned the established forms and settled traditions of his art, and spoke out his message in an irregular, half-rhythmical chant according to a fashion of his own, unrestrained, audacious, vociferous, demanding the attention and calmly challenging the judgment of the world. In his eyes his poetic contemporaries were weaklings and sentimentalists. "Do you call these genteel little creatures American poets?" he asks.* He longs for a poetry as large, strong-limbed, free, elemental, and democratic as the genius of our Republic.

* *Democratic Vistas.*

In his first poem he thus triumphantly announces his own arrival:

"No dolce effectuoso I;
  Bearded, sunburnt, gray-neck'd, forbidding, I have arrived,
  To be wrestled with as I pass for the solid prizes of the universe."

He belongs to no school and bows to no precedents; he is the declared enemy to all conventions:

"I wear my hat as I please, indoors or out."

We cannot account for him, or tell from whence he comes; we only know that in some way he appears,— "untamed," as he asserts, and "untranslatable,"— to sound his "barbaric yawp over the roofs of the world." It is now nearly half a century since Whitman made his startling, not to say theatrical, entrance, yet the man and his work remain to be "wrestled with." There has grown up about him an ever-increasing mass of controversy and criticism. In this country John Burroughs has hailed him as the poet-prophet of our age and country; in England his work has been received with enthusiasm by such cultured and fastidious critics as William Michael Rossetti and John Addington Symonds. He has had neglect, ridicule, and abuse; but the circle of his devotees, though small, is probably increasing. To the vast body of readers his work is still repellent, bewildering, or altogether unknown. His poetry defies all ordinary critical tests, and the legitimate differences of opinion in regard to it are still so great that his ultimate place in our literature remains uncertain.

It certainly seems as though Whitman were fitted in one respect to be the poet of our people. None of

Whitman's life.

our great writers lived in such a free, intimate, and daily relationship with the · laborers in the factory, the shop, or the field; none came in a more simple or natural contact with the average man. Whitman belonged to the people, not merely through sympathy, but by his birth and habit of life. He was born at West Hills, Long Island, in 1819. He came of sound but humble ancestry, partly English and partly Dutch. His father, a carpenter by trade, removed to Brooklyn while Whitman was yet a child, and there the boy attended the public school until he was thirteen. He learned type-setting, and for twelve years of his young manhood worked as a compositor in New York. His eager, inquiring contact with the varied life of a great city during this time was his real education. New York was his university. With a marvellous power of observation and sympathy he explored and absorbed the life which surged about him. "He went on equal terms with every one," says his biographer; "he liked them and they him, and he knew them far better than they knew themselves."* He thus realized the idea of human friendliness which he suggests in one of his poems:

"Stranger, if you passing meet me and desire to speak to me,
    why should you not speak to me?
And why should I not speak to you?"

* Bucke's *Life of Whitman*, p. 19.

To this knowledge of life in New York a yet wider experience was added. In 1849 he started on a leisurely progress through the Southern, Western, and Middle States. He was a part of much of the life he saw, for from time to time he settled down and earned enough money to enable him to continue his journey. On his return to Brooklyn he was newspaper editor and house-builder, but he worked merely to provide for his daily needs; his real ambition was to speak out what was in him. His force accordingly went into the writing of his first poem, *Leaves of Grass*, which appeared in 1855. The book, which was slow in gaining any notice, was helped forward by a very favorable opinion from Emerson.

Whitman had now studied our democracy in all the daily avocations of peace; his next great experience of it came through our Civil War. His brother, who was in the Federal army, was wounded at the opening of the struggle, and Whitman left Brooklyn to attend him. After some experiences at the front, Whitman was nurse for several years in the army hospitals at Washington, injuring his magnificent health by his devotion. The war and Whitman's experiences in it were the occasion of several books. *Drum-Taps*, which contains some of his best poetry, appeared in 1865, and his *Memoranda During the War* ten years later. After the close of the war Whitman remained at Washington until 1873, as clerk in one of the Government offices, but was stricken with paralysis in that year and compelled to give up his position. A long period of invalidism and poverty followed, during which he bore himself with a cheerful serenity, wonderful in a man who had delighted in the abundant energy of a superb physique. In 1874 he moved to Camden, New Jersey, and there lived simply and obscurely until his death in 1892.

There was about Whitman something robust, large, and primitive. His early education was inadequate, and he was not a wide reader at any time; but he loved and knew men and nature, and lived in a wonderful companionship with them. Intensely individual by conviction as well as by his disposition, he was comparatively shut off from that life which comes to us through books. Whatever the defects of his work, we feel back of it, if we read it not in parts but as a whole, the imperative pressure of a strong if often wilfully eccentric personality. Confused, incoherent, full of offenses against taste and art, with outlandish words, slang, and elementary French phrases floating as on a weltering sea of words, we yet feel under all an indefinable sense of personal power.

Whitman's work.

Whitman feels himself, and in his own strange fashion makes us feel, the greatness and wonder of America. "These United States themselves are essentially the greatest poem," he wrote in his preface to *Leaves of Grass.* Their "crowning glory," he says elsewhere, "is to be spiritual and heroic." * Such a realization of what we are and may be is unfortunately rare in us and in our

His view of life.

* *A Backward Glance o'er Travelled Roads.*

literature. This feeling for our country, the greatest political expression of democracy, was nearly related to Whitman's intense belief in the importance of the individual. He aimed to be the poet of the " average man "; he believed that the essence of life consists in the free development of each individual. But while he insists on the sacredness of the individual, he emphasizes with equal force the sacredness of those bonds which should bind all individuals together. Perhaps more than anything else, he is the poet of that great ideal of human brotherhood which lies at the base of a true democracy. It is his aim to sing " the song of companionship," to write " the evangel poem of comrades." He declares that " the main purpose of these States is to found a superb friendship," up to this time " latent in all men."

How far Whitman succeeded in expressing these and other large conceptions in an artistic form is yet an open question. There is no doubt that at times he is exceedingly felicitous in his **His poetic form.** use of words, and that many passages in his poems unite a remarkable beauty with a subtle rhythmical charm. On the other hand, if we call the great bulk of his work poetry, it must be not merely by enlarging the borders of poetic art, but by reconstructing our fundamental conceptions of the nature of poetry itself. Two examples of his peculiar manner may be given: one, of his favorite method of cataloguing places or objects in an interminable succession; the other, of the purely prosaic character of his ordi-

nary phraseology. In a passage on the *Broad-Axe* he
tells us what the axe can make:

> "The axe leaps!
> The solid forest gives fluid utterances;
> They tumble forth, they rise and form,
> Hut, tent, landing, survey,
> *   *   *   *   *   *
> Hoe, rake, pitchfork, pencil, wagon, staff,
> Saw, jack-plane, wedge, mallet, rounce,"—

and so on in a pitiless enumeration, until we feel that
he has confused the function of the poet with the
duties of an invoice-clerk. The other passage is taken
almost at random from the same poem:

> "To use the hammer or the saw (*rip or cross-cut*),
> To cultivate a turn for carpentering, plastering, painting."

These instances do not show Whitman at his best, yet
they fairly represent the average quality of hundreds
of pages. If they have any touch of poetry in them,
the world's poetic sense has been perverted from the
days of Homer until now.

A hardly less serious shortcoming is the over-
strained, incoherent vein of rhapsody in which Whitman's work abounds. One of his ablest admirers,
John Addington Symonds, admits that his most serious fault is a kind of "forcible feebleness." * In
much of Whitman's work we find merely a weak
diffuseness, a boisterous violence and extravagance of
expression, instead of the compactness, precision, and
quiet reserve of a true strength. The power in Whitman's poetry impresses us as the native force and

* *Walt Whitman. A Study*, p. 141.

sincerity of the man, painfully struggling to make itself felt through a clumsy and inadequate means of expression.

In judging either of Whitman or of his theories of art it is not enough to admit that there is an element of power in the man himself, that his views are sometimes inspiring or his aims high: we must rather ask whether he has the poet's gift of musical and beautiful speech, the power to create that which will permanently delight, uplift, and console? It is not enough to say that Whitman is an original genius because he differs from all other poets; it is easier to differ from the great poets than to resemble them. It is easy for a writer to mistake a studied eccentricity for originality; but we must remember that something more is required than a departure from the ordinary principles of composition in order to create a literature that shall be truly national, and that to violate any essential principle of poetic art is to violate the immortal laws of beauty on which it rests. That Whitman is different is in itself neither for nor against him; the ultimate test of his work will be in its power to move men.

Assuming to be the poet of our democracy, Whitman's work is in fact as utterly removed from the people as he himself was close to them in his daily life. The scholars Longfellow and Lowell are the poets of thousands of humble homes; Whitman is as yet the admiration of a little clique among the most cultured upper class. Called the founder of a national American literature, by a singular irony he is better known

to the intellectual aristocracy of England than among
the people of his own land. Whether he will ever be
our poet as Burns is the poet of Scotland, is a matter
for individual judgment. In the meantime it may
help us to apply to him his own test:

" The proof of a poet should be sternly deferred till
his country absorbs him as affectionately as he has
absorbed it."

.

STUDY LIST.

TAYLOR AND WHITMAN.

1. Bayard Taylor. (*a*) Among the shorter poems
"The Bedouin Song," "Nubia," the classical study
"Hylas," and "A Song of the Camp" may be read as
favorable examples of Taylor's poetic powers. "The Quaker
Widow " is interesting as an idyllic presentation of a phase
of life not often treated in our verse. The longer narrative
poem "Lars: A Pastoral of Norway" should not be passed
over. It is a beautiful study of the life in Norway and in
Taylor's own section of Pennsylvania ; the fierce primitive
passions and rude customs of Norwegian life are contrasted
with the placid and peace-loving existence of the Quakers.
The story is well told, and the poem abounds in admirable
descriptions of nature. "Views Afoot "will give a fair idea
of Taylor's ability as a writer of travels, and "The Story
of Kennet " of his work as a novelist.

(*b*) BIOGRAPHY AND CRITICISM. The best life of Taylor
is that by Albert H. Smyth in the American Men of Letters
Series (1896). See also *The Life and Letters of Bayard
Taylor*, by Marie Hansen Taylor and Horace E. Scudder,
and, especially for criticism, Stedman's *Poets of America*.

2. Walt Whitman. (*a*) POEMS.—Whitman's work is so
diffuse, voluminous, and unequal that it will be found best

to approach him through one of the volumes of Selections, in which we are given examples of his best manner only. Any one or all of the following selected editions of his poems will be found convenient: *Poems; Selected and Edited by William Michael Rossetti* (with a critical introduction by the editor), London, 1880; *Selected Poems by Walt Whitman* (Webster & Co., 1892); *Selected Poems* in the Camelot Classics, with an introduction by Ernest Rhys. Among the poems or selections worthy of especial notice the following may be mentioned: "O Captain! my Captain," a lament on the death of Lincoln, one of the best known of Whitman's poems, and one of the most regular in its poetic form; "The Mystic Trumpeter," "Out of the Cradle Endlessly Rocking," "When Lilacs Last in the Dooryard Bloom'd." "Pioneers! O Pioneers," which deals, as its name implies, with the great westward migration, shows Whitman's large feeling for country. The "Beat! Beat! Drums!" from "Drum-taps," is full of martial vigor and spirit, while the "Come Up from the Fields, Father," a pathetic study of simple home-life, shows the war from another aspect.

(*b*) PROSE.—*Specimen Days in America*, in the Camelot Classic Series, is convenient as an introduction to a study of Whitman's prose. The account of his experience in the Washington hospitals in this book gives us some idea of that tenderness and strength which undoubtedly formed a part of Whitman's singular, and in some respects disappointing, character. *Democratic Vistas*, the preface to the *Leaves of Grass*, and *A Backward Glance O'er Travelled Roads*, help us to understand Whitman's views on poetry as an art, and on American literature and society. See also *Autobiographia; or the Story of a Life*, by Walt Whitman. Selected from his prose writings (Webster & Co., 1892).

(*c*) BIOGRAPHY AND CRITICISM. Only a few books from

the growing mass of Whitman literature need be given here. Life, by William Clarke (London, 1892), is a short and convenient biography, with critical comments. The longer life by Richard Maurice Bucke (1883) ranks high as an authority. John Burroughs, who writes as a personal friend as well as an enthusiastic admirer of the poet, has given us his critical views and personal impressions in *Walt Whitman as Poet and Person*, and *Whitman: a Study* (1896). Among the many essays on this subject we may mention that of J. A. Symonds, entitled "Democratic Art, with Special Reference to Walt Whitman," in *Essays Speculative and Suggestive*, vol. ii., and that of Edward Dowden on "The Poet of Democracy," in *Studies in Literature*.

CHAPTER V.

GENERAL SURVEY OF LITERATURE SINCE THE WAR.

Any attempt at a critical estimate of the work of those writers who have risen into prominence since the Civil War would be out of place in an elementary study like the present. When we try to form a clear conception of the general character of the period as a whole, we are confused by the vast amount of writing produced within that time, and by the large number of writers in many departments of literature, whose work would naturally claim the attention of the historian. If one could master all that has been published in the United States within the last thirty years, in itself an almost impossible task, one could not safely undertake to sift the permanent from the transient or to pronounce upon the relative merits of authors many of whom are just entering upon their work. In these matters we must wait patiently for the test of time: we are too close to see clearly or to judge impartially, too much influenced by individual prejudices or likings; and any criticism under such conditions would be little more than an expression of partial knowledge and personal impressions. Yet to avoid any reference to the history of our literature during this recent period, to omit all consideration of its present conditions or future prospects, would be to leave our study obviously incomplete. It seems best, therefore, to refer briefly to a few movements which, so far as we can now determine, have marked our literary history since the Civil War, attempting no criticism of recent or living writers, but contenting ourselves with a passing mention of a few prominent names for the purpose of illustrating the general trend of the literature whose course they have helped to determine.

As we look to-day over the whole field we are impressed with the ever-widening area over which our literary activity is becoming distributed. When Irving wrote, a great part of the country was still unconquered or even unexplored; our civilization and enterprise

The wider distribution of our literature.

have now overflowed the narrow limits of the Eastern settlements, and have spread from sea to sea. Along the Pacific coast are populous towns and mighty cities, while the great plains of the middle West, so lately the home of the Indian and the buffalo, are being converted into a region of grain-fields or pasture-land, from which we supply the markets of the world. Throughout this vast extent of territory prosperous towns have sprung up, to be new centers of wealth and of the life of the intellect. The public-school system, established so long ago in New England, has followed in the train of settlement and become a well-established and important element in the life of these new communities of the West. As wealth, luxury, and refinement increase among us, as they spread continually over a wider area, and as education becomes more general throughout the country, our literature is gradually passing beyond its old geographical boundaries, and the literary life of the older Eastern cities is being more and more shared by Chicago, St. Louis, and other cities of the West.

But while we see that the West and the South are gaining in importance as factors in our literary history, the prominence of New York as a center of literature has been an undoubted feature of this recent period, especially since the passing of the great writers of the New England school. It is not hard to understand why this should be the case. Though in itself distinctly mercantile rather than literary in tone, New York is the largest, the richest, and the most cosmopolitan of our great cities, and as such it is a natural commercial center for our literature. It supports some of our best daily and weekly papers, thus attracting many writers who, like Bryant, Taylor, or Stoddard in an earlier time, find it desirable to combine journalism with literature; it contains many of our largest publishing-houses, and, more than all, it is the home of a large proportion of our leading magazines. A city which holds out such rewards to the successful literary worker naturally draws many writers to itself. Young writers, or untried aspirants for literary distinction, seek New York somewhat as the youth of England go up to try their fortunes in London, and many more who do not actually live in New York look to her magazines and publishing-houses as the best market for their work. The great

The place of New York in recent literature.

illustrated monthlies of New York are known to all of us, and they fill an enormous place in the mental life of our country. Without stopping to mention many others of more recent date, *Harper's Monthly* (founded 1850), *Scribner's Magazine* (first series, 1870–1881; second series, 1889–), and *The Century Magazine* (1881) have been the medium for much that is best in our recent literature, and have been the means of introducing many of our best writers to their public. Through them, for instance, nearly all of the latest group of Southern story-writers gained a hearing and rapidly won their way into favor. Through *Harper's*, moreover, George William Curtis long delighted us with his wise and kindly comments on life, books, and manners; through it William Dean Howells expounded his views of the art of fiction· and through it Charles Dudley Warner is to-day giving us his mature reflections on men and things. This literary influence and importance of New York is consequently one of the features of our literature during the period under review. There we find some of our best living critics, such as Edmund Clarence Stedman and George E. Woodberry; some of our foremost story-writers, such as Frank R. Stockton, Thomas A. Janvier, and Richard Harding Davis,—all these, however, Philadelphians by birth; there we find such poets and writers as Richard Watson Gilder, the editor of *The Century ;* E. L. Godkin, the editor of *The Nation* and the author of some careful studies on the peculiar problems of our democracy; F. Marion Crawford, F. Hopkinson

Smith, Brander Matthews, and many more. With New York we associate the later work of the novelist William Dean Howells. Henry James, Howells's co-worker in fiction, is a New Yorker by birth, but on the whole a very large proportion of these so-called New York writers have been born elsewhere. Indeed so many different sections of the country speak through rather than directly out of New York, that the city may be fairly thought of as representing more than any other center the literary life of the country at large.

Besides all this, New York and the Middle States have had an important share in the creation of a school of fiction, the growth of which has been one of the leading features of our recent literary history. The large place which fiction has come to occupy in our literature is too obvious to be overlooked. The period we are considering has given us little poetry of a high order, except that produced in their old age by the poets of the former time; it has not been remarkable for the depth or eloquence of its weightier prose, or for the brilliancy and insight of its literary criticism, but in its fiction it has made a distinct and notable contribution to literature. How are we to think of this new fiction as compared to that which preceded it?

Realistic fiction.

Our first great story·writers, while they dealt with American life, instinctively turned aside from those commonplace and prosaic phases of it with which they were daily brought into contact, and selected those more picturesque and romantic themes which borrowed some charm from remoteness and unfamiliarity. Take, for example, the work of the four great masters of the earlier period. Irving recreated the vanished life of Manhattan, or sought refuge in the legends of one of the most picturesque of American streams; Cooper found his romantic coloring in the Indian, and in the dangers and freedom of border life; Hawthorne, who complained of the difficulty of writing a romance about a country where there was nothing but a "commonplace prosperity," contrived to envelope even his stories of American life with a magical moonlight atmosphere which withdrew them from the light of common day; while Poe, the master of the terrible and the grotesque, was, in his own way, as remote as Hawthorne from the bustling, money-seeking world that surrounds us. But when we recall the best-known novels and short stories written in America within recent years, we see at once that by far the greater number of them differ widely from the romantic stories of the four great writers just mentioned in subject, character, and aim. Following the lead of certain great contemporary novelists in Russia, France, and Spain, many of our later fiction-writers have aimed to reproduce, with an unrelieved and unswerving truth and minuteness, just those every-day aspects of American society which their great predecessors instinctively idealized or ignored. A so-called "realistic" school of fiction has consequently risen up among us, which, according to one definition, "aims at embodying in art the common landscape, common figures, and common hopes and loves and ambitions of our common life."

In nearly every great section of our huge country keen-eyed observers have been recording in fiction one or another of the almost innumerable phases of American society. Taken together, these studies give to the careful reader a fairly accurate notion of our composite national life. But life in this country is as yet such a roughly-pieced patchwork of local differences, that the novelist who aims at a faithful reproduction of it often gets no further than a study of some particular locality, which he paints over and over again up to the extreme limits of endurance. The last thirty years has given us a long procession of these local studies: it has produced writers who are practically specialists on some particular and often narrow plot of ground. We have had experts on the old lady of the New England village, on the Tennessee mountaineer and the plantation negro; or, among the novelists who have taken a somewhat wider outlook, we have had elaborate studies of society life in Boston, Washington, Newport, Philadelphia, or New York.

The recognized leaders in this realistic movement are WILLIAM DEAN HOWELLS (1837–) and HENRY JAMES (1843–). For a quarter of a century Howells has been a prominent figure among our men of letters, and in **William Dean Howells.** many ways he impresses us as one of the most representative authors of his time. He is not college-bred, but he has studied the American in the West

and in the East. Residence abroad has given him
the opportunity of seeing our country as a whole in
the perspective which one gets from a foreign point
of view. Born in 1837, at Martin's Ferry, in the
Ohio Valley, he began his career as type-setter, journalist, and poet. He wrote a campaign life of Lincoln in 1860, and was our consul at Venice from
1861 to 1865. Through an early visit to Boston he
had made the acquaintance of Lowell and Holmes,
and after his return to America he lived for a time
in Boston, where he was received into that chosen
circle of poet-scholars which included Longfellow
and Lowell. He was editor of the *Atlantic Monthly*
from 1872 to 1881, after which he removed to New
York, and in 1886 assumed the charge of the Editor's Study in *Harper's Monthly*.

Howells has by no means confined himself to novel-
writing. He is the author of many witty little plays
or farces; he is poet and literary critic, and has given
us essays on the Italian poets and some charming
descriptions of Venetian life; but it is as a leader of
the realistic movement in fiction that he now chiefly
concerns us. *Their Wedding Journey*, the beginning
of his work as a novelist, appeared in 1871; but since
then his manner and methods have materially changed
as his theory of the art of fiction has taken shape.
In a long succession of books he has given us the
results of his conscientious analysis and painstaking
observation of the most obvious and unexceptional
aspects of American society. Carefully shunning the
depths or the heights, he has striven with an un-

wearied patience to bring before us the average life
of the average man and woman, withholding no detail
which others might avoid as trivial, which might
help to make his picture real.   His books are full of
characters which are the unmistakable outcome of
our peculiar conditions.   Silas Lapham, struggling on
the perilous edge of social recognition; Bartley Hub-
bard, the slangy, up-to-date young journalist; Lydia
Blood, the "Lady of the Aroostook," the New England country girl passing through the complexities
of a more sophisticated society, innocent, independent, thinking no evil, and so un-afraid.   And such
characters move against a background of more than
photographic reality and distinctness.   We are in
Boston in *The Minister's Charge* or *A Woman's Reason*, keenly alive to the fountain in the Common or
the confusing procession of trolley-cars; we are in
New York in *A Hazard of New Fortunes*, being initi-
ated into the mysteries of the boarding-house system
or watching the trains on the elevated roads.   When
we reflect that Howells has not only given us as a
novelist wonderfully successful examples of his theories of art, but that he has, as a critic, preached these
theories from the vantage of an editor's chair, we can
gain some idea of the influence which he has ex-
ercised upon our recent fiction.

Henry James has worked side by side with Howells, and on the same general lines.   His first book,
A Passionate Pilgrim, a collection of short   **Henry
James.**
stories, is indeed full of an ideal and
romantic beauty and grace, but he soon abandoned

this early manner for work full of cleverness and penetration, but of a strikingly realistic kind. His long acquaintance with life abroad and his opportunities for the study of the American in Europe have made him pre-eminent in what has been called the "international novel,"—novels that introduce Europeans and Americans in those relations which are the outcome of our closer intercourse with the Old World.

Besides these two leaders of realism—the one a native of, the other closely identified with, New York—there are many recent novelists in the Middle States with whose work the future historian of our literature will doubtless have to reckon. Prominent among these are Rebecca Harding Davis, first known for her powerful story *Life in the Iron Mills* (1861); Ellen Olney Kirk, Helen Hunt Jackson, and Margaret Deland.

While New York has been thus prominent, New England has not lacked some notable writers in recent years, some of whom have been clearly leaders in the especial line to which they have devoted themselves. In fiction, New England life, particularly in the country districts and the smaller towns, has been portrayed with minuteness and fidelity by such writers as Elizabeth Stuart Phelps Ward, Harriet Prescott Spofford, Sarah Orne Jewett, and Mary E. Wilkins. Arthur Sherburne Hardy has produced novels notable for their strength and finish of style. Blanche Willis Howard, whose entertaining story *One Summer* was most fa-

Recent writers of New England.

vorably received, has given us in *Guenn*, a story of
artist life in Brittany, one of the strongest and most
masterly works of fiction produced in America in
recent years. JOHN FISKE has become widely known
as a scientist and philosophical thinker, and more
recently as one of our ablest writers on American
history. The labors of a group of writers in this
last-named field—JUSTIN WINSOR (1831–1897), the
author of a scholarly and elaborate history of America;
HENRY ADAMS, HENRY CABOT LODGE, and others—
are too important to be passed over. Indeed it may be
said here that outside of New England as well as within its limits an increasing attention to our country's
history and institutions has been one of the distinctions of these later years. In the South the labors of
Professor HERBERT B. ADAMS, of Johns Hopkins
University, Baltimore, have been instrumental in
raising up a school of capable students and historians
of our institutions and our past. The Middle States
have given us the admirable works of Professor
WOODROW WILSON, of Princeton University, and of
JOHN BACH McMASTER, Professor of American History at the University of Pennsylvania.

Returning to the later literature of New England,
we find but little poetry of a high order compared to
the fuller utterance of the preceding period. Yet,
within its carefully defined and often narrow limits,
the poetic art of THOMAS BAILEY ALDRICH is of
the finest and most finished kind. Master of the
shorter and lighter lyrical forms, Aldrich's prose
as well as his verse is distinguished by delicacy
of workmanship and refinement of tone. CELIA

THAXTER, whose life was passed on the Isles of Shoals off the coast of New Hampshire, did some good work both in prose and verse, and some of her shorter poems, such as *The Little Sandpiper* and *The Tryst*, though slight, possess unmistakable poetic feeling. Another poet of later New England, EDWARD ROWLAND SILL (1841–1887), has enriched our literature with some sonnets and short poems of unusual power and depth of thought. Though born in Connecticut, the greater part of the productive period of Sill's life was spent in the far West. He was for a time professor in the University of California, but his early death in Ohio cut short a career full of promise. But he was essentially a New Englander from first to last. He was not an imitator of Emerson,—indeed his verse has a distinctly individual note,—but he expressed after his own fashion that inner spirit of New England that we find also in Emerson's verse. He has the same deep love of nature, and his work is pervaded by that high seriousness and philosophic depth which is characteristic alike of Emerson and of the would-be-emancipated Puritanism of which he was the representative. Sill left but little verse, yet he left enough to show us that in him we lost a true poet, filled with noble ideals of life and beauty, and endowed with the faculty of insight into the heart of things.

Let us now attempt to form some general conception of the place and part of the South and West in our recent literary history. While New York, the mighty metropolis of the Middle States, has been, as has been said, the greatest commercial center for our literature during recent years; while New England, although gradually losing her supremacy, has continued to hold an important place in our intellectual and literary life,—it seems probable that the most significant and promising literary developments have come from the South.

Literature in the South.

With the close of the Civil War the Southern States entered upon a new and momentous era in their history. They had fought to the end for the maintenance of the old *régime* with a desperate and heroic determination; they had given of their best, and the war left them weakened and impoverished. But terribly as the South had suffered, it showed a remarkable power of recuperation; for the inevitable changes consequent upon the war brought with them a new principle of growth, and opened the way, painful and difficult as it seemed, to a broader and healthier development. Slavery, which had been the basis of the social and agricultural system of the South, had become more and more a bar to progress. The abolition of slavery freed the South from a burden and a peril; it brought with it the advance of the Southern States on new lines, it united them more closely to the rest of the country, and enabled them to share in the forward movement of the nation as a whole. Within ten years after Lee's surrender many grave political and industrial problems had been successfully met, and the reorganization of the South in harmony with our national life had been substantially accomplished. With these changes in the social, industrial, and edu-

cational conditions, with the fuller development of
the South's internal resources, the infusion of Northern elements, and the quickening contact with the
life of the world without, has come the rapid rise of a
new group of Southern writers and the entrance of a
comparatively new force into our literature.

During the years immediately after the war the
South needed all her energies for the difficult task of
readjustment to her changed conditions, but as her
hardest problems began to press less heavily, and as
she felt the stimulus of new forces stirring within
her, this new life began to find a voice. Accordingly,
about ten or fifteen years after peace was established,
one Southern writer after another won his way into
public favor, chiefly through the pages of the great
Northern magazines. The writers of this new school
devoted themselves almost entirely to fiction; there
were a few verse-writers among them, but the short
story was, on the whole, their favorite literary form.
For the most part they treated, with picturesqueness and pathos, of various phases of Southern life in
the present and in the past. It is true that Simms,
Cooke, and others of an earlier generation had given
their stories a similar setting, but the new writers
presented the many-sided life of the South in its
more out-of-the-way and less familiar aspects, or
else treated it with a freshness and fidelity born of
a keener perception of its peculiarities or its charm.
Thus GEORGE W. CABLE has taken for his theme the
life of the Creoles in his native city of New Orleans,
MARY N. MURFREE (Charles Egbert Craddock) has

taken us into the remote mountain regions of Tennessee, while THOMAS NELSON PAGE has set us in the
midst of the landed gentry of old Virginia,   **Recent**
and, with such writers as JOEL CHANDLER   **writers.**
HARRIS, RUTH MCENERY STUART, and IRWIN RUS-
SELL, has given the negro a place in literature.   A
mere allusion to a few of these recent Southern writers
is all that is possible for us here.   GRACE KING, like
Cable, is known through her portrayal of the Creole
life and character; RICHARD MALCOLM JOHNSTON,
whose work dates, however, from a much earlier period, has continued his delineation of Georgia scenes;
and more recently JAMES LANE ALLEN has given us
from Kentucky work characterized by thoughtfulness
and beauty, with a deep and almost primitive hold
on the life of nature.

When we attempt to understand and measure this literature of the new South, we cannot but feel that it
has already brought a fresh and welcome impulse, and
that we are justified in looking to it for still further
and perhaps greater triumphs.   The war divides these
younger writers from the old South, whose glories they
love to revive in art.   An abrupt change has removed
all that generous and splendid life of the past into the
proper perspective for the literary artist.   Its broad
plantations, its ample manor-houses, full of comfort,
ease, and repose; its gentlemen of a vanished school,
simple and high-minded, irascible but kindly: living
like patriarchs among their troops of slaves,—all these
things, seen through a softening light of memory, re-
ceding and yet familiar, give to the Southern writer

a peculiarly rich and romantic background. The
negro alone, as revealed to us by Page or Harris in
fiction, and by Russell in dialect verse; his unconscious humor, his delicious peculiarities, his quaint
superstitions and folk-lore, has given to these creations of the recent South an element before almost
unknown to literature.

But these Southern story-writers have done more
than give us studies of new localities: we
feel instinctively a different quality in their
work. If we contrast it with the productions of New England, intellectual, self-examining,
self-conscious, we feel the richer coloring, the warmer
blood, and quicker pulses of the South. Read the
most characteristic of Hawthorne's stories, and then
turn to the *Mars' Chan'* or *Meh Lady* of Thomas
Nelson Page. It is like passing from the world of
thought to the world of action, from the analysis of
life to living. The fine-spun problems of mind and
conscience have no place in this world, but instead we
have a story of which men and women never tire,
which is almost as old in all its essential elements as
human life. It is a world to be alive in, a young
world, where the men are full of knightly courtesies
and knightly courage, and where the women are good
and fair; a world of young heroes who can lead a
cavalry charge up the slope, to fall under the very
lips of the cannon; of simple-hearted slaves whose
lives are too narrow to hold anything beyond an un-
questioning and indestructible fidelity; of women who
seem to belong with those heroines of Homer, Shake-

North and South. (margin note)

speare, or Scott whom the world supposes itself to
have outgrown. Or let us put such a book as Cable's
Grandissimes beside such a keen and clever study of
Boston as Howells's *A Woman's Reason*, and it is like
the tropic warmth of the Gulf Stream after the chill
of Northern waters; let us place the fair, gentle, placid
Priscilla, that old-time Puritan ideal of maidenly perfection, beside one of Cable's heroines, a creature of
life, impulse, and movement, with a " sparkle of the
Gallic blood," vivacious, sensitive, appealing, change-
able,—and we shall know that, whatever else this
Southern literature may be, at the least it is different.

And as there is in the work of these writers a
fuller throb of action and motion, there is also a
warmth and glow of color in many of
their descriptions of nature which seem   **Nature in
Southern**
to carry with them the atmosphere of the   **literature.**
South. The earlier work of LAFCADIO
HEARN, who, though not a native American, may be
associated with this Southern group, has in it an
extraordinary richness, an unrestrained, emotional
quality which contrasts sharply with the manner of
the North. *Chita*, one of his earliest stories, is alive
with the glow of the Southern imagination, with the
raptures of one who has absorbed nature through
every sense. Cable, too, has given the Southern landscape a place beside that of New England in our
literature. It is before us in many a charming passage, distinct in outline, warm and glorious with color,
and bathed in the lucid clearness of the Southern sky.

On the whole, while we must not undervalue the

earlier literature of the South, it seems safe to conclude that the changes consequent upon the war have brought with them a new and powerful impulse to literary production. It has been truly said that over much of that earlier literature there is "the trail of the amateur, the note of the province, the odor of the wax flower"; to-day the South can boast of many professional men of letters who, relieved of the drawbacks which handicapped their predecessors, belong not to the South merely, but to our American people.

Side by side with this literature of the new South we find the scattered beginnings of a literature which is not merely written in the West, but Western, transporting us to yet other conditions and surroundings, and portraying them with freedom and vigor. These Western writers, like those of the South, have had the advantage of a background that holds out magnificent opportunities to the poet and the novelist. For the great literary artist the West is indeed a new land, full of yet unwritten stories of heroic achievement, of tragic failures, and fabulous successes. There, has been seen in our own day the primitive contest of man with his fellows and with the stubborn forces of nature. Over the vast spaces of this Western world a new migration of the nations has swept; wave after wave, a confused, restless mass of humanity, drawn from the Old World and the New; stirred often by lawless passions, yet somehow, out of turbulence, creating order, security, and law. When gold was discovered in California in 1849, and thousands

The literature of the West.

of fortune-hunters swarmed to the Pacific slope, and to the wild life of the mining-camp, with its feverish excitements, its dangers, and its chances of sudden wealth, a new field was opened, not only to the gold-hunter, but to the writer of fiction.   It is hardly too much to say that it was through these mining-camps of California that the West made its first real entrance into literature.   Its first great interpreter in literature was FRANCIS BRET HARTE.   **Francis Bret Harte.** Bret Harte belongs to the East by birth, and to the West by adoption.   Born in Albany, New York, in 1839, he went to California when about six-teen, and was by turns school-teacher, miner, and type-setter.   He drifted into journalism, and in 1868 was selected as the first editor of the *Overland Monthly*, a magazine whose establishment is one of the milestones in the development of Western literature.   The first of his many stories of Western mining life, *The Luck of Roaring Camp*, appeared in the second number of the *Monthly*, and gained him instant recognition in the East.   It was followed by *The Outcasts of Poker Flat*, *Miggles*, and a long succession of other stories in the same vein.   Recognizing the possibilities of a new subject, he had claimed it for literature, and his success was assured.

This rising Western literature found its poet in CINCINNATUS HINER MILLER, or Joaquin Miller as he is more generally called, a native of Indiana, who, like Bret Harte, had spent some time in the gold-diggings of California.   Miller's first book of poems, *Songs of the Sierras*, appeared in 1871, a year after

Bret Harte's first collection of stories had been issued. In the same year JOHN HAY, in his *Pike County Ballads*, celebrated in vigorous verse the rugged virtue and unsuspected tenderness hidden under the roughness of many a homely hero of the West. Hay, like Miller, was a native of Indiana, a State which has also given General LEW WALLACE, JAMES WHITCOMB RILEY, and EDWARD EGGLESTON to literature. In these early verses of Hay's, with their Western vernacular, their strong but simple rhythm, their New World heroes, the captain of the Mississippi steamboat or the Western stage-driver, we seem to hear the prelude to a new literature of democracy. Hay is but one of those who have stood before this life of the West in its heroism, its coarseness, its interminable wastes of commonplace, and endeavored to convert the mass of raw material to the poet's use. Bret Harte's spirited and unconventional verses on the ruder aspects of Western life have been followed by those of EUGENE FIELD (1850-1896), the Chicago journalist; its mere every-day side, in all its monotonous drudgery or hopeless commonplace, has been essayed by such writers as WILL CARLETON, who rose to popularity by his *Betsey and I are Out* (1871), and JAMES WHITCOMB RILEY. However we may regard these attempts to embody the ordinary lives of thousands of our people in the forms of art, they must at least interest us as experiments and as indications of the widening area of our literature. Nor is it only in this homely verse that the less dramatic and drearier side of existence in the great West has found its chroniclers; such writers as EDWARD EGGLESTON, JOSEPH KIRKLAND, E. W. HOWE, MARY HALLOCK FOOTE, OCTAVE THANET (Miss French), HAMLIN GARLAND, and CAPTAIN CHARLES KING have familiarized us through their prose with many of its varied aspects. Kirkland, a native of New York State, who passed the greater part of his life in Chicago, has not shrunk from depicting in *Zury* (1887) the dead level of existence in the agricultural solitudes of the Middle West, in all its isolation, sordidness, and privations, with a pitiless realism and an unquestionable power. Eggleston, well known by his *Hoosier Schoolmaster* (1871), *Roxy* (1878), and other books, Howe, and Garland, have made places for themselves in different portions of the same vast field. Mary Hallock Foote, in such books as her *Led Horse Claim*, depicts the life of the mining-camp; while Captain Charles King admits us into the little world of the Western army-posts. In sharp contrast to the writers who aim to bring before us the ruder aspects of the West is H. B. FULLER, who takes us into the rush of the greatest of the Western cities in his two novels of Chicago, *The Cliff Dwellers* (1893) and *With the Procession* (1895).

Such a recital of a few names gives us but an imperfect idea of the true scope and nature of the literature of the West, now just springing into life. We find in it a promising note of self-confidence and enthusiasm, with an intense local pride. One of the best of its younger writers, Hamlin Garland, has defiantly asserted its freedom from the literary stand-

ards of the past.   He has announced that the day
of the East, with its over-cautious adherence to foreign
models, is over, and that the day of the West is at
hand.   He has declared that "the past is not vital,"
and that in the great Middle West, "emancipated"
from tradition, the true American literature is to be
born.* We should not put this aside as vain boasting;

**Character-
istics of the
Western
literature.**
the spirit that seeks to repudiate our in-
debtedness to the intellectual life of the
English people may be both foolish and
immature, but it has in it an element of
self-reliance that is a good omen for the future.   It is
true that our writers have, as a whole, shown too
little of that confidence in their own strength which
one would naturally expect in a young people, and if
the West has something of the ignorant recklessness
of youth in literary matters, it is, after all, to youth
that the future belongs.   As yet Western literature
is largely experimental, but when we think of the
daring, the resources, the magnificent reserve of
energy in that great region, we must thankfully
acknowledge that out of this prolific West a broader,
bolder, and more national literature may yet come.

One characteristic feature of our recent literature
—its humor—we have reserved for a separate mention.   Probably no other element in our literature is
so distinctly and exclusively American.   Imitative
as much of our serious work may be, our humor

---

*The Literary Emancipation of the West.   The *Forum*,
XVI. p. 156.   See also *The Arena*, V. 669 ; and H. Garland's
Crumbling Idols.

is unmistakably a genuinely national production.
Even the English, while their perception of the American joke is apt to be delayed and uncer-
tain, admit that our humor is ours alone.   **American
                                              humor.**
They may call it "vulgar," or "rudi-
mentary," or "middle-class," but they acknowledge
that we are at least entitled to say of it, "A poor
thing, sir, but mine own." A leading English critic
and essayist, for instance, writes: "The Americans
are of our own stock, yet in their treatment of the
ludicrous how unlike us they are! As far as fun
goes, the race has certainly become differentiated." *
In fact, humor is a characteristic element in our literature, because it extends far beyond purely literary
limits and is a characteristic element in the American
people. Neither our poetry nor our scholarship rests
on such a broad basis of popular appreciation. Our
sense of the ludicrous is not the possession of a limited
class; it is a national trait. It declares itself in the
funny columns of countless newspapers, in our popular songs, our minstrels, our theatres, our slang; it is
stamped on thousands of funny stories that, handed
on from one to another, traverse the whole country
with wonderful swiftness. No wonder, then, that
when some of this popular sense of humor gets into
literature we recognize in it marks of a national trait.

Our American humor in its different manifestations is of so many different grades that it is difficult
to speak of it as a whole. Our best writers, such

---

* Andrew Lang. Article on "American Humor," in *Lost
Leaders*, p. 70.

as Irving, Lowell, and Holmes, have created works
which from the firm and enduring quality of their
humor are fairly entitled to be called classical; but
from such masterpieces as *The History of New York*
or *The Biglow Papers* we descend through innumerable gradations to the crude coloring and broadly
farcical fun of certain of our illustrated papers, or to
the yet wider realms that lie beyond the range of
print. Much of our most characteristic humor lies
in an uncertain region somewhere between these two
extremes, and we might mention many writers who
furnished fun to our fathers or grandfathers, whose
works are now little more than empty names.

The last thirty years has been especially rich in
humorous writings of a distinctly original character.
We need not ask how many of these works which
amuse us will continue to amuse our descendants: it
is enough to say that at least they have filled a large
space in the period we are considering. These years
have given us HENRY W. SHAW (1818–1885), known
to most of us as "Josh Billings"; CHARLES FARRAR
BROWNE ("Artemus Ward") (1834–1867); and
SAMUEL LANGHORNE CLEMENS, or "Mark Twain."
Besides these are many others: DAVID ROSS LOCKE,
prominent after the war, under the pseudonym of
"Petroleum Vesuvius Nasby," as a political satirist;
EDGAR WILSON NYE, or "Bill Nye"; ROBERT J.
BURDETTE, of the *Burlington Hawkeye;* and countless
others of varying shades of merit. If we look at the
work of these writers as a whole, without any attempt
at specific criticism, it is evident that it is broadly

representative, because the essential elements of its
humor are a structural part of our national character.
It has, in the first place, an underlying basis of sound
morality and hard common sense. It often sins
against good taste, but seldom against good morals;
on the contrary, we can often detect under its extravagance and absurdity a definite moral purpose. "Josh
Billings," in his *Farmer's Allminax* (1869), is another
Franklin, as shrewd and as sensible as "Poor
Richard," but with a distinctly higher moral tone.
Take away the thin disguise of bad spelling from
Shaw's best sayings, and we find the typical American
who "thinks straight and sees clear," the teacher
of the people who can pack the essence of a subject
into a homely epigram. This absence of any display
of sentiment, this mingling of sound sense and a
profound seriousness of purpose with a quaint or
humorous expression, is characteristic not only of
Franklin, but of that broadly representative American, Abraham Lincoln.

A still more conspicuous trait in our American
humor is its lack of reverence. As a people we find
a genuine schoolboy's pleasure in the dese-
cration or belittling of anything solemn,   **Our lack of
reverence.**
venerable, or impressive, and we have a
corresponding fear of betraying either enthusiasm or
emotion. The purpose of Mark Twain's famous
books of travel is said to be the ridicule of the rhap-
sodies of the American tourist in Europe; but to
some of us even shallow raptures are better than a
cynical levity. In his *Innocents Abroad*, whatever

its purpose, we see the typical American Philistine, turned loose among the proudest achievements of civilization, poking fun at Michael Angelo, winking familiarly in the most inopportune places, and habitually flippant in the presence of things consecrated to reverence.* This "unwearying search after the comic side of serious subjects" and "after the mean possibilities of the sublime" runs through an enormous proportion of our humorous literature. We find material for jesting in our enthusiasms, our aspirations, and our beliefs, while some of our most serious national problems and gravest national perils —the corruption of politics or dishonesty in business

Exaggeration as an element in our humor. —furnish stock subjects for the cheap wit of the newspaper paragrapher. With the same coolness, levity, and jaunty self-sufficiency we Americans have delighted in playing base-ball under the shadow of the Sphinx, or in instituting a Wild West Show in the Coliseum. The culmination of our impervious audacity is shown in the story of the progressive traveller who blew out the light, believed by the pious to have been burning in a certain shrine for a thousand years, with the triumphant exclamation, "Well, I guess it's out now!" Another element in our humor is the daring absurdity of its exaggeration: thus we are told of the Texas cows, so thin that it takes two men to see one

---

* It is but just to remind the student that Mark Twain has done some excellent work of a quite different character. He is here alluded to simply as a humorist.

of them, and of the express train that went so fast that the mile-posts looked like a pale fence.

Looking at our American humor as impartially as we can, we must acknowledge that, while it is almost invariably clever and amusing, it often fails in those deeper and finer elements which give to the work of the world's greatest humorists a more enduring quality. The masters of humor do not deal in broad farce only; they do not place their chief reliance on the travesty of the sacred or the admirable; they are not merely amusing,—they are rather lords of that dubious border-land, full of pathetic suggestion, which lies between laughter and tears. While our humor is not without these finer elements, they are subordinated, on the whole, to a good-natured cynicism or a boisterous fun.

The work of our humorists is, nevertheless, a wholesome and a hopeful element in our national literature. It has behind it the power of an enormous popular sympathy and a crude but vigorous native force; back of it is a great nation, dexterous, nimble-witted, alert; a nation that thinks and lives fast, with a keen sense of the ludicrous, and an almost invincible good-humor. We have already contributed in no small degree to the innocent "gaiety of nations," and we can hardly doubt that humor will continue to be one of the distinctions of our literature in the years to come.

We began our study by remarking that in its origin our literature was a literature of sections: we declared that its history was, before all, the story of the drawing together of this group of isolated literatures into a comparative unity, out of which a more truly national literature might come. After completing our survey of literary progress during the latest

Conclusion. period we are better able to realize that the local differences impressed so deeply upon the great sections of the country from the first are not even now wholly effaced. Looking back over our past we know that these differences are the inevitable result of many causes, and that nothing can obliterate them but time. It is not merely for convenience that we have continued to classify our writers, as far as possible, according to the section which produced them. We have still a literature of New England, another of the Middle States, another of the South, and yet another of the West, each distinguished by characteristics of its own. As yet, a truly national literature can hardly be said to exist, for such a literature must have back of it a homogeneous people with a distinctive national character and ideals. Shakespeare does not stand for his native county of Warwickshire; he stands for England and the English type. We cannot imagine that even a genius equal to Shakespeare could so stand for America, for the American types and the American ideals are yet too varied and uncertain. But if we are not yet a nation in this deeper sense, we can see that out of much confusion one national character is taking form. One terrible menace to union has been met and overcome; modern methods of transportation and communication have helped and are still helping to bind together our widely scattered population, and the spread of

a practically uniform system of popular education is
continually bringing Americans into a closer union
and establishing between them the bond of a common
ideal.   These things are legitimate causes of encouragement so far as our literary future is concerned.
We are inclined to speak hopefully of that future,
but by no means with a foolish confidence.   So far our
literature, with all its successes, is but little more
than the earnest of something greater to come.   Its
share in the higher life of man must depend largely
on the faithfulness of the American people to their
highest ideals.   If we believe that a noble future lies
before our democracy, we will believe that it lies before our literature likewise.   There is no lack of inherent ability in us; we can do what we will.   If as
a nation we can be saved from the dangers of great
possessions, if we can resist the thousand insidious
influences which are corrupting our national character, and give that which is best in us free play,
American literature, like that of Greece, Rome, or
England, will take its place among the most precious
and imperishable possessions of our race.

APPENDIX

TABLE I.—COLONIAL ERA, CIR. 1607—CIR. 1765.

ENGLISH HISTORY AND LITERATURE.	AMERICAN HISTORY.	NEW ENGLAND LITERATURE.	MIDDLE STATES LITERATURE.	SOUTHERN LITERATURE.
James I., reigns 1603-1625. Dekker and Webster's "Westward Ho!," 1607. Milton, born 1608. Chapman's "Translation of Iliad (Books I. to XII.)," 1610. Shakespeare's "Tempest," 1610. King James' Version of the Bible completed, 1611. Samuel Butler, born 1612. Jeremy Taylor, born 1613. Chapman's "Translation of the Odyssey," 1614. Raleigh's "History of the World," 1614. Beaumont, died 1616. Shakespeare, died 1616. Raleigh, died 1618. Ben Jonson, Poet Laureate, 1619. Bacon's "Novum Organum," 1620.	Landing of English at Jamestown, 1607. Quebec founded, 1608. Hudson River discovered, 1609. Lake Champlain discovered, 1609. Hudson Bay discovered, 1610. Dutch trading-post established on Manhattan Island, 1613. John Smith explored the New England coast, 1614. First negro slaves imported into Virginia, 1619. First representative assembly in the United States, 1619. Landing of Pilgrims, 1620.	The Pilgrim Fathers: Mayflower Compact, written 1620. Bradford and Winslow: "A Relation or Journal," written 1620-1621, published 1622.		John Smith (1580-1631): "A True Relation of Such Occurrences and Accidents of Note as hath Happened in Virginia," 1608 (London). William Strachey: "A True Repertory of the Wrack and Redemption of Sir Thomas Gates, Knight," etc., 1610. John Smith: "A Map of Virginia, with a Description of the Country, the Commodities, People, Government, and Religion" (Oxford),1612. "A Description of New England," 1616.

TABLE I.—COLONIAL ERA, CIR. 1607—CIR. 1765—*Continued*

ENGLISH HISTORY AND LITERATURE.	AMERICAN HISTORY.	NEW ENGLAND LITERATURE.	MIDDLE STATES LITERATURE.	SOUTHERN LITERATURE.
Burton's "Anatomy of Melancholy," 1621. Shakespeare, First Folio, 1623. Charles I., reigns 1625-1649.	First Indian Massacre in Virginia, 1622. New Amsterdam settled by Dutch, 1623.	William Bradford (1588-1657): "History of Plymouth Plantation," 1630. (Written from about 1630 onward.)		John Smith (with others), "The General History of Virginia, New England, and the Summer Isles," 1624.
Bacon's Essays (final form), 1625. John Fletcher, d. 1625. Bacon, died 1626. Middleton, died 1627. Bunyan, born 1628. Petition of Right, 1628. Dryden, born 1631. Donne, died 1631. Locke, born, 1632. Milton's "L'Allegro," and "Il Penseroso," 1632. George Herbert, died 1633 Milton's "Comus" (acted), 1631. Ben Jonson, died 1637. Dekker, died 1637. Milton's "Lycidas," written 1637.	Salem founded, 1628. Boston founded, 1630. First colonization of Maryland, 1634. First important colonization in Connecticut, 1635. Harvard College founded, 1636. Roger Williams founded Providence, 1636. The Pequot War, 1637. First printing-press in America set up by Stephen Day, at Cambridge, 1639.	John Winthrop, (1588-1649): "The History of New England," 1630. (Written from 1630-1648.) William Wood (1580?-1639): "New England's Prospect," (with map), 1634. William Pierce: "An Almanac for 1639; Calculated for New England," 1639. (First almanac printed in the Colonies.)		George Sandys (1577-1644): Translation of the Fifteen Books of Ovid's "Metamorphoses," 1626.

TABLE I.—COLONIAL ERA, CIR. 1607—CIR. 1765—*Continued*

ENGLISH HISTORY AND LITERATURE.	AMERICAN HISTORY.	NEW ENGLAND LITERATURE.	MIDDLE STATES LITERATURE.	SOUTHERN LITERATURE.
Burton, Ford, and Massinger, died 1640. Wycherley, born 1640. Milton's "Reason of Church Government urged against Prelacy," 1641.		Richard Mather (1596-1669), John Eliot (1604-1690) and others: "The Whole Book of Psalms Faithfully Translated into English Metre," 1640. (The Bay Psalm Book; first English *book* printed in America.)		
English Civil War began, 1642. Newton, born 1642.	John Eliot began to preach to the Indians, 1646.			
Sir T. Browne's "Religio Medici" (auth. ed.), 1643. Milton's "Areopagitica," 1644.	Stuyvesant, Governor of New Netherlands, 1646.	Roger Williams (1606-1683): "The Bloody Tenet of Persecution for Cause of Conscience," 1644.		
Charles I., Trial and Execution of, 1649. The Commonwealth, 1649.		Nathaniel Ward (1570-1653): "The Simple Cobbler of Agawam," by "Theodore de la Guard," 1647.		
Jeremy Taylor's "Holy Living," 1650 Charles II., crowned at Scone, 1651. Otway, born 1651. Hobbes's "Leviathan," 1651. Jeremy Taylor's "Holy Dying," 1651.		Anne Bradstreet (1613-1672): "The Tenth Muse lately sprung up in America, or Several Poems," 1650.		

TABLE I.—COLONIAL ERA, CIR. 1607—CIR. 1765—*Continued*

ENGLISH HISTORY AND LITERATURE.	AMERICAN HISTORY.	NEW ENGLAND LITERATURE.	MIDDLE STATES LITERATURE.	SOUTHERN LITERATURE.
George Herbert's "Country Parson," 1652. Cromwell, Lord High Protector, 1653. Walton's "The Complete Angler," 1653. Cromwell, died 1658. The Restoration, 1660. Charles II., reigns 1660–1685. The East India Company incorporated, 1660.		John Eliot (1601–1990): Translation of the New Testament into Algonquin, 1661. (The Holy Bible, 1663.) Michael Wigglesworth (1631–1715): "The Day of Doom, or a Poetical Description of the Great and Last Judgment," 1662.		John Hammond: "Leah and Rachel; or, The Two Fruitful Sisters, Virginia and Maryland," 1656 (?).
Defoe, born 1661. Butler's "Hudibras," Part I., 1663; Part II., 1664; Part III., 1678. Prior, born 1664. Waller's Poems, 1664. Great Plague in London, 1665. Great Fire in London, 1666. Shirley, died 1666. Cowley, and Jeremy Taylor, died 1667. Swift, born 1667. Milton's "Paradise Lost," 1667.	Settlement of North Carolina, 1661. New Netherlands conquered by the English; New Amsterdam became New York, 1664. First permanent settlement of New Jersey, 1665.	"God's Controversy with New England," 1662.		George Alsop: "A Character of the Province of Maryland," 1666.

TABLE I.—COLONIAL ERA, CIR. 1607—CIR. 1765—*Continued*

ENGLISH HISTORY AND LITERATURE.	AMERICAN HISTORY.	NEW ENGLAND LITERATURE.	MIDDLE STATES LITERATURE.	SOUTHERN LITERATURE.
Pepys's Diary, ended May 31, 1669. Dryden, Poet Laureate, 1670. Milton's "Paradise Regained" and "SamsonAgonistes," 1671. Steele and Addison, born 1672. Rowe, born 1673. Herrick and Milton, died 1674. Bunyan's "Pilgrim's Progress," Part I., 1678; Part II., 1684. Hobbes, died 1679. Samuel Butler, died 1680. Dryden's "Absalom and Achitophel," 1681. Sir T. Browne, d. 1682. Bunyan's "Holy War," 1682. Izaak Walton, d. 1683. James II., reigns 1685-1688. Cotton's "Translation of Montaigne's Essays," 1685.	Hudson Bay Company incorporated, 1669. "Old South" Church, Boston, founded 1669. Mississippi River discovered, 1673. Printing-press set up at Boston, 1674. King Philip's War, 1675. "Bacon's Rebellion" in Virginia, 1676. William Penn founded Philadelphia, 1682. Charter of Massachusetts declared forfeited, 1684.	Anne Bradstreet: "Several Poems Compiled with Great Variety of Wit and Learning," 1678. Cotton Mather (1663-1728): "An Elegy on the Much-to-be-Deplored Death of that Never-to-be-Forgotten Person, Rev. Mr. Nathaniel Collins," 1685.	Daniel Denton: "A Brief Description of New York," 1670. William Penn (1644-1718): "Brief Account of Pennsylvania," 1683.	

TABLE I.—COLONIAL ERA, CIR. 1607—CIR. 1765—*Continued*

ENGLISH HISTORY AND LITERATURE.	AMERICAN HISTORY.	NEW ENGLAND LITERATURE.	MIDDLE STATES LITERATURE.	SOUTHERN LITERATURE.
Waller, died 1687. Bunyan, died 1688. Gay and Pope, b. 1688. The English Revolution, 1688. William and Mary, reign 1689-1702. Richardson, born 1689. Locke's "Essay Concerning Human Understanding," 1690. Dryden's "Translation of Virgil," 1697. Hogarth, born 1697. Dryden, died 1700. Thomson, born 1700. Queen Anne, reigns 1702-1714. Defoe's "Shortest Way with the Dissenters," 1702. Pepys, died 1703. John Wesley, born 1703. Locke, died 1704. Swift's "Battle of the Books," and "Tale of a Tub," 1704.	William Bradford set up printing-press at or near Philadelphia, 1685. First paper-mill in United States erected at Germantown, 1690. William and Mary College chartered, 1692. Yale College founded, 1700. Printing-press in Maryland, 1700.	Cotton Mather: "Memorable Providences relating to Witchcrafts and Possessions," etc., 1689. "Public Occurrences," Boston, Sept. 25, 1690. (Sometimes called the first American newspaper.) Increase Mather (1639-1723): "A Further Account of the New England Witches," 1692. Cotton Mather: "Wonders of the Invisible World," 1693. Cotton Mather: "Magnalia," etc., 1702. "The Day Which the Lord has Made," 1703. The Boston News Letter, established Apr. 24, 1704. (The first newspaper in what is now the United States.)	Almanack printed by William Bradford, Philadelphia, 1687. William Penn: "The Excellent Privilege of Liberty and Property," 1687. Daniel Leeds (Compiler): "The Temple of Wisdom," 1688. Gabriel Thomas: "An Historical and Geographical Account of the Province and County of Pennsylvania and New Jersey," 1698.	Robert Beverley (?-1716): "History of Virginia," 1705.

TABLE I.—COLONIAL, ERA, CIR. 1607—CIR. 1765—*Continued*

ENGLISH HISTORY AND LITERATURE.	AMERICAN HISTORY.	NEW ENGLAND LITERATURE.	MIDDLE STATES LITERATURE.	SOUTHERN LITERATURE.
Evelyn, died 1706. Union of Scotland and England as Great Britain, 1707. Fielding, born 1707. William Pitt, Lord Chatham, born 1708. Steele, Addison, and others: *The Tatler*, 1709. Rowe's Edition of Shakespeare, 1709. Hume, born 1711. Steele, Addison, and others: *The Spectator*, 1711. Sterne, born 1713. Pope's "Windsor Forest" and "Ode for Saint Cecilia's Day," 1713. George I., reigns 1714–1727. Nicholas Rowe, Poet Laureate, 1715. Wycherley, died 1715. Pope's "Translation of the Iliad." (Books I. to IV.), 1715. Gray, born 1716.	Thomas Hutchinson, born 1711.	Cotton Mather: "Good Lessons for Children," Verse, 1706. Cotton Mather: "Bonifacius; an Essay upon the Good that is to be Devised and Designed," 1710.		"Ebenezer Cook, Gentleman": "The Sot-Weed Factor, or A Voyage to Maryland," 1708.

TABLE I.—COLONIAL ERA, CIR. 1607—CIR. 1765—*Continued*

ENGLISH HISTORY AND LITERATURE.	AMERICAN HISTORY.	NEW ENGLAND LITERATURE.	MIDDLE STATES LITERATURE.	SOUTHERN LITERATURE.
Addison, died 1719. Defoe's "Robinson Crusoe" (Part I.), 1719. Prior died, Collins and Smollett born, 1721. Defoe's "Journal of the Plague Year," 1722. Sir Joshua Reynolds and Adam Smith, born 1723. Ramsay's "Gentle Shepherd," 1725. Swift's "Gulliver's Travels," 1726. Newton, died 1727. Gay's Fables, 1727. George II., reigns 1727-1760. Goldsmith, born 1728. Congreve and Steele, died 1729. Burke, born 1729. Defoe, died 1731. Cowper, born 1731. Theobald's Edition of Shakespeare, 1733. Butler's "Analogy of Religion," 1736. Gibbon, born 1737.	Samuel Adams, born 1722. James Otis, born 1725. Printing-press established in Charleston, S. C., 1730. Franklin originated the Library Company of Philadelphia, 1731. Washington, born 1732. Georgia settled, 1733. John Adams, born 1735. Patrick Henry, born 1736.	The Boston Gazette established, 1719. James Franklin: *The New England Courant*, Boston, 1721. Roger Wolcott (1679-1767): "Poetical Meditations," 1725. (?) "Hoop Petticoats Arraigned and Condemned by the Light of Nature and Law of God," 1726. Mather Byles (1707-1788): "A Poem on the Death of King George I., and the Accession of George II." 1727. Cotton Mather: "Boanerges: A Short Essay to Strengthen the Impressions Produced by Earthquakes," 1727. Samuel Sewall (1652-1730): Diary (manuscript finished), 1729.	*The American Weekly Mercury* established, Philadelphia, 1719. James Logan (1674-1751): "In Laudem Pennsylvaniæ Poema," 1729. George Webb: "Batchelors-Hall," (a Poem), 1731. Benjamin Franklin (1706-1790): "Poor Richard's Almanac" (begun), 1732. James Logan: "Cato's Moral Distichs Englished in Couplets," 1735.	First Almanac in Virginia, 1731. *The Virginia Gazette* established, 1736. (First newspaper in the State.)

TABLE 1.—COLONIAL ERA, CIR. 1607—CIR. 1765—*Continued*

ENGLISH HISTORY AND LITERATURE.	AMERICAN HISTORY.	NEW ENGLAND LITERATURE.	MIDDLE STATES LITERATURE.	SOUTHERN LITERATURE.
Richardson's "Pamela," 1740. Fielding's "Joseph Andrews," 1742. Pope, died 1744. Swift, died 1745. Thomson, died 1748. Richardson's "Clarissa Harlowe," 1748. Smollett's "Roderick Random," 1748. Fielding's "Tom Jones," 1749. Sheridan, born 1751. Gray's "Elegy in a Country Church-yard," 1751. Richardson's "Sir Charles Grandison," 1753. Fielding, died 1754. Crabbe, born 1754. Johnson's "Dictionary of the English Language," 1755. Battle of Plassey, 1757.	Thomas Jefferson, born 1743. The first Bible printed in America, by Christopher Sower, (German, in Germantown (in German), 1743. Princeton College founded, 1746. University of Pennsylvania founded, 1749. James Madison, born 1751. King's College (now Columbia) founded, 1754. Braddock's defeat, 1755. First newspapers in North Carolina and in Connecticut, 1755.	Jonathan Edwards (1703-1758): "Sinners in the Hands of an Angry God," 1741.	Benjamin Franklin: *The General Magazine and Historical Chronicle for all the British Plantations in America* (monthly), 1741. John Webbe: *The American Magazine* (monthly), 1741. James Logan: Translation of "De Senectute," 1744. Benjamin Franklin: "Hypothesis for Explaining the Several Phenomena of Thunder-Gusts," etc., 1750. John Bartram (1699-1777): "Observations," (Travels to Lake Ontario), 1751. Benjamin Franklin: "Plan of Union for the Colonies" (printed?), 1754. William Smith (1728-1793): "History of New York from the First Discovery to the Year 1732," 1757.	

TABLE I.—COLONIAL ERA, CIR. 1607—CIR. 1765—*Continued*

ENGLISH HISTORY AND LITERATURE.	AMERICAN HISTORY.	NEW ENGLAND LITERATURE.	MIDDLE STATES LITERATURE.	SOUTHERN LITERATURE.
Johnson's "The Idler," 1758–1760. Collins, died 1759. Burns, born 1759. Johnson's "Rasselas," 1759. George III., reigns 1760–1820. Richardson, died 1761. Hogarth, died 1764. Ann Radcliffe, b. 1764. Percy's "Reliques of Ancient Poetry," 1765.	Capture of Quebec, 1759. Writs of assistance in Massachusetts, 1761. Printing-press established in Georgia, 1762. College of Rhode Island (now Brown University) established, 1764. Stamp Act, 1765 (repealed 1766).	Jonathan Edwards: "A Treatise on Original Sin," 1758. James Otis (1725–1783): "Rights of the British Colonies Asserted and Proved," 1764.	*The American Magazine and Monthly Chronicle for the British Colonies,* 1757–1758. Benjamin Franklin: "Father Abraham's Speech," 1758. Thomas Godfrey, Jr. (1736–1763): "The Prince of Parthia" (written), 1758. (Acted in Philadelphia, 1767.) "The Court of Fancy," Poem, 1762. "Philadelphiensis," "The Manners of the Time." A Satire. 1762. "Juvenile Poems on Various Subjects, with the Prince of Parthia, a Tragedy," edited by Nathaniel Evans, 1765.	*The Georgia Gazette* established at Savannah, 1763. (First newspaper in Georgia.)

TABLE II.—BEGINNINGS OF NATIONALITY, CIR. 1765—CIR. 1815.

ENGLISH HISTORY AND LITERATURE	AMERICAN HISTORY	NEW ENGLAND LITERATURE	MIDDLE STATES LITERATURE	SOUTHERN LITERATURE
Goldsmith's "The Vicar of Wakefield," 1766. Maria Edgeworth, born 1767. Sterne's "Sentimental Journey," 1768. Sterne, died 1768. Gray's Poems, 1768. Lord North, Prime Minister, 1770. Wordsworth, b. 1770. Goldsmith's "The Deserted Village," 1770. Smollett's "Humphrey Clinker," 1771. Scott, born 1771. Gray and Smollett, died 1771. First edition of the "Encyclopædia Britanica," 1771. Warren Hastings, Governor-General of India, 1772. Coleridge. born 1772. Letters of "Junius," collected edition, 1772.	Dartmouth College founded, 1769. The "Boston Massacre," 1770.	Timothy Dwight (1752–1817): "America," a Poem, 1772.	Benjamin Franklin: "Autobiography," begun, 1771, published (complete ed.) 1868. Philip Freneau (1752–1832) (with Brackenridge): "The Rising Glory of America," 1772.	

TABLE II.—BEGINNINGS OF NATIONALITY, CIR. 1765—CIR. 1815—*Continued*

ENGLISH HISTORY AND LITERATURE.	AMERICAN HISTORY.	NEW ENGLAND LITERATURE.	MIDDLE STATES LITERATURE.	SOUTHERN LITERATURE.
Goldsmith, died 1774. Southey, born 1774. Burke's Speech on American Taxation, 1774. Chesterfield: Letters to his Son, 1774.	"Boston Tea Party," 1773. First Continental Congress, 1774. Boston Port Bill, 1774. Battles of Lexington and Bunker Hill, 1775.		Thomas Paine (1737-1809): "Common Sense," 1776, "The Crisis" (No. I.), 1776. (Last two numbers, 1783.)	Thomas Jefferson (1743-1826): The "Declaration of Independence," 1776.
Jane Austen, Lamb, and Landor, b. 1775. Burke's Speech on Conciliation with America, 1775. Sheridan's "The Rivals," 1775. Gibbon's "Decline and Fall of the Roman Empire" (Vol. I.), 1776.	Washington took command of the American Army, July 3, 1775. Siege of Boston, 1775. "Declaration of Independence," 1776. Boston evacuated by the British, 1776. Articles of Confederation adopted by Congress, 1777.	John Trumbull (1750-1831): "M'Fingal" (Canto I.), 1775.	Francis Hopkinson (1737-1791): "The Battle of the Kegs," 1779.	
Adam Smith's "The Wealth of Nations," 1776. Sheridan's "School for Scandal," 1777. Hazlitt, born 1778. Frances Burney's "Evelina," 1778.	Burgoyne's surrender, 1777. Independence of the United States acknowledged by France, 1778.			

TABLE II.—BEGINNINGS OF NATIONALITY, CIR. 1765—CIR. 1815—*Continued*

ENGLISH HISTORY AND LITERATURE.	AMERICAN HISTORY.	NEW ENGLAND LITERATURE.	MIDDLE STATES LITERATURE.	SOUTHERN LITERATURE.
Moore, born 1779. Johnson's "Lives of the Poets," 1779.	Paul Jones's victory with the *Bonhomme Richard*, 1779. Surrender of Cornwallis, 1781. Articles of Confederation ratified by all the States, 1781.	John Trumbull: "M'Fingal," complete, 1782.	Philip Freneau: Poems, 1786.	Thomas Jefferson: "Notes on the State of Virginia" (London), 1787.
Susan Ferrier, b. 1782. Frances Burney's "Cecilia," 1782.		Timothy Dwight: "The Conquest of Canaan," 1785.	Alexander Hamilton (1757–1804) (with Madison and Jay): *The Federalist*. (First collected edition), 1788.	
Cowper's "Table Talk," 1782.	First English Bible published in America 1782.	Joel Barlow (1764–1812): "The Vision of Columbus," 1787.		
Crabbe's "The Village," 1783.	Independence of the United States acknowledged by England, 1782.		Benjamin Franklin: "Antobiography" from 1757 to 1759 written, 1789.	
Cowper's "The Task," 1785.	Treaty of Paris, 1783. The Constitution of the United States, 1787.			
De Quincey, b. 1785.				
Impeachment of Warren Hastings, 1786.	Shays's Rebellion in Massachusetts, 1787.			
Byron, born 1788.				
White's "Natural History of Selborne," 1789.	George Washington inaugurated first President, 1789.	Susanna Haswell Rowson (1761–1824): "Charlotte Temple," 1790.	Thomas Paine: "Rights of Man," Part I., 1791; Part II. 1792.	
Adam Smith, d. 1790.	Vermont admitted, 1791.			
Boswell's "Life of Johnson," 1791.	Kentucky admitted, 1792.			
Shelley, born 1792.				

TABLE II.—BEGINNINGS OF NATIONALITY, CIR. 1765—CIR. 1815—*Continued*

ENGLISH HISTORY AND LITERATURE.	AMERICAN HISTORY.	NEW ENGLAND LITERATURE.	MIDDLE STATES LITERATURE.	SOUTHERN LITERATURE.
Burns' Poems, 1793. Gibbon, died 1794. Ann Radcliffe's "Mysteries of Udolpho," 1794. Carlyle and Keats, born 1795. Burns, died 1796. Coleridge's Poems, 1796. Burke, died 1797. Hood, born 1798. Cowper, died 1800. Macaulay, born 1800. Coleridge's Translation of "Wallenstein," 1800. Maria Edgeworth's "Castle Rackrent," 1800. John Henry Newman, born 1801.	The Whiskey Insurrection, 1794. Tennessee admitted, 1796. John Adams, President 1797. Washington became the Capital of the United States, 1800. Thomas Jefferson, President 1801.	Phillis Wheatley Peters (1753?-1784): Poems, 1793. Joel Barlow: "Hasty Pudding," 1796.	Thomas Paine: "The Age of Reason," 1794. (Part II., 1795.) "The Columbian Muse," a Selection of American Poetry, New York, 1794. Philip Freneau: New Poems (1768-1794), 1795. Joseph Hopkinson (1770-1842): "Hail Columbia," written 1798. Charles Brockden Brown (1771-1810): "Wieland," 1798. "Ormond," 1799. "Arthur Mervyn," Part I., 1799; Part II., 1800. "Edgar Huntley," 1801. "Clara Howard," 1801. "Jane Talbot," 1801. William Clifton (1772-1799): Poems, 1800. Joseph Dennie (1768-1812): Established The Portfolio (Philadelphia), 1801.	George Washington (1732-1799): Farewell Address, 1796.

TABLE II.—BEGINNINGS OF NATIONALITY. CIR. 1765—CIR. 1815—*Continued*

ENGLISH HISTORY AND LITERATURE.	AMERICAN HISTORY.	NEW ENGLAND LITERATURE.	MIDDLE STATES LITERATURE.	SOUTHERN LITERATURE.
Maria Edgeworth's "Moral Tales," 1801. Union of Great Britain and Ireland, 1801. Jane Porter's "Thaddeus of Warsaw," 1803. War between England and France, 1803. Maria Edgeworth's "Popular Tales," 1804. Scott's "Lay of the Last Minstrel," 1805. Battles of Trafalgar and Austerlitz, 1805. J. S. Mill, born 1806. Coleridge's "Christabel," 1806. Lamb's "Tales from Shakespeare," 1807. Moore's "Irish Melodies," 1807. Wordsworth's Poems, 1807. Scott's "Marmion," 1808. *Quarterly Review* established, 1808. Jane Porter's "Scottish Chiefs," 1810.	Ohio admitted, 1802. Bowdoin College founded 1802. Louisiana purchase, 1803. Fulton's steamer "Clermont" on the Hudson, 1807. The Embargo Act, 1807.	Joel Barlow (1755-1812): "The Columbiad," 1807. Fisher Ames (1758-1808): Speeches and Writings, 1809. Isaiah Thomas (1749-1831): "History of Printing in America," 1810.	*The New York Evening Post* established, 1801.	William Wirt (1772-1834): "Letters of a British Spy," 1803; "Life of Patrick Henry," 1817. John Marshall (1755-1835): "Life of Washington," 1804.

TABLE III.—LITERATURE OF THE REPUBLIC, CIR. 1809—CIR. 1897.*

ENGLISH HISTORY AND LITERATURE.	AMERICAN HISTORY.	NEW ENGLAND LITERATURE.	MIDDLE AND WESTERN LITERATURE.	SOUTHERN LITERATURE.
George III., reigns 1760–1820.	Lincoln, born 1809.	Samuel Woodworth (1785–1842):	Washington Irving (1783–1859):	
E. B. Browning, born 1809.	Madison, President, 1809.	"New Haven, A Poem Satirical and Sentimental," 1809.	"Salmagundi" (with J. K. Paulding), 1807–1808.	
Tennyson, born 1809.		"The Old Oaken Bucket."	" Knickerbocker's History of New York," 1809.	
C. Darwin, born 1809.			"Sketch-Book," 1819–1820.	
Campbell's "Gertrude of Wyoming," 1809.		Benjamin Silliman (1779–1864):	" Bracebridge Hall," 1822.	
Shelley's "Zastrozzi," (an early romance), 1810.		"Travels in England, Holland, and Scotland," 1810.	" Life and Voyages of Columbus," 1828.	
E. Gaskell, born 1810.			" The Alhambra," 1832.	
Southey's "Curse of Kehama," 1810.		Edward Everett (1794–1865):	" Life of Washington," 1855–1859.	
Scott's "Lady of the Lake," 1810.		"Defence of Christianity," 1814.		
Thackeray, born 1811.	War with England, 1812.	"The Progress of Literature in America," 1824.		
Jane Austen's "Sense and Sensibility," 1811.	Louisiana admitted, 1812.			
R. Browning, born 1812.	Battle of Lake Erie, 1813.	John Neal (1793–1876):		
Byron's "Childe Harold," 1812–1818.	Washington entered by the British, 1814.	"Keep Cool," 1817.		
Shelley's "Queen Mab," 1813.	Treaty of Peace with England, 1814.			
Wordsworth's "The Excursion," 1814.				
Scott's "Waverley" novels, 1814–1831.				

* In this table the chronological position of an author is determined by the date of his first important publication. He is assigned to the section of the country in which the bulk of his work has been produced.

TABLE III.—LITERATURE OF THE REPUBLIC, CIR. 1809—CIR. 1897.—*Continued*

ENGLISH HISTORY AND LITERATURE.	AMERICAN HISTORY.	NEW ENGLAND LITERATURE.	MIDDLE AND WESTERN LITERATURE.	SOUTHERN LITERATURE.
Battle of Waterloo, 1815. Coleridge's "Christabel," 1816. Charlotte Bronte, born 1816. Moore's "Lalla Rookh," 1817. Keats' Poems, 1817. *Blackwood's Magazine* established, 1817. Coleridge's "Biographia Literaria," 1817. Keats' "Endymion," 1818. J. A. Froude, born 1818. C. Kingsley, born 1819. J. Ruskin, born 1819. George IV., reigns 1820–1830. Shelley's "Prometheus Unbound," 1820. Mary Ann Evans (George Eliot), born 1820. Herbert Spencer, born 1820. Tyndall, born 1820.	Battle of New Orleans, 1815. Indiana admitted, 1816. Monroe. President, 1817. Mississippi admitted, 1817. Illinois admitted, 1818. Florida purchased from Spain, 1819. Alabama admitted, 1819. Maine admitted, 1820. The Missouri Compromise, 1820.	James Gates Percival (1795–1856): "Poems," 1821. "The Dream of a Day," 1813. Richard Henry Dana (1787–1879): "Dying Raven," 1821. "The Buccaneer," 1827. Catherine Maria Sedgwick (1789–1867): "The New England Tale," 1822. "Hope Leslie," 1827. Noah Webster (1758–1843): "Dictionary of the English Language," 1828. Lydia Maria Child (1802–1880): "Hobomok," 1824. "Progress of Religious Ideas," 1855.	William Cullen Bryant (1794–1878). "The Embargo" (second edition, enlarged), 1809. "Thanatopsis," (in *North American Review*), 1817. "Poems," 1821. "Thirty Poems," 1869. Translation of "The Iliad," 1870. Translation of "The Odyssey," 1871–1872. "Orations and Addresses," 1873. James K. Paulding (1779–1860): "The Backwoodsman," 1818. Fitz-Greene Halleck (1790–1867): "Fanny," 1819; (with additions) 1821. "Alnwick Castle, and Other Poems," 1827. "Poems," 1847, 1852, 1858.	

TABLE III.—LITERATURE OF THE REPUBLIC, CIR. 1809—CIR. 1897—*Continued*

ENGLISH HISTORY AND LITERATURE.	AMERICAN HISTORY.	NEW ENGLAND LITERATURE.	MIDDLE AND WESTERN LITERATURE.	SOUTHERN LITERATURE.
De Quincey's "Confessions of an Opium Eater," 1821. Keats, died 1821. Lamb's "Essays of Elia," 1822–1824. M. Arnold, born 1822. Shelley, died 1822. Landor's "Imaginary Conversations," 1824–1824. Byron, died 1824. *Westminster Review* established, 1824. Hood's "Whims and Oddities," 1826. E. B. Browning's Poems, 1826. Dante G. Rossetti, b. 1828. *The Athenæum* established, 1828. *The Spectator* established, 1828. Repeal of Test and Corporation Acts, 1828. Catholic Emancipation Act, 1829.	Missouri admitted, 1821. U. S. Grant, born 1822. "Monroe Doctrine," 1823. J. Q. Adams, President, 1825. University of Virginia opened, 1825. Jackson President, 1829.	Henry Wadsworth Longfellow (1807–1882): "Poems," 1826. "Hyperion," 1839. "Voices of the Night," 1839. "Poems on Slavery," 1842. "Evangeline," 1847. "Hiawatha," 1855. "Ultima Thule," 1880. "In the Harbor," 1882. Nathaniel Hawthorne (1804–1864): "Fanshawe," 1828. "The Scarlet Letter," 1850. "The House of the Seven Gables," 1851. "The Marble Faun," 1860. "Dr. Grimshaw's Secret," 1883. Charles Sprague (1791–1875): "Prize Poems," 1824. "Poems," 1841.	Joseph R. Drake (1795–1820): "Poems by Croaker and Company" (with Halleck), 1819. "The Culprit Fay, and Other Poems, 1835. James Fenimore Cooper (1789–1851): "Precaution," 1820. "The Spy," 1821. "The Pioneers," 1823. "The Last of the Mohicans," 1826. "The Pathfinder," 1840. "The Deerslayer," 1841. James Kent (1763–1847): "Commentaries on American Law," 1826–1830.	

TABLE III.—LITERATURE OF THE REPUBLIC, CIR. 1800—CIR. 1897—*Continued*

ENGLISH HISTORY AND LITERATURE.	AMERICAN HISTORY.	NEW ENGLAND LITERATURE.	MIDDLE AND WESTERN LITERATURE.	SOUTHERN LITERATURE.
Tennyson's "Poems, chiefly Lyrical," 1830. William IV., reigns 1830-1837. Opening of the Liverpool and Manchester Railway, 1830. Reform Bill passed, 1832. *Chambers' Journal* established, 1832. Scott, died 1832. Sir Edwin Arnold born 1832. R. Browning's "Pauline," 1833. E. B. Browning's translation of "Prometheus Unbound," 1833. Carlyle's "Sartor Resartus," (in *Fraser's Magazine*), 1833. Emancipation of Slaves Act, 1833. "Penny Cyclopædia," 1833. S. T. Coleridge, died 1834.	Nullification Act of South Carolina, 1832.	William Ellery Channing (1780-1842): "Discourses, Reviews and Miscellanies," 1830. John Greenleaf Whittier (1807-1892): "Legends of New England," 1831. "Mogg Megone," 1836. "Voices of Freedom," 1849. "Snow-Bound," 1866. "At Sundown," 1892. Joseph Story (1779-1845): "Commentaries on the Constitution of the United States," 1833. George Bancroft (1800-1891): "United States History," 1834-1874.	Nathaniel Parker Willis (1806-1867): "Sketches," 1827. "Pencillings by the Way," 1835, 1844. "Paul Fane," 1856. *New York Herald* established, 1835. *New York Tribune* established, 1841. *Graham's Magazine* established, 1841. J. Bayard Taylor (1825-1878): "Ximena," 1841. "Book of Romances, Lyrics, and Songs," 1851. "Hannah Thurston," 1863. Translation of "Faust," 1870-1871. "Critical Essays and Literary Notes," 1880. Herman Melville (1819-1891): "Typee," 1846. "Moby-Dick," 1851.	Edward Coate Pinkney (1802-1828): "Rodolph, and Other Poems," 1825. Henry Clay (1777-1852): "Speeches in the House of Representatives," 1826. William Gilmore Simms (1806-1870): "Lyrical and Other Poems," 1827. "Atalantis," 1832. "The Yemassee," 1835. "The Partisan," 1835. *The Southern Review* established, 1828. Edgar Allan Poe (1809-1849): "Tamerlane and Other Poems," 1827. "MS. found in a Bottle," 1833. "The Raven and Other Poems," 1845.

TABLE III.—LITERATURE OF THE REPUBLIC, CIR. 1809—CIR. 1897—*Continued*

ENGLISH HISTORY AND LITERATURE.	AMERICAN HISTORY.	NEW ENGLAND LITERATURE.	MIDDLE AND WESTERN LITERATURE.	SOUTHERN LITERATURE.
Lamb, died 1834. W. Morris, born 1834. Dickens's "Sketches by Boz" (as a serial), 1834. Browning's "Paracelsus," 1835. Municipal Reform Act, 1835. Dickens's "Pickwick," 1836–1837. Victoria, reigns 1837. Swinburne, born 1837. Carlyle's "French Revolution," 1837. First electric telegraph, 1837. Rise of trades unions and Chartism, 1837. Dickens's "Nicholas Nickleby," 1838–39. Thackeray's "Catherine," 1839. Penny post established, 1840. Queen Victoria's marriage to Prince Albert of Saxe-Coburg, 1840.	Arkansas admitted, 1836. Texas a republic, 1836. Van Buren, President, 1837. Michigan admitted, 1837. Independent Treasury Act, 1840.	Ralph Waldo Emerson (1803–1882): "Historical Discourse at Concord," 1835. "Nature" (Anon.), 1836. "Essays," 1st Series, 1841; 2d Series, 1844. "Poems," 1847, 1865. "Natural History of Intellect," 1893. Oliver Wendell Holmes (1809–1894): "Poems," 1836, 1846, 1849, 1850, 1862. "Autocrat of the Breakfast-Table," 1858. "Professor at the Breakfast-Table," 1860. "Elsie Venner," 1861. "The Guardian Angel," 1867. "Over the Tea-Cups," 1890.	Thomas Buchanan Read (1822–1872): "Poems," 1847. "The New Pastoral," 1855. "Sheridan's Ride," and others, 1865. George H. Boker (1823–1890): "The Lesson of Life and Other Poems," 1847. "Plays and Poems," 1856. "Poems of the War," 1864. Richard H. Stoddard (1825–): "Footprints," 1848. Complete editions of Poems, 1880. *Harper's Magazine* established, 1850. Henry Rowe Schoolcraft (1793–1864): "History, Conditions, and Prospects of the Indian Tribes," 1851–1855.	John J. Audubon (1780–1851): "Birds of America," 1830–1838. "Quadrupeds of North America," 1846–1850. John Pendleton Kennedy (1795–1870): "Swallow Barn," 1832. "Horse-Shoe Robinson," 1835. "Rob of the Bowl," 1838. A. B. Longstreet (1790–1870): "Georgia Scenes," 1835. *The Southern Literary Messenger*, 1835–1864. *The Southern Quarterly* established, 1842. Charles E. Gayarré (1805–): "Louisiana; its History as a French Colony," 1851–1852.

TABLE III.—LITERATURE OF THE REPUBLIC, CIR. 1809—CIR. 1897—*Continued*

ENGLISH HISTORY AND LITERATURE.	AMERICAN HISTORY.	NEW ENGLAND LITERATURE.	MIDDLE AND WESTERN LITERATURE.	SOUTHERN LITERATURE.
Robert Peel, Prime Minister, 1841. Carlyle's "Heroes and Hero Worship," 1841. *Punch* established, 1841. Dickens's "American Notes," 1842. Macaulay's "Lays of Ancient Rome," 1842. Southey, died 1843. Wordsworth: Poet Laureate, 1843. Macaulay's "Essays" (republished from *Edinburgh Review*), 1843. Ruskin's "Modern Painters," 1843-1860. Factory Bill, 1844. Repeal of Corn Laws, 1846. Charlotte Bronte's "Jane Eyre," 1847. Thackeray's "Vanity Fair," 1847-1848. Lord John Russell, Prime Minister, 1847. Macaulay's "History of England," 1848-1860.	Wm. H. Harrison, President, 1841. Tyler, President, April 4, 1841. University of Michigan opened, 1841. Morse telegraph in the United States, 1844. Polk, President, 1845. Texans admitted, 1845. Florida admitted, 1845. War with Mexico declared, 1845. Iowa admitted, 1846. Smithsonian Institution organized by Congress, 1846. City of Mexico captured, 1847. Wisconsin admitted, 1848.	Wm. Hickling Prescott (1796-1859): "Ferdinand and Isabella," 1837. "Conquest of Mexico," 1843. "Conquest of Peru," 1847. "Philip II.," 1855, 1858. George Ticknor (1791-1871): "History of Spanish Literature," 1849. "Life of Wm. Hickling Prescott," 1863. James Russell Lowell (1819-1891): "Class Poem," 1838. "Poems," 1841, 1848. "The Biglow Papers," 1st Series, 1848. 2d Series, 1866. "A Fable for Critics," 1848. "Among my Books," 1870, 1876. "My Study Windows," 1871. "Essays and Addresses," 1891.	George Wm. Curtis (1824-1892): "Nile Notes of a Howadji," 1851. "The Potiphar Papers," 1853. "Prue and I," 1856. "Address on James Russell Lowell," 1892. Richard Grant White (1822-1885): "Shakespeare's Scholar," 1854. "Studies in Shakespeare," 1885. Henry Reed (1808-1854): "Lectures on English Literature," (published) 1855. "Lectures on the British Poets," 1857. Walt Whitman (1819-1892): "Leaves of Grass," 1855. "Drum-Taps," 1865. "Democratic Vistas," 1870.	

TABLE III.—LITERATURE OF THE REPUBLIC, CIR. 1809—CIR. 1897—*Continued*

ENGLISH HISTORY AND LITERATURE.	AMERICAN HISTORY.	NEW ENGLAND LITERATURE.	MIDDLE AND WESTERN LITERATURE.	SOUTHERN LITERATURE.
M. Arnold's "The Strayed Reveller and Other Poems," 1848. E. Gaskell's "Mary Barton," 1848. M. Edgeworth, died 1819. Free libraries established, 1850. Wordsworth, died 1850. Tennyson: Poet Laureate, 1850. Tennyson's "In Memoriam," 1850. Duke of Wellington, died 1852. Thackeray's "Henry Esmond," 1852. Moore, died 1852. Kingsley's "Hypatia," 1853. Crimean War, 1854-1856. *Saturday Review* established, 1855. Froude's History of England, 1856-1869.	Peace with Mexico, 1848. Gold discovered in California, 1848. Taylor, President, 1849. Fillmore, President, 1850. California admitted, 1850. Pierce, President, 1853. Kansas-Nebraska Act, 1854.	Richard Henry Dana, Jr. (1815-1882): "Two Years before the Mast," 1840. "The Seaman's Friend," 1841. *The Dial*, published, 1840-1844. William Ware (1797-1852): "Julian, or Scenes in Judea," 1841. Theodore Parker (1810-1860): "Transient and Permanent in Christianity," 1841. Sylvester Judd (1813-1853): "Margaret," 1845. William Wetmore Story (1819-1895): "Poems," 1847, 1856. "Roba di Roma," 1862. "Poems," 1885.	*Putnam's Monthly Magazine* established, 1853. Charles Godfrey Leland (1824-): "The Poetry and Mystery of Dreams," 1855. "The Hans Breitmann Ballads," (in *Graham's*), 1856. "Abraham Lincoln and the Abolition of Slavery," 1879. Evert A. Duyckinck (1816-1878), and George L. Duyckinck (1823-1863): "Cyclopaedia of American Literature," 1856. John T. Trowbridge (1827-): "Neighbor Jackwood," 1857. "The Emigrant's Story," 1874. Miriam C. Harris (1834-): "Rutledge," 1860. "Missy," 1882.	Francis Lieber (1800-1872): "Civil Liberty and Self-Government," 1853. Mary Virginia Hawes ("Marion Harland") (1831-): "Alone," 1854. "The Hidden Path," 1855. John Esten Cooke (1830-1886): "The Virginia Comedians," 1854. "Virginia," (A History), 1883. "My Lady Pokahontas," 1885. Paul Hamilton Hayne (1830-1886): "Sonnets and Other Poems," 1855-1857. Complete edition, 1881. Henry Timrod (1829-1867): "Poems," 1859, 1873.

TABLE III.—LITERATURE OF THE REPUBLIC, CIR. 1809—CIR. 1897—*Continued*

ENGLISH HISTORY AND LITERATURE.	AMERICAN HISTORY.	NEW ENGLAND LITERATURE.	MIDDLE AND WESTERN LITERATURE.	SOUTHERN LITERATURE.
Indian Mutiny, 1857. Siege of Lucknow and Cawnpore Massacre, 1857. Thackeray's "Virginians," 1857-1859. George Eliot's "Scenes of Clerical Life," 1858. Jews admitted to Parliament, 1858. Tennyson's "Idylls of the King," 1858-1886. Darwin's "Origin of Species," 1859. George Eliot's "Adam Bede," 1859. Macaulay and De Quincey, died 1859. *Macmillan's Magazine* established, 1859. *Cornhill Magazine* established, 1860. Reade's "The Cloister and the Hearth," 1860. George Eliot's "Silas Marner," 1861. Prince Consort, died 1861.	Buchanan, President, 1857. The Dred Scott decision, 1857. Minnesota admitted, 1858. Oregon admitted, 1859. John Brown's raid, 1859. Secession of South Carolina, 1860. Lincoln, President, 1861. Confederate States organized, 1861.	Henry Theodore Tuckerman (1813-1871): "The Characteristics of Literature," 1849. "America and her Commentators," 1861. Francis Parkman (1823-1893): "The California and Oregon Trail," 1849. "The Conspiracy of Pontiac," 1851. "Pioneers of France in the New World," 1865. "Montcalm and Wolfe," 1884. Edwin Percy Whipple (1819-1886): "Essays and Reviews," 1848. "Literature of the Age of Elizabeth," 1869. "American Literature," 1887.	William Dean Howells (1837-): "Poems of Two Friends" (with John James Piatt), 1860. "Venetian Life," 1866. "Their Wedding Journey," 1871. "The Lady of the Aroostook," 1879. "The Rise of Silas Lapham," 1885. "The Quality of Mercy," 1892. Edmund Clarence Stedman (1833-): "Poems, Lyric and Idyllic," 1860. "The Victorian Poets," 1875. "Poets of America," 1885.	

TABLE III.—LITERATURE OF THE REPUBLIC, CIR. 1809—CIR. 1897—*Continued*

ENGLISH HISTORY AND LITERATURE.	AMERICAN HISTORY.	NEW ENGLAND LITERATURE.	MIDDLE AND WESTERN LITERATURE.	SOUTHERN LITERATURE.
Swinburne's "Rosamund," 1861.	Firing upon Fort Sumter, 1861.	Donald Grant Mitchell (Ik Marvel) (1822–):	Rebecca Harding Davis (1831–):	
E. B. Browning, died 1861.	Battle of Bull Run, 1861.	"Reveries of a Bachelor," 1850.	"Life in the Iron Mills," 1861.	
	Kansas admitted, 1861.	"Dream Life," 1851.	"Waiting for the Verdict," 1867.	
Thackeray, died 1863.	Battle of Shiloh, 1862.	"Pictures of Edgewood," 1869.	"Dallas Galbraith," 1868.	
Spencer's "Principles of Biology," 1864.	Battle of *Monitor* and *Merrimac*, 1862.	"American Lands and Letters," 1897.	"Frances Waldeaux," 1897.	
	Emancipation Proclamation, 1863.			
Landor, died 1864.	Battle of Gettysburg, 1863.	Harriet Beecher Stowe (1812–1896):	David Ross Locke (Petroleum V. Nasby) (1833–1888):	
	Surrender of Vicksburg, 1863.	"Uncle Tom's Cabin" (serial), 1851.	"The Nasby Papers," 1864.	
Matthew Arnold's "Essays in Criticism," 1865–1888.	West Virginia admitted, 1863.	"The Minister's Wooing," 1859.		
	Sherman's March to the Sea, 1864.	"Oldtown Folks," 1869.	Charles F. Browne (Artemus Ward) (1834–1867):	
Ruskin's "Sesame and Lilies," 1865.	Nevada admitted, 1864. Surrender of Lee, 1865.	Richard Hildreth (1807–1865):	"Artemus Ward: His Book," 1862.	
	Assassination of Lincoln, 1865.	"The White Slave," 1852.	"Artemus Ward: His Panorama," 1869.	
	Johnson, President, 1865.	"History of the United States," 1849–52.	Emma Lazarus (1849–1887):	
Fortnightly Review established, 1865.	Thirteenth Constitutional Amendment, 1865.	Jones Very (1813–1880):	"Poems and Translations," 1866.	
	Vassar College opened, 1865.	"Essays and Poems," 1839.	"Songs of a Semite," 1882.	

TABLE III.—LITERATURE OF THE REPUBLIC, CIR. 1809—CIR. 1897—*Continued*

ENGLISH HISTORY AND LITERATURE.	AMERICAN HISTORY.	NEW ENGLAND LITERATURE.	MIDDLE AND WESTERN LITERATURE.	SOUTHERN LITERATURE.
Bryce's "The Holy Roman Empire,"1886. George Eliot's "Felix Holt," 1866. Ruskin's "Crown of Wild Olives," 1866. Swinburne's "Poems and Ballads," 1866. *Contemporary Review* established, 1866. Disraeli Prime Minister, 1867. Parliamentary Reform Bill, 1867. Browning's "The Ring and the Book," 1868. William Morris's "The Earthly Paradise" (Vols. I. and II.), 1868. Gladstone, Prime Minister, 1868. Matthew Arnold's "Culture and Anarchy," 1869. Blackmore's "Lorna Doone," 1869. Lecky's "History of European Morals," 1869. *The Academy* established, 1869.	Tennessee readmitted (the first reconstructed State), 1866. The Atlantic Cable permanently laid, 1866. Reconstruction Act, 1867. Purchase of Alaska, 1867. Nebraska admitted, 1867. Impeachment of President Johnson, 1868. Fourteenth Constitutional Amendment, 1868. Cornell University opened, 1868. University of the South opened, 1868. Arkansas, North Carolina, South Carolina, Louisiana, and Florida readmitted,1868. Grant, President, 1869.	Henry David Thoreau (1817–1862): "Walden," 1854. "Summer," 1884. "Winter," 1887. "Autumn," 1892. William Winter (1836–): "The Convent," 1854. "English Rambles," 1883. "Shakespeare's England," 1886. John Lothrop Motley (1814–1877): "The Rise of the Dutch Republic," 1856. "The History of the United Netherlands" (1860–1868). "John of Barneveld," 1874. Francis James Child (1825–1896): Edited English and Scottish Ballads, 1857–58. *Atlantic Monthly* established, 1857.	S. Weir Mitchell (1829–): "The Wonderful Story of Fuz-Buz," 1867. "Hepzibah Guinness," 1880. "Roland Blake,"1886. "Hugh Wynne, Free Quaker," 1897. John Burroughs (1837–): "Notes on Walt Whitman," 1867. "Wake-Robin," 1871. "Fresh Fields," 1884. F. Bret Harte (1839–): "Condensed Novels," 1867. "The Luck of Roaring Camp," 1870. "In the Carquinez Woods," 1883. "Susy," 1893. Henry C. Lea (1825–): "Studies in Church History," 1869. "History of the Inquisition of the Middle Ages,"1887–1888.	

TABLE III.—LITERATURE OF THE REPUBLIC, CIR. 1809—CIR. 1897—*Continued*

ENGLISH HISTORY AND LITERATURE.	AMERICAN HISTORY.	NEW ENGLAND LITERATURE.	MIDDLE AND WESTERN LITERATURE.	SOUTHERN LITERATURE.
Dickens, died 1870. Disraeli's "Lothair," 1870. Newman's "Grammar of Assent," 1870. D.G.Rossetti's Poems, 1870. Darwin's "Descent of Man," 1871. George Eliot's "Middlemarch," 1871. Charles Lever, d. 1872. Dobson's "Vignettes in Rhyme," 1873. Pater's "Studies in the Renaissance," 1873. Green's "A Short History of the English People," 1874. Leslie Stephen's "Hours in a Library," 1874-1879. Charles Kingsley, died 1875. Victoria, Empress of India, 1876. Harriet Martineau, died 1876. George Eliot's "Daniel Deronda," 1876.	Reconstruction completed, 1870. Fifteenth Constitutional Amendment, 1870. Treaty of Washington, 1871. Geneva award, 1872. Financial crisis, 1873. Wellesley College opened, 1875. Centennial celebration at Philadelphia, 1876. Colorado admitted, 1876.	John Godfrey Saxe (1816-1887): "The Money King and Other Poems," 1859. Theodore Winthrop (1828-1861): "Cecil Dreeme," and "John Brent," 1861. John Foster Kirk (1824-): "History of Charles the Bold," 1863-1868. Henry Howard Brownell (1820-1872): "War Lyrics and Other Poems," 1866. Harriet P. Spofford (1835-): "The Amber Gods and Other Stories," 1863.	Thos. Bailey Aldrich (1836-): "The Story of a Bad Boy," 1869. "Marjorie Daw and Other People," 1873. "Mercedes and Later Lyrics," 1883. Samuel L. Clemens (Mark Twain) (1835-): "Innocents Abroad," 1869. "Tom Sawyer," 1876. "Huckleberry Finn," 1884. Charles Dudley Warner (1829-): "My Summer in a Garden," 1870. "Back-Log Studies," 1872. "A Little Journey in the World," 1889.	Sidney Lanier (1842-1881): "Tiger Lilies," 1867. "Poems," 1876. "The Boy's Froissart," 1878. "The Science of English Verse," 1880. "The English Novel," 1883.

TABLE III.—LITERATURE OF THE REPUBLIC, CIR. 1869—CIR. 1897.—*Continued*

ENGLISH HISTORY AND LITERATURE.	AMERICAN HISTORY.	NEW ENGLAND LITERATURE.	MIDDLE AND WESTERN LITERATURE.	SOUTHERN LITERATURE.
Spencer's "Principles of Sociology" (Vol. I), 1876. *The Nineteenth Century* established, 1877. Lecky's "History of England in the 18th Century" (begun), 1878.	Johns Hopkins University opened, 1876. Hayes, President, 1877.	Thomas Wentworth Higginson (1823-): "Out-Door Papers," 1863. "Larger History of United States," 1884. "Women and Men," 1887.	Elisha Mulford (1833-1885): "The Nation," 1870. *Scribner's Monthly Magazine* established (1870): Afterwards *The Century,* 1881. Edward Eggleston (1837-):	
Edwin Arnold's "The Light of Asia," 1879. Meredith's "The Egoist," 1879. Outbreak of Zulu War, 1879.	Resumption of specie payments, 1879.	Henry W. Shaw (Josh Billings)(1818-1885): "Josh Billings: His Sayings," 1866. "Farmers' Allminax," 1869.	"The Hoosier School-master," 1871. "Roxy," 1878. "Duffels, 1893. John Hay (1839-): "Pike County Ballads," 1871.	
Spencer's "Data of Ethics," 1879. George Eliot, d. 1880. Gladstone, Prime Minister, 1880. Lang's "Ballades in Blue China," 1880.		Edward Everett Hale (1822-): "The Man Without a Country," and Other Tales," 1866. "Ups and Downs," 1871. "In His Name,"1873.	Cincinnatus H. Miller ("Joaquin Miller") (1811-): "Songs of the Sierras," 1871. "Poems" (complete edition), 1882. "Songs of the Mexican Seas," 1887. Horace Howard Furness (1833-): "Variorum Edition of Shakespeare," Vol. I, 1871.	
Lord Beaconsfield and Carlyle, died 1881. D. G. Rossetti's "Ballads and Sonnets," 1881. Stevenson's "Virginibus Puerisque," 1881.	Garfield, President, 1881. Garfield shot, 1881. Arthur, President,1881.	Louisa M. Alcott (1832-1888): "Little Women," 1868-1869. "Old-Fashioned Girl," 1870. "Jo's Boys," 1886.		

TABLE III.—LITERATURE OF THE REPUBLIC, CIR. 1809—CIR. 1897—*Continued*

ENGLISH HISTORY AND LITERATURE.	AMERICAN HISTORY.	NEW ENGLAND LITERATURE.	MIDDLE AND WESTERN LITERATURE.	SOUTHERN LITERATURE.
Darwin, D. G. Rossetti, and Anthony Trollope, died 1882. J. R. Green, died 1883. Drummond's "Natural Law in the Spiritual World," 1883. Stevenson's "Treasure Island," 1883. Charles Reade, d. 1884. Lang's "Custom and Myth," 1884. Dobson's "At the Sign of the Lyre," 1885. Bill for "Representation of the People," 1885.	Brooklyn Bridge opened, 1883. Civil Service Reform Bill passed, 1883. Washington Monument completed, 1884. Cleveland, President, 1885.	Edward Rowland Sill (1841-1887): "The Hermitage and Other Poems," 1868. "Poems," (published) 1888. Elizabeth Stuart Phelps Ward (1844-): "The Gates Ajar," 1886. "A Singular Life," 1895. Helen Hunt Jackson (1831-1885): "Verses," 1870, 1873. "Ramona," 1884. "Sonnets and Lyrics," 1886.	Frank R. Stockton (1834-): "Roundabout Rambles," 1872. "Rudder Grange," 1879. "The Lady, or the Tiger?" 1884. "The Squirrel Inn," 1891. Lew Wallace (1827-): "The Fair God," 1873. "Ben-Hur," 1880. Henry James, Jr. (1843-): "A Passionate Pilgrim," 1875. "Roderick Hudson," 1875. "Daisy Miller," 1878. "The Portrait of a Lady," 1881. "Essays in London," 1893. Hubert Howe Bancroft (1832-): "The Native Races of the Pacific States," 1875.	Maurice Thompson (1844-): "Hoosier Mosaics," 1875. "The Witchery of Archery," 1878. "Poems," 1892. Frank O. Ticknor (1822-1874). "Poems," 1879. George W. Cable (1844-): "Old Creole Days," 1879. "The Grandissimes," 1880. "Dr. Sevier," 1884. "The Silent South," 1885.

TABLE III.—LITERATURE OF THE REPUBLIC, CIR. 1809—CIR. 1897—*Continued*

ENGLISH HISTORY AND LITERATURE.	AMERICAN HISTORY.	NEW ENGLAND LITERATURE.	MIDDLE AND WESTERN LITERATURE.	SOUTHERN LITERATURE.
Dowden's "Life of Shelley," 1886. Tennyson's "Locksley Hall Sixty Years After," 1886. Stevenson's "Kidnapped," 1886. Matthew Arnold, died 1888. Bryce's "The American Commonwealth," 1888. Kipling's "Plain Tales from the Hills," 1888. "Encyclopædia Britannica" (9th edition completed), 1888.	Bryn Mawr College opened, 1885. Statue of Liberty dedicated in New York Bay, 1886.	Celia Laighton Thaxter (1836-1894): "Poems," 1872. "Among the Isles of Shoals," 1873. "The Cruise of the Mystery," 1886. John Fiske (1842-): "Myths and Myth-Makers," 1872. "Outlines of Cosmic Philosophy," 1874. "The Destiny of Man," 1884. "The American Revolution," 1891. "The Discovery of America," 1892. J. Boyle O'Reilly (1844-1890): "Songs from the Southern Seas," 1872.	Richard Watson Gilder (1841-): "The New Day," 1875. "The Poet and His Master," 1878. "Poems," 1887. Ellen Olney Kirk (1842-): "Love in Idleness," 1877. "The Story of Margaret Kent," 1885. "Sons and Daughters," 1887. *The Dial* established (Chicago), 1880. *The Critic* established, 1881. F. Marion Crawford (1854-): "Mr. Isaacs," 1882. "Saracinesca," 1887. "Sant' Ilario," 1889. "Marion Darche," 1893. "Katharine Lauderdale," 1894.	Constance F. Woolson (1848-1894): "Rodman the Keeper," 1880. "Anne," 1882. "Jupiter Lights," 1889. Joel Chandler Harris (1848-): "Uncle Remus," 1880. "Free Joe," 1887. Thomas Nelson Page (1853-): "Marse Chan," *The Century*, 1884. "In Old Virginia," 1887. "Elsket," 1891. "The Old South," 1892.

TABLE III.—LITERATURE OF THE REPUBLIC, CIR. 1809—CIR. 1897—*Continued*

ENGLISH HISTORY AND LITERATURE.	AMERICAN HISTORY.	NEW ENGLAND LITERATURE.	MIDDLE AND WESTERN LITERATURE.	SOUTHERN LITERATURE.
Robert Browning, died 1889.	Harrison, President, 1889.	Blanche Willis Howard (1847-): "One Summer," 1875. "Aunt Serena," 1883. "Guenn," 1883.	James Whitcomb Riley (1852-): "The Old Swimmin' Hole and 'Leven More Poems," 1883. "Poems Here at Home," 1893.	Richard Malcolm Johnston (1822-): "Dukesborough Tales," 1883. "The Primes and their Neighbors," 1891.
Stevenson, "Master of Ballantrae," 1889.	North Dakota, South Dakota, Washington, and Montana admitted, 1889.			
Cardinal Newman, died 1890.	Idaho and Wyoming admitted, 1890.	Sarah Orne Jewett (1849-): "Deephaven," 1877. "A Country Doctor," 1884.	Edgar Watson Howe (1851-): "Story of a Country Town," 1882. "The Moonlight Boy," 1887.	Mary N. Murfree (Charles Egbert Craddock) (1850-): "Where the Battle was Fought," 1881. "In the Tennessee Mountains," 1884. "The Prophet of the Great Smoky Mountains," 1885. "In the Stranger People's Country," 1891.
William Watson's "Wordsworth's Grave," 1890.				
Barrie's "The Little Minister," 1891.	International Copyright Act, 1891.	Henry Cabot Lodge (1850-): "Life and Letters of George Cabot," 1877. "Historical and Political Essays," 1892.	"A Man Story," 1888. John Bach McMaster (1852-): "History of the People of the United States," begun 1883. Mary Hallock Foote (1847-): "Led-Horse Claim," 1883. "In Exile," 1891. H. C. Bunner (1855-1896): "Airs from Arcady and Elsewhere," 1884. "Short Lives," 1890.	
Hardy's "Tess of the D'Urbervilles," 1891.				
Kipling's "Life's Handicap," 1891.				

TABLE III.—LITERATURE OF THE REPUBLIC, CIR. 1809—CIR. 1897.—*Continued*

ENGLISH HISTORY AND LITERATURE.	AMERICAN HISTORY.	NEW ENGLAND LITERATURE.	MIDDLE AND WESTERN LITERATURE.	SOUTHERN LITERATURE.
Freeman and Tennyson, died 1892. Stopford A. Brooke's "History of Early English Literature," 1892. Gladstone, Prime Minister, 1892. Crockett's "The Stickit Minister," 1893. Benjamin Kidd's "Social Evolution," 1894. Rosebery, Prime Minister, 1894.	University of Chicago opened, 1892. Cleveland, President, 1893. World's Fair at Chicago, 1893.	Henry Adams (1838-): "Life of Albert Gallatin," 1879. "John Randolph" (American Statesmen Series), 1882. Justin Winsor (1831 1897): "Reader's Handbook of the American Revolution," 1880. "Christopher Columbus," 1891. Thomas R. Lounsbury (1838-): "James Fenimore Cooper," 1882. "History of the English Language," 1879. "Studies in Chaucer," 1891.	Edith M. Thomas (1854-): "A New Year's Masque," 1884. "Lyrics and Sonnets," 1887. Margaret Deland (Campbell) (1857-): "John Ward, Preacher," 1888. "Sidney," 1890. "Philip," 1894. The *Forum* established, 1886. *Scribner's Magazine* re-established, 1887. F. Hopkinson Smith (1838-): "Well-Worn Roads," 1886. "Colonel Carter of Cartersville," 1891. "A Gentleman Vagabond and Some Others," 1895. Joseph Kirkland (1830-1894): "Zury," 1887. "The McVeys," 1888.	Lafcadio Hearn(1850-): "Strange Leaves from Strange Literature," 1884. "Chita," 1889. "Out of the East," 1895. Grace Elizabeth King: "Bonne Maman," 1886. "Monsieur Motte," 1888. "Earthlings," 1889. Irwin Russell (1853-1879): "Dialect Poems," 1888.

TABLE III.—LITERATURE OF THE REPUBLIC, CIR. 1809.—CIR. 1897.—*Continued*

ENGLISH HISTORY AND LITERATURE.	AMERICAN HISTORY.	NEW ENGLAND LITERATURE.	MIDDLE AND WESTERN LITERATURE.	SOUTHERN LITERATURE.
Salisbury, Prime Minister, 1895. Alfred Austin: Poet Laureate, 1895. Walter Pater, died 1896. William Morris, died 1896. Du Maurier, Coventry Patmore, and "Tom" Hughes, died 1896. The Diamond Jubilee, 1897.	Sesquicentennial of Princeton University, 1896. McKinley, President, 1897.	Arthur Sherburne Hardy (1847-): "But Yet a Woman," 1883. "Passe Rose," 1889. Mary E. Wilkins: "A Humble Romance," 1887. "A New England Nun," 1891. "Jane Field," 1892. "Pembroke," 1894.	Eugene Field (1850-1896): "Culture's Garland," 1887. "A Little Book of Western Verse," 1889-90. Hamlin Garland (1860-): "Main-Travelled Roads," 1891. "Crumbling Idols," 1894. Alice French (Octave Thanet) (1850-): "Stories of a Western Town," 1893. Richard Harding Davis (1864-): "Gallegher and Other Stories," 1891. "The Exiles," 1894. "Soldiers of Fortune," 1897. Henry Blake Fuller (1857-): "The Cliff Dwellers," 1893. "With the Procession," 1895.	James Lane Allen: "Flute and Violin," 1891. "A Kentucky Cardinal," 1895. "The Choir Invisible," 1897. Ruth McEnery Stuart: "A Golden Wedding," 1893. "In Simpkinsville," 1897.

INDEX.

A

Abolition, influence on literature. See SLAVERY.

Acadia, 179

Adams, Charles F., cited, 77

Adams, Henry, 315; cited, 72, 157, 162

Adams, Herbert B., 315

Adams, John, 99; *Works* (C. F. Adams), 77

Adams, Samuel, 93, 99, 150

Addison, Joseph, influence on American literature, 252; imitated, 83, 85, 91, 119, 123

Ages, The (Bryant), 142, 147

Al Araaf (Poe), 265

Alcott, A. Bronson, 172

Alcuin, a Dialogue on the Rights of Women (C. B. Brown), 109

Alden, John, 180

Alden, Joseph, cited, 148

Allan, John, 265, 266

Allen, A. V. G., cited, 72

Allen, James Lane, 319

Allston, Washington, 155

Almanac, the first American, 26

Alnwick Castle (Halleck), 152

America, scope of the term, 1 et seq.; growth of education in, 18, 19, 24-26, 28, 33-35; the printing-press in, 18, 19, 26, 34 the first newspaper in, 26; the first American book, 37; the establishment of nationality, 75 et seq.

America (Dwight), 103

America Independent (Freneau), 103

American authors, despised abroad, 115

American Biography (Sparks), 49, 112

American books, despised abroad, 115

"American Cicero," the, 93

American Commonwealth (Bryce), 37, 228

American Flag, The (Drake), 153

American history, 8

American humor, 152, 207, 211-216, 326-331; the first masterpiece of, 120, 121

American Humorists (Haweis), 244, 245

American literature, the term, 1 et seq.; its growth, 2 et seq., 13 et seq.; takes place among the literatures of the world, 115

American Literature (Nichols), 112

American Literature (Richardson), 72, 112

American Literature (Tyler). See HISTORY OF AMERICAN LITERATURE.

American Literature (Whipple), 130, 178, 247

American Magazine, The, 70

American Note-Book (Hawthorne), 194

369

Pancoast's Introduction to
English Literature.

By HENRY S. PANCOAST.   556 pp.   12mo. $1.25 net.

" It asumes a study *of* and not *about* English literature; it assumes that one author differeth from another in glory and influence, and that in an introductory course only those of predominant influence can be studied."—*Prof. E. E. Wentworth, Vassar College.*

" It treats of movements—is not merely a catalogue of names and a record of critical ratings. Not even the dullest pupil can study it without feeling the historical and logical continuity of English literature."—*Nation.*

It describes the political and social conditions of the successive periods ; notes foreign as well as domestic influences ; emphasizes the relations of literature to history.

"Its criticism is of a kind to stimulate investigation rather than to supplant it."—*A. J. George, Newton (Mass.) High School.*

The nineteenth century, for the first time in such a book, receives its fair share of attention.

In style it is "interesting," says *Prof. Winchester of Wesleyan University (Conn.),* "readable and stimulating," says *Prof. Hart of Cornell,* "interesting and sensible," says *Prof. Sampson of Indiana University,* "attractive," says *Prof. Gilmore of Rochester University,* "well written," says *Prof. Czarnomska of Smith College.*

It is fully equipped with teaching apparatus. The "Study Lists" give references for collateral reading, and, in the case of the most suitable works, hints and suggestive questions. Comparative chronological tables, a literary map of England, and a plan of Shakespeare's London are included.

HENRY HOLT & CO., 29 W. 23D ST., NEW YORK.

FRANCKE'S SOCIAL FORCES IN GERMAN LITERATURE.

By Prof. KUNO FRANCKE of Harvard.

577 pp. 8vo. $2.00, *net.*

A critical, philosophical, and historical account of German literature that is "destined to be a standard work for both professional and general uses" (*Dial*), and that is now being translated in Germany. Its wide scope is shown by the fact that it begins with the sagas of the fifth century and ends with Hauptmann's mystical play " Hannele," written in 1894.

" The range of vision is comprehensive, but the details are not obscured. The splendid panorama of German literature is spread out before us from the first outburst of heroic song in the dim days of the migrations, down to the latest disquieting productions of the Berlin school. We owe a debt of gratitude to the author who has led us to a commanding height and pointed out to us the kingdoms of the spirit which the genius of Germany has conquered. The frequent departures from the orthodox estimates are the result of the new view-point. They are often a distinct addition to our knowledge. . . . To the study of German literature in its organic relation to society this book is the best contribution in English that has yet been published." — *The Nation.*

" It is neither a dry summary nor a wearisome attempt to include every possible fact. . . . It puts the reader in centre of the vital movements of the time. . . . One often feels as if the authors treated addressed themselves personally to him; the discourse coming not through bygone dead books, but rather through living men."—*Prof. Friedrich Paulsen of University of Berlin.*

" A noble contribution to the history of civilization, and valuable not only to students of German literature, but to all who are interested in the progress of our race."—*The Hon. Andrew D. White, ex-President of Cornell University.*

" For the first time German literature has been depicted with a spirit that imparts to it organic unity . . . rich in well-weighed, condensed judgments of writers . . . not mere rewordings of the opinions of standard critics. . . . The style is clear, crisp, and unobtrusive; . . . destined to be a standard work for both professional and general uses."— *The Dial.*

HENRY HOLT & CO., 29 W. 23D ST., NEW YORK.

January, 1898.

English Readings for Students.

English masterpieces in editions at once competently edited and inexpensive. The aim will be to fill vacancies now existing because of subject, treatment, or price. Prices given below are NET, *postage eight per cent. additional.* 16mo. *Cloth.*

Arnold (Matthew): Prose Selections.
Edited by LEWIS E. GATES, Asst. Professor in Harvard. xci + 348 pp. 90c.

Includes The Function of Criticism, First Lecture on Translating Homer, Literature and Science, Culture and Anarchy, Sweetness and Light, Compulsory Education, "Life a Dream," Emerson, and twelve shorter selections, including America.

> Bliss Perry, *Professor in Princeton:*—" The selections seem to me most happy, and the introduction is even better if possible than his introduction to the Newman volume. Indeed I have read no criticism of Arnold's prose which appears to me as luminous and just, and expressed with such literary charm."

Browning: Selected Lyrical and Dramatic Poems.
With the essay on Browning from E. C. Stedman's "Victorian Poets." Edited by EDWARD T. MASON 275 pp. 60c.

Burke : Selections.
Edited by BLISS PERRY, Professor in Princeton. xxvi + 298 pp. 60c.

Contents. Speeches at Arrival at Bristol, at Conclusion of the Poll ; Letters to the Marquis of Rockingham, to the Sheriffs of Bristol, and to a Noble Lord; Address to the King ; Selections from The Sublime and the Beautiful, from Thoughts on the Present Discontents, from Speech on the Nabob of Arcot's Debts, from Impeachment of Hastings (2), from Reflections on the Revolution in France (7, including Fiat Money).

> Edward Dowden, *the Author and Critic:*—"They seem to me admirably chosen and arranged, and the introduction brings various aspects of Burke's mind truly and vividly before the reader."

Coleridge : Prose Extracts.
Edited by HENRY A. BEERS, Professor in Yale College. xix + 148 pp. 50c.

The selections, varying in length from a paragraph to ten or twenty pages, are mainly from *Table Talk* and *Biographia Literaria*, but also from *Notes on Shakespeare* etc.

De Quincey: Joan of Arc; The Mail Coach.

Edited by JAMES MORGAN HART, Professor in Cornell University. xxvi + 138 pp. 50c.

The introduction sketches De Quincey's life and style. Allusions and other points of unusual difficulty are explained in the notes. This volume and the Essays on *Boswell's Johnson* (see below) are used at Cornell for elementary rhetorical study.

Ford: The Broken Heart.

A Spartan Tragedy in verse. Edited by CLINTON SCOLLARD, Professor in Hamilton College. xvi + 132 pp. 50c. (Buckram, 70c.)

A play that in its repressed emotion and psychological interest furnishes a marked contrast to the feverish "night pieces" common when it was written. Charles Lamb wrote "I do not know where to find in any play a catastrophe so grand, so solemn and so surprising as this" [of *The Broken Heart*].

Johnson: Rasselas.

Edited by OLIVER FARRAR EMERSON, Professor in Adelbert College. lvi + 179 pp. 50c. (Buckram, 70c.)

This book is chosen as fairly illustrating the style, thought, and personality of the great literary dictator of the eighteenth century. The introduction treats of Johnson's style, the circumstances under which *Rasselas* was written, and its place in the history of fiction. The text is based on the first edition. The notes explain allusions and trace the sources of some of Johnson's materials.

Lyly: Endimion.

Edited by GEORGE P BAKER, Professor in Harvard College. cxcvi + 109 pp. 85c. (Buckram, $1.25.)

Lyly's plays really show him to a better advantage than does the *Euphues*, by which he is chiefly remembered, and his place in English dramatic history makes it desirable that one at least should be easily accessible,

Macaulay and Carlyle: Essays on Samuel Johnson.

Edited by WILLIAM STRUNK, Jr., Instructor in Cornell University. xl+191 pp. 50c.

These two essays present a constant contrast in intellectual and moral methods of criticism, and offer an excellent introduction to the study of the literary history of Johnson's times.

Marlowe: Edward II. With the best passages from TAMBURLAINE THE GREAT, and from his POEMS.

Edited by the late EDWARD T. McLAUGHLIN, Professor in Yale College. xxi+180 pp. 50c. (Buckram, 70c.)

Edward II., besides being Marlowe's most important play, is of great interest in connection with Shakespere. The earlier chronicle drama was in Shakespere's memory as he was writing *Richard II.*, as various passages prove, and a comparison of the two plays (sketched in the introduction) affords basis for a study in the development of the Elizabethan drama.

Newman: Prose Selections.

Edited by LEWIS E. GATES, Professor in Harvard College. lxii+228 pp. 50c. (Buckram, 90c.)

The selections lead the reader through some of the more picturesque and concrete passages of Newman's prose, to his impeachment of the liberal and irreligious tendencies of the age, his insistence on the powerlessness of science to make men moral, his defense of supernaturalism, his ridicule of English prejudice against Catholics, his statement of the Catholic position, and finally to two powerful imaginative pictures of supernatural interferences in the natural world-order.

Tennyson: The Princess.

Edited by L. A. SHERMAN, Professor in the University of Nebraska. [*In preparation.*]

Postage 8 per cent. additional.

HENRY HOLT & CO., 29 W. 23d St., New York.

Specimens of Prose Composition.

16*mo.*   *Cloth.*   *Per volume*, 50c., NET.

Prose Narration.

Edited by WILLIAM T. BREWSTER, Tutor in Columbia College. xxxviii +209 pp.

Includes Selections from Scott, Thackeray, Hawthorne, Jane Austen, George Eliot, Stevenson, and Henry James. Part I. Elements of Narrative—Plot, Character, Setting, and Purpose. Part II. Combination of the Elements of Narration. Part III. Various Kinds of Narrative. Part IV. Technique of Good Narrative.

Prose Description.

Edited by CHARLES SEARS BALDWIN, Ph.D., Instructor in Yale College. xlviii+145 pp.

Includes: Ancient Athens (Newman); Paris Before the Second Empire (du Maurier); Bees (Burroughs); Byzantium (Gibbon); Geneva (Ruskin); The Storming of the Bastille (Carlyle); La Gioconda, etc. (Pater); Blois (Henry James); Spring in a Side Street (Brander Matthews); A Night Among the Pines, etc. (Stevenson).

Exposition.

Edited by HAMMOND LAMONT, Professor in Brown University. xxiv+ 180 pp.

Includes : Development of a Brief ; G. C. V. Holmes on the Steam-engine; Huxley on the Physical Basis of Life; Bryce on the U. S. Constitution ; "The Nation" on the Unemployed; Wm. Archer on Albery's " Apple Blossoms"; Matthew Arnold on Wordsworth.; etc.

Argumentation. MODERN.

Edited by GEORGE P. BAKER, Professor in Harvard College. 16mo. 186 pp.

Lord Chatham's speech on the withdrawal of troops from Boston, Lord Mansfield's argument in the Evans case, the first letter of Junius, the first of Huxley's American addresses on evolution, Erskine's defence of Lord George Gordon, an address by Beecher in Liverpool during the cotton riots, and specimen brief. ──────────

Postage 8 per cent. additional.

HENRY HOLT & CO., 29 W. 23d St., New York.